END OF BENEVOLENCE

THE SYNMEN CHRONICLES - BOOK ONE

DAVID GUDMUNDSON

END OF BENEVOLENCE

To my amazing mom

CONTENTS

PART ONE

THE GREAT ADVANCE

I'LL BE LAST

THE WORLD WAS PERFECT, forged of beauty and bliss. Everyone's lives were perfect too, full of wonder and kindness. Every day since the very first day, happiness had dominated sadness, trust had conquered fear. But it hadn't been enough. Seeking more, nearly everyone had gone. Only a few remained. Tomorrow, they'd be gone too.

KEN AND NORA SAT TOGETHER, looking out over the lake, its surface shimmering in the morning sun. Their two children, Jen and Jax, played in the sand about twenty feet from shore.

"We're so lucky," said Ken, playfully bumping his shoulder into Nora's.

"Want to get lucky?" she asked, bumping him back.

Ken smirked. "I'm glad we waited to the end." He waved toward the lake where several boats floated aimlessly, rocking gently. A quarter mile away, dozens more lined a deserted dock. "It's like we have the whole world to ourselves. Every-one's gone."

"Not everyone," said Nora, pointing at a dog trotting

along the shore. "Must be holdouts nearby. Anyone transferring would have dropped their pets off at a pen by now."

"What if we'd been born earlier?" asked Ken.

"We'd be older, have more kids, maybe even grandkids," said Nora, grinning.

"I mean a lot earlier. We'd not have met Stevens. We'd have died. Our kids too."

"I wonder about our kids sometimes."

"Honey."

Nora sighed. "I know. I still wonder. Don't you?"

"We grew up. Remember? We were happy, but bored. We've always wished we could be young again. Jen and Jax will get to be young forever, and we'll be together forever."

"I know, honey. Do you ever feel scared, about transferring?" she asked.

"Honestly? I think so. If I do, it vanishes so fast I hardly notice. Do you?"

Nora crossed her arms, hugging herself. "A little, especially lately. Thankfully, not for long."

"That's how fear works, honey, sadness too."

"I know. I love you."

Ken leaned in and kissed her. "Let's go get lucky," he said.

When they parted, they saw their daughter running toward the dog.

"Jen, honey, we're leaving," shouted Nora.

"I want to pet it, Mommy," Jen yelled back.

"She sure loves dogs," said Ken.

"Who doesn't? They've been bred for thousands of years to love people, especially children." Nora looked up and down the shore. "Where are its owners?"

"Doggieees!" squealed Jax, scrambling to stand.

Still a toddler, Jax lost his balance and plopped back down. Laughing at their baby boy, Ken and Nora saw two dogs now stood at the shore. One was playing with something splashing in the shallow water.

"Jen, come get Jax so he can pet the dogs too," Ken shouted.

Their daughter ran back to Jax and lifted him to his feet. His little legs wobbled, but he managed to keep his balance. Jen took his hand and walked to the lake, Jax toddling beside her.

"Jen cried when I dropped off Snuggles," said Ken, getting up to join his children.

"Really? She was sad?"

Ken frowned, but only for a moment. "Sort of. She'd cry, again and again, but couldn't maintain it."

"No one can. One of the mysteries of the universe," said Nora.

"Maybe we'll learn why in the Great Advance. Stevens says we'll understand everything once there."

"He's such a great man."

"Mommy?"

Nora and Ken looked up and now saw four dogs. Two were sniffing Jen, aggressively, forcing her back. One bumped her. Jax had fallen and was crawling toward the lake.

"Honey, something's wrong," said Nora.

Suddenly, Jax screamed, a short, terrible screech that came to an abrupt stop. Ken and Nora raced to their children. Both saw what had upset little Jax, what the dog had been "playing" with. Snuggles lay in the shallow water at the edge of the lake, unmoving, her white coat muddied and pink with blood. Nora grabbed Jax and turned him away. Ken reached to pick up Jen. She resisted and tried to run to get Snuggles.

"Daddy, you said they'd take care of her," Jen cried.

Ken knelt down and pulled Jen close. Dogs panted all around them, six now. *Where are the dogs' owners?* he wondered. A large dog appeared at their side, gaunt, its coat ragged, white foam dripping from its mouth, its breath wretched.

"Honey, let's go," said Nora, shying back, bumping into two dogs behind her.

Snuggles shook, then stilled. Jen struggled to break free and run to help. Ken held her tight.

"Jen, stay with your mother," he said, guiding Jen to Nora. "I'll get Snuggles."

A small wave washed over their dog, rocking her still body. Ken moved toward her. Snuggles was only ten feet away.

"Hurry, honey," said Nora.

Snuggles shook again. She raised her head, saw Jen, and wagged her tail.

"My daddy will save you, Snuggles," said Jen.

The gaunt dog lunged at Snuggles, knocking Ken to the ground. It snatched their pet by the neck, crunched and shook her with two quick shakes, then turned and looked at Ken and Jen, Snuggles clenched in its mouth. White foam and blood intermingled, dripping down Snuggles's leg.

"Daddy, help!" screamed Jen.

Ken looked back. A dozen dogs now surrounded his family. Jen stood between Nora's legs. A tall bony dog stalked inches away, growling at her face. A smaller dog tugged at Nora's pant leg, growling furiously. Nora held Jax high, struggling to maintain her balance, and kicked the dog. It yelped and scampered away. Ken rushed toward his family.

"Ken, look out!" shouted Nora.

He fell forward, slammed from behind. Teeth ripped his back. He swung around and punched the dog's throat, stunning it. Scrambling to his family, Ken grabbed Jen and lifted her away from the dogs.

Ken and Nora stood together, surrounded, holding their children. Fear came to each, subsided, then returned with a fury, again and again. A skinny dog, ribs showing, lunged. Ken kicked, sending the dog tumbling. The dog stood, growling softly, glaring at Ken.

Dozens of dogs, all kinds, large and small, some strong and recently groomed, most gaunt and sickly, all starving, surrounded the family. The dogs crept closer, heads low, inches above the ground. There would be no escape.

Ken and Nora held their children tight, kicking away each dog that attacked. They heard a humming sound. Nora was squeezing Jax, her arm protecting his neck, her hand pressing his face into her shoulder. She relaxed the pressure, allowing Jax to breathe more freely. Jax wasn't humming. He was singing.

Jen began singing too. Ken and Nora looked lovingly into each other's eyes. Neither felt the battle between fear and happiness raging in their minds.

"Maybe we'll still be together forever," said Nora, her eyes glistening in the morning sun.

Out of the corner of his eye, Ken saw a large, dark movement. Jen stopped singing. Ken's heart sank.

"Daddy, look!" cried Jen.

Only ten feet away, a large boy ran toward them, his big legs pumping, his running hindered by a large brown bag he held with both hands.

An instant later, the boy plowed into the dogs, tripped and fell. Arms and legs flailing, he rolled across the ground. Dogs yelped, jumped away, and turned back, eyeing the boy. His bag had burst, its contents scattered across the sand. A dog sniffed an item from the bag, then plopped down and began eating.

The boy scrambled to his feet and backed away, shielding Ken, Nora, and their two children. The dogs ignored them, fighting over the strewn contents from the boy's bag. Once at a safe distance, they stopped. The boy looked back at the beach.

"Those dogs are starving," he said.

For the first time, Ken and Nora got a good look at the boy. He was actually a young man with large legs, beefy arms, and round, boyish cheeks. Jen jumped from Ken's arms and ran to the man.

"You saved us!" she cried, hugging his leg. Nora touched the man's arm.

"Thank you," she said. The young man didn't reply, his gaze still on the dogs. He pointed at a gaunt shepherd lying on the beach about fifty feet away, its hind legs twitching. He bent over and removed Jen's arms from his legs.

"I hurt that dog," he said, moving toward the beach.

"No, stop!" yelled Ken, grabbing the man.

"I have to help it," said the man.

Ken held on, but the man was strong. "Nora, help me!"

Nora stepped into the path of the man, still holding Jax. "Please stay with us," she said. "We can help the dog when it's safe."

"Mommy, he's bleeding!" cried Jen, holding out the man's injured hand.

Ken tore off his shirt sleeve and wrapped it around the man's hand. Nora brushed sand from the man's clothes and smoothed his tousled hair. He seemed to relax.

"I'm big so I fall a lot."

"You're perfect and a hero!" said Jen.

The man blushed. "I like helping people. My mother taught me how."

"Thank you for helping us," said Nora.

"Are you guys holdouts?" asked the man.

Jen smiled. "No, we're transferring this afternoon. We were just visiting the beach one last time. Without you, we'd have missed the Great Advance!"

The man brightened. "I work for the Great Advance. I help people transfer. After everyone transfers, I'll transfer. My mother was first and I'll be last."

Ken and Nora startled. Both now knew the name of the young man who had saved them.

"What was in the bag?" asked Jen.

"Lunch."

"You eat a lot," said Jen.

"Jen!" said Nora.

The man answered with an air of gravity. "I make lunch for everyone at the station."

"Lucky for us," said Ken.

They watched the dogs until only a few remained. The injured shepherd lay still. Nora stayed with the children while the young man and Ken checked on the dog. They returned without the dog. Jen took the man's hand.

"Can we walk with you to the transfer station?" she asked.

The man smiled. Nora kissed him on the cheek. Jax leaned from Nora, reaching for the young man. Ken, Nora, and Jen laughed.

"Would you like to carry Jax?" Jen asked.

2

LAST DAY

BOBBY PETTED HIS DOG, Candy, as she slept in the corner of the window nook, warmed by the afternoon sun. He watched his big brother, Mikey, who'd never seemed so anxious. Bobby was anxious too, about what would become of Candy after they were gone.

"Have you seen my green shirt?" asked Mikey, taking off his t-shirt.

"That shirt's green," said Bobby.

Mikey tossed his shirt to the floor. "I might have spilled something on it during lunch," he said, looking in his closet.

Bobby pointed at two shirts folded neatly atop a dresser, both green, his brother's favorite color. "What about those two shirts?" he asked.

Candy woke, cracking open her eyes, looking at Bobby.

"I meant the green shirt I had on yesterday," said Mikey, looking under his bed.

Bobby resumed petting Candy, his fingers gently caressing her forehead. The shaggy poodle sighed and closed her eyes.

"The shirt Angel gave you?" asked Bobby.

"Yes, that one."

"You going to Angel's? Did you ask Mom?"

"Mom will let me. It's our last day. Where's my shirt?"

"Mikey, I'm sad for Candy," said Bobby.

Upon hearing her name, the dog stood up, licked Bobby's face, and lay down again. Beneath her, Bobby spotted Mikey's green shirt and noticed Mikey saw it too. Mikey sat down beside Bobby and rubbed Candy's belly.

"I wish Candy could go with us too," he said. "Can you imagine, chasing her around the whole universe? How would we clean up after her?"

"Mikey."

"I'm sorry, little brother. I'll think of something."

"Promise?" asked Bobby.

Mikey stood up and grabbed one of the other shirts from atop the dresser. "I promise, little brother," he said, before rushing out the door.

Alone in Mikey's bedroom, Bobby massaged Candy's tummy while looking out the window. He saw the valley below and the work area where his father sat each morning watching the sunrise and delivering his speech to the whole world. He saw the picnic table where his family had just had lunch and thought about how his father had surprised them, coming home in the middle of the day for a family meal. He saw his baseball glove on a bench, a ball tucked inside. Today's baseball game was canceled at the last minute. Too many players were gone. He heard his father's voice downstairs and smiled. His father hadn't returned to work yet!

Bobby ran downstairs to ask his father to play catch, then stopped when he heard his mother talking about Mikey. He knew he shouldn't eavesdrop, but couldn't help himself.

"Honey, thank you for coming home for lunch. I'm so happy we'll be a family forever, but I'm not sure Mikey is excited about the Great Advance."

"I admit, I'm getting a little anxious too, though of course it doesn't last. Becky, can you believe it? By this time tomorrow, I'll have given my last speech, and we'll be in the transfer line ourselves. I need to get back to the transfer station. Did the boys leave?" asked his father.

"I think Bobby went upstairs. Mikey went to see Angel. She's nice. I like her. Do you think . . ."

"Do I think what?"

"You know, do you think Mikey and Angel are in love?"

Bobby wondered what his mother meant. Of course, Mikey and Angel loved each other. Everyone loved everyone.

"I don't know," said his father. "They're young, only seventeen, but they seem to spend all their free time together."

"We did it, and we barely knew each other."

"Did what?"

Seconds of silence passed. Bobby worried he'd been caught. Peeking around the corner, he saw his mother and father kissing. He'd seen them kiss before, but not like that. He pulled his head back when they parted.

"Ha! You mean, are they making love?" said his father. "No, Becky, I don't think so. Angel's parents wouldn't approve.

"That wouldn't have stopped you."

His father laughed. "Probably not."

Bobby was confused. He knew what love was, but what was making love?

"Let's eat breakfast tomorrow, family breakfast," said his mother. "We'll eat right after your morning speech. Then we'll walk to the transfer station together."

Bobby waited for his father to answer. He peeked, wondering if they were kissing again. He saw his father looking out the kitchen window onto the deck. His mother came up behind him, put her arms around his waist, and her chin on his shoulder.

"Are you okay, honey?"

"Tomorrow morning's speech is my last chance to save the holdouts. I'm worried I can't convince them it's safe," he replied. "Becky, what do you want to do on our last evening?"

"Make love to you."

"Shhh! Bobby might hear you!"

Bobby nearly stepped out to reveal himself, thinking he was about to be discovered, then stilled after hearing his mother.

"Bobby can't hear us. My Stevens, my lover, my hero, father of my boys, leader of the Great Advance, I'm so proud of you."

"We both know you still lead the Great Advance, and flattery will absolutely get you what you want, but only if you tell me what you want," he said, laughing.

Bobby saw his parents kissing again, long and tenderly.

"Oh, that," his father said.

"Go check on the transfer station. When you get back, I want you to make love to me one last time."

He laughed. "If you insist, my dear. I'll be back by eight if the transfer lines aren't too long. It'll still be light enough to play catch with Bobby. I broke another promise yesterday. I told him I'd come home early to play catch, but I forgot for the third time in a row."

"You could play with Bobby now. He's upstairs."

"I can't. I'm due at the transfer station."

"If you're late getting home tonight, you and Bobby can play tomorrow. Who's running the station tomorrow? Not you, I hope."

"No, not me, but we'll be in line, honey," he replied. "And I should be there in case something happens."

"Your team can handle things for a few hours. Tell them you need to go home for a bit. Bobby would love to play catch with you on the last day."

"What if something goes wrong?"

"What could go wrong? Besides, it's not like the world is going to end," she said, laughing.

"That's not funny . . . well, it is a little," he said chuckling.

Bobby heard the front door open. He had to lean further around to see. He saw his parents embracing at the front door.

"What are we doing when you get back?" his mother asked.

"Playing catch with Bobby, if I get back in time."

"Funny. Then what?"

"Making love with you, one last time."

Bobby again wondered what making love was. It sure sounded important and seemed to be more than just kissing.

When his father left for work, Bobby walked toward the door and stopped behind his mother. The street was completely deserted except for his father. There was no one left on their entire block. His mother startled, then turned toward Bobby.

"Bobby, I thought you were upstairs," she said.

"Sorry, Mom."

"Are you okay?"

Bobby nodded.

"Why don't we go to the square? We can stop by Angel's house to get Mikey and easily be back before dark."

"They might be making love," said Bobby.

"Bobby!"

BOBBY and his mother left to pick up Mikey, taking a self-driving local transport unit. The streets were empty.

At Angel's house, Bobby hesitated to knock, afraid he'd be interrupting Mikey and Angel's private time. Angel's parents answered and went to get Mikey. He seemed sad to leave but brightened when Angel whispered in his ear.

Bobby overheard her say, "I'll see you tonight." He didn't understand what Angel meant. He knew it would be impossible for Mikey to see Angel later that night. After visiting the square, they'd be going home and straight to bed. Walking to the transport unit where their mother waited, Bobby learned what Angel meant.

"Bobby, tonight's our last night, ever," whispered Mikey. "Angel and I are sneaking out, and you're coming with."

For the longer trip from Angel's house to the square, Becky, Mikey, and Bobby's transport unit flew upward and attached itself to a high-speed transportation cluster. The translucent barrier around their transport unit flashed green when their unit was safely secured to the cluster.

Bobby looked around, expecting to see people in other transport units as on previous trips to the square. Instead, they were surrounded by dozens of units, each packed with boxes. Only the transport unit directly in front of them contained other passengers, a mother and her toddler son. Mikey made a face at the toddler, making him laugh out loud.

"Mom, what are the boxes for?" asked Bobby.

"The boxes contain supplies for holdouts," Becky said. "Some transport units have become unreliable. Those no longer safe for people have been redeployed to distribute food, water, medicine, and other provisions to local stocking centers."

Bobby saw the toddler's mother startle and glance anxiously around her transport unit. Then she smiled and addressed his mother.

"I feel sorry for holdouts," she said, without a hint of fear in her voice. "Even if the supplies do last, once the climate controls and sea walls break down . . . not to mention the wild animals."

The toddler held out his hand, offering Mikey a lollipop. Mikey laughed and shook his head.

"What's his name?" Becky asked the mother.

"Benjamin," she replied, squeezing her son's leg, then motioning toward Bobby and Mikey. "Our kids are so lucky. Imagine roaming the universe, exploring for all of eternity, still with the curiosity of a child. Have you used the demo-portals and seen how much fun children are having who've already transferred? They're so happy."

"We're going to the demo-portals now," said Bobby.

The translucent barrier around the mother and toddler's transport unit twinkled yellow.

"Wait, this isn't our stop," the mother said, looking outside. The twinkling yellow barrier turned orange, indicating the transport unit would soon separate from the main cluster.

"Oh no," she said. "Is our transport unit failing? We're in the middle of nowhere. We'll miss the last day of the Great Advance!"

Bobby saw his mother quickly pull a small tablet from her purse, tap the screen hurriedly, then shout to get the woman's attention.

"Miss, stay exactly where your transport unit drops you off!" his mother yelled. "Another unit will be by to pick you up in ten minutes."

The woman nodded just as the barrier flashed red and separated from the cluster, leaving an empty space where the transport unit had been. Within seconds, another unit packed with supplies took its place.

"Mom, what happened?" Mikey asked.

"They'll be fine," said his mom, looking at her tablet. "A working transport unit is on the way to pick them up now. Your father was afraid of something like this, so he gave me override access to the transportation system."

Bobby watched the unit containing the mother and toddler set down on the deserted roof of a large warehouse. Not a person could be seen in the area surrounding the warehouse. He looked up at his mother.

"What if we hadn't been here?"

"Bobby, did you see the wrapper on that kid's lollipop?" asked Mikey. "It said 'Great Advance'."

"All the little kids have them lately," Bobby replied, still looking at his mother.

THE VISIT to the square wasn't as fun as usual. Most people had already transferred. Mikey and Bobby engaged the demo-portals to talk with their friends who were gone. All of them were happy and encouraged Mikey and Bobby to join them. When their turn was up, the brothers exited their demo-portals and rejoined their mother.

"Look at everyone," said Becky. "They're so excited. The demo-portals were a great idea, not just to validate that people will be truly happy in the Great Advance but to convince people they should go."

Two small children burst from another demo-portal, running toward their parents and squealing with laughter.

"Mommy, Daddy, can we transfer now? Can we, please?" begged the children.

"First thing tomorrow morning," their father replied, giving each child a kiss and a hug.

An older man emerged from a demo-portal, smiling and giving a thumbs-up sign to the sky. He saw Becky, Bobby, and Mikey looking at him.

"My wife transferred early to be with her sister who was gravely ill and bedridden," he said. "Now they're zooming around the universe together!"

"We'll all be in the Great Advance tomorrow," Becky replied to the man.

"Can't wait!" he said.

Bobby tugged his mother's hand. "Mom, I'm worried about Candy. My friend Troy said his dog got loose and is running wild."

"I know, honey," his mom said. "Let's go in case your father gets home early."

ARRIVING HOME, the house was quiet.

"Bedtime," said Becky.

Mikey and Bobby hugged their mother and went upstairs.

"Sleep in my room tonight, Bobby. I'll wake you up when it's time to go," whispered Mikey.

"Have you ever snuck out before?"

"Are you scared?"

"No. Well, a little. Have you?"

"Don't worry," said Mikey. "A lot of our friends will be there, the ones who are still here, anyway. Go to sleep. I'll wake you up when it's time to go."

Bobby didn't worry, but he didn't fall asleep. He lay in the darkness, thinking about Troy's dog, about leaving Candy behind, and about his father not having time to play catch. Sadness came, then quickly vanished. Soon, Bobby looked forward to sneaking out.

A few hours later, he heard Mikey whisper, "Bobby?"

"What?"

"You awake? Time to go."

"Are you sure we won't get caught?"

"We won't get caught."

"What if Candy barks?"

"We'll pet her, and she'll be fine. Besides, she's sleeping. Don't bump her getting out of bed."

"Who will be there?"

"Everyone. Everyone who hasn't transferred, I mean. Some of your baseball team might be there."

"I think they're all gone."

"Oh, well, you'll still know people."

"Mikey?"

"What, Bobby?"

"Will Ronnie and Rachel be there?"

"Yes. Rachel is stopping by Angel's place on the way. Why?"

"They're holdouts. Father says we should stay away from holdouts."

"Their parents are the holdouts. It's not their fault," said Mikey.

"I know. It's not fair. Do you think they're going to die?" asked Bobby.

Mikey got out of bed and reached for his shoes.

Bobby remained under the covers. "You left your clothes on."

"C'mon, Bobby. Get up. We'll be late."

Bobby got up. Mikey laughed. "You left your shoes on? Take them off. It'll be quieter. We'll put them on once we get outside."

"So, you have snuck out before."

"Yeah, a few times, lately."

"What if Candy barks when we sneak back in?" asked Bobby, taking off his shoes.

"She won't. I've done this before, remember. You didn't even wake. Let's go." Mikey nudged the bedroom door open, peeked down the hallway, and verified the coast was clear with a thumbs-up signal to Bobby. They walked past their parents' bedroom and down the stairs.

Normally, the front door was open, but it was kept closed now due to the wild dogs. As quietly as he could, Mikey opened the door and they stepped out of the house. Bobby waited on the porch while Mikey eased the door shut. A minute later, the boys were walking down the sidewalk. It was the middle of the night, but it wasn't dark. Light from the stars made it easy to see. Block after block, most of the homes they walked by were empty. Arriving at a large open field that bordered the houses, Mikey stopped and pointed out into the field.

"See that hill? That's where we're going. From the top, you can see the whole lake. Look, kids are there already."

"Not many," said Bobby.

Mikey took Bobby's hand and walked into the field. They had only taken a few steps when a voice startled them.

"Hey, Mikey, wait up."

Bobby recognized the voice.

"Hi, Rachel. Hi, Ronnie," said Mikey. Rachel was seventeen, same as Mikey. Ronnie was ten, Bobby's age. They were friends.

Mike frowned. "Where's Angel?"

"She got caught," replied Rachel. "I'm so sorry, Mikey."

"It's okay. It's not like it's the end of the world or anything," said Mikey. Bobby sensed his brother's disappointment.

"Maybe you can still see her tomorrow morning?" suggested Rachel.

"Maybe," said Mikey. "Thanks for bringing Ronnie."

Rachel looked up at the hill. "It wasn't easy. He almost chickened out. I told him Bobby was coming. Where is everyone? I only see a few kids."

"I don't know. Let's go see," said Mikey.

Bobby eyed Rachel and Mikey but kept quiet. The four children walked through the field toward the hill. Mikey walked with Rachel. Bobby and Ronnie followed close behind.

"You and Angel were together earlier, weren't you?" asked Rachel.

Mikey shook his head. "We were never alone. Hey, maybe there's a way to do it in the Great Advance."

Bobby suspected Mikey was talking about making love. Whatever that involved, it required being alone.

"My dad says there isn't," said Rachel. "He says that's one reason why we're not going."

"I was just kidding. It's just… it's our last day."

"I'm so sorry. I know Angel really wanted to come." Rachel took Mikey's hand. "She loves you, Mikey."

As they walked up the hill, a plan came together in

Bobby's mind. When they saw the other side of the hilltop, the four children gasped in surprise.

Lying on their backs on the flat gentle slope were dozens of their friends, all lying side by side, hand in hand, looking up at the stars. Before them, a lake shimmered in the moonlight. It was quiet except for hushed voices and occasional laughter. Barking dogs could be heard in the distance.

Mikey, Rachel, Bobby, and Ronnie formed a new row at the top of the hill. Over time, many more children came. The whispering and laughing subsided until the night was perfectly quiet. It was Bobby who broke the silence. He spoke as softly as he could, but everyone heard.

"Ronnie?"

"What, Bobby?"

"Do you think you can take care of my dog, Candy?"

"I'll ask. I'm sure my dad will say yes," replied Ronnie.

A boy from the row below sat up and turned around. "You're a holdout?" he asked Ronnie. At the boy's question, several other children sat up too.

"Yes, my brother and I are," Rachel answered for him.

"Are you afraid?" asked the boy.

More children sat up. The Great Advance was so all-consuming that most people didn't understand why anyone would be a holdout. Rachel and Ronnie didn't feel threatened or intimidated. No one had ever felt that way.

"I feel afraid of the Great Advance sometimes," admitted Rachel, "especially before we became holdouts, but never for very long. How about you?"

"Sometimes," said the boy, "but the feeling goes away."

Many other children agreed they had also been afraid or sad, but the feelings always vanished. Most of the time, everyone felt happy about going. They talked about how friends they'd seen in the demo-portals all loved the Great Advance.

Another boy, Charley, who was about the same age as

Mikey, said his friends who'd already transferred loved the Great Advance too, but he was also a holdout.

"My parents want me to grow up," he said.

The children went silent. One by one, they lay back down beneath the stars. Growling and scampering sounds could be heard from the direction of the lake. A boy several rows down from Mikey and Bobby sat up.

"Charley, can you please take my dog?" he asked. "She's tiny and a very good dog."

"I'll ask my parents," said Charley, "but I don't think they'll let me. My baby sister got attacked by a dog yesterday."

The children sat up, all exclaiming at once.

"What!"

"No way!"

"Is your sister okay?"

"How'd that happen?"

"Dogs don't attack people!"

"It wasn't our dog," said Charley. "My mom says it had white foam on its mouth. There was a whole pack. They attacked my dad too, but he chased them away."

"Maybe the dogs were hungry?" asked a child.

"That's not possible," said another. "My dad said that after people transfer, their dogs are cared for in feeding areas."

"My mom said sickness made the dog attack," said Charley. "She thinks a lot of the dogs are sick."

"What about your baby sister?" asked Mikey.

Charley sniffled, then answered without a hint of sadness. "She's sick. She might die."

"You should go on the Great Advance," said Bobby. "That'll save her."

"I know, my parents are talking about maybe going now."

The children lay back down. The night air was cool, and the stars were beautiful. Two girls began singing. Other joined. Scampering sounds came from the bushes. The children quieted, listening. Many began to leave. Mikey, Bobby, Rachel, and Ronnie left last. Rachel and Ronnie said goodbye at the bottom of the hill. Before they separated, Ronnie promised Bobby he'd take care of Candy. Mikey and Bobby walked alone across the field.

"Mikey?"

"What, Bobby?"

"You knew Rachel and Ronnie would be there. You made sure Ronnie would be there."

"Yes, Rachel was picking up Angel," replied Mikey.

"I mean Ronnie. You got Rachel to bring Ronnie. You knew I'd ask him to take Candy."

"I thought you might," said Mikey.

"Thank you, Mikey."

"You're welcome, little brother."

Mikey and Bobby reached the edge of the field that butted up against their neighborhood. Bobby thought about Mikey and Angel, and about how Mikey had planned on seeing Angel on the hill that night, one last time. He knew Mikey loved Angel and wanted to be with her, just like his mother wanted to be with his father.

"I'm sorry Angel couldn't come," he said.

"You overheard me and Rachel talking?"

Bobby nodded. "What if you could see Angel tomorrow?"

"I'll see her tomorrow, in the transfer line," said Mikey, shrugging.

"No, I mean, what if you could see Angel tomorrow for real?"

"For real?"

"Alone, in private, I mean," said Bobby.

Mikey scoffed. "That's not possible. We'll be going separately to the transfer station. We'll be with our families. People will be everywhere. I might not even get to see her before she transfers."

"But what if it was possible?"

"Where could we be alone? People will be everywhere."

"At home."

"We'll all be in the transfer line with our families," said Mikey.

"What if we could walk back home?"

Mikey laughed. "Kid brother, can you just tell me what you're talking about?"

"Tomorrow, we'll be at the end of the line because Dad's in charge. Remember at dinner last night, Dad said we probably won't transfer until late afternoon. Maybe not until night."

"So?"

"So, it's barely a mile walk home. You and Angel can easily go home, make love, and get back to the transfer station."

"It's more than a mile. Wait, did you just say, 'make love'?"

"I heard Rachel talking," replied Bobby.

Mikey shook his head. "Do you even know what making love is? Never mind. What if Angel transfers before I get there?"

"You'll have to find her before that."

"Her parents will never let her go with me. They didn't leave us alone the whole time I was at her house earlier today."

"They'll let her go if Dad goes with us," said Bobby. "Everyone trusts Dad."

"Bobby, I love you, but you're crazy."

"What if Dad went with us?" asked Bobby, unwilling to relent.

Mikey stopped, picked up a rock, and looked at a tall tree towering above them in the night sky. "If Dad went with us, Angel's parents would let her go with me, and you'd be the best brother in the entire universe, for all time." Mikey threw the rock, hitting the tree with a loud thwack. "But it doesn't matter, Dad's not going to do that."

The two brothers arrived home and snuck back into the

house. Candy sat at Mikey's bedroom door, waiting. She whined a little and slapped her tail on the floor, but she didn't bark.

"Little brother, sleep here, like when we were little."

"Really?"

Mikey patted the bed, and Candy jumped onto it. "All three of us. There's room."

Within seconds Mikey fell asleep, but Bobby lay awake. He waited a few minutes, then slipped out of bed. Careful not to wake Mikey, he tiptoed down the hallway to his parents' bedroom and crept up to his father's side of the bed. His dad was sound asleep. Bobby tapped him on the shoulder and his dad woke.

"What is it, Bobby? Is everything okay?"

"Dad, I want to play catch, one last time."

"Right now? It's too dark, Bobby."

"Not now, tomorrow, before we transfer. Out front like we always do. Can we?"

"How about in the morning, after my speech?"

"In the afternoon, before we transfer," said Bobby.

"Maybe, Son. We'll talk about it in the morning, after my last speech."

"Promise?"

"I promise. Now, go to bed. If we're going to play catch, I need you to be wide awake. I've got a new curveball to try out."

Bobby remained by the bed. He had one more thing to do.

"Is everything okay, Son?"

"What about Mikey?"

"He can play with us too."

"I mean, what does Mikey want most on his last day?"

"I honestly don't know. I'll ask him first thing tomorrow morning."

Bobby smiled, kissed his father, and ran back to bed.

STEVENS LOOKED over at his wife, who was still sound asleep. He'd come home late and exhausted, but thanks to Becky, his speech was ready, and it was a good one. They'd made love for hours.

He thought about the coming morning, their last day, his last speech. He looked forward to seeing the sunrise one last time. Now, thanks to Bobby, he'd be playing catch one last time, too. The Great Advance was the most important advance in the history of their society, but as their last day approached, the little things were increasingly important.

But what will happen to the holdouts? he worried. Becky had encouraged him to appeal to the little things tomorrow to convert those who remained. He wasn't exactly sure what that meant. She'd told him to listen carefully, that it might mean something different for every holdout.

Bobby came to mind next, such a good boy, such a smart boy. They'd play catch right after his speech. No, Bobby wanted him to talk to Mikey first. After his speech, he'd find out what Mikey wanted to do one last time, what Mikey wanted most on his last day. Then he'd play catch with Bobby.

Stevens fell asleep dreaming about his family being together forever in the Great Advance.

3
LAST SUNRISE

STEVENS WOKE up early to watch the last sunrise and give his last speech.

He'd begun delivering his morning speeches several years ago. On the first morning, the brightness of the sunrise had bothered him. On the second morning, its boldness annoyed him, so he turned away. On the third morning, a ray of orange snuck from behind a cloud and warmed him. The next, a brilliant array of colors overwhelmed him. From then on, he'd eagerly awaited the sunrise each morning. He wanted to share it with his family, so he began sketching its beauty in a journal.

Watching sunrises made Stevens happy and sad.

Happy, not because the sunrise was exciting and beautiful, but because the sunrise seemed alive. Stevens imagined how happy he'd soon feel seeing millions of sunrises, all across the universe, all at once.

Sadness was harder to describe because Stevens couldn't stay sad very long. The moment he felt sad, he became happy. Sadness had always been like that, suddenly appearing, then vanishing, replaced by happiness. He could make himself sad. It wasn't hard. He just thought about never seeing a sunrise again.

While awaiting the last sunrise, Stevens wondered how many other things he'd miss because he had never taken the time to notice. He'd have all the time in the world now. No, not in the world, in the universe.

Thinking about Mikey and Bobby, Stevens picked up the synaptic imager. He'd taken the device home from the lab, so his sons could sense the sunrise at its full brilliance without using their eyes. But they were still asleep. They would never know this last sunrise. That was okay. His sons would soon know millions of sunrises, and every single one would be experienced directly by their minds.

The sunrise was nearly at its brightest. Focusing the synaptic imager at the horizon, Stevens pressed "Record" and held the imager against his forehead. Without eyes filtering the sensation, waves of beauty immersed his mind.

"Would you like some coffee, Rob honey?" asked his wife, pulling up a chair beside him.

"Thank you," he replied, setting down the synaptic imager. Becky always asked if he wanted coffee after she'd already made it. Without Becky, Stevens knew he'd have been a scientist. Instead, she'd made him the most loved and important man in the world.

"Thanks for staying up with me last night. I know you're tired, but your last speech is important. The holdouts need you."

"I'm glad you pushed me," he said, sipping the coffee. "If not for you, none of this would be possible."

He saw Becky look at the horizon. The sunrise was disappearing. Only a soft orange glow remained. He transferred the sunrise from the synaptic imager to his journal, letting it take up all the remaining pages.

"I recorded this morning's sunrise," he said. "It's not the same as in person, but would you like to see it?"

"I think I'll wait for the real thing," she said, smiling.

He put his journal down. "I like when you call me Rob. You're the only one that still does."

Becky leaned over and kissed him on the cheek. "You're Stevens to the world, but you'll always be Rob to me."

She opened the journal revealing a sketch of a sunrise. "I tried to wake the boys. I know how much you wanted all of us to join you. But they're too tired from last night. I took them to the square last night to use the demo-portals one last time."

"Did you use one too?" Stevens asked, knowing the answer. His wife didn't need to. The demo-stations, outfitted with hundreds of portals, had been her idea to help people who'd become afraid, and his wife was fearless. She'd formally left the program a few years ago to raise Mikey and Bobby, but remarkably, her commitment and influence on the program remained strong. Stevens had been fearless too, until William's letter.

"No, it was too late," she said.

"Were their friends there?" Stevens asked.

"Yes, some of them," she said softly. "Bobby cried for almost a minute when he found out Troy's dog Blackie was running wild."

"Bobby's always known we can't bring pets."

"It's hard for Bobby, honey. He can't stay sad for long, so whenever he thinks about Candy staying behind, it hurts all over again. It's like you thinking of your father."

Stevens winced.

"I'm sorry. If your father was alive, he'd be proud. You know he would. Your mother too. The whole world loves you and depends on you."

"I know," he replied. "Candy's a good dog. I'm going to miss her."

They sat for a few more minutes together. The sunrise was over, and the sun was beating down on them. He didn't mind, but she did. Wiping sweat from his brow, Stevens wondered if he'd miss being too hot.

"What's wrong, Rob, really?" she asked. "We'll be transferring today. It's what we've been working for."

"The lines have gotten long, honey, hours long lately."

"Why? Our transfer station is only for the local neighborhood and families of employees working on the Great Advance."

"I don't know. It's just taking longer. People are more hesitant, taking more time, and we only have one chair. Also, there are more holdouts than we thought. We're not sure why, exactly." His voice trailed off. He knew one reason for the lines.

Their local transfer station had been sized for two transfer chairs, the second not needed, except as backup. About six months before, the ten-chair regional transfer station began experiencing unexpectedly long lines. Spare chairs, stored far away in deep underground containers, would have taken several days to retrieve, so Stevens had sent the backup chair to the regional station to relieve the congestion. Since the first transfer three years ago, not a single chair anywhere on the planet had broken, so no one had thought to return the backup chair. During the last several weeks, when the bulk of Great Advance employees were scheduled to transfer, Stevens remembered the backup chair and requested it be shipped back. Unfortunately, it disappeared in transit.

"The transportation system has completely broken down in the proximity of the regional transfer station," he'd been informed.

Out of an abundance of caution, despite no chair failures after billions of transfers, Stevens ordered his team to wait a few minutes between transfers to allow the chair to cool off, reducing the chance of a breakdown. The waiting period caused the lines. Thinking of the lines, he felt a pang of worry, then relief when the feeling disappeared.

"I'm starving," he said.

"Time to get breakfast going. I'll get the boys up." Becky leaned over and kissed him on the cheek. "Bacon?"

"Extra bacon," he replied. "When the boys wake up, can you tell them to see me?"

"Right after your speech, I'll have them come out."

Alone again, without a sunrise to wonder about, Stevens turned to work. It was his last morning and his last speech. With his thoughts, he commanded a holographic display to appear in front of him, adjusted the image to full brightness against the morning sun, and studied the morning reports. Transfer stations all around the world were on schedule, with no problems. It was their last day too. Some had already shut down.

Stevens looked at the infrastructure reports—more transportation failures. They'd be walking to the station later this morning, for sure. Next, he brought up the health and safety report and froze, in shock, then quickly calmed. Three new sightings of wild animals, one near the transfer station. Dozens of dog attacks, including an entire family at the lake. Stevens shuddered, thinking about how his boys often played on the shore. Thankfully, today was the last day. The second incident: a baby girl bitten in her backyard. She might die. Stevens knew her parents were holdouts. Maybe now they'd join the Great Advance.

INSIDE THE KITCHEN PREPARING BREAKFAST, Becky looked out at her husband, excited about their new beginning. His strength and commitment were as strong as ever, but increasingly, over the last few weeks, she sensed something else: regret, fatigue? She couldn't tell what. It seemed to have begun when Billy started working at their local transfer station. Rob had begun talking again about Anna's lab mishap. No, not the mishap, William's letter about the mishap, and how it had affected Billy. That was almost twenty years ago. Whatever the cause, Rob's mornings on the deck, and trying to convince the remaining holdouts, were wearing on him.

The night before had been wonderful. They had made love and stayed up late working on his speech. Her beloved Rob was tired. That was okay. After today, neither of them would ever need to sleep again and would be loving one another forever in the Great Advance.

4

LAST HOLDOUT

JIMEE WAS A GENIUS. Not a run-of-the-mill one in-a-hundred-years genius who might discover a new theory about how the world works.

Jimee was a different kind of genius. She had a gift of clear, unclouded observation. When other people saw a flock of birds overhead, Jimee saw two hundred thirty-seven birds, nineteen flapping their wings exactly in sync, twenty-two flapping exactly out of sync from the nineteen, and the rest flapping at various unique rates. When other people heard a pack of dogs barking, Jimee heard twelve dogs barking. When other people felt rain or snow on their skin, Jimee felt forty-three drops of rain per second. She could tell whether a snowflake hit her arm on a flat side of the flake or an edge.

Jimee was a good person. She loved the pure goodness inherent in everyone everywhere. Her power of observation enabled her to notice two odd things about people, though. When in large crowds, where few people knew each other, Jimee sensed that everyone seemed to be connected somehow, except for herself. She felt apart from everyone, even from people she knew. The observation didn't bother her. She liked being different and knew everyone loved her for who she was.

Jimee wondered if her being different was related to her

second observation about people. She noticed that something seemed to make people happy and actively prevented them from being sad or afraid. In school, Jimee told her teacher about her observation. Jimee's teacher laughed and patted her head.

"This is how people have always been," her teacher said. "People are always happy and good, and always will be."

Jimee wasn't convinced. Something else seemed to be at play. No matter the circumstances, even when people had cause to be upset, they rarely expressed fear, anger, or frustration, and when they did, they recovered quickly, apologized, and returned to being genuinely nice to one another. The only time people were sad was when they lost a loved one or a friend to old age or an accident.

Jimee's curiosity about fear and sadness grew. Her gift of observation allowed her to determine who had recently lost someone close to them, and by the tone of their voice, how long ago.

Mysteriously, when someone became sad, Jimee detected something rise up and suppress the sadness, reducing it until it was gone and replacing it with happiness. As far as Jimee knew, she was the only one who questioned the struggle between happy and sad.

Her childhood had been challenging. Her father died when she was a baby, and her mother when she was three. Jimee was a good student but had a difficult time fitting in at school. On a planet populated with loving and supportive people, Jimee grew up learning to accept her genius and any anxiety her great observational powers caused her.

But she missed her mother. Her memory of her mother's death drove her to understand the struggle between happy and sad. She had no idea how to go about it, so she decided to study everything. Her mother would have liked that.

At the very least, Jimee reasoned, if she learned everything, she might also discover why everyone except her seemed connected. Maybe the connection between people and the struggle between happy and sad were related. So she studied everything—history, science, math, philosophy, medicine, art, music, but she couldn't find the answers she was looking for.

JOIN THE GREAT ADVANCE! Jimee remembered the first time she saw the slogan of the Great Advance in a college hallway where she worked. The building was twelve thousand three hundred and forty-two years old, one of the oldest buildings in existence. The floor had been soft white without a speck of dirt or a scuff mark anywhere. The walls of the building were self-cleaning glass, not a fingerprint to be seen. Displays were integrated into the walls, flashing messages or streaming videos. Children often ran at the glass wall, laughing. The wall changed colors to warn of a collision, then changed to a soft foam, safely catching and bouncing the children back to the middle of the hallway. Jimee had never played that game when she was little, but she remembered watching her friends play. The materials science enabling the morphing glass had fascinated her until she understood how simple it was.

Despite her genius and excellent grades, Jimee hadn't gone to college. Unlike mandatory high school, colleges had to be joined. Jimee preferred her isolated uniqueness. Fortunately, she found a job maintaining the planet's old infrastructure, which valued her genius and allowed her to be alone. For Jimee, it became the perfect job because it supported her curiosity about happiness and sadness.

Second only to the Great Advance, which recruited the best scientists, maintaining old buildings was considered the most scientifically and technically challenging job on the planet. Due to her genius of observation, Jimee found the job easy.

Tens of thousands of years before she was born, the population growth necessitated the development of a fully integrated planet infrastructure. Seemingly natural on the surface, the planet's infrastructure had become an interconnected system, deeply intertwining every building. Even the seemingly serene residential neighborhoods and dense forests were superimposed upon sophisticated, aged infrastructure.

Before long, it had become risky and impractical to rebuild the aged, interconnected framework. Preserving, reinforcing and refurbishing replaced rebuilding, but projects that had once taken years now took decades.

Safety had become an issue, which, tragically, Jimee knew well. Her mother's job had been maintaining the forests. She'd died while working on forest infrastructure critical for the planet's air supply.

Noticing aging was important to maintaining old infrastructure. The key was seeing aging before it created damage. Jimee saw the significance in the most insignificant things. Once she observed the aging, other people would make repairs.

She worked alone and liked working alone. Many of her coworkers worked together, but rarely with Jimee. Occasionally, if an observation was uncertain, the coworkers asked her for a second opinion before reporting an issue to the fixers. Sometimes, for especially insidious aging issues that might require relocating thousands of people, the infrastructure observers met as a group before reporting the problem. Jimee never required second opinions.

The oldest buildings on the planet were located at colleges with vast libraries and computer archives. All day long, during breaks and even while working, Jimee studied in the colleges, researching the conundrum of happy versus sad.

Jimee loved her job. It was unheard of for people not to like their jobs. She sometimes wondered how everyone could be happy at their work. Many bad jobs had been automated, but it seemed that bad jobs still existed, and people were happy with those jobs for some reason. She suspected it had to do with the battle between happy and sad.

As she worked and observed the most infinitesimal things, she completely ignored the plethora of Great Advance messages that flashed from the walls of the hallways.

Hope for the Great Advance

The Great Advance is Almost Here!

The Great Advance Needs More Scientists—Please Apply

Then, one day, the wall displays flashed a brand-new message.

Join the Great Advance!

Jimee became a holdout the instant she saw the message because she didn't join things, especially things crowded with people who didn't understand what they were joining.

A few days after she saw the new message, one of Jimee's coworkers called a group meeting. Except for Jimee, all twenty coworkers were exactly on time for the meeting, causing a brief wait in the hallway while filing into the room. Jimee, however, arrived twenty-seven seconds late in anticipation of the delay. There was a large conference table in the middle, but no one sat down. They all stood facing outward, toward displays built into the walls. The group waited for the coworker who'd called the meeting to project the issue onto the displays.

"Do you all mind sitting down?" asked Terri, the group leader. Everyone sat except Jimee, who didn't like groups and planned to end the meeting by solving the issue within seconds after it was described.

"Jimee, do you mind sitting down, please?" asked Terri.

She complied. Terri had been a close friend of Jimee's mother and had kept in touch with Jimee while she was growing up. After high school, Jimee wandered aimlessly, not caring to join anything. Terri had sought her out and offered her a job as an observer.

"You've all seen the new message?" asked Terri.

Jimee expected the small holographic displays to emerge from the conference table to display the message, but nothing happened.

"I heard the fixers are leaving their jobs," a coworker said.

"They're quitting?" asked another coworker.

"No, the fixers have been reassigned to build transfer systems for the Great Advance," replied Terri.

"Makes sense. Everyone knows fixers build the most reliable equipment," offered a different coworker. "There's no reason to fix anything anymore."

"That's not why I called you all here," said Terri.

"The Great Advance project will need observers too, won't they?" asked another. "They can't build reliable equipment without us."

"I agree. Fixers need to know what to strengthen," said another.

"Are you guys joining the Great Advance?" asked another. "I signed up the second I saw the new message. I'm going the first week, I think."

"When will that be?"

"They haven't set a date yet. Supposedly, a couple of years from now the transfer systems will be ready."

"They'll need observers, won't they? To guarantee the transfer systems work perfectly for everyone."

"We can't guarantee anything."

"No, but if the transfer equipment is designed to work forever, it will likely work for a few years until everyone is transferred."

"That's why they need the fixers."

"And why they need us."

"Everyone," said Terri. "You are discussing very important things. But let me tell you why I called you here. If everyone can stop talking and focus for a minute, I can answer most of your questions."

Everyone paused except Jimee, who hadn't been talking. She stifled the urge to voice the error, which would have required talking.

"You've all heard the wonderful news," said Terri. "The Great Advance has entered a new phase. Scientists estimate in another three years the program will begin. Using prototype systems, they've resolved all technical problems. The technology is safe. The technology works. Now it's a matter of manufacturing and mass-producing reliable transfer equipment. Special design teams are being formed. The scientists who designed the prototypes need to be assisted by the best production, reliability, and safety people on our planet."

Jimee stifled the urge to interrupt and voice a second error. All of her colleagues were indeed the best, except one, and Terri knew it. That was a deliberate mistake.

"Jimee, do you have a question?" asked Terri.

Jimee shook her head, thankful she hadn't been asked if she had an observation.

Terrie continued. "Reliability and safety are where we come in. Some members of our team and members from several other teams around the planet have been selected to join the design teams. It's a great honor, not only because we were selected, but because we've been identified as the best of the best among the tens of thousands of reliability and safety experts in our organization. So, for the next three years until the Great Advance begins, some of you will work with the design teams." Terri paused for questions.

"Not all of us?" asked a coworker.

"How long until the Great Advance begins?" interrupted a coworker.

"Good question, Eugene. Three years is the estimate," said Terri.

Everyone nodded approvingly as if Eugene had asked a good question, except Jimee, who winced, thinking of her mother. She wondered how it was possible for Eugene to be so oblivious.

He was older, about the same age that Jimee's mother would have been had she lived, and he'd maintained the same forest her mother had. Jimee's mother died because an access hatch had been left open in the forest, an act of carelessness. Accidents were learning experiences, so no one was blamed. However, Jimee suspected Eugene was at fault. By checking the records, Jimee discovered Eugene had been assigned to the same area as her mother the day before the accident.

"Are you okay?" Terri asked Jimee.

"Yes, thank you," replied Jimee.

"When do we start?" asked a coworker.

"We start immediately, but as I was saying, not all of us. The survival systems still need to be maintained, so those of you inspecting essential infrastructure, including forests, disposal, communications, transport clusters, wild animals, and food and water will continue in your current jobs. Those of you assigned to inspect static infrastructure, including buildings, roads, and bridges, will be reassigned to transfer design teams."

Everyone nodded except Eugene. Jimee sensed his disappointment and quickly thought of a plan to test happy versus sad.

"That makes sense," said a coworker assigned to food safety. "We won't be needing thousand-year-old buildings anymore, but we have to eat until every last person transfers."

"That's right," said Terri. "We'll need to keep the survival systems running until the last week. Those of you maintaining survival systems will transfer last. Those of you on the long-term infrastructure teams report to the main lobby of the Great Advance tomorrow morning. Tell them your name. Each of you is already assigned to a design team. Any questions?" There were none. "Okay, thank you."

"Ma'am, I have a request," said Jimee, eyeing Eugene. He

seemed so disappointed that he wasn't listening. She worried her plan would fail.

"Yes, Jimee. What is it?"

Jimee waited, looking at Eugene. He noticed and looked back. Holding Eugene's gaze, Jimee continued. "I'd like to request someone take my place."

"Why?" asked Terri.

"I'll go in her place," said Eugene.

Jimee smiled inside. Her plan was working. "I'm a hold-out. I'll trade with Eugene," she said. "I know the forest well."

Terri waited, giving the other coworkers an opportunity to speak up. No one did. She asked the remaining long-term infrastructure people if they were okay joining design teams. All of them were excited about the opportunity.

"Are you sure, Jimee?" asked Terri.

"Yes." Jimee readied her mind. If her plan was to work, she had to be ready. Everyone on the planet was so wonderful and kind that, since her mother's death, Jimee had rarely been genuinely sad and never angry. Her plan was to get angry and to observe if something came and took her anger away.

"Thank you, Jimee," said Eugene, extending his hand.

Prepared for the anger Jimee knew would come, she grasped Eugene's hand. Resentment and animosity overcame her. She squeezed. He winced. She registered her every emotion. Happiness didn't come. Her heart raced. Her stomach tightened. Her anger grew. She squeezed harder.

"You're welcome," Jimee said, glaring at Eugene.

She felt his hand pop. He jerked, trying to pull away. She sensed his fear, then sensed happiness come, but not to her. Happy came only for Eugene. She released his hand. She felt his fear fade, overcome by happiness. Eugene smiled. Jimee seethed.

"Really, Jimee, thank you so much," he said, patting her arm.

Shaking slightly, unaided by happiness, Jimee mustered

strength from within herself and calmed her anger. Her plan had worked, but the result was unexpected. She was different from everyone else. Why?

"It's decided then," said Terri. "I'll swap your names. Jimee, tomorrow, please report to the forest safety division. Thank you, everyone."

5

SYSTEMS FAILURE

JIMEE MAINTAINED the forests for the next three years, spending most of her time in the forest where her mother had worked. She discovered that she liked the assignment better than her former job analyzing buildings. In the forest, Jimee was truly alone.

The spot where the hatch had been left open had long since been cleared, and she went there often to eat lunch, to contemplate, and to study her books. The forest held no libraries or computers, so Jimee brought her own books. She stored them in the compartment beneath the ground where her mother had fallen. Jimee imagined studying with her mother. While studying, she remembered the appearance and sudden vanishing of her mother's fear. The memory made Jimee study harder.

She also liked the absence of displays in the forests. In buildings, displays were integrated into doors, walls, and tables, everywhere, for people to receive information and communicate. They even popped up in open spaces using holographic images and were tastefully and artistically tuned to the preferences of nearby people. Jimee's preference was for no displays. If she was alone in a room, displays would be off because of her preference, but if anyone else entered the room, they would be activated.

Jimee's apartment had two displays, one wall-mounted and the other holographic, but they were never activated. For three years working in the forest, she never saw an operating display.

One morning as Jimee was getting ready for work, both displays in her apartment turned on. The wall-mounted one beeped and flashed a message.

Hello, Jimee. Please report to the animal safety division.

She was careful not to nod or make any motion the display might interpret as a response. Jimee didn't like to talk to people. She liked talking to machines even less. The holographic display projected an image of a man sitting on a short stool on a deck. Behind the man was a beautiful house. To the side of the house, she could see the edge of one of the forests that she maintained. The man started speaking.

"Hello, my name is Stevens. Yesterday, our people officially began the journey to the Great Advance with our first two transfers. I'm happy to tell you—" Jimee pushed a button to turn off the display, but it wouldn't turn off.

"Display off," she commanded, overcoming her distaste for talking to machines.

Surprisingly, the display stayed on. Mandatory holo-broadcasts were usually limited to major storm warnings or other safety announcements. Jimee considered trying the mute button, then decided it didn't matter because she was leaving.

She left for work, leaving the holo-comm system mid-broadcast, and doing as instructed, reporting to the animal safety division. In addition to Jimee, there were forty-three other workers. She assumed they had received the same message on their displays. The lobby was busy with people, but most of them were leaving. This was odd given that they should have been arriving for work in the morning. A woman greeted Jimee and the others with a big smile.

"Hi, everyone. Thank you for coming," she said. The workers approached the woman, gathering around her in a semicircle. "It's such a wonderful day. Did you hear?" she asked.

"Hear what?" asked a worker.

"The transfers started yesterday! Not only that, the animal safety division was selected to be one of the first teams to transfer."

"What about the animals?" asked a worker. "Some of them are very dangerous."

"We've put them in pens."

Jimee didn't react, but several others did, visibly wincing. The woman noticed.

"It's cruel, we know," she said. "It's just until everyone has transferred. Then the pens will automatically release the animals. Can you all excuse me for a minute? Hey!" she shouted at someone behind Jimee.

A man who was leaving the building stopped and turned around. "Hey, Sue! See you tomorrow," he shouted.

"What time are you getting there?" asked Sue.

"I'm in the second group. I'll be getting there about ten," he replied.

"I'm in the first group. Get there early, okay?"

"I will. See you tomorrow!" The man waved as he disappeared through the door.

Sue returned her attention to Jimee and the workers, with an even bigger smile than before. "Sorry about that interruption. So, where was I? Oh, I remember. In addition to maintaining the forests, we're going to ask you to maintain the pens."

"You mean with the wild animals?" asked a worker.

Sue laughed. "No, silly, we know you aren't trained to care for wild animals. That's why we built fully automatic pens. All you have to do is maintain them. If the pens are working, the animals will be kept safe and away from people. The pens will do everything for the animals, including automatically feed them."

For the next several months, Jimee worked to maintain the forests and the wild animal pens. At the forest offices or the wild animal offices, she sometimes encountered coworkers and discovered many of them were holdouts. Like Jimee, they had all been assigned double duty, at both the forests and the pens. Some pens broke down, but never so badly that animals escaped.

Around the third month, Jimee noticed dogs inside the pens. She asked about the dogs and learned from another holdout that they had been pets of families that had transferred. The dogs didn't last long in the pens. Jimee reported that the dogs were being killed by wild animals, but nothing changed. Jimee and her coworkers decided to help the dogs. Whenever they saw a dog in a pen, they let it out.

Every morning before she went to work, the holographic display of the man called Stevens was projected into the middle of her apartment. Jimee listened to his speech a few times. Stevens always talked about the Great Advance, carefully addressing people's concerns in a direct and thoughtful manner. He respectfully described reasons people didn't want to go: fear of a system malfunction, worry about the unknown, or holding on to the present. Stevens described how people had overcome system-related concerns after the first million trouble-free transfers, but that worries about the unknown was more difficult to overcome. To help people with their worry about the unknown, Stevens asked everyone to visit special demo-stations installed by the Great Advance program. People could use demo-portals built into actual transfer chairs to communicate with others who had already engaged the transfer. While the demo-portal was only a window and not an actual transfer, the excitement in the voices of those who had already transferred helped people overcome their fear of the beyond.

Stevens described how people were unaware of what they truly cherished, and how much they would miss the beauty in everyday things, until their scheduled time of transfer actually arrived. He described how it wasn't uncommon for people to back out seconds before their transfer. In time, Stevens stressed, with counseling and support, even the most hesitant person would become enthusiastic about transferring to the Great Advance.

Jimee was impressed by Stevens's speech, but it didn't affect her determination to remain a holdout. After a few months of hearing the speeches and maintaining the forests and animal pens, Jimee's wall display flashed a new message.

Hello, Jimee. Please report to the food and water division.

A few months later, Jimee's wall display flashed another message.

Hello, Jimee. Please report to the transportation division.

And a month later, a new message flashed.

Hello, Jimee. Please report to the communications division. That was the last message to report to a new division.

Jimee and other holdouts around the world were maintaining all the vital systems for the entire planet. They held large meetings to discuss strategies for maintaining them. During the calls, some holdouts expressed resentment but said they couldn't hold the feeling for long. Others expressed appreciation because they were learning important things that would help them survive once everyone else transferred.

Many holdouts changed their minds and joined the Great Advance, so the systems became harder to maintain. Anticipating system failures, the holdouts stockpiled food and water in various locations around the planet. One day, the animal pens failed. Jimee felt sad seeing the wild animals starve to death. She sensed sadness in her colleagues too, but only momentarily. Jimee realized she'd likely never learn why happy vanquished sad in others but never within herself.

She and her colleagues worked hard, keeping the forests

alive to provide clean air, and maintaining the food, water, transportation, and communications systems.

One morning, a large video conference meeting was called for the remaining workers—nearly all were holdouts. They were informed that the last day of the Great Advance would be in two months. There had been delays. The workers were asked to maintain vital systems until then. Jimee and a few holdouts from around the planet who were especially gifted at math modeled the problem. The uncertainty was how many holdouts would convert or quit in the final weeks. Jimee and her coworkers reported that maintaining food, water, and air was feasible, but the transportation and communications systems might break down during the final weeks and would certainly fail before the last day. The workers were thanked for their service. The meeting ended, and the screens switched to display positive messages about the Great Advance.

Jimee watched and started to feel anxious. Her world had long ago developed past the point where people could survive without a trained workforce to run and maintain the sophisticated planetary infrastructure necessary for basic services. Food, medicine, and climate control were global services that required the support and maintenance of millions of specially trained people working together—people who had already transferred. The worldwide availability of these services over the centuries had enabled the population to focus on science, society, enlightenment, and culture. Without modern technology and expert support personnel, basic survival would not be possible for more than a generation or two.

Jimee understood that staying behind would mean a life of hardship not experienced on the planet for centuries. She would be facing those new challenges with a small group of holdouts. To survive would require a new kind of society to deal with a new reality. Everything would need to be forged anew.

Jimee wasn't sure why she should transfer, but she knew why she should stay behind. She was still looking to understand the conflict between happy versus sad and needed more time. If she joined the Great Advance, she might never find the truth.

6
LAST SPEECH

STEVENS TOOK A DEEP BREATH. He was ready but nervous, knowing his speech was his last chance to change the minds of holdouts. He would broadcast to every person on the planet as he had done every day since the Great Advance was formally approved.

Nearly everyone on the planet had transferred. From the Great Advance project, only Stevens, the staff assigned to operate the transfer machines, and their families remained. By the end of the day, the final hundred thousand people would transfer. There were still a few thousand holdouts who didn't want to go. Some were frightened, some didn't want to leave a beloved pet, or, Stevens now surmised, some didn't want to leave watching sunrises or playing catch behind.

He focused his mind. A few thought commands later, a holo-channel was established to connect Stevens to every remaining person. Less than a second later, a holographic projection of him appeared in front of each holdout. Loud sirens blasted from the system's speakers, guaranteeing attention to Stevens's last broadcast.

He began his speech.

JIMEE WAS one of the last holdouts listening to Stevens. She sensed something different about him, then realized he was sad. Even through the holographic display, Jimee could tell. This morning, the tone of sadness in Stevens was strong and unusual, staying longer before being pushed away. She knew Stevens had not lost a loved one or a friend. Something different was causing his sadness. Then she noticed something odd. Stevens was sweating. It was odd because people rarely got sick. Maybe he was hot from the sun, or maybe from a battle within him, between happy and sad.

She focused on every sound, every pattern, every frequency, and on the specific words Stevens chose. She followed his eyes. He'd glance at a holo-image of a holdout and become sad, then his tone would change as if something was interfering, rejecting the sad, beating it back. He'd glance at another holdout, and the cycle would repeat. He glanced at her. His sadness surged. Jimee gasped. She was one of the holdouts! She was making Stevens sad!

"This is my last worldwide address. After today, our civilization will have completed the Great Advance. We begin a new chapter in our existence and embrace the entire universe. We move forward from our physical world into a spiritual world. For thousands of years, we have lived a glorious existence on this planet. In the beginning, there was hunger, so we created tools and learned to farm and hunt. There was cold, so we discovered fire. There were wild animals, so we learned to live peacefully with all creatures. There was disease, so we discovered medicine. With each advance, our bond with our planet and our love for each other grew stronger. We are born alone, but with each generation, our civilization developed a deep understanding of our world, our universe, and ourselves."

As Stevens's speech unfolded, Jimee was satisfied the communications system was working well. She and her fellow holdouts had worked tirelessly to keep it running but knew the communication system would completely fail shortly after the broadcast. All available power was being diverted to the transfer stations.

Jimee had seen enough. The off switch on her display had been disabled, so she bent over to access the power unit to unplug herself from the planetary communications system and was surprised to feel a prickling on her thigh. She recognized that the feeling came from a photograph of her mother that was in her pocket.

Smiling, she imagined her mother telling her to listen to Stevens, to be respectful, not to disconnect, even if she wasn't going on the Great Advance.

"Over the centuries, our people came to understand that our achievements were never unique or separate, but instead were a way to unify everyone in common goals and advancements. The Great Advance is the ultimate destiny for our souls. Every advance we have taken together. Our ancestors built ships and crossed the seas. Our forefathers created spaceships and explored the solar system. Over the last century, some of your grandparents and some of your parents made the ultimate sacrifice to enable this final journey, the Great Advance."

Jimee tried to focus on Stevens but felt another prickling on her leg. She reached into her pocket, took out the photograph, and looked at the picture of her mother. She smiled, knowing whatever caused happy to overcome sad had nothing to do with her feelings for the picture. Her mother had been beautiful.

"Imagine the boundless happiness of your children in the Great Advance, at the peak of their wondrous curiosity, no longer bound to a single world already explored, their every discovery already known centuries before. Once in the Great Advance, your children's infinite curiosity will be matched by the infinite wonders of the universe."

Still listening to Stevens, Jimee remembered her mother

and their last day together. It had been Jimee's third birthday. It was the day she took her mother's photograph. It was also the day her mother fell through the hatch in the forest.

REALIZING his speech was having little effect, Stevens leaned forward and raised his voice. "Every advance, we have taken together. The Great Advance is the release of our souls from a planet that was once infinitely vast but now limits and confines us. The Great Advance will release our souls from physical bodies that were once a mystery of creation but now constrain and limit our growth."

He paused, frustrated. He could see from the attention feedback on his holo-comm panel that he was losing people. They couldn't turn the system off, but they could turn the volume down so low that he was nearly muted. Almost everyone had done so.

This is their last chance, and they won't listen, he thought. *They are all going to die.* Stevens considered ending his speech early, giving up.

Let them die, he told himself, growing angry. *All the education, all the explanations about the Great Advance and still the holdouts don't want to go.*

He reached to turn off the holo-comm system, then felt something reenergize him, fade his frustration, leaving only sadness. Then the sadness faded too. Instead of turning the system off, Stevens turned up the volume. Leaving the holo-comm system, he ran into his office. With a large black marker, he wrote two lines on a blank piece of paper in large block letters.

JIMEE SENSED Stevens's sadness and felt sad too, but unlike Stevens's, her sadness remained. She looked down at the photograph. A tear splashed onto her mother. Jimee remembered holding the camera.

"Take the picture, Jimee," her mother had said.

7

PLEASE BLINK, MOMMY

* Jimee, three years old *

"TAKE THE PICTURE, JIMEE."

"I just push the button, Mommy?"

"Yes, honey, but not too hard."

"It's heavy."

"I know, honey. It's old. Daddy loved antiques. Am I still centered?"

Jimee pushed the button.

"You took it? Was I centered?" Jimee's mother asked.

Jimee hadn't known how to use the camera, but by observing the relative position of her mother and the camera, she had known her mother was precisely centered.

"I took it, Mommy," Jimee said.

"Did you hear the click?"

"Yes, Mommy. It clicked."

Jimee actually heard three clicks, one when she pushed the button, another when an invisible crack in the casing shifted under pressure of the first click, and a third when the camera advanced the film for another picture. Jimee's mother walked over, took the camera, and patted Jimee on the head.

"That's a real click, not the electronic clicks other cameras make," her mother said. She knelt down beside Jimee and gave her a hug. "I can't believe you're three years old already."

"Why, Mommy? Wasn't I born three years ago?"

"Oh, Jimee, I love you."

"There were three clicks," Jimee said.

"Three? There should have only been one."

Jimee wondered if she could show her mother the source of the second click without taking apart the camera. Her mother would never allow that.

"Maybe Daddy made the second click," said Jimee.

"Oh, Jimee, you're such a good girl," her mother said softly.

Jimee looked at her mother. To a three-year-old girl as different as Jimee, her mother was her everything. Even more so for Jimee, since her father had died shortly after she was born.

She knew her mother had an important job taking care of plants and trees that made clean air for everyone. When her mother worked in the distant part of the forest, she often took Jimee for company, causing her to miss school. Jimee didn't mind. She didn't like school.

Her dislike for school wasn't because children picked on her. No one was ever picked on. Jimee didn't like school because she had to pretend to be dumb to fit in. With her mother, Jimee could be herself. Her mother knew she was different, and that she didn't relate to others, not even to her teachers. For Jimee's sake, her mother began planning her work to maintain the far edges of the forest more frequently.

Her mother recognized Jimee's genius and had dedicated herself to developing her daughter's potential. She would point out the tiniest things, even pollen and dust specs and teeny little bugs, and ask Jimee to describe them. She liked when her mother explained things that she could feel but not see, like wind and sound. Her mother explained that invisible things could be powerful, like gravity and magnetism, and sometimes clashed, like hot and cold.

"Try to understand everything, Jimee," her mother would say after explaining something particularly complex. Then she would laugh and say, "Everything is a lot of things. Might take a million years, so we better keep learning!"

Jimee laughed with her mother when she said this, although Jimee didn't understand why it was funny. Jimee knew math. The planet wasn't big enough to take that long to understand everything. The universe might be, though.

Jimee's mother held up the camera. "In honor of your first picture on your daddy's camera, this roll is for you," she said, patting Jimee's head before picking her up. "We'll be home soon, honey."

The dense forest made slow going. There were no trails. Jimee couldn't see the ground beneath the plants.

"The wilderness is denser than it would be if allowed to grow normally," her mother explained.

Jimee liked that her mother talked in great detail while they walked. Whatever Jimee didn't understand, she remembered and asked about later, after they got home. While walking, her mother explained how plants had been bred to grow extra thick. It made the air better for the people. Jimee already knew that.

"We water and feed the soil from a network of tunnels below. That's how we get the plants to grow so thick," her mother said. Jimee didn't know that.

"Can I walk by myself, Mommy?"

"Can you stay right behind me?"

"I will."

"Wait, I have an idea." Her mother took off her jacket and then her shirt. She tied the shirt sleeve to the belt strap on the back of her pants and handed the other sleeve to Jimee. "Here, hold on to this."

Jimee took the sleeve. Her mother put her jacket back on.

"Don't let go."

"I won't."

"Squint your eyes when we walk. If your eyes get scratched by a branch, it really, really hurts. Can you remember to squint your eyes?"

"Yes, Mommy," said Jimee, knowing she would only squint when her mother checked on her. She didn't need to squint, because she could see every twig on every branch, every edge of every leaf, and anything that might poke and scratch her eyes well before it actually scratched her eyes.

"You promise?"

"I promise."

"Okay, let's go."

They started walking again, slowly. Jimee knew her mother was worried about Jimee tripping in the dense brush. Her mother stopped several times to make sure she was okay. Each time, Jimee squinted and tightened her grip on the sleeve just before her mother turned. One time, Jimee squinted so hard, she didn't see a branch. The branch scratched her cheek and made her cry. Jimee's mother knelt down and hugged her.

"Oh, my little Jimee," she said, wetting her fingers in her mouth, then rubbing the wetness over the scratch. Jimee was surprised how much better it made her feel. She squinted her eyes even tighter and squeezed the sleeve to show her mother that she was a good girl. Her eyes were squinted so tightly that she could barely see her mother.

"You're so cute."

To impress her mother even more, Jimee squinted her eyes until she couldn't see her mother at all. Jimee heard her mother laugh and felt more wetness on her forehead, then a smooching sound, then a coolness as the forest air touched her wet forehead. Jimee had felt that smooching wetness before, every night when her mother kissed her goodnight. Tightening her grip on the sleeve, she readied herself to go and heard her mother stand up.

"Stay close, honey, we'll be home soon."

Jimee wanted to wipe her forehead but didn't. She didn't want her mother to see. At home in bed, Jimee would wait until her mother had gone before wiping the wet kiss away.

Through her squinted eyes, she saw her mother turn to start walking. Then she heard two sounds she'd never heard before, a swishing and a yelp. The next instant, the sleeve jerked, yanking Jimee forward onto her chest, dragging her. The sleeve ripped from her tiny hands. She heard a scream, a loud thud, then nothing. She opened her eyes. Her mother was gone.

"Mommy?"

Jimee heard the wind, weaving through trees high above, birds, rustling in nearby bushes, twigs and specks of dirt, shifting under insect's tiny feet. She heard thousands of sounds. Each sound she processed. Each sound she recognized. None came from her mother. Suddenly, Jimee heard her mother breathe. The wetness on Jimee's forehead felt warm.

She crawled forward and saw that her mother had fallen down a hole and wasn't moving. Jimee crawled to the side of the hole where it was less steep and crept down. A minute later, she was at her mother's side.

"Mommy?"

Jimee's mother lay on her stomach, struggling to breathe. Jimee touched her shoulder. She felt her mother struggle to move, then grow still. She saw her mother's hair, matted wet, dripping dark red. Jimee knew it was blood.

She lay down beside her mother, her face on the ground, sideways facing her mother, an inch away. Jimee felt the warmth of her mother's breath and looked into her mother's eyes. Jimee and her mother had looked at each other many times before, but not like this, not so deeply. Her mother started to shake. Jimee reached out and touched her mother on the cheek.

"I'm afraid, Jimee," her mother whispered.

Jimee felt her mother's fear, and it made her afraid too. She snuggled closer, so close their noses touched. She felt something invisible and warm push her mother's fear away. Jimee's fear remained strong and unabated.

"Don't be afraid, Jimee."

Jimee heard a thousand sounds. The loudest sound of all was the quiet within her mother.

"Everything is a lot of things, Mommy. Wake up, it might take a million years."

The next moment, the wetness on Jimee's forehead felt cold. Her mother's eyes looked different. Jimee leaned in and kissed her mother's cheek, a wet kiss, just like her mother gave. Eyes an inch apart, Jimee saw that her mother wasn't blinking. She tried not to blink either.

"Please blink, Mommy."

Jimee lay still for a long time, a million years, she imagined. Her mother's eyes were open but weren't looking. Jimee closed her mother's eyes with her tiny fingers as gently as she could.

"Don't be afraid, Mommy."

8

DON'T BE AFRAID

WHERE IS STEVENS? wondered Jimee, wiping a tear from her cheek. It felt strange, the wetness on her face. Another tear came. She was careful not to let it drop onto her mother's picture.

STEVENS RAN BACK to his holo-comm system, clutching the sign. He knew he'd been gone too long. Holdouts weren't even looking at the holo-comm. Many had wandered away. He pressed the emergency alert button, emitting a loud alarm. It worked. Everyone looked. Stevens held up the sign.

STAY AND DIE. GO AND LIVE FOREVER.

No more speeches, Stevens thought. Ten seconds passed. Twenty seconds. One minute. No one seemed to move. He worried that the communications system had failed. Then he saw people start moving.

Good, it's still working. To his dismay, one by one, the holdouts walked away from their holo-comm systems, shaking their heads.

No, don't go! Stevens couldn't understand why they wanted to die.

Sadly, he switched all holo-systems from mandatory to voluntary and watched as his audience panel showed the hold-outs disconnecting en masse. Out of frustration, he pressed the emergency alert button again, sending another alarm blasting through the communications system, hoping to regain at least one holdout's attention. He waited, still holding the sign. The audience count fell, pausing at a few hundred remaining viewers, then continuing to zero.

"No wait! Not zero. One," Stevens said aloud. There was one holdout still watching.

He zoomed his display to better see the holdout, hoping to recognize who it was. He didn't. He brought up the holdout's records. Her name was Jimee. Her father had died when she was a baby. Her mother had died three years later from a fall in the forest. Rescuers found Jimee nearly starved to death, lying next to her mother. Jimee had been delirious and whispering to her mother. When the rescuers tried to pick up Jimee, she had clung to her mother's neck, not letting go.

"Don't be afraid, Mommy," she had been repeating over and over.

Excited by a new idea, Stevens took the sign down. He flipped it over and wrote a new message.

JIMEE SAW STEVENS, visibly excited, take the sign down and write a new message. She stared at the sign. It read:

DON'T BE AFRAID

Jimee was not afraid. Not before she saw the sign, not after the sign. She knew Stevens had accessed her history. The sign reminded her of what her mother had said every time they were in the forest.

"Understand everything," her mother had said. Her mother's words made Jimee realize joining the Great Advance might enable her to find the answers she sought. In the Great Advance, she could explore the universe to discover the connection between happy and sad.

Jimee pressed the button to change her status from a holdout to a transfer. She saw Stevens smile. Transfer instructions streamed onto her display. She smiled back.

9

KISSED BY THE GREAT ADVANCE

Anna stared at the display. Her life was perfect. Her every dream had come true except one, until now.

Congratulations, Anna. Your health monitor indicates you're going to have a healthy baby boy!

Anna quickly sent a reply to her doctor. *Don't tell William! I want to surprise him!*

She couldn't wait to tell her husband, William, that he was going to be a daddy. Her excitement pushed her to walk as fast as she could, one hand on her flat belly, laughing at herself for imagining she could already feel her baby kicking.

She'd wondered about being pregnant during the Great Advance, but William had assured her it wasn't a problem because the project would be phased to accommodate everyone. Besides, the Great Advance was at least a decade away. The timing was perfect!

Her walk to the Great Advance headquarters, where William worked as a top scientist, took about twenty minutes. She went to an outside deck where they normally met for lunch. Realizing lunch was still an hour away, she walked inside to find him.

The building was enormous, but Anna knew where to go based on William's many tours. She went to his office first, but he wasn't there, so she went to his laboratory. Anna reached to open the lab door, then stopped. Bubbling with excitement, she touched her tummy and imagined the door opening. Standing in the doorway would be her beloved William. She'd take his hand, place it on her belly, and say: "William, meet your new son, Billy!"

Laughing at the image, Anna knocked on the door, but no one answered. She heard a whirring noise. William probably couldn't hear her knocking, so she tried the door. It was locked. She knocked again and stood on her toes to look through the window of the door but couldn't see anything. The window had been covered from the inside with some kind of shiny metal material.

She decided to go back to the deck to wait for William, then remembered she still had his access card in her purse. One day, he'd left his card at home and had gotten a new one. He'd told Anna to keep the old card as a backup in case he lost his card again.

Anna used the card to open the lab door and walked inside. The laboratory was empty. That was the last thing she remembered.

"ANNA?"

William sounded far away. She couldn't see. She realized her eyes were closed.

"Move the sensor all around her head, William," said a second voice, closer and tinny sounding. "Hold the scanner on top of her head."

"How is she?" asked William.

Anna felt a cool, hard surface touching her head. Her beloved William sounded concerned.

"Move the scanner back and forth, in small circles, all around her head," said the second, close-up voice.

"Doctor, how is she?" demanded William.

"She's excellent, William," replied the doctor. "Her brain looks absolutely normal."

Anna's eyes felt heavy. *What had happened?* She struggled to see. Shortly, she made out a man sitting next to her, holding a small black ball over her head: her William. The doctor's voice came from inside the black ball. Another man stood behind William.

"Scan her forehead," said the doctor from inside the black ball. William's hand moved in front of Anna's eyes, blocking her view. Soft green lights flashed from the ball, tracing a scanning pattern from her eyes to her forehead.

"She's perfect, William," continued the doctor. "Her brain's mature, so the impulses from the lab equipment didn't hurt her at all."

Anna's eyes snapped fully open. She grabbed William's hand and jerked it from her head to her belly.

"Anna, what's wrong?" asked William.

Anna frantically moved the black ball in circles on her belly.

"Doctor, what's she doing? Anna, stop. The doctor says you're okay," said William.

The voice from the black ball spoke again. "William, Anna's pregnant."

Anna recognized the voice as her doctor.

"What?" exclaimed William.

She tightened her grip on his hand. "William, it's our Billy," she said.

"Oh, my love," said William. He kissed her. She felt his happiness.

The man behind William stepped forward. Anna recognized him as Stevens, the head of the Great Advance program, the most loved and famous man in the world, and a friend of William's.

"Congratulations!" he said, patting William on the back. "Anna, I'm so happy you're okay."

William leaned in and kissed her. "Not just okay, absolute perfection," he said.

Anna beamed.

"What happened, William?" Stevens asked.

William sat back, still holding Anna's hand. "We were running synaptic experiments for the Great Advance chairs. The laboratory was secured. Not even my staff had access. Anna was looking for me and had an access card that I forgot to return. She must have entered during a transfer surge."

Anna reached up and wiped a tear from William's cheek. "Doctor, how is the baby?" she asked.

"The baby is fine," replied the doctor. "No, better than fine. The baby looks perfect, to use William's words, absolute perfection."

Anna giggled with joy.

"What did you mean when you said she would be okay because her brain is mature?" asked Stevens.

Anna looked anxiously at the black ball on her belly.

"I only meant that Anna's brain is fully developed, so she was able to respond reflexively by shutting down and going to sleep," said the doctor. "Anna conceived recently, so the baby's brain structure isn't formed yet. The impulses likely had no effect."

"So, Billy is going to be okay?" asked William.

"Absolutely," said the doctor. "Anna, can you come to my office tomorrow for a comprehensive checkup?"

Anna was too happy to answer. The black ball clanged to the floor. She pressed William's hand against her tummy.

"William, meet your son, Billy!" she said.

"Billy will be truly special," said Stevens. "Your son has been kissed by the Great Advance!"

10

L-O-V-E

ANNA FELT a little hand on her leg. Billy wanted to be picked up. At two years old, he still couldn't walk or talk, and she worried something was wrong. The pediatrician couldn't discover a reason for his delayed development. Billy's father had asked special brain doctors to examine the boy, but they said Billy looked perfectly normal to them as well. She picked up her son and set him down on the countertop so he could watch. Billy was a big boy for his age. Anna worried she soon would no longer be able to carry him.

Billy extended his hand out to Anna, balled into a fist. His little finger stuck out. Anna laughed and kissed his little finger.

"You want to write Daddy's secret message today?" she asked.

She always wrote with her little finger. It was harder, and sometimes she made mistakes and had to start over, but it seemed more special that way. Anna wrote the same way every day, by dragging her little finger through the peanut butter, careful to push deep enough, but not so deep that her finger hit the bread, and mindful of the width of each letter so the whole word would fit without having to scrunch the last few letters.

An important step before the writing was the spreading.

Peanut butter had to cover the whole slice, and it had to be smooth. Ridges and clumps made writing harder, especially the clumps. One good thing about clumps was that they caused a larger glob to build up on her little finger, and the glob had to be licked off. Anna always let Billy lick the buildup from her finger. She imagined it was extra essence left behind by the word she was writing.

Anna remembered the first time she had written in the peanut butter. She had written the word *love*, then turned the bread over and hid the secret message on the inside of the peanut butter and jelly sandwich. Every day since then, she'd brought William a peanut butter sandwich with the special word. They would sit together and talk while William told Anna of his work on the Great Advance, played with Billy, and ate his sandwich with Anna's hidden message of love.

Anna finished spreading the peanut butter and showed Billy the perfectly smooth layer she had made on the bread, explaining: "Even perfect things can be made better. That's what the Great Advance is about. Your turn. Make it better!"

She scooted Billy closer. Holding him against her chest, she guided his little finger toward the peanut butter. The *l* was scraggly, the *o* less scraggly, and the *v* and *e* were perfect.

"Your daddy will be so proud," she said.

Smiling, Billy held his little finger up for her to see. A big glob of peanut butter clung to the tip.

"Go ahead, Billy. Have a little love," she said.

He opened his mouth to eat the glob of peanut butter, then stopped and thrust his hand toward his mother. Her eyes began to water as the glob of love melted in her mouth.

"Oh, Billy," she whispered. She didn't know what else to say. She couldn't remember any other words.

"Mommy," Billy said.

His first word! Anna couldn't wait to tell William. He would be proud. Anna wrapped the sandwich and lifted Billy into his stroller.

On the walk over to William's office, Billy said, "Mommy," many more times.

"Good boy, Billy. Now say *daddy*," Anna said. "We're going to see Daddy at his work. Say *daddy*."

"Mommy," Billy said again.

They arrived early and went straight to the deck. Since her lab mishap while pregnant with Billy, Anna hadn't gone inside William's workplace. She lifted Billy out of his stroller and set him down to play. Anna didn't give him any toys because he preferred to play with his hands or feet and gaze around to take in all the happenings around him. She often took Billy to the park to be with other children his age. He had fun at the park, but he didn't play with the children. He sat and watched them, sometimes laughing at the funny things they did. Anna knew Billy wanted to play with the other children but didn't know how. Although not a single mother ever said anything negative, Anna sensed that the other mothers were relieved Billy didn't play with their children because he was so big.

While Anna and Billy waited, the door to the deck opened and two employees came out to eat lunch. She didn't know their names, but she recognized them. They were scientists in the Great Advance and worked with William. They had only taken a step onto the deck when they saw Anna and stopped.

"Oh, wait, I forgot something," one of the employees mumbled, backing up through the door.

"Have you seen William?" asked Anna, but the door had closed behind the scientists.

She knew something was wrong. She waited another few minutes and was about to call William when the door opened, and Stevens came out onto the deck. Anna had only seen Stevens a few times since her lab mishap, but she knew he and William were close friends.

"Hello, Anna. Hi, Billy," said Stevens.

He sat down beside her. Billy crawled over and tugged on his pant leg. Anna wanted to ask about William, but she couldn't summon the courage. She waited for Stevens to say more. Stevens reached out and touched her hand. Billy went still, watching Stevens. Anna closed her eyes, hoping when she opened them, she would wake from a dream and see William.

"Anna, William has been in a terrible accident," Stevens said.

Anna tasted the peanut butter in her mouth. She started to cry. She felt a tug on her knee, opened her eyes and saw Billy. He was standing and holding the sandwich.

"Daddy?" asked Billy.

11

WHOLE GREAT BIG GIGANTIC UNIVERSE

AFTER WILLIAM'S DEATH, Anna began teaching Billy about his father and the Great Advance. The project had always been special to them. Generations of their family had worked on the Advance long before it was renamed the Great Advance. Billy's father, his grandparents, his great-grandparents, and many generations before had been scientists who had dedicated their lives, and even given their lives, to the Advance.

Anna showed Billy pictures of relatives posing by early versions of the transfer prototypes and old articles proclaiming the systems would soon be fully operational and safe. She taught him that his father had been a top scientist on the Great Advance, one of the greatest scientists ever, and that no one had died since his father's sacrifice.

The project's leadership honored William as a hero. They said what they'd learned from his accident enabled them to make the system completely safe. Anna told Billy that his father used to hold him and tell him that one day, if they were lucky, they'd all be together forever in the Great Advance.

"You might even be one of the scientists who completes the Great Advance, your father used to say."

Anna knew Billy would never be a scientist. Billy couldn't learn to read or do math. He looked at everything simply. He was good at recognizing people's feelings and helping people feel better, which puzzled Anna because others didn't seem to feel connected to Billy.

She first realized Billy's gift while telling him about his father. Billy seemed to sense her getting sad, even before she felt sad herself. He'd say something sweet, or touch her on the arm, or look at her in his unique Billy way and make her feel better.

She knew his ability wasn't especially useful because no one was ever sad for long. Whenever something bad happened to someone, their sadness came and went away without Billy's help. Nonetheless, Anna did everything she could to help Billy develop his gift for helping people.

Every night, she read him books. She loved holding him in her arms and telling him stories of brave men and women helping people overcome great challenges.

After each story, Billy told his mother, "I want to be brave and help people too."

Her reply was always the same. "The best way to be brave is by helping people. One day you might help people who are in a lot of trouble, and then later, after you did the helping, someone might call you brave."

"Like Daddy?" Billy would ask her.

"Yes, like your father," she would reply. "He helped everyone in the world by working on the Great Advance."

"Why not the whole universe, Mommy? I want to help everyone in the whole great big gigantic universe!"

12

CROSSWALK GUARD

On Billy's first day of school, his mother said, "Billy, you are growing up. You're going to learn things, but you're different and could have a hard time fitting in. Still, you are going to have a beautiful life, and you'll be great because you have a special gift. You know how to help people feel good. Most people don't need help feeling good, and when they do, it doesn't last long. Still, helping is what makes you special. Always ask yourself, 'Do I help people feel better when they are around me?' When you help people, they will remember you." She hugged him. "Never forget, you will be great."

For the rest of the boys and girls, the first day of school was a time of nervousness, giggling, and making new friends, a day to remember. For Billy, the first day of school was a time of being by himself while in a crowd of other children. He wanted to play with them but didn't fit in. He just watched the other boys and girls and imagined playing with them.

Billy liked his teachers. He knew they worried about him, but he didn't know why. The teachers would sometimes sit with him while he watched the other children play.

Billy couldn't do homework. He had a hard time with numbers and remembering things, so his teachers didn't require him to do the assignments. He told his teachers about his mother reading him stories about brave leaders helping people, so they developed a special learning program for him. They read him stories from the history of his people, and he learned about ancient times, before climate control, when people rescued others from terrible storms. Billy learned that millions of people once got sick and needed to be saved. He heard stories about brave captains of great ships that crossed oceans to discover new lands and form new countries.

As the years passed, Billy's helping made him one of the most loved kids at school. Eventually, the children began playing with him, including him in things and inviting him to play baseball. Billy liked playing right field because he could see everything from there, and he almost never needed to run after a ball. Standing all by himself in the outfield, Billy felt part of something.

A year before his high school graduation, everything changed. He was old enough that his mother and teachers allowed him to walk home by himself. To get home, he had to cross a street, and he became good at crossing streets because he looked out for the transport units. Billy knew the units would never hit a kid. Most flew in the sky, but older versions drove on the streets. His mother and teachers told him that the units had sensors designed to watch out for children. A kid hadn't been hit by a transport unit in a long, long time. They were perfectly safe, but some were big and loud and made him nervous.

One day, Billy got to the street along with twenty or thirty other kids, some much younger than him, between four and five years old. As he walked toward the crosswalk, some kids cut over to a field next to the street to play. They threw balls, played tag, or sat talking on the grass in small groups. They were laughing and having fun. Billy watched and wanted to play with them, but his mother had told him that if he wanted to walk home, he had to walk straight home so she wouldn't be worried.

As he was about to cross the street to walk home, two boys began flying huge kites, the largest he'd ever seen. The kites were beautiful and made loud flapping sounds in the wind. All the kids stopped what they were doing to watch. The boys had tied the kite strings around their waists. They were having great fun chasing each other across the field as the kites jerked and yanked the two boys in crazy directions.

If Billy had been experienced with kites, he might have seen the danger. The youngest boy's kite was too big for him. The wind that day was tumultuous, and Billy could feel it pushing him as he stood watching the kites. Suddenly, a big gust grabbed the kite flown by the smaller boy, lifting him off the ground. The boy screamed as the kite pulled him up, higher and higher.

The kite flew straight up with the boy flailing wildly at the end of the string. A moment later, the gust of wind dissipated, leaving the little boy and his kite suspended in midair before the kite began falling toward the ground. The kite recaught the air and swept sideways, straight toward Billy and a group of small boys and girls on the edge of the crosswalk.

BILLY WOKE up in the hospital. His mother told him what had happened. Billy had shoved a group of five or six children standing in front of him out of the path of the screaming boy, who then smashed into Billy's chest. The force of the collision slammed Billy onto his back, knocking the wind out of him. Somehow, Billy managed to wrap his arms around the boy. That would have been the end of the incident, if not for the kite and the transport unit in the street. The resistance from Billy's weight caused the kite to swing high in the air, then over the street, and then down toward the street. Billy lay on his back, wheezing and clutching the little boy as the kite became tangled with a speeding transport unit, jerking the little boy, and Billy, who held on. The unit dragged Billy and the boy toward the street, smashing them into a barrier that separated the street from the sidewalk. Billy took the full impact of the barrier, still holding the boy. The kite string broke upon impact, leaving Billy unconscious and bleeding on the side of the street. The little boy didn't have a scratch on him.

As his mother told him the story, Billy saw that she was happy. He felt her happy-sad tears fall on his arm, so he reached with his other hand to touch her, but his hand wouldn't move. Looking over, he saw why. The two boys who had been flying the kites were holding his hand. They looked alike, except one was a bigger than the other.

"Are you two brothers?" asked Billy.

The smallest boy was lifted up by his parents and set down carefully on the bed next to Billy.

"You're a hero, Billy," whispered his mother into his ear.

A few days later, Billy was released from the hospital, still wearing a few bandages and with a cast on his arm. The school welcomed him back with a big celebration. Billy liked that the kids talked with him more than before, both during class and on the playground.

One morning, he was called to the principal's office.

"Billy," the principal said, "we have a problem with the younger students. Since the crosswalk incident, they have been afraid to cross the street to go home. The teachers have suggested that you be a crosswalk guard for the kids getting out of school. Your job would be to help them feel safe crossing the street to go home."

Billy was confused. He knew transport units always stopped for kids in the crosswalk. Everyone knew that. There was no reason to be scared. But he'd never been asked by a grown-up to help before.

"Yes, I'd like very much to be a crosswalk guard," said Billy.

He loved his job as crosswalk guard. Each day, Billy was excused from class early to put on his uniform to get to the crosswalk before the younger kids. When the bell rang, the kids poured out of school, in small groups of one or two at first, and then as a huge crowd. Billy was their hero, and the kids obeyed his instructions. Billy formed small groups to walk together across the street. He knew what it felt like to be isolated and made sure every child felt included on his crosswalk.

After a few months, the crosswalk became crowded. Children whose parents had picked them up now asked them to walk home just so they could cross the street with Billy. Children who lived on the opposite side of the school would go to Billy's crosswalk and then walk all the way back around the school to get home. During all of this, Billy remained Billy, a kind, simple, thoughtful boy, apart from everyone but working to help children feel included. The more Billy's popularity grew, the more he was surrounded by children every afternoon at the crosswalk.

Billy remained the crosswalk guard for the rest of that year. At the graduation ceremony, he sat proudly with his class. The cheers were loudest when Billy's name was called.

After the ceremony, Billy and his mother returned home and found a man waiting for them. Billy saw that his mother recognized the man and was happy to see him, but he felt his mother become a little sad as well. The man was dressed in official looking clothes, and he seemed very nice. He had a thick envelope in his left hand. He reached out to Billy to shake hands. It was the first time Billy had ever shaken hands. The man introduced himself as the leader of the Great Advance.

"Hello, Billy. My name is Stevens. Nice to see you again," said the man.

"Nice to see you too," said Billy, although he didn't remember ever seeing the man before.

"Have you considered what you're going to do now?" Stevens asked.

"Billy is thinking about college," answered his mother.

"That's great!" said Stevens.

"Would you like to come inside?" Billy's mother asked.

"I'd love to," Stevens replied.

Billy felt nervous. He couldn't remember another man being in their house before.

Billy's mother led them into the living room and motioned for the man to sit. Billy sat across from him. The coffee table between Billy and Stevens was stacked with the books that his mother read to Billy every night—stories of the Great Advance and other adventures and explorations.

"I'll make tea and be right back," Billy's mother said, leaving Billy and Stevens alone in the living room. They sat silently until she returned. She set a cup of tea on the coffee table in front of Stevens and sat down next to Billy.

"It's nice to see you again," his mother said. "How are your two boys?"

Stevens took a sip of tea. "They are excellent, thanks to your son."

Billy was confused by his mother's familiarity with the man. With a slight increase in formality, Stevens turned to Billy.

"What were you thinking of studying?"

Billy was smarter than he used to be. He knew that the man was probably just being nice, or perhaps asking a question people often ask before asking the question they'd come to ask.

"I don't know," said Billy.

"What was your favorite subject in school?"

"I like to help people. Anything that involves helping would be something I'd study," said Billy.

Stevens smiled. "That's why I'm here, Billy. The Great Advance needs help. We think you can help us."

"What kind of help?" asked Billy's mother. "He's only a boy."

"I'm grown up now, Mommy," said Billy.

"We need Billy's kind of help," said Stevens. "The Great Advance is something people have been working on for the last several thousand years. Everything may be ready very, very soon. For a long time, forever almost, the Great Advance has been a theoretical impossibility, a what-if possibility of the mind merging with the universe. As we've advanced scientifically, the Great Advance is becoming more than a theory, Anna. It's becoming an aspiration."

Billy tried to stop his mind from wandering. It was disrespectful, but often happened when people spoke with long sentences and big words. He waited for Stevens to stop talking. He knew what to say at the end.

"Generations of scientists worked on the project. As is the way of our people, each generation along the journey to the Great Advance yearned for the possibility, but consistent with the wisdom of our people, they and we have debated the efficacy of such an endeavor."

"That's nice," said Billy.

"Scientists, like your father and grandparents," said Anna.

"Yes, Billy, like that," said Stevens.

Billy noticed his mother was smiling.

Stevens reached for his tea and took a sip. "Your books?" he asked, motioning to the books on the coffee table. "You like to read?"

Billy didn't answer. He didn't like telling people he couldn't read. Now that he was older, he didn't like people knowing his mother still read to him. It wasn't that anyone would make fun of him. Everyone was kind and supportive, but Billy didn't want the man to know.

"I like the stories," he replied.

"Those are wonderful books, indeed," said Stevens. "The history of our people. The history of our advances are stories of adventure and journeys of discovery. We have had exhila-rating ventures into the unknown. With each step forward, our people became better, smarter, stronger, safer, and we advanced our understanding of ourselves and our world."

"Billy knows all the stories by heart," Billy's mother said.

Stevens spent the rest of the afternoon with Billy and his mother. He talked about Billy's father as one of the great scientists. Billy told Stevens about his school and his job as a crosswalk guard. His mother showed Stevens pictures of Billy and his father when Billy was a baby. Stevens told them stories about the bravery and sacrifice of early pioneering scientists of the Great Advance. Billy's family had been heroes begin-ning hundreds of years ago.

Eventually, Stevens came out with the real question he'd come to ask. "Billy, will you help us on the Great Advance?"

Billy didn't know what Stevens meant. He looked at his mother, then back. "I don't know science things," he said quietly.

"I don't need scientists, Billy. I need you. I need your help, your special kind of help." Stevens motioned to the books on the table. "Just like in your books. Billy, our people will experi-ence a great journey with exciting discoveries and new knowl-edge. Now that the journey is actually upon us, some people will become uncertain. They will worry about leaving the comfort of what they know. People fear the unknown. Just like in your books, every advance needs a leader to help people see the future and be strong and brave."

"Why would people be afraid?" Billy asked.

Stevens leaned forward and smiled. "Like the street, the transport machines, and the crosswalk, the Great Advance is safe, but a few accidents from long ago have concerned people, and some are frightened of what might happen in the Great Advance."

"My father had an accident," said Billy, remembering his

father had been the last person to die testing the project. He sensed his mother sadden and took her hand.

"Your father was a great man, a hero," said Stevens, nodding.

Billy was quiet for a minute, thinking. "My school principal said everyone believed the crosswalk was safe, but it wasn't."

"Billy!" whispered his mother.

"That's a good analogy," said Stevens. "The Great Advance is like the crosswalk. Hundreds of years ago, machines used to hit people in crosswalks, but science fixed that. Now crosswalks are very safe. Only when a sudden wind came up, a one-in-a-million chance, was it unsafe."

Billy tried to think of how to say that if one chance in a million actually happened, it became one chance in one.

"How would Billy help the Great Advance?" Anna asked.

"Billy, I'm here to ask you to help us help people, to help everyone in the world feel safe, to help people be excited about crossing over to the Great Advance, just like you do for children crossing over your crosswalk."

"Will I get a uniform, like the crosswalk?" asked Billy.

"Yes, similar to what your father wore," replied Stevens.

THE NEXT MORNING, Billy's mother gave him a hug and a kiss as he left for his first day on the job at a division of the Great Advance called the Program of Education and Excitement for the Great Advance. Billy's job would be to meet with people, teach them about the project, and help everyone see how wonderful the Great Advance would be.

Billy was good at his job, better than anyone in the division. At first, he met with one or two people at a time, then families, then large groups. Over the next year, he helped to calm and provide comfort to millions of people who had concerns about the Great Advance.

Though he still lived with his mother, his job required that he travel. Billy liked that part of his job and brought his mother a gift from everywhere he went. As much as he liked his job and traveling to faraway places, he still loved returning home. His mother would be waiting at the front door with a peanut butter sandwich and his favorite books about heroes helping and saving people. Billy would eat his sandwich, imagining the secret message written inside, and tell his mother about all the people he helped feel safe about the Great Advance.

13

LIKE MY DADDY WANTED ME TO

BILLY WAITED ON THE PORCH. He was happy. He'd been working for the Great Advance for a year and had helped many people change their minds from holding out to transferring.

The morning's holdout report showed that a woman named Teena and her four-year-old son Timmy were holdouts, and that meant they needed help. Billy loved helping people. He knocked on their door again. It was his third visit to the woman's home, and each time, no answer. Billy's resolve to help grew each time. He'd just decided to leave and return the next day when the door cracked open.

"Hi, my name is Billy."

"Hi, Billy," the woman replied.

Billy was moved by her kind voice. She reminded him of his own mother, only her voice was softer, almost a whisper. He smiled. "Can we talk?"

The woman opened the door another inch. Her face was as kind as her voice but impassive. Billy maintained his smile. Most people smiled back. She didn't. He saw that she was looking at the Great Advance insignia on his jacket.

"Nice to meet you, Billy, but I've already decided. Timmy and I aren't going."

Billy nodded. His job was recruiting holdouts to the Great Advance, but he'd never recruited anyone who'd told him their mind was made up. That was disrespectful. He'd come to help by recruiting her, but now helping meant making her feel better.

"What's your funnest thing to do?" he asked. "Mine is when my mother reads me stories."

"What?"

"I can read by myself, though. I graduated." Behind her, Billy saw her son sitting on the floor surrounded by books. "Wow, can Timmy read?" he asked.

Teena looked at her son. When she looked back at Billy, she'd opened the door farther and was smiling. "He's a good reader. He knows math too."

Billy's face brightened. "Maybe he'll be a scientist when he grows up, or a teacher."

The woman's smile vanished. "Most of the scientists are transferring. Teachers too."

For the first time that he could remember, Billy didn't know what to say or how to help. The woman thanked him for stopping by and closed the door.

At home that night, Billy couldn't stop thinking of the mother and her son. He got up and went into the living room and opened his favorite books, with the biggest pictures, but they didn't help. His mother came out and read to him. Billy soon fell fast asleep. The next morning, he returned to the home of Teena and little Timmy.

"Would it be okay if I read to Timmy?" he asked.

Without a word, Teena opened the door wide, welcoming Billy inside. The living room was impeccable. Timmy sat on the floor in front of a couch, reading a book.

"Sit down, Billy," said Teena. "I'm glad you came back. Timmy asked about you after you left."

Billy sat on the couch. "Hi, Timmy. What are you reading?" he asked.

Timmy held up his book. Billy recognized it as a slate, the same as he'd used in school to learn reading and writing.

"A book my daddy and me wrote," the little boy said.

Billy fidgeted. He knew from the holdout report that Timmy's father had died in an accident only three months before.

"His daddy died in a transport crash on the way home from work," Teena said, confirming what he remembered from the report—but there was something else.

Billy thought hard, confused. Everyone knew transports were perfectly safe. Thousands of them had whisked people around the planet for hundreds of years without incident.

Teena walked over to a desk, grabbed a pamphlet, and walked back to sit down beside Billy. "Here, the recruiter before you gave me this," she said. Billy recognized the pamphlet. It was a brochure for the Great Advance, the same one he'd given to hundreds of people.

"Look," she said, pointing to a phrase on the cover. "I feel myself getting angry whenever I read it, but the feeling vanishes. I wish I could stay angry."

Billy stared at the brochure, reading every word, but he already knew what it said. He'd memorized it long ago.

Join the Great Advance!
As safe as Transports you take every day!
Not a single Transport accident in over 500 years!
One billion Transfer tests without a single failure!
Guaranteed Safe!

"We were holdouts before my daddy died," said Timmy.

"Why?" asked Billy.

"You want to read my book to me?" asked Timmy.

Billy looked at Teena, who was sliding off the couch to sit beside Timmy. Billy did the same.

"It's a book about what I want to be when I grow up," said

Timmy, handing Billy the slate, then nestling his chin in the crook of Billy's arm. "It's called *Timmy*."

"I like it already," said Billy.

Teena put her arm around Timmy. Billy began reading.

The book began the day Timmy was born and had additions every few weeks. Timmy's father wrote about all the things Timmy might become—an artist who would help people see beauty, a teacher who would help people learn, an administrator who would help people live. Billy read about Timmy becoming an athlete, a scientist, or a doctor, or all three; about being a husband, a father, and maybe one day soon, a brother.

"That was when I was a baby," said Timmy. "My part is next. My daddy wrote it, but it was me." Timmy's first entry was that he wanted to be his mommy so he could love his daddy, and also be his daddy so he could love his mommy.

"My daddy said I have to be myself," said Timmy.

Billy read about Timmy wanting to be a star so he could twinkle. Every day for a month, Timmy wrote about being a star. The next month, Timmy wanted to be the sun to make people warm, then grass and snow so children could play, then the moon so parents could read to children at night.

"How did you think of all those things?" asked Billy.

"I told Daddy I wanted to be a dog to lick kids' faces, but he didn't write that," Timmy said.

Teena laughed. "I think your daddy thought you were poking fun."

Billy continued reading. Since Timmy had begun contributing, the book had new entries almost every day. Each day, Timmy imagined being something new. The last page was dated but blank. Timmy took the book from Billy.

"His daddy died that day," Teena explained. "Timmy, honey, what are you writing?"

"The ending," said Timmy, holding up the book.

The last page read:

I wish
I could grow up
Like my daddy wanted me to

"Oh, Timmy," Teena said.

Timmy handed the book to Billy and jumped up from the floor.

"I'm going outside to play, Mommy. Thank you, Billy!" he shouted, running outside. Alone, Billy and Teena remained on the floor.

"Now you see why we're holdouts?" asked Teena.

Billy stared at the last page. "I want to help people, forever," he said. "In the Great Advance, I will be able to help people forever."

"You helped Timmy," said Teena, touching Billy's arm.

With his finger, Billy traced Timmy's last wish in the book. "I don't remember my father."

"Billy, I'm so sorry," said Teena.

"Maybe my father died so I could be anything I want in the Great Advance."

14

A SOFT MIST

AFTER MEETING TEENA AND TIMMY, Billy's success in helping holdouts join the Great Advance further increased. One day, Billy and all his colleagues were called to a meeting for everyone in the Great Advance program. At the meeting, Billy encountered Stevens, who immediately smiled and stopped to talk. Billy rarely saw Stevens, but whenever they crossed paths, Billy felt proud that Stevens, the most respected person on the planet, would stop and say hello and ask about his mother.

After everyone was seated in the auditorium, Stevens walked onto the stage. Around the auditorium were dozens of large screens displaying people in auditoriums all around the world, all from the Great Advance. Stevens waved to the crowd and began speaking.

"My name is Stevens." Everyone laughed at his humble humor as his voice boomed through auditoriums around the planet.

"Today, we begin our journey to the Great Advance! Our system is ready! After hundreds of years of science, the system is operational!" Cheers, excitement, and energy filled the room. Smiling broadly, Stevens waited for the cheers to subside, then continued.

"Transfer stations to the Great Advance are in place all

over the world." He pointed at the video screens. "Starting tomorrow, transfer stations will begin operation. Tomorrow, our people begin a new journey!"

The Great Advance employees stood, cheering and hugging. Everyone was happy, including Billy. Then Billy began to think about his mother. He knew how important the Great Advance was to her. She would want to be here for this celebration in remembrance of his father. An image appeared on the screens.

"Do you know who these people are?" Stevens asked, pointing to the projected image.

The screens displayed pictures of a family posing next to an ancient version of a Great Advance system. Billy gasped.

"Our people have achieved greatness over thousands of years. We began as only a cell in a drop of water. Advancing and evolving, time and time again, we journeyed into the unknown. We learned, grew, united, and advanced our civilization."

Billy stared at the screens, hardly listening. The pictures were from his house! The members of the family were his relatives! Billy wanted to go home and get his mother. He backed through the crowd as Stevens continued.

"These people are the original heroes of the Great Advance. They were also the first pioneers and voyagers of the synaptic transfer, the foundational invention of the Great Advance."

Almost to the back of the crowd, Billy saw the exit sign. The crowd was cheering loudly, transfixed by Stevens and the photographs. At the exit's large double-wide doors, Billy turned to look. The picture displayed on the screen was his father. Billy ran to get his mother. She would be so proud. He hoped he could get her back in time.

With every worker in the auditorium, the hallway was empty. Doors automatically opened, then shut behind him as he raced down a hallway. Billy ran fast, his big feet pounding the floor. He'd be outside soon, then home, then back with his mother. She would get to see the wonderful tribute to his father. Stevens's voice boomed from hallway speakers as Billy ran.

"Today, I'm honored to introduce you to Anna, a descendent of the original heroes of the Great Advance."

"Thank you, Mr. Stevens."

Billy froze, then turned and raced back down the hallway to the nearest video screen. He saw his mother on stage with Stevens. Billy watched, alone in the hallway, while thousands watched inside and millions more from auditoriums all around the world. Cameras zoomed in on Stevens and his mother. Billy saw that his mother was happier than he had ever seen her. The camera panned to the right. Something rose slowly from beneath the stage.

"Tomorrow, my friends, the transfer of our people to the Great Advance begins. Tonight, we honor its original heroes by transferring their descendants."

Rising from the stage was a large platform with two large, shiny steel chairs with soft white cushions covering the seats and armrests. Billy recognized the chairs as *transfer chairs*!

Stevens walked over to Billy's mother, took her hand in his, and led her to one of the chairs. Gently, and angling his body so the camera could see, he strapped her into the chair. Then Stevens turned toward the audience again.

"Now, I would like you to meet Anna's son, Billy, who happens to be the most successful educator in the entire Great Advance program. Billy, would you please join us on stage?"

Billy, in the hallway, stared at the screen. He heard an excited hush and saw everyone looking for him making his way to the stage. Stevens walked to the edge of the stage and peered into the crowd to where Billy had originally been standing. Billy heard his mother's voice.

"Billy, honey, isn't this wonderful? I wanted to surprise you. Stevens said we could be the first. You will be a hero like in the stories and like our relatives in the pictures." Her voice was soft and warm, just like at home.

"Mother, I'm coming!" Billy yelled at the video screen. He ran back down the hallway to the auditorium.

"Billy, are you there? Come on up, honey."

Billy ran as fast as he could. When he got to the first set of doors, they didn't automatically open, and Billy crashed and fell to the floor. Gasping for breath, he tried to open the doors, kicking and ramming them with his shoulders. He heard Stevens talking.

"Billy will be here. I saw him earlier. Where did he go?"

"I'm outside!" yelled Billy at the screen. "Locked out!"

It was no use. He knew they couldn't hear him. He shrank down to the floor against the wall of the hallway and watched. Stevens continued looking for him. A photograph of Billy flashed across the screen, and the audience helped look. His mother sounded sad as she called for her son. Billy knew he'd ruined the inaugural transfer that had been planned for him and his mother. The amazing, wonderful, excited energy that had filled the auditorium transformed to support and love. Everyone basked in connected empathy. Except Billy.

"People, we thank you for your support and patience here today."

The camera zoomed back, now showing Billy's mother in the transfer chair. In the chair intended for Billy sat a scientist who had worked with Billy's father. Everyone cheered.

"We have a new plan," announced Stevens. "Instead of Anna and Billy leading us into the Great Advance, Anna, the great-great-great-great-great-great-granddaughter of our original hero, and Lou, a close colleague and friend of Anna's husband, William, will transfer tonight in place of Billy. Billy, a hero and leader in his own right, and the greatest recruiter and educator of the Great Advance, will be the last to transfer. Billy will stay and help us, and educate us, and make us comfortable with the Great Advance, all the way to the very last person."

Billy could only stare at the screen. He knew instantly what Stevens meant. Billy would be alone, without his mother until he transferred. The crowd cheered their support, but in a subdued manner. The screen centered on Billy's mother and the scientist, then zoomed in on her. Billy saw his mother looking desperately for him, trying to smile. Billy felt happy for his mother. He knew how honored she was by William and her family's Great Advance contributions.

"I'm proud of you, Billy," she said, her eyes glistening.

Billy began to cry.

Everything happened quickly after that. Stevens addressed the audience, reminding them of the great honor they'd soon witness. Then he knelt in front of Billy's mother and the scientist, thanked them for their leadership, got up, stepped behind the chairs, and placed his hands on the control switches for each machine. The audience went silent.

Billy sat in the hallway opposite the locked doors, watching as the display focused on his mother and the scientist. The scientist's eyes were closed. Billy's mother still scanned the audience. Stevens was speaking, indicating that he would throw the transfer switch momentarily. Billy saw his mother shift her eyes from the audience to the camera. She seemed to be looking right at Billy.

"See you soon, Billy. Love you," she said.

Then Stevens pulled the transfer switches. A soft mist surrounded the two transfer chairs. When the mist faded, the chairs were empty. The Great Advance had officially begun.

———

THE NEXT MORNING, Billy woke up alone in his home for the first time in his life. He went into the living room and looked at the pictures of his relatives, the same ones Stevens had displayed to the audience the night before. Billy already missed his mother, suddenly realizing of all the pictures of their relatives, there were no pictures of her. She existed only in his memory, at least for now. He believed his mother would be waiting for him in the Great Advance. Billy took a picture of his father off the shelf. Where was his father? Was he with his mother? He wished he had a picture of his mother.

Before Billy could contemplate further, he heard a knock at the front door. It was Stevens. Billy looked at the picture of his father. Billy's mother had told him that Stevens and Billy's father had been good friends who worked together for years. He knew that his father had asked Stevens to help during an experiment and something had gone terribly wrong. Stevens had been the last person to see Billy's father before he died.

Billy invited Stevens inside. They sat down while Billy explained what happened the night before. They talked together for a long time. Stevens told Billy his father was a hero and his mother had become a hero too.

"Billy, you should be very happy for her," Stevens said.

"It's just that the house seems empty now."

"You will be with her again. She's probably here with us now, but we can't tell."

"But not my father? Mother said you pulled the switch for him too, in my father's laboratory."

"No, Billy, your father did not make it."

"But Mother said you pulled the switch, like last night."

"Your father and I were doing tests. The chairs weren't transferring then. I'm sorry, Billy."

"It's okay."

Stevens paused briefly, then spoke softly. "Billy, do you think you can keep helping us?"

"Everyone is already excited to transfer," replied Billy.

"Everyone who attended the ceremony last night was excited, yes. But there are many people who haven't decided to transfer. They need a leader to help them have the courage to cross over to the Great Advance, like when you helped children cross the street. Until the very last day, there will be many holdouts that you can help. When the people learn that you will be the last to transfer, they'll see how brave you are, and that knowledge will help them be brave."

Billy didn't feel brave and was pretty sure he wasn't a leader, but he knew one thing for sure. "I want to help," he said.

Stevens smiled. "Thank you. I'm happy you'll keep helping us. We still have a lot of work to transfer everyone on the planet."

As he and Stevens shook hands, Billy promised to help everyone that he possibly could. Stevens was almost to the street when Billy thought of something and called out.

"Mr. Stevens, how'd you know about the crosswalk?"

Stevens stopped and looked back at Billy. "Billy, don't you remember me? I was in the hospital when you woke up after the crosswalk incident. My sons, Bobby and Mikey, were the boys flying the kites. You saved Bobby. You were very brave. Bobby would've died if not for you."

Billy remembered, but he did not recall feeling brave. If anything, he'd felt afraid. "I was just helping," he said.

Stevens laughed. "You'll meet Bobby and Mikey again. We'll all transfer together on the last day. It'll be fun!"

15

LAST DAY

STEVENS WAS RELIEVED. He had just given his last speech and maybe he'd saved another holdout. The morning reports said the last day of the Great Advance was going smoothly. He could smell the bacon and fresh-brewed coffee. Becky was preparing breakfast, their last family meal. Stevens heard the door to the kitchen squeak open.

Not going to be fixing that, he thought, grinning.

"Hi, Dad," said Bobby, emerging from the kitchen.

"Where's my glove? Let's play catch!" said Stevens, remembering his promise from the night before and getting up to get his glove.

"Not so fast. Breakfast will be ready in ten minutes!" shouted Becky.

"After breakfast then," said Stevens.

"Can we play in the afternoon instead?" asked Bobby.

"Bobby, we'll be in line," said Stevens.

"But Dad, yesterday the line was hours long. I heard everyone was leaving for last chances at doing things."

"That's true," said Becky. "Mikey, are you up? Come down for breakfast!" she shouted.

Stevens and Bobby walked to the kitchen and sat down at the breakfast table.

"I don't know, Bobby," said Stevens. "We'd be gone too long."

"It's barely over a mile. You'd be back in an hour, two tops," said Becky.

"We're walking, honey."

"What about the car the boys and I took to the demo-station?"

"Most of the remaining transports failed last night. I allocated the few that are left to people who live farther away."

"Well, you're head of the program. Something tells me they'll wait for you," she said, smiling. "Besides, it's not like I don't still have a little say with your team. I might even help on the transfer platform."

"The team would love that," said Stevens.

"Yay!" cheered Bobby.

Stevens was still hesitant but saw how excited Bobby was, so he agreed. Mikey came down the stairs.

"What's all the cheering about?" Mikey asked through a yawn.

Stevens remembered the night before. "Mikey, can I talk to you?"

"Sure, Dad. Is everything okay?"

Bobby ran over to Mikey and whispered in his ear, causing Mikey to frown. "I don't know, Bobby."

"In private, please," said Stevens. Bobby and Becky left the room. Stevens and Mikey talked together in hushed voices. When breakfast was ready, Becky called them three times before they finally appeared.

"What were you two talking about?" asked Becky.

"Nothing," said Mikey, winking at Bobby.

"I saw that," said Becky.

"Father son stuff," said Stevens.

After breakfast, the boys ran upstairs, and Stevens explained.

"I like it. No, I love it," said Becky, grinning. "But Angel's parents will never allow it."

"That's what I said," replied Stevens. "Honey, are you sure you're okay with this? I won't do it if you don't want me to. Mikey will understand."

Becky laughed. "Like father, like son."

"More like his mother, if I remember correctly," said Stevens with a wink.

"I admit, I wish I'd have thought of it. What about Angel's parents?"

"The boys have a plan."

"With both Mikey and Bobby going with you, tell your team I'll be helping them on the platform for sure," said Becky. "Wait, did you say the *boys* have a plan?"

"Yes, Bobby's in on it," said Stevens.

"Bobby's idea, probably," said Becky, laughing again.

The remainder of the morning was a happy one. The four tidied up the house as if they were readying for a family vacation and wanted everything in place when they returned. Stevens and Bobby made a show of arranging their baseball gloves and a ball, placing them just inside the front door.

"Your things are out on the deck, honey," said Becky. "Don't you want to put them away? Can you bring me the coffee cup?"

Stevens started walking outside, then stopped. It was late morning. The sun was high in the sky. It was hot with no wind. He thought of his mornings on the deck the past year.

"No, honey, I think I'll leave my journal and coffee cup just as they are."

THEY ALL LEFT their house for the transfer station a few hours later, joking and arguing about whether the distance to the station was more or less than a mile.

"We won't arrive until after one o'clock," said Mikey.

"Did you call Angel?" Stevens asked.

Mikey nodded. "She said she'll try to stall."

They stopped at Rachel and Ronnie's house along the way so Bobby could drop off Candy. Then Stevens, Becky, Mikey, and Bobby walked the rest of the way to the transfer station. As predicted, it was crowded. The line reached across the field and wound back toward the station.

Becky frowned. "How many people are transferring today?"

"About eight hundred, depending on holdouts," replied Stevens. "By now, two or three hundred have already transferred."

"People are still arriving," said Becky.

"A lot of family breakfasts," said Stevens.

Bobby grabbed Mikey's arm. "I see Angel. She's up front," he said.

"Let's go get her," said Mikey.

Stevens shook his head. "Not yet. She's still about fifty people from the platform. There's plenty of time."

The transfer station was a simple structure, a twenty-square-foot platform raised eight feet off the ground. A shiny steel transfer chair stood in the middle, with soft, inviting white cushions covering the comfortable-looking seat and armrests. A helmet attached to a flexible rod hung behind the chair. Thin safety railings surrounded the platform, with stairs leading up to the top.

The line of people led straight to the bottom of the stairs. People buzzed with excitement. Children darted around, giggling and playing games. Parents talked, reminiscing and promising to explore the universe together once in the Great Advance.

"First things first," Stevens said, leading Becky, Mikey, and Bobby to the end of the line. He recognized almost everyone. They had worked for him in the Great Advance program and had stayed behind to make sure the synaptic transfer system ran smoothly. Not that it was necessary. The system was perfectly safe and designed to operate continuously, so their presence had never been needed. Still, it would have been disastrous if the technical expertise for the Great Advance transferred and there was a system failure. Once transferred, it was impossible to return.

With the local station now so congested, it might be dark before everyone transferred. Stevens looked around. Everyone was happy. The line was a good thing, he decided, part of the plan.

"Honey, the line isn't moving," said Becky. "The system isn't broken, is it?"

"It's not broken," he said, but her question momentarily unsettled him.

Days ago, the Great Advance had passed beyond the point of no return. So many people had transferred that if anything went wrong, no matter how unlikely, the system would be impossible to repair. The remaining people would not get to transfer. Those who stayed behind would face terrible hardships. No one would now survive the commonplace challenges from past centuries due to society's total reliance on globally maintained infrastructure to meet basic needs.

"I see what you meant by long lines," Becky said.

"They'll probably install the backup chair soon," said a woman in front of them.

"I heard the communications system is down," the woman's husband said.

"That's okay. It's part of the plan," Stevens said to Becky, loud enough for the family in front to hear. "By now, everyone has transferred except us, and the regional transfer station is off-line, so no need for communications anyway."

He winked at Mikey. "The delay is part of the plan, isn't it, Mikey?"

Mikey grinned sheepishly at his mother, then looked down the line. "We better hurry. Angel can't stall forever."

"Mikey, remember, if her parents don't let her go with you, that's the way it is," Becky said.

"I understand, Mom."

"Excuse me, Mr. Stevens, could you check to see if something has gone wrong?" asked a woman in line.

"Sure, I'll be right back. I'm sure it's nothing," he said, speaking louder than before. Winking at Becky, he added, "Bobby, come along. Let's see what's going on with the line."

"Take your time, Mr. Rob Stevens," said Becky, giving her husband a hug. "I'll go up to help on the platform after you leave. Have fun."

Taking Bobby's hand, Stevens walked toward the front of the line to see what was causing the delay.

"See you in a few, Mom. Love you," said Mikey, following behind.

BECKY WATCHED people fawn over her husband. Everyone recognized him as he walked down the line. They either worked for Rob on the project or recognized him from his morning broadcasts. Many people stepped out of line to shake hands or introduce themselves.

Becky wished his parents could see their son now. They'd have been proud of him. His father had disapproved of Rob's career choice and blamed Becky.

She knew his father was right. She'd recruited Rob as a bright young man into the newly founded Great Advance program. He hadn't even graduated from college yet. How could she have known she would fall in love?

She remembered the family dinner when she'd first met his parents thirty years ago and wished she hadn't been so brash.

16

WHY DO YOU CALL IT GREAT?

* Thirty years earlier *

BECKY HELD HER TONGUE. Rob had warned her the dinner might start awkwardly, and he was right.

"I want to be a scientist, Dad, but I want to do this more."

"Why history, Son? After you graduate, there's a spot waiting for you on the Advance team. You can eventually be a leader of that team."

"I'll still be part of the Advance," replied Rob. "Just not as a scientist."

"What do you mean? The Advance is pure science. How can you help the Advance without being a scientist?"

Becky had an opinion about that and began to speak, but Rob poked her leg and cut her off.

"Can we talk about this after dinner, Dad?" asked Rob, looking at his mother, who came to the rescue.

"Betty, what are you studying?" his mother asked.

"Her name is Becky, Mom."

"Oh, I'm sorry."

"That's okay, Mrs. Stevens," said Becky, taking her turn to poke Rob's leg. "Was Betty over for dinner last week?"

"Yes. I mean no, I . . ." replied Rob's flustered mother.

Rob's father jumped in, saving his wife. "No, I don't think that's correct. Betty was here two weeks ago. Bridget was here last week."

Everyone laughed.

"You see, Becky," said Rob. "I have the coolest parents in the world."

"When did you two first meet?" asked Rob's father.

Becky thought for a few seconds. "About four weeks ago, I think it was. The last three weeks I was with Reggie, Rex, and Roger."

Everyone laughed heartily.

"Touché!" said Rob's father.

"I told you dinner would be a little crazy," said Rob.

"Okay, everyone, let's eat," said Rob's mother.

The meal was simple but elegant: chicken and fish, spinach, rice, and berries. The dining table was old and heavy. The dinnerware was thin porcelain from centuries long past with faint cracks visible on each piece. Rob's father was a scientist from the most elite team of the Synaptic Advance, but he was also a man of strong tradition. The dining table and dishes had been in his family for generations. In the center of the table was a thousand-year-old bottle of wine, preserved by specially treated glass. The setting was traditional and formal, but the meal was full of fun and joking.

Becky had a wonderful dinner with Rob's family, talking about music, art, history, and politics. When they were almost done eating, Rob's mother asked Becky how she'd met Rob.

"We met at test day, at the university," replied Becky. "I've graduated, but I work as an administrator in the History Department."

"Test day? Rob, you tested already, didn't you?" his mother asked.

"Yes, I did, but this test qualifies me for a brand-new program."

"In the History Department?" asked Rob's father.

"Yes, but it's still part of the Advance. Tell him, Becky."

Becky finished off her wine before speaking. "Testing is rigorous to find qualified students who can succeed in the new program. Of all the students tested, only one has qualified thus far," she explained.

"What's your job as an administrator?" asked Rob's father.

"To recruit students. The most qualified have mostly committed to other programs, such as becoming scientists in the Advance."

"How do you recruit?" asked Rob's mother.

"We just tell them about the program. Many want to join after that, but most aren't qualified."

"Can you recruit me?" asked his father.

Becky raised her eyebrows. "Mr. Stevens, you?"

"Dad, stop," said Rob.

"Becky, he's playing," said his mother.

Rob's father's voice raised slightly. "I'm serious. My son wants to forfeit his spot in the top scientific team for the Advance, and I don't know why."

Becky looked at Rob, surprised.

"Dad, I just took the test last week. I haven't had time to explain. Becky, you don't have to explain this."

"I want to," said Becky. "You haven't described the program to your parents, so of course they don't understand."

"How did you get involved in the program?" asked Rob's mother.

"I studied history," replied Becky. "The new program is a cooperation between the History Department and the Great Advance."

"Great?" asked his father.

"She's leaving out the part that her master's thesis was the catalyst for the whole idea," said Rob.

"You keep saying that," Becky said, smiling. "We don't know that's true. Practically the whole History Department was studying the subject by then."

"I don't understand what history has to do with the Advance. The Advance is about the future," said his father. There was an uncomfortable pause. "I'm sorry, I didn't mean that the way it sounded."

"That's okay," said Becky. "History can be about the future too."

"Let me serve dessert and you can tell us about the program," said Rob's mother.

Rob helped his mother clear the table. Becky and his father made small talk until dessert was served, then Becky began to describe the program.

"It helps to start with some history. Long ago, long before this dining table was created, it was easy." Becky paused.

"What was easy?" asked Rob's mother.

"She baited you to ask that," said his father, taking a sip of wine.

Becky smiled and continued. "Before science and technology created sophisticated tools, basic safety wasn't assured. Imagine what it was like. You could die at any moment. Killed by wild animals, droughts, floods, or freezing cold. It was easier then, by far. Anyone could do it. Everyone needed it."

"Needed what?" asked Rob's mother.

"It's hard to believe people lived like that," said Rob, shaking his head.

Becky eyed Rob's father. He was listening intently, letting his wife ask questions. She continued, knowing he'd be weighing in soon. "Our people persevered and made continuous advancements. We invented tools to build homes and advanced architecture. We gathered in cities to support each other, but there were many challenges."

"Like what?" asked Rob's mother.

"Like sickness," said Rob. "They had doctors and medicine, but not enough for everyone. Many diseases had no cure. There was overcrowding and pollution. Social planning wasn't perfect then."

"That's right," said Becky. "It was an amazing time of advancement and progress for our people. However, for the individual person, there were still many challenges. It was still easy, and everyone needed it."

"Okay, I'll bite. What was the 'it' that was easy that everyone needed?" asked Rob's father.

Becky looked at him, acknowledging his question, but not answering. "Now things are different," she went on. "We have advanced. Everyone is safe. No one goes hungry. No one has been ill in over a thousand years. Success and happiness are a certainty. Everyone is content."

"That's good, right?" asked his mother.

"No, not for the Great Advance," replied Rob.

"Why do you call it 'great'?" asked Rob's father. "It's called the Synaptic Advance, or just the Advance."

Becky continued as if she hadn't been interrupted. "People today have everything they need. Everything is provided. There is nothing to sacrifice for anymore. What was once a very natural thing, what was once crucial to survival and to advancement, we've lost. We took it for granted, so we don't even know it's gone." She smiled at Rob and took a sip of wine. "This new program will get it back."

"I think I understand what you are saying," said Rob's father.

"I don't," said Rob's mother.

"It's a leadership program," said Rob, taking over for Becky. "We've grown so content that we don't need leadership to take us anywhere new."

"That's not true. We have leaders everywhere, of the planet, of nations, of cities," said his father. "Good ones. They wouldn't allow it."

"No, sir, we no longer have leaders. We have administrators," said Becky. "They exist to provide services to the population, maintain infrastructure, and distribute resources. Important things, but administrators aren't leaders. They have no following and aren't taking us anywhere. The planet's administrators are simply providers, supporting whatever the people wish. Leadership is required for people to want to go somewhere new, to take risks."

"Becky's right, Dad. Administrators work very hard to serve people's every need, which keeps things status quo. They keep things running smoothly, making only incremental changes, because things are already perfect, and people want things to stay that way."

Becky let her zeal get the best of her. "Without leadership, the Advance and all of its promise will never leave the laboratory," said Becky. "It will never be great."

"There's that word 'great' again," interjected Rob's father. "Becky, why do you call it great?"

"Why not?" asked Rob's mother.

"We might even discover other people in the Advance, people who have already transferred from some other planet in the universe," said Becky.

"No chance," said Rob's father. "With long-range synaptic scanners, we've already scanned the universe at a particle level. There's life everywhere, but not sentient, not evolved. We are the only people in the universe."

Becky realized Rob's father would not be convinced. She worried about Rob remaining excited about the program. "The Advance was wonderful as a theory to study, and to imagine the possibilities. Now, with recent discoveries . . ."

"Discoveries by Dad's science team," said Rob.

Becky nodded, lightly touching Rob's leg. "Now, the Advance is no longer a scientific impossibility. As exciting as the idea is, it also represents the unknown. It represents risk. The Advance means leaving everything behind, as our ancestors did when they crossed the seas. Unfortunately, the Advance is beginning to lose support because people are content with what they have. That's why we need a new kind of leader."

"The Advance needs a leader to help people see the potential of the program," said Rob. "Dad, that could be me."

Relieved, Becky continued. "Until now, the head of the Advance was a scientist. The next leader will come from our new leadership program, someone we can train to be a true leader like the greatest leaders from our history. People will be excited about the Advance. The Synaptic Advance will become the Great Advance!"

Rob's father stiffened. "You intend to manipulate everyone."

"No, we want people to understand a possible new future for humanity," said Becky.

"Humans aren't meant to exist in the particle fabric of the universe," said Rob's father. "That's why it's empty now."

Becky smiled. She'd heard that argument before. "This continent had no people once."

"That's not the same thing," said Rob's father.

Becky couldn't stop herself. "Were the moons around our planet meant for people? Not only is there no air on our moons, but it's impossible to survive the heat and the cold."

"Becky," said Rob.

She went on unabated. "Was the bottom of the ocean meant for people? Thanks to science, and leadership, the moons and the oceans host entire cities now."

"Shouldn't we let people choose?" asked Rob's mother.

"There's no choice if the program remains in the laboratory," said Becky. "Rob's test results show he's the perfect candidate. If he accepts, he will become the leader of the Great Advance!"

BECKY STEPPED to the side of the line to see better, as Rob, Mikey, and Bobby reached the front of the line. She saw

Angel's parents recognize Rob and immediately defer to his presence.

Becky thought of how far she and Rob had come. He had wildly exceeded all expectations. To prove the wisdom of his choice to his father, Rob had dedicated himself to the program, studying every leader in history, practicing motivational techniques, and running group simulations in order to persuade holdouts to join the Great Advance. Behavioral scientists from the Great Advance worked with the historians analyzing every detail, even Rob's name.

Becky still called her husband Rob, but everyone else called him Stevens. It had been her idea to change Rob's name to Stevens for the sake of creating an even stronger following. "Mr. Stevens" had been too formal. Dropping "Mr." while using his last name created a nice blend of familiarity and power, and it worked. People became increasingly attracted to Stevens's leadership. Before long, his influence extended far beyond the Great Advance to encompass the entire planet.

Their commitment was so great, they'd even delayed having children. When Mikey was born, she'd stayed with the Great Advance but only part time. When Bobby was born, she'd quit, but her passion for the program remained strong. She loved being a mother as much as she had loved putting the "Great" in the Great Advance.

A voice from behind her startled Becky.

"Ma'am, your husband is the greatest man in the world. We are all so lucky."

Becky smiled.

17

JIMEE MEETS STEVENS

JIMEE ARRIVED at the transfer station early. She wasn't sure why, but she wanted to meet Stevens in person before embarking on the Great Advance.

Confident she'd arrived before him, she went to the check-in table. Part of the check-in process was a body scan to detect any belongings a person might be wearing that could cause errors in the transfer process. Jimee's scan detected nothing that might hinder the system's performance, but something caught the attention of the attendant.

"Is that a paper photograph?" the attendant asked. "We have some just like it at my house."

"Yes," replied Jimee, scanning the distance for Stevens.

"Can I see?"

Jimee withdrew an envelope from her pocket, removed the photograph, and handed it to the attendant.

He studied it, looking up at Jimee, back at the photo, and again at Jimee. Despite trying to ignore the attendant so she could look for Stevens, Jimee sensed something unusual about him, a solitary strength, a kind aloofness. She couldn't tell which.

"That's a picture of my mother," she said, looking at the attendant. Besides being unusually big and having a bandaged hand, he was just another kind person like everyone else, but seemed simple, and projected an independence and a self-contained strength Jimee had never sensed before.

"Your mother's pretty," he said. "Has she already transferred? Do you think you will be able to recognize her in the Great Advance?"

Jimee pondered the question as she looked for Stevens. Recognition had been a question since the very beginning of the program. How would people recognize each other without physical bodies or audible voices? Nobody was sure because transfers were one-way only. It had been argued that if two people knew each other, their souls would recognize one other. Recognition had been definitively proven only recently with the introduction of the demo-portals.

"I hope I recognize my mother, and that she recognizes me," continued the attendant.

"What?" asked Jimee, distracted by his unusual aura.

She saw Stevens and his family in the distance. They had just arrived. Forgetting about the attendant and the photograph of her mother, she ran to get in line in ahead of Stevens, cutting into the line near the front. She immediately saw that her haste had been unnecessary. Stevens and his wife stopped repeatedly to talk with people and were several hundred people behind Jimee when they finally got in line.

To talk with him, Jimee decided to let people pass her until Stevens and his family were right behind her. Then, even if he was still busy talking with others, she would still be able to recognize him in the Great Advance by looking for the person who transferred right after her.

The line moved slowly. One by one, the person in front walked up and sat in the transfer chair. Attendants carefully strapped in each person and pulled the switch. A soft mist enveloped the body, the mist cleared, and the chair was empty. Whenever Jimee got close to the front, she found an excuse to step out of line and lose a few places. When Stevens finally got to the front, Jimee planned to strike up a conversation. She hoped he would be happy to see her after learning that she was the last holdout from the morning broadcast.

The line stopped moving. Jimee saw that the problem wasn't an issue with the system, but an argument of some kind. In a world of pure harmony and goodwill, arguments were rare and always polite and respectful. That didn't mean there were never disagreements. Jimee moved closer to learn what the argument was about. A teenage girl at the front of the line was arguing with her parents.

"Honey, it's our turn to transfer. Everyone is waiting. Your mom's going first, then you, then me, as we discussed. Okay, Angel?" asked the father.

"Can't I go tonight?" pleaded the girl.

Jimee instinctively did the calculations, four hundred thirteen people in line, two-foot average spacing, single file up front, reaching seven people wide in back, an average width of three, just over two hundred seventy-five feet long now. Assume one hundred more people to arrive. That would be five hundred thirteen still to transfer. Not good. The girl was right. It was 1:31 now. At the recent average of fifty-three seconds per transfer, it would be 9:04 before everyone transferred, over an hour past sundown. Jimee recalculated. Thirty-five seconds between transfers would be required to transfer everyone by 6:30, allowing a nice buffer before nightfall. She wondered if she should let the attendants know.

"Angel, honey, why the change of heart all of a sudden? Are you afraid?" asked the girl's mother.

Jimee could see that the girl wasn't afraid at all. Whatever was bothering her, it wasn't fear. The girl looked back toward the end of the line. Jimee's gift of observation provided the answer. The girl was looking back at Stevens's family, specifically, at Stevens's older son.

"Please, Mom," begged Angel.

The discussion continued for several minutes. Jimee

watched with interest, observing Stevens's older son acknowledge the girl with a smile and a nod. The next moment, Stevens and his two sons left the line, walking toward the front.

The attendants running the transfer station sat quietly, not interfering or pressuring the family in any way. Jimee wondered if they had seen this scenario play out before. They had probably learned long ago that these situations were so personal that there was nothing they could do or say to help.

"Father, I promise I want to go. I just want more time. I'll go with Mikey and his parents, I promise!" the girl insisted.

"You saw Mikey yesterday," said her mother.

Jimee sensed the people in line behind the family getting restless, but everyone was careful to be quiet and not pressure the family. Stevens arrived with his two sons. The entire group turned to acknowledge them.

"Hi, everyone. Is everything okay?" asked Stevens.

"Mikey!" exclaimed Angel.

"Mr. Stevens, this is my wife and my daughter Angel. We've always wanted to meet you," said the father, extending his hand to Stevens.

"Nice to meet you," said Stevens, shaking hands. "This is my son Bobby, and it looks like at least one of you knows Mikey. Is there anything I can help with?"

Jimee watched Angel's parents. Their respect and deference for Stevens was palpable. Angel's parents asked if Angel could stay behind for a short while and transfer with Stevens's family.

"That would be fine," Stevens replied. "We'd be happy to have her."

Angel's parents hugged their daughter and told her they'd be waiting for her in the Great Advance. Stevens stayed for another few minutes, watching each parent get strapped into a chair. Smiling, each blew kisses to Angel, who blew kisses back. A mist enveloped each parent, and when the mist cleared, the chairs were empty.

Jimee realized something was afoot when Stevens looked down the line and waved to his wife. He then walked with Bobby, Mikey, and Angel down the street. Bobby was skipping and hopping and kicking pebbles down the street. Mikey and Angel held hands.

She watched them go, losing her chance to talk to Stevens. Why were they leaving the transfer station on the last day? She felt a hand gently touch her shoulder.

"Sweetie, are you okay? You're next in line," said a man behind her.

Startled, Jimee turned toward the man. He held a baby, barely a month old. His wife and three small children crowded around him. One, a girl, held out a lollipop for Jimee.

"It's cherry. You can lick it," she said.

Jimee saw the two other children had lollipops too. The mother leaned into Jimee, smiling conspiratorially.

"We told them if they can still taste the lollipop while being transferred, they might be able to taste it forever. I wish I'd have thought of it, but we got the idea at a Great Advance seminar."

Jimee forced a smile, backed out of line, and hurried to catch up with Stevens.

The street, and in fact the world, was nearly deserted. Stevens and the kids could easily have seen Jimee following, but they never looked back. The group walked until they came to a house and went inside.

Alone in front of the house and unsure what to do, Jimee moved closer. Just as she arrived on the front sidewalk, Bobby burst out the front door and ran into the yard in front of the house.

"C'mon, Daddy!" he yelled.

"Right behind you!" Stevens said, emerging from the

house carrying a ball and two gloves. "Here you go!" He tossed the ball and one of the gloves to Bobby.

Laughing, Bobby somehow managed to catch them both, and they began playing catch.

Jimee could tell Stevens and his son played together a lot. Each of them instinctively knew whether the ball would be thrown high, low, to the left, or to the right. Every time one of them began to throw the ball, the other would begin extending his glove in anticipation before the ball left the other's hand. Standing there on an empty street, watching Stevens and his son playing catch, Jimee knew she had never felt such a connection.

"Hello, young lady," said Stevens, not breaking his throw-catch rhythm with Bobby.

She sensed Stevens was genuinely saying hello without any irritation they'd been followed. "Hi."

"Wanna play catch with us?" asked Bobby. "I can get Mikey's glove."

Jimee desperately wanted to experience the connection, or whatever it was that Stevens and Bobby were feeling, and she'd never played catch before. "No. I just. I wanted to . . . I'm just curious."

"About what?" asked Stevens, stretching to catch a wild throw from Bobby.

She didn't know the answer. She wanted to ask about the sign Stevens had made during his speech earlier that morning. She felt confused, a rare and uncomfortable feeling for her. She did want to play. Maybe she could learn something. Why didn't she say yes?

"I'm Jimee, the one you saved during this morning's broadcast," she said finally, instantly getting Stevens's attention.

Feeling him look more closely at her, she wondered what he saw. A thin, gangly, and to all appearances, weak young woman, the poor little girl whose mother had died when she was a baby, or the last holdout to join the Great Advance? Jimee knew she wasn't actually weak. Everyone on the planet had been healthy and strong for thousands of years.

"Thank you for joining us," he said. "We can talk on the way back."

The intensity of Stevens and Bobby's play increased, mesmerizing Jimee. She noted every detail. The sound of the ball smacking into the pocket of the glove. The glove's leather stretching as it opened. Fingers clenching and releasing the ball. The ball whirring, spinning through the air. The smell of leather and oil on Stevens's glove. The smell of dead frogs and snakes on Bobby's glove. Jimee's father had died when she was still a baby. Jimee had never been athletic nor played ball at school. Watching Stevens and Bobby, she understood that a boy playing catch with his father was entirely different from a boy playing ball with other kids.

Jimee sensed that Stevens and his son playing catch had opened a window in the universe, a web of invisible connections. Their play had temporarily realigned the fabric of the universe. Fabric threads that normally stood apart now formed a connection, a bond between a father and his son. Jimee saw a connection not of this world but of something else, something spiritual, something inherent to the universe, something amazing and good. Neither Stevens nor Bobby saw the connecting threads. They just played catch. Jimee watched, fascinated by the threads connecting father and son. Time warped. The sound of Bobby's voice snapped Jimee out of her trance.

"Thank you, Daddy, that was fun," said Bobby with a big smile.

Jimee felt the spiritual web between father and son ease back into the fabric of the universe.

"Let's get Mikey and Angel," said Stevens. "Jimee, we'll be right back. You can come inside with us if you like."

She walked to join them. Her legs felt stiff. Amazingly,

three hours had passed. Impossible. How could that be? Stevens seemed unaware. Bobby led the way into the house, followed by Jimee. Stevens held the door open.

Inside, she felt another connection, similar to what she had sensed outside. She sensed soft tentacles emerging from the ceiling and reentering, as if wrapping around something upstairs, coming from Stevens's older son, Mikey, and the girl, Angel.

Bobby, still holding both gloves and the ball, grinned. Jimee eyed the boy. Mikey and Angel had likely been upstairs the whole time, and Bobby somehow knew it.

"You two wait here. I'll be back in a few minutes," said Stevens.

"Can we wait for you outside on the deck, Daddy?"

"Sure, Bobby. Show Jimee the way," Stevens replied, before walking upstairs.

18
THE TRUTH ABOUT ANNA'S LAB MISHAP

STEVENS WENT to Mikey's bedroom and was about to knock on the door when he realized he was rushing unnecessarily. He still had plenty of time to get back to the transfer station and decided to give Mikey and Angel more time together. He continued down the hallway into his home office, which he rarely used since he'd begun delivering the morning broadcasts from his deck.

Stevens sat at the desk. It had been his father's. On the far corner, he saw a picture of himself and Becky with Anna and his onetime best friend, William. He felt the soft coolness of the leather chair on his legs and smelled the old wood of the desk. He wondered if he'd miss possessions in the Great Advance, or if he'd miss the feel and smell of things, like chairs and desks. But things weren't important, he reminded himself. Family was. He'd be together forever with Becky, Mikey, and Bobby once they transferred. Anna wouldn't have William, but she would have Billy. More than that, Stevens thought, everyone would have everyone in the Great Advance.

He looked at William in the picture. William was beaming, proud he was about to have a baby boy. Stevens saddened for a moment, remembering William's letter. He opened the drawer. The letter was exactly where he'd placed it years ago. He picked it up and read:

My dearest Rob,

You are a wonderful and amazing friend. I smile when I think of you. As your closest friend, I think you deserve to know the truth. As your best friend, my duty is to tell you the truth. A million times, I have failed to tell you.

The truth makes me angry and sad, so when I try to bring it up, suddenly I feel a warmth and a lightness overcome my anger, and then we are laughing with each other, and I can no longer tell you. Instead, we talk and share stories of our families and discuss our important work on the Great Advance.

The last time we were together, you showed me a photo of your new baby boy, Bobby. He's beautiful. That evening, I showed the picture to Anna. She laughed and said Bobby was the cutest baby ever. She loved his baseball pajamas. Then Anna and I looked at our first family photo. Anna loved that photo. I did too. Do you remember? You were there on the day of Anna's lab mishap and took a picture of me and Anna rubbing our little Billy inside her belly. The truth about the lab mishap is what makes me angry and sad, and what I need to tell you.

My dear friend, Rob, I write this letter to share the truth. I know the warmth and the light will come for my anger and sadness, but I need to stay angry so I can finish writing this letter. Looking at our first family photo and thinking about my beautiful Billy will give me the strength to complete the letter.

You were right, Rob, when you said the Great Advance kissed our Billy and made him special. Anna and I were happy and excited to imagine something as wonderful as the Great Advance blessing our unborn baby boy. Since then, I have learned how Anna's mishap in the laboratory of the Great Advance changed Billy.

The Great Advance took Billy's connectedness. Billy doesn't belong. He isn't part of the rest of us. He plays alone. He doesn't have friends, not real ones. When Billy has to be strong, the strength comes only from within.

Importantly, the reason for my letter isn't about Billy. Thanks to his loving mother and our kind and loving society, Billy will be okay. Rob, I'm worried for everyone else and the Great Advance.

ONCE TRANSFERRED, WILL THE GREAT ADVANCE TAKE FROM OTHERS WHAT IT TOOK FROM BILLY?

I've put Billy's picture down. The warmth and light have come, and my anger has faded, but not my resolve. With Billy's strength, I will soon learn more.

Meet me in my laboratory tomorrow morning when you arrive. I have several experiments you can help me with that might help us understand.

Your trusted friend, William

Stevens stared at the sentence William had capitalized. William's accident happened the following morning. He'd joined William in the laboratory and was assisting when something went wrong. An investigation revealed that William had configured the transfer chair in an unsafe manner. William's team reviewed his laboratory records and journals to discover what William was working on. They found many notes and peculiar references to his son, Billy, but nothing that revealed what William was investigating.

Stevens had never shared the letter with anyone, not with Anna, not with the scientists who'd investigated William's accident, and not with his executive team for the Great Advance. Only with his wife, Becky, who'd encouraged him to keep the letter private. Everyone knew Billy was a beloved little boy, loved by everyone. Making the letter public would only hurt Anna and cause undue concern for Billy.

Worse, people were already anxious about the Great Advance. If anyone had found out about William's letter, there would have been many more holdouts, and the Great Advance could have been delayed indefinitely, hurting everyone.

19
SUNRISE

JIMEE WAS WATCHING Stevens walk up the stairs when Bobby's sweaty hand grabbed hers and pulled her across the living room, through glass doors, and onto the deck. The terrain from the deck sloped downhill as far as she could see, providing a view of the city that stretched all the way to a distant sea. The city was still, no sounds, no movement in the distance. Jimee tried to imagine what it would be like if people were still there.

Several chairs were arranged on the deck to overlook the city. One chair was heavily worn. Beside it, a small table held a half-full coffee cup, a journal, and an electronic pen.

"That's where my daddy sits every morning," said Bobby.

"Where do you sit?" Jimee asked, knowing it wasn't on the deck since only one chair showed use.

"Up there, in my room," said Bobby, pointing to a window on the upper floor of the house.

She looked, but her attention was drawn to the room next to Bobby's, from which she felt the pulsing fabric of the universe bending and glowing as threads of spiritual connection surged through the walls.

"That's my brother Mikey's room," said Bobby. "Sometimes I sleep in his room, like when I was little."

Jimee could only stare, entranced and overwhelmed by the wonderful feeling radiating from Mikey's room.

"Are you okay, ma'am? Hey! Are you okay?" Bobby yelled, tugging Jimee's arm.

"Oh, sorry. Yes, I'm fine."

She was more than fine. She'd never felt better in her life. She was beginning to understand the wonder of transferring to the Great Advance, where beautiful, happy, joyous feelings of love would flow freely between people, unencumbered by the physical realities of time and space.

The spiritual bonds from the upstairs room surged stronger and stronger, flowing out from the house into the valley below. Jimee sat down in Stevens's chair and looked at the city. She imagined how happy the people would feel if they were still alive and in their homes, or at work or play. Jimee remembered her childhood, and her difficulty fitting in. She thought of her dislike of groups and her job working all by herself and suddenly realized she wanted to be with the rest of her people in the spiritual connectedness of the Great Advance. She would finally belong to something.

Remembering what Bobby said about Stevens sitting in his chair every morning, Jimee thought of how Stevens must have looked forward to his morning speeches. Sitting in his chair now, Jimee's curiosity overcame her. She reached for Stevens's journal.

Watching Bobby playing on the deck, she realized that he felt the connectedness too. Bobby's play seemed filled with light, as if he were floating, dancing in harmony with something in the universe. The something touched him, caressing him, moving through him, spinning Bobby with its intertwining threads.

Bobby's arms flung out as if he were opening up to the universe. He hugged himself, holding the joy and keeping it for himself. Spinning around and laughing, Bobby's arms opened, offering himself and his joy to the universe and joining with whatever it was that he felt.

Every nerve in her body felt on fire, energized. Time slowed. The pulsing fabric from Mikey and Angel became gentle waves, with peaks cresting far apart, leaving quiet calm behind. Bobby stilled, then danced again, in harmony with the waves. Jimee looked at Stevens's journal. The cover was soft, old, and faded from the sun. She opened it to find the pages were anything but old. Each was a high-capacity computer system, designed to store the kind of complex information only a synaptic scientist in the Great Advance might require.

Inside were Stevens's notes about his speeches. Each started on a new page and spanned two or three pages. Jimee recognized the speeches.

Stevens had meticulously planned changes from speech to speech to encourage people with different concerns to join the Great Advance. Jimee's gifts of observation and minute detail were matched by Stevens's understanding of people and how to motivate them to follow him into the Great Advance, to belong, to learn, to discover all there was, everywhere.

At that moment, Jimee wanted nothing more in the world than to join others in the Great Advance. She wondered how she could have been foolish enough to be a holdout. Awash in the pulsing, connecting fabric of the universe, Jimee closed her eyes. She felt a small breeze touch her face and knew it was Bobby's spinning. Could this be the paradise Stevens was hinting about in his speeches? Couldn't be. Not yet. This wonderful feeling on the deck with Bobby was just a sample of what could be. Bobby began to sing.

Jimee opened her eyes and turned a page of the journal. She found not another speech but a sketch of a sunrise. Turning the page again, she found another sunrise, more beautiful somehow. On the next page, another sunrise, beautiful again. Page after page was filled with sunrises. Like

Stevens's speeches, each morning the sunrise changed slightly, growing more enchanting each time.

Bobby stood on the railing, balancing in the glowing fabric of the universe. Behind Bobby across the valley, Jimee saw the horizon that presented the sunrise to Stevens each morning. Bobby stood on his toes, his arms stretched to the sky, twirling on the railing. Jimee tensed. It was three feet down to the deck, and a one-hundred-foot drop to the cliffs below, but Bobby seemed incapable of falling.

Jimee looked up at Bobby on the rail, then beyond Bobby to the horizon. Suddenly, in her mind, she recognized a pattern in Stevens's sketches, in the changes from one sunrise to the next. What was it?

Oblivious now to the waves of warmth from Mikey and Angel, and from Bobby's dancing, Jimee turned back to Stevens's first sunrise. Quickly, she paged through drawing after drawing.

A bug landed on the page, a gnat. Careful to not hurt the gnat, Jimee shook the page. The insect flew off, joining a swarm of gnats a dozen feet away. Seconds later, the swarm moved closer. Several gnats landed on the lip of the coffee cup. They seemed to be looking at her.

Jimee turned the page. Instead of a drawing, she saw the icon of a synaptic recording. She quickly flipped through the remaining pages. All were dedicated to the recording. Jimee had never seen a synaptic recording, but she'd read about them. Scientists used synaptic imagers in the laboratories of the Great Advance to record synaptic energy. She knew that to experience the recording, she only had to close her eyes and touch the page.

Jimee looked at Bobby dancing, with the horizon beyond, as she basked in the warm waves from Mikey and Angel. She took a deep breath, closed her eyes, and placed her palm on the page. Wondrous beauty immersed her mind. She gasped, unable to breathe. Her eyes watered. Her skin hurt. She dropped the journal to the deck and leaned back, in shock.

Within the beauty, hidden by the beauty, Jimee had sensed a message. The journal lay on the deck, still open on the page of the sunrise recording. Her hand no longer touched the page, but the message continued screaming at Jimee. It had burned into the bottom of her soul. It was a warning, and a threat.

STAY AWAY OR DIE!

20

THE GNAT

SWEAT POURED from Jimee's face. She felt sick. Bobby was singing. Rubbing her eyes, Jimee saw Bobby dancing on his toes, twirling on the rail, laughing. Her stomach hurt. The connecting waves were softer now, smooth ripples flowing from the upstairs bedroom. Jimee looked up. Mikey and Angel emerged onto the deck of the upstairs bedroom.

"Is that really your brother?" Angel asked.

"That's him all right. He's the best!" answered Mikey through his laughter.

To Jimee it felt like the world was ending, because, she suddenly knew, it was. Something in the sunrise had warned against the Great Advance. The sun seemed so hot, beating down on her neck.

Who or what had sent the warning? Souls recently transferred as part of the Great Advance? No, that didn't make sense. Recently transferred souls could easily send warnings via the demo-portals, and to Jimee's knowledge, none had.

Who else could it be? Life that already lived in the Great Advance or souls that had transferred long ago, long before life on her home planet? If so, why use the sunrise? Why not simply warn the souls already in the Great Advance? Why not just use the demo-portals?

Stevens walked out onto the deck.

"Daddy, look at me. I'm a butterfly!" called Bobby, twirling on the rail on one foot, perfectly balanced.

"Bobby, what are you doing?" shouted his father.

"Watch!"

Bobby danced on the railing. His eyes were closed, arms outstretched, back arched, head thrown back, basking in the afternoon sun. Then, in a swift, smooth movement, he straightened, and on the ball of one foot, the toes of his other foot pointed out to the side, Bobby spun like a top until he came to a stop.

Poised perfectly on the rail, Bobby readied his next move. The next instant, Jimee sensed he had lost his balance. Maybe it was his father calling out to him or Mikey's laughter, or maybe Bobby sensed Jimee's shock from reading the journal.

"Go, Bobby!" shouted Mikey from above.

"He's good," said Angel.

"Bobby, that's amazing. Now get down," said Stevens.

Jimee realized Bobby didn't know he'd tipped past the point of no return, couldn't hear the frantic pounding of his own heart, didn't know he was about to fall off the railing to the rocks a hundred feet below. Bobby, and then Stevens, Mikey, and Angel would only realize what was happening after Bobby began falling. Bobby's beaming smile would soon vanish.

Just then, Jimee heard the whine of gnats. The swarm flew at Bobby, several into his right ear. Instinctively, Bobby raised his right arm to swat the gnats. The sudden movement caused him to regain his balance. Still beaming, Bobby turned toward his audience and took a deep bow.

"Thank you, Daddy," Bobby said, pulling himself up. "I'm ready to go back to the transfer station now!"

"We are too!" shouted Mikey. "Little bro, you're awesome!"

Jimee felt something land on the back of her hand and

looked down. It was a gnat, the same gnat that had landed on the page of the journal. One of its legs was broken.

Bobby must have hit the gnat when he swiped at it, she thought.

"Who's that girl in the chair down by Bobby?" asked Angel. "She looks sick."

"Back we go," said Stevens. "Your mother will be nearing the front of the line by now, if she's not helping on the transfer platform."

Jimee stood up slowly. The gnat flew from her hand and joined the swarm, its leg dangling awkwardly. She closed her eyes, consciously burning the image of the gnat into her memory. Was the gnat related to the warning in the sunrise, the energy in the fabric, or just a coincidence?

"Napping in my favorite chair?" asked Stevens. "You should see the sunrises from here in the morning."

"I can imagine," she said, opening her eyes. The gnat swarm was gone. Everything seemed as it should be. Her wits returned quickly.

"Sir, it's 5:35," she said. "Everyone should be transferred within an hour or two."

"What! How?" asked Stevens.

"Assuming they sped up from fifty-three seconds per transfer to—"

"I meant, where'd the time go?" Stevens interjected.

"Sorry, sir. You and Bobby played catch for three hours and eleven minutes. You were upstairs for twenty-two minutes."

Jimee saw Angel wink at Mikey, who grinned broadly. Stevens rubbed his shoulder. Jimee's mind raced. The waves from the fabric affected time, even for her. The sunrise had tried to warn Stevens. A gnat had saved Bobby.

Bobby ran to this father and grabbed his hand. Together, father and son left the deck, followed by Jimee. Mikey and Angel came down the stairs, and all five left the house to return to the transfer station.

Walking down the street, everyone felt happy. Bobby seemed especially happy. Jimee wondered if that was caused by the residue from being immersed in the fabric waves when he and his father played catch. Mikey poked fun at Bobby's dancing. It was good-natured fun that made even Jimee smile. Bobby, still holding his father's hand, joked back with Mikey.

"Daddy, in the Great Advance, we will be able to think, right?" asked Bobby.

"Yes, Son, better than we can now because we'll no longer be limited by our brains," replied Stevens.

"So, does that mean Mikey and his small brain will no longer be the stupidest one in our family?" asked Bobby.

Everyone laughed. Jimee managed a nervous smile. She'd always associated her uniqueness with her brain.

How will I change in the Great Advance? she wondered, suddenly concerned. *How will the attendant, who seemed simple, change?*

"Ow!" yelled Bobby, feigning a hurt shoulder when Mikey smacked him. He recovered quickly and laughed. "Hit away, big brother. Last chance!"

Angel whispered into Mikey's ear. Mikey's eyes lit up. "Dad, after we transfer, if my supposedly tiny brain no longer makes me stupid, does that mean Bobby's big, fat, math brain no longer makes him a smarty-pants?"

"Pick up the pace, boys," said Stevens, walking faster.

Bobby, Mikey, and Angel jogged to keep up. Jimee stopped in her tracks, overwhelmed by Mikey's question.

"Jimee, you okay?" Stevens shouted to her from a block ahead.

Jimee didn't reply. She wasn't okay about the warning, she wasn't okay about the gnat, and she wasn't okay about losing her uniqueness when she lost her brain.

Stevens stopped, causing the children to stop too. "Jimee! Hurry!"

"I'll get her," said Bobby, running toward Jimee.

"No wait, Bobby," said Stevens. "She's a holdout. I'll save her. You kids go on ahead. Your mother will be waiting. Tell her I'm helping a holdout. Let the attendant know we'll be there in thirty minutes. Wait for us, and we'll all transfer together." He looked at the horizon. "It'll be nice, just after sundown."

"No problem, Dad," Mikey answered.

The kids continued on to the transfer station. Stevens walked back to Jimee. She waited quietly as he approached.

"Are you okay?" he asked.

She wanted to answer but didn't know what to say, where to start. The warning hardly mattered now. The entire planet had already transferred.

"Jimee, talk to me." Stevens pointed to a porch of a house nearby. "Those chairs look comfortable. How about we sit for a bit?" He walked up to the porch and sat down.

A dozen narrow, aging wooden steps led up to the porch. Jimee guessed that whoever on her safety team had been responsible for maintaining the neighborhood had been reassigned to the Great Advance long ago.

She stayed where she was in the middle of the street and looked up at him on the porch. She imagined him sitting on his deck every morning, planning his speeches to persuade everyone to join the Great Advance. All the while, something in the sunrise had been warning him.

"Why?" whispered Jimee.

"Jimee, talk to me."

"Why?" she asked again, louder.

"I don't know. You seem upset," replied Stevens.

Jimee turned away. It was getting late and the sun would be going down soon. She faced toward the horizon, toward the setting sun.

"I've never really watched a sunset," said Stevens. "The view from our house doesn't face that way."

She stared at the blue sky in the distance and reimagined

the fabric of the universe weaving together as she had witnessed it on Stevens's deck. Abruptly, she turned back toward Stevens. "Why leave? Why did you insist everyone leave?" she demanded.

"What happened?" asked Stevens. "What changed at—"

"What's the answer to Bobby's question?" Jimee interrupted. "Mikey's question too. Why didn't you answer their questions?"

He shrugged. "I don't know. I'm the leader of the Great Advance, but I'm not a scientist."

"I think you do know," she said. "You've been leading the Great Advance for almost your entire life. You tested the transfer on many people, so tell me the truth."

After a few minutes, Stevens reached over and touched the chair next to him. "Come sit, and I will as best I can."

Jimee didn't move. "Why lie?"

"What?"

"About lollipops."

"Jimee, I don't know what you are talking about."

Stevens tapped the chair again. Jimee didn't budge. She sensed he was telling the truth about the lollipops.

"Please, Jimee."

Giving in, Jimee walked up the stairs, automatically stepping over a broken step at the top, and sat down next to Stevens. The sky was turning deeper blue, so the sun would set soon. If Stevens had been truthful, this would be his first sunset since drawing the sunrises.

"Jimee?"

Jimee didn't reply. She was thinking about the boys' questions. She was wondering about sunrises. She was thinking about the gnat. "Will I be the same in the Advance?" she asked.

"No, you will be a better version of yourself. You will be the essence of you for the first time, unhindered by any physical constraints," said Stevens.

A gnat landed on the porch railing in Jimee's line of sight to the sunset. Jimee tensed. Could it be a coincidence? It had to be. She noticed a swarm of gnats hovering in the distance.

"What if we aren't the first to transfer?" Jimee asked. "What if others have transferred before us, or already live in the Great Advance, and they don't want us there?"

"We'll be the first. Space travel over the last thousand years has revealed no sentient life, and our most sensitive Great Advance scanners have discovered no sentient life either, not physical, not spiritual. What makes you ask that?"

Jimee studied Stevens. He was sincere. Nonetheless, the warning in the sunrise had to have come from someone or something.

"As a people, we have made great progress," he added.

"That's how your speeches start," said Jimee, squinting to see the gnat against the glare of the sun.

"From nothing, our civilization has achieved everything."

"What do you mean, everything?"

"Our society became safe and strong because we loved one another, everyone connected to everyone, yes?"

"Yes," replied Jimee, but thought to herself, *except me, and maybe the attendant.*

Stevens continued. "Unlike the animals and the birds, we learned to roam freely. We advanced from the bottom of the ocean to the land and sky, and then into space, yes?"

"In machines," replied Jimee, watching the gnat and the advancing sunset. The gnat rotated slightly to face Stevens. Was it limping? Frustrated by the glare of the sun, Jimee couldn't be sure. The gnat was a black silhouette against the brightness.

"Unlike the insects," said Stevens, "which live and die with no identity, humans are not programmed to be only one simple thing."

Programmed? By who? she wondered. The gnat rotated toward Jimee. She saw that it was definitely limping.

"From the beginning of time, the animals, the fish, the birds, and the insects have stayed the same, while humans evolved toward perfection, exploring everything, understanding everything, mastering everything."

The gnat turned back toward Stevens. Jimee could clearly see its broken leg.

"Not sunrises and bugs," said Jimee under her breath.

"What?"

Jimee didn't reply. Stevens continued.

"So, the question is: What is the next step for a people who understand everything?"

To realize they don't know anything, thought Jimee.

"We free ourselves from the physical realm to enable ourselves, not just to connect to each other, but to connect to everything, to become a part of everything. For all of our progress, for all of our science and technology, our DNA has not changed. Our people are an advanced people. As individuals, we enjoy civilization's advancements, but as individuals of physical form, we remain separated, and after a short time, perish. Physically, we have stalled while our minds have advanced. A newborn baby today is the same physically as a baby of our ancient ancestors. We have eradicated disease. We grow perfect food. We can repair broken bones. Still, we die, and while alive, we are just as susceptible to accidents as in times past. The universe is billions of years old. Humans live less than a nanosecond in comparison. In that nanosecond of life, humans are defined not by their souls, but by their DNA, by genetics. A lucky few possess DNA with the capacity for genius, leadership, athletics, or artistic talent. Still, all humans are limited by the physical body and brain."

Jimee wondered if the gnat was listening. It came to her that of all she'd studied, she hadn't studied bugs and sunrises. She imagined neither had changed much in the billions of years since the beginning of the universe.

"Jimee, what if you could free yourself from the limitations of your legs? Even if you walked every day of your life, you would only see a fraction of the planet. What if you could free yourself from your lungs? You would no longer be trapped above water or below space. What you know, how you think, what you accomplish, occurs in the nanosecond of your life. Physical existence is a prison. You and I should be free to evolve into whatever we want to be. To accept physical limitations limits our true potential."

The sunset was minutes away. The gnat hadn't moved.

"You didn't see the message in the sunrise," said Jimee.

"What?" asked Stevens.

Jimee saw the gnat turn to look at the sunset. The sun touched the horizon, and the sky burst forth in a dazzling array of colors. It seemed the sunset knew this would be the last sunset ever seen on that horizon, so the brilliance of all future sunsets radiated, all at once. Captivated, she didn't see the gnat fly away. Maybe the sunset was trying to communicate one last time, in a final attempt to warn them away from the Great Advance. Stevens and Jimee watched in silence as the sun disappeared below the horizon.

"Beautiful," said Stevens softly.

"The holdouts don't have a chance to survive. You know that, don't you?" asked Jimee. She sensed him tense.

"Before the transportation system broke down, we created stockpiles of food, water, medicine, and other supplies, all over the world," he said.

"Supplies won't be enough. Hundreds of years ago, the entire population became completely dependent." said Jimee, sensing his sadness. She realized he knew, and cared, but his passion for the Great Advance took precedence. She sensed his sadness dissipate. She felt the need to bring it back, to prolong it.

"Even if the supplies do last, the climate controls will fail —storms, tidal waves, droughts, famine, disease."

"Jimee," Stevens pleaded.

She couldn't stop herself. "Holdouts won't stand a chance against the animals. Humanity will cease to exist."

"Dad! Dad!" yelled Mikey.

Jimee saw Mikey running down the street from a couple blocks away. He seemed frantic.

"Yes, Son, we're coming!" shouted Stevens, getting up and moving toward the steps, while looking back at Jimee. "No, Jimee, humanity will exist forever in the Great Advance."

She rose, then froze. Stevens's foot was coming down on the broken step. She heard a whine. Stevens stopped. He'd heard it too. He slapped his neck. The whine stopped.

That gnat just sacrificed itself to save Stevens! Jimee thought.

"Thankfully, there're no bugs in the Great Advance," he said, grinning, then stepped forward again.

"Wait!" said Jimee, reaching out.

She was too late. Stevens's entire weight came down on the broken step. It gave way. Reflexively, he grabbed Jimee's arm. The two tumbled down the steps onto the sidewalk.

"Dad!" yelled Mikey, running toward them.

Jimee rolled onto her hands and knees. Stevens had cushioned her fall, and she hadn't been hurt.

"Stevens, are you okay?" she asked.

Mikey leaned over his father. "Dad, your neck!"

Jimee scrambled over to Stevens and saw he was badly hurt. He lay on his back with his head at an impossible angle, turned so far to the side that his nose pushed into the ground. Mikey started crying.

"Stevens, can you feel your legs?" asked Jimee.

He didn't reply. Mikey began to shake. Jimee didn't know what to do. Stevens's eye was open. She saw it blink. She was afraid. The blink reminded her of her mother.

"I think you broke your neck. Can you talk?"

Unsure what to do, she crouched and bent down face-to-face with Stevens. His eye was still open. He blinked again.

"Why doesn't he answer?" asked Mikey hysterically.

"Stevens, if you can hear me, blink three times," she said.

He blinked three times.

"He can hear and see us. Mikey, go into the house and get a large blanket. Hurry!"

Mikey ran up the porch steps into the house. Jimee sat down next to Stevens and reached out to hold his hand. It felt warm. She squeezed, then realized Stevens likely couldn't feel her touch. Where was Mikey? She examined Stevens. His neck was turning purple. He was bleeding internally. His only chance at survival was to transfer.

Mikey burst from the house with a blanket. Jimee carefully edged it under Stevens. Taking each end of the blanket, they shuffled slowly to the transfer station. Jimee made a quick calculation. Assuming Mikey had walked to the station and run all the way back, he'd spent only twelve minutes at the station before leaving to get his father.

"Mikey, what happened at the station?" Jimee asked.

Mikey began to answer, then tripped, nearly dropping his father.

Jimee didn't ask again, knowing she'd find out soon, in sixty-eight minutes at their current pace.

Rounding the last corner, Jimee saw Bobby, Angel, Becky, and an attendant sitting near the transfer station. They were the only ones left. It was getting dark fast. Streetlights flickered on, providing an eerie glow. Bobby ran to meet them with Becky close behind. Jimee recognized the attendant as the one she'd met earlier that morning. The attendant's arm was around Angel's shoulders. Angel was crying.

Stevens blinked helplessly as Jimee explained to Becky what had happened. Becky immediately took charge, directing the attendant to help carry Stevens the final block to the transfer station. Angel saw Stevens and began crying again.

She ran away from the group, disappearing behind a large building. Mikey ran after her. Jimee and the attendant hurriedly carried Stevens up to the steps to the transfer chair, with Becky at his side, stabilizing the blanket. Bobby followed, crying.

A terrible stench came from the chair. The white leather was stained brown. Jimee retched and nearly fell. The whole platform smelled of feces. Behind the transfer chair lay piles of dirty shirts that had been used to wipe the chair.

"Transfer Rob, then Bobby," Becky directed the attendant. "I'll get Mikey and Angel."

Becky turned to Bobby, who stood a few feet away, staring at his father. Stevens's eyes had turned red. Blood drooled from his mouth.

"Bobby, honey, be brave. Daddy will be okay."

"Mikey and Angel went that way," said the attendant, pointing. "Behind the building, where we laid the bodies."

"Bobby, stay here!" Becky said. She ran down the steps and disappeared into the darkness.

"Bodies, what bodies?" asked Jimee.

21

PICKLE

OUT OF THE corner of his eye, Stevens saw Bobby. Was it Bobby? With his head hanging at an extreme angle, Stevens couldn't be sure.

It wasn't supposed to be like this, he thought. He knew he might miss the Great Advance if Billy didn't transfer him soon. He felt no pain but knew his neck had to be visibly broken. Mikey's reaction on the porch had said it all. Stevens saw a pool of dark saliva forming on his lap. He didn't have long. He strained to see Bobby, who stood about six feet away.

Father's and son's eyes met and connected.

STEVENS REMEMBERED the mornings before baseball games. Everything seemed brighter. The air was fresher. He'd be in the kitchen cooking pancakes, waiting for Bobby. The night before, he'd have laid Bobby's baseball uniform on the foot of Bobby's bed, freshly cleaned and perfectly folded.

Walking to a game together, they didn't talk. They didn't need to. On game mornings, they were connected, just like when playing catch in the front yard.

Stevens wheezed. Blood spattered his chest. He squeezed his eyes shut, then forced them open. He saw a tear dripping down Bobby's cheek.

A game was underway. Bobby was at bat. He swung and missed. The pitch smacked into the catcher's glove. Bobby spit, touched his hat, and tapped the dust off his shoes. He swung again, a base hit, a triple!

"Take a big lead, Bobby. You're fast. You can get back," shouted Bobby's coach.

"Go, Bobby!" cheered his teammates.

Stevens didn't cheer. He didn't need to. Bobby took a twenty-foot lead, scowling at the pitcher. Crouched and ready, Bobby stared down the pitcher, who glared back.

The pitcher stepped back from the rubber and began walking toward Bobby, angling toward third. Stevens saw Bobby's focus shift away from the pitcher to himself in the stands. He felt Bobby's joy.

Stevens heard a dripping sound. He saw drops hit the soft fabric of his pants, pooling dark red. He smelled his bowels. Someone's hands clasped his face and pushed him against the headrest of the transfer chair.

Stevens felt Bobby's surprise at suddenly seeing the pitcher so close.

"Bobby, get back!" shouted Bobby's coach.

The pitcher laughed and held the baseball out for Bobby to see.

Bobby dashed for home. The pitcher gave chase, then threw the ball. Bobby reversed to third. The catcher gave chase. The first baseman covered home. The catcher threw. Bobby reversed. The first baseman caught the ball, blocking his path. Bobby reversed, again and again, trapped in a pickle. The crowd quieted. Time stopped. A lone cheer reverberated through the universe.

Stevens tried to talk, to tell Bobby he'd score the winning run, but his mouth wouldn't work.

"Go, Bobby," yelled Stevens.

Bobby sprinted for home. The ball whizzed by. Bobby dived. Dust mushroomed. The umpire's arms swept outward.

"Safe!" he yelled.

Bobby leaped to his feet. Both teams poured onto the field, congratulating Bobby and celebrating the greatest play ever played.

Stevens rejoiced, knowing the connection with his son would last forever in the wonder of the Great Advance.

22

BECKY

JIMEE LOOKED out from the platform for Angel, Mikey, or Becky, but it was too dark to see. Dogs growled in the distance, thirteen of them.

"Hold his head while I get some tape," the attendant instructed Jimee.

Bobby stood a few feet away. Stevens was nonresponsive. It was critical to transfer him immediately. The attendant taped him across the chest and shoulders, then looped the tape under his chin and around his ears, securing Stevens's head to the back of the headrest where the synaptic transfer receptors were located.

"You can let go now," said the attendant. "The tape should hold him for a successful transfer."

Jimee let go. She could hear Stevens's breathing, barely.

"Stand back," said the attendant.

Jimee moved back. The attendant pulled a lever on the armrest. There was a slight humming sound. A rush of air swirled around Stevens, followed by a sweet-smelling mist.

"That's for the bugs," said the attendant. "It stops bugs from transferring with the person. The mist kills the bugs."

"Why does it matter?" asked Jimee. "I thought only people could transfer."

"That's true, but bugs mess up the transfer somehow," replied the attendant.

The humming stopped, and the swirling mist dispersed into the air. Stevens lay perfectly still. He was no longer breathing.

"Help me get him out," the attendant said, motioning to the tape holding Stevens's head in place.

Jimee didn't move. "I thought the body was dispersed by the system," she said.

"The chair is supposed to vaporize the bodies, but it's broken. There's no one left who can fix it," said the attendant.

"Why not get one of the demo-chairs? Or a chair from the regional station?"

"The transportation system's broken. Vehicles don't work anymore. Communications broke too."

Jimee nodded, realizing either location was at least a two-day walk away, and if the stations had been taken off-line, the chairs might not be functional anyway.

The attendant pointed at a flashing green light on the display of the Stevens's chair. "The transfer system still works, but we have to remove the bodies."

"So, where . . . ?"

"Over there, behind that building," said the attendant.

Jimee realized the attendant was referring to the building where Mikey, Angel, and Becky had disappeared.

"Pull the tape off," said the attendant.

She knew Stevens's body was dead, but she couldn't help pulling the tape off carefully, as if trying to avoid hurting him. The tape had fully covered his ears, as the attendant had been careful to make sure Stevens's head was fixed in place for a proper transfer. Being extra gentle around his face, Jimee pulled the tape off his left ear and was stunned to see the gnat, the same gnat she had seen on the porch, the same gnat with the broken leg. Stevens must have hit the gnat, trapping it inside his ear just before his fall! Jimee's mind raced. The mist? Did the mist kill the gnat? No! The tape would have protected the gnat from the mist! Jimee looked up at the night sky as if she was looking for Stevens and the gnat.

"What happens if a bug were to transfer with a person?" she asked.

No longer secured by the tape, Stevens's head fell forward. Blood oozed from his mouth. Jimee felt sick.

"Grab him under the armpits. I've got his legs," the attendant instructed.

Together, they picked up Stevens's body. Jimee noticed how the attendant expertly guided his legs out of the chair, no doubt from an afternoon of practice. Suddenly overcome by nausea, she lost her grip and twisted Stevens's torso to maintain it, causing the attendant to lose his balance. They both fell, dropping Stevens on the floor.

"It's okay, he's waiting for us in the Great Advance," said the attendant, pointing to a corner of the transfer station. "We'll put him over there, in that corner."

Jimee and the attendant hoisted Stevens again. They had just set down his body when Jimee saw Bobby. He had moved to the far corner of the transfer platform. Jimee was grateful for the attendant. Without his help, Stevens wouldn't have made it to the Great Advance.

"Can you get the others?" asked the attendant. "I'll transfer Bobby."

Jimee left Bobby with the attendant and walked around the building to the right of the transfer station. Immediately, she saw why everyone had been upset, and why the attendant had been so skilled at removing Stevens's legs from the chair.

There were two hundred and eleven dead bodies. The kids must have arrived after the breakdown of the subsystem that vaporized bodies after a transfer. Becky must have sent Mikey back to get Stevens. The bodies had been carried from the transfer station, past the people in line, to the opposite side of the building. Jimee imagined how horrible that must have been.

The first few dozen bodies were stacked in neat rows, hands folded across their chests as if asleep. Whoever carried these people must have been as careful as the attendant had been with Stevens. But the magnitude of the bodies, which lay in progressively more haphazard stacks, must have over-whelmed the attendant and other handlers quickly.

The poor attendant, Jimee thought. Sensitivity and care had given way to horror. The shock of witnessing what was meant to be a painless and blissful transfer of a loved one to a new life had transformed into something ugly and primitive. The attendant likely had help in the beginning, but as people continued to transfer and bodies piled up, he'd carried the bodies all by himself.

Stevens's wife seemed in charge. She must have helped. Angel had been crying. She had probably helped too. Surely Bobby had only watched, young as he was, and so had no task to distract him from the horror.

In the darkness, a soft glow emerged along the horizon. Dead people lay on the grass. The night was silent, not a breath or a heartbeat. Then Jimee heard growling, as if to defy the silence. At the edge of the bodies, the dogs prowled. They stared at her, heads low to the ground, growling softly.

Where had Mikey and Angel gone? She scanned the hill-side that stretched straight up toward the soft glow that would soon be another sunrise. The children were nowhere to be found. Jimee made her way around the bodies. As she approached the far edge of the field, a pack of dogs darted into the darkness. Jimee concentrated and slowed her breathing. She shouldn't have been surprised by the dogs. Calming herself, she heard a soft gurgling sound and trained her ears on the new sound. It came from where the dogs had been. An injured dog that needed help, maybe? She walked toward the sound—and saw Stevens's wife, Becky.

Jimee fell to her knees and vomited, fighting to regain control.

She felt a tug on her pant leg, panicked, and kicked. She heard growls and panting. How many? She stood up, clutching dirt. She had read: never run from a wild animal. Make noise, shoo it away. Fear brought back her focus. Twenty-three dogs, most scattered in the distance. Two up close.

Jimee yelled, stumbled, and threw the dirt at the dogs. They jumped back, staring with yellow eyes glowing in the night. The two nearest her wore collars. Becky lay on her side. Jimee remembered, she'd let the dogs out. She knelt and listened. Becky wasn't breathing. She touched Becky's neck. It was sticky and wet. Becky was dead.

WHEN JIMEE ARRIVED BACK at the transfer station, the attendant was sitting on the floor next to the bodies of Bobby and Stevens. Bobby's head lay in the crook of Stevens's arm.

"You transferred Bobby," Jimee said weakly. It was all she could say.

The attendant looked out into darkness, then back at her questioningly. "You couldn't find them?"

Jimee sat down beside the attendant, shaking her head.

"You can transfer. I'll wait for them," he said.

"We'll wait for them together," said Jimee. Numbly, she sat down beside the attendant. In the cool darkness, they searched the night for Mikey and Angel. Hours passed. Every second seemed forever.

"That was a baseball field. I played right field," said the attendant, indicating where they'd taken the bodies.

Another hour passed. Jimee thought of Stevens and Bobby playing catch. Hours had seemed seconds.

"You transfer," said Jimee. "I'll wait for Mikey and Angel."

Dogs growled in the darkness of the field, fighting over something. Jimee tried not to count. There were forty-eight dogs.

"Becky?" asked the attendant, his eyes wide.

Jimee nodded, unable to answer. Hours passed.

"Where we laid the bodies, that was right field," said the attendant.

"I've never played," said Jimee.

The streetlights flickered out. Jimee knew the backup power to the grid had gone down. The larger animals would now escape the pens. There would be more than wild dogs roaming soon.

"You should transfer," she said.

"I'm supposed to be last."

"You will be last."

Jimee looked out into the early morning darkness. There was a hint of light on the horizon. The attendant got up and instructed Jimee on the operation of the transfer chair. She strapped him to the apparatus.

"Wait," he said. "I have your picture."

"Picture?" asked Jimee, looking up at the coming sunrise.

"Of your mother. It's in my shirt pocket."

Jimee took the picture. "What's your name?"

"Billy."

Jimee pulled the transfer switch. It was difficult, removing Billy from the chair, and impossible without banging his body into various parts of the transfer apparatus. When his head fell forward and hit a steel rod protruding from the armrest, Jimee realized the chair had been designed to be easily entered, not exited. Angling him carefully, Jimee eventually extracted Billy from the chair and laid him beside Bobby and Stevens. Except for the mark on his forehead from the steel rod, he looked asleep.

Exhausted, Jimee sat next to Bobby, facing the hillside. She looked out at the hill in the distance. The sun was just beginning to peek over the horizon.

In the distance, Mikey and Angel appeared walking together up the hill, holding hands. Jimee yelled for them, but they didn't hear.

At the top of the hill, Mikey and Angel appeared as silhouettes, with the bright orange glow of the sunrise behind them. Mikey and Angel kissed, becoming one in the shimmering light, and continued kissing while the sun rose behind them. The sun shone so brightly, Jimee's eyes watered, and she was forced to look away. When Jimee looked again, Mikey and Angel were gone. She stood up to leave the platform. There was nothing left to do now but go home.

Blocking Jimee's path from the platform were the bodies of Stevens, Bobby, and Billy. Something moved on the attendant's forehead. It was a gnat. The gnat stared at Jimee and Jimee stared back. Jimee thought of Bobby dancing, of the sunrises, of Stevens's journal, of her mother, of everything there was to know, and how now no one would come to know any of it, including Jimee. She heard her mother's favorite saying in her mind.

"Everything is a lot of things, might take a million years, so we better get started!" Jimee changed her mind.

Positioning herself in the transfer chair, she strapped herself into all the straps she could reach. Slowly, so as not to lean too far out of the chair, especially her head, which had to stay firm against the interface, she reached behind the chair for the transfer switch, grasping. It was too far away. She strained, stretching her shoulder. She felt a pop. Her fingers reached the switch. She looked at the bodies of Stevens, Bobby, and Billy. Dogs circled the station, fifty-seven. Three leaped up the platform stairs.

Jimee pulled the switch.

PART TWO

HELTER SKELTER

23

NOTHINGNESS

Nothingness was the first sensation, then emptiness, then freezing cold and burning hot.

There was a star, the hottest location in the universe, then nothingness again.

There was light, millions of sunrises on millions of planets, each opening a new day. Too bright. Close eyes! Can't. No eyes.

There was dizziness, no reference in the nothingness. Falling! Can't. No up. No down.

There was endlessness in the nothingness, an instant and an eternity, the same, different, meaningless. Time had no meaning in the Great Advance.

Mommy, help me, thought Jimee in the nothingness. Crying out, no voice, no mommy, no nothing. Reaching out, no arms, no feeling, no ears, no . . .

"Jimee." Sensing a thought.

"Jimee. It's me, Stevens." Recognizing.

"Where? Nowhere," thought Jimee.

"Here, and there," said Stevens.

"Mikey, Angel, your wife . . ." Jimee thought.

"I know, Jimee. We know."

"Bobby?" asked Jimee.

"He's here."

"Hi, Jimee," said the attendant, Billy.

"Hi, Jimee," said Bobby.

"Mother, that's Jimee. She transferred me," said Billy.

"Hi Jimee. Nice to meet you," said Anna.

Jimee slowly became aware of her new existence, sensing Stevens, Bobby, Billy, Anna, and millions of other spirits. She sensed every person from their planet who had transferred, all at the same time. All of them were joyous and happy, just as Stevens had said they'd be.

Still disoriented, Jimee reeled through the nothingness of her disembodied state. How was it possible to be here and there, but not be anything at all? Jimee remembered Mikey and Angel below on a distant planet, Bobby's dead body lying next to Stevens, the dead bodies surrounding Stevens's wife. Jimee heard and felt Stevens's voice, and millions of other voices, all at the same time.

"Jimee, try to relax. You will get used to it. You were the last to transfer."

Jimee let herself drift, soaking up the happiness that seemed all around her.

"You left our little girl behind!"

Icy cold slammed into Jimee, feeling of both anger and sadness. She cried out in pain. She thought of the wild animals getting loose.

"Oh no!" cried the father.

"Please, stay out of Jimee's thoughts. She tried to help. Let her get oriented," said Stevens.

Jimee felt a strong, warm presence surround her. She recognized the presence as the attendant, Billy.

"You will feel better, soon," Billy said.

She felt instantly better, then screamed, realizing she'd floated into the sun. But the white-hot center of the sun didn't burn. Jimee was a soul. She had no body, no skin, no nerves, nothing a white-hot star could burn.

"You left our daughter!"

Jimee felt anger from Angel's father. Something tore at her consciousness, the mother's agony. Jimee realized that her soul, no longer protected by flesh and bones, was exposed and naked in a sea of souls. Stevens, Billy, and the others could sense her every thought.

"You will learn to protect yourself from the thoughts of other souls," Stevens said.

"I can help by wrapping around you as a shield, if you like," offered Billy.

Jimee didn't reply. She thought of the people she'd left behind. She sensed Stevens's sadness about Becky and Mikey. She sensed Angel's parents' anger. She observed that their sadness and anger persisted, unabated, despite the boundless happiness of millions of others.

"I'm sorry, Stevens," Jimee said, suddenly reeling as her thoughts intensified Stevens's grief. Bobby joined his father, consoling him.

"Where is the happy that comes for the sad?" thought Jimee.

"You tried to save them, Jimee," said Stevens. "What do you mean by happy coming for sad? Focus on relaxing. You had a tough transfer because you weren't properly attached to the interface. The transfer worked, but barely."

"Becky was killed by dogs," Jimee thought, losing control again. She wondered if she should tell Stevens.

"I know, Jimee. That wasn't your fault."

"You can read my thoughts?"

"You can sense me, and I can sense you," said Stevens. "All the souls sense each other. You will learn to control and guide your thoughts, anywhere, and to anyone you want. You'll learn to keep your soul private too."

Jimee struggled to understand. "I can nod, but I have no neck. I can shiver, but I have no body."

Stevens motioned toward Billy. "That's how it works,

Jimee. You see me point, but I have no arms. You hear me speak, but I have no mouth. It's all in our thoughts now."

With Stevens's and Billy's support, Jimee grew accustomed to her new spiritual existence. She learned that Stevens had been in agony about losing Mikey and Becky, and that Bobby and Billy consoled him before Jimee's transfer.

She drifted through their home planet, sensing only animals, insects, and primitive life. Not a single holdout remained.

She wondered how Stevens could have recovered so quickly, and why holdouts had died so quickly on her planet until she realized untold time had passed—time meant nothing to a soul.

As PROMISED by the Great Advance program, the disembodied souls became explorers of the universe. Souls soared from one solar system to another, reveling in their new existence. Millions of souls thanked Stevens for bringing them to their new home. Except for the tragedies on the last day of transfer, the Great Advance had brought wondrous happiness to everyone who had transferred, just as Stevens had promised.

Jimee explored, but she didn't zoom through galaxies with the other souls. When she had been physical, Jimee's genius had isolated her, so she was accustomed to being alone and didn't feel the need to be around other souls in the Great Advance. In short order, she learned that the universe was teeming with primitive, nonsentient life, and that every soul she sensed was from her home planet. Stevens had been right. They were the only people in the universe, and the first to transfer.

Jimee's genius for observation and unanswered questions had driven her to look for answers in the Great Advance, and she wasn't disappointed. Every speck of dust was new and exciting, a world within, as interesting to Jimee as the most massive planet. Every pattern in every sunrise on every planet could be studied.

She learned many new things observing planets and particles. Sunrises, however, revealed nothing and remained a mystery. At first, Stevens accompanied Jimee on many of her explorations, but Jimee's focus shifted from sunrises to the tiny particles, and Stevens lost interest. Jimee continued her research, all the while enjoying the irrepressible happiness of all the transferred souls. She began to sense something else within the happiness. For a while, she couldn't tell what it was —boredom, she decided.

Jimee approached Stevens. His mind still contained sadness, and she sensed him yearning for something.

"Are you getting bored like the others?" she asked, too forcefully. Thousands of souls overheard. They zoomed closer to hear more.

"No, Jimee. I'm not bored," he said.

Jimee didn't reply. She had just discovered new vibrating nanoscopic particles, so small she hadn't noticed them before.

"Jimee, why do you say I'm bored?" repeated Stevens.

Millions of souls were listening now. Jimee remained focused on the vibrating particles. There was something wonderful about them. What was it? The particles vibrated in harmony and seemed connected. A warm energy somehow passed between them, seemingly connecting particles separated by millions of other particles. Pondering them, she realized Stevens was right. It wasn't boredom she sensed. Completely self-absorbed, she asked herself a series of questions.

Why did souls seem to be looking for something, even though they zoomed around the universe, able to see everything? She sensed sadness in some.

"Jimee, what do you mean?" asked Stevens.

Why did sadness now exist in more souls, no longer vanquished by happiness?

"Jimee, are you okay?" asked Stevens.

Jimee wondered if the energy passing between the particles was the same as she'd observed passing between Stevens and Bobby while playing catch and exuding from Mikey and Angel from Mikey's bedroom.

"Jimee, we don't understand," said Stevens.

Were the gnat, sunrise, and particles connected? If so, before the Great Advance, had souls once been connected too?

"Jimee, everyone's listening."

Jimee wondered if the Great Advance was a terrible mistake.

"Jimee, stop! You're upsetting the souls."

24

LONELINESS

ONE BY ONE, the millions of souls that had gathered around Jimee and Stevens drifted away, leaving only four: Jimee, Bobby, Stevens, and far off in the distance, Billy. Jimee returned to her study of the particles. Time passed, maybe thousands of years, maybe millions. Jimee couldn't tell. Time had no meaning to a soul.

"The souls all went to the planets, you know," said Bobby. "That's where they go. Me too. Except Billy, he never goes. He's hovering over there."

"What would souls be doing on the planets?" asked Jimee.

"Many hover around our home planet too," said Bobby.

This interested Jimee, and she allowed herself to separate from a particle and extend her soul out to different regions of space. Bobby was right. Millions of souls were tightly packed around multiple planets.

She extended to their home planet. The souls were concentrated in thick clusters all over the planet. Each cluster centered on primitive life. Jimee zoomed closer, attempting to see if the souls were somehow affecting the life.

"They cluster together because they're lonely," said Bobby.

Jimee looked at Bobby quizzically. He hadn't actually said the word *lonely*, because the word hadn't existed on their home planet. People on their home planet had been fully connected, full of love and support, so while people might have been physically alone, they had never felt lonely. Instead, Bobby projected the feeling of a person who felt isolated and cut off from others. Jimee recalled her physical existence and realized she recognized the feeling.

"Do you feel lonely like the others?" asked Stevens.

She was surprised how effortlessly Stevens conveyed the word *lonely*. He must have been feeling lonely too.

"Yes, I feel lonely, like the others," replied Bobby.

"I've sensed the feeling in both of you," said Jimee. "I think it started with boredom and is getting worse."

"Is loneliness what's driving souls toward planets?" asked Stevens.

Jimee didn't know. She suspected the answer was related to the particles and connectedness somehow. "Describe this lonely feeling," she said.

Bobby answered first. "The souls seem sad, but they don't know why."

Jimee listened to the souls around another nearby planet, careful to keep her distance. Again, they clustered around primitive life. Sensing the souls, Jimee found what she was afraid she'd find. They longed for their physical existence and exuded their collective longing upon the primitive life.

"The sadness is worst among clusters of souls," she observed. "I think their sadness came from being lonely."

"How can that be?" Stevens wondered openly. "Souls are all together, intermingling."

Why isn't happiness rising up to overcome the sadness? wondered Jimee, keeping her question private.

"I'll check, Dad," said Bobby, letting his essence drift among the souls around their home planet.

Jimee and Stevens followed Bobby and waited, hovering in deep space far from the planet. Bobby zoomed to the planet, straight into the thickest, saddest cluster of souls he could find.

"Ugh!" he yelled. Shocked and frightened, Bobby zoomed back to his father and Jimee.

"What is it Bobby? What did you feel?" asked Stevens.

"Unloved, empty, outcast, abandoned, hopeless, sad, angry." Like the word *lonely*, Bobby couldn't articulate all of those feelings, so he projected them exactly as he'd experienced in the midst of the cluster of anguished souls.

Jimee had never felt such abject and total loneliness. She and Stevens reacted involuntarily, shooting away from the source of their pain, leaving Bobby abandoned in empty space, utterly alone in the complete blackness of nothingness.

25

ICY-BLACK SPECK

"JIMEE! STEVENS!" shouted Billy, zooming toward them.

Jimee felt Billy's strength, absorbed it, and recovered. She didn't realize what had happened until Billy spoke.

"Where'd Bobby go?" he asked.

Jimee sensed all around her. Bobby had vanished.

"Bobby!" Stevens shouted. "Oh, no, where's Bobby!" Frantically, Stevens searched for his son, stretching his soul across the solar system. Jimee worried he would tear himself to shreds.

"I thought Bobby was here with you and Stevens," said Billy.

Jimee believed she knew what had happened to Bobby. The same had nearly happened to her and Stevens, and would have if not for Billy.

"Bobby's gone," she said.

"Help me, Jimee!" pleaded Stevens.

"I'll search the planet," said Billy, zooming off.

"Wait, Billy!" shouted Jimee. "When looking for Bobby, stay near the planet and other souls. Don't zoom into areas of the universe where you are totally alone."

"I won't," promised Billy before racing away.

Jimee turned to Stevens. He was zooming from soul to

soul, asking everyone to help him search for Bobby. She tried to get his attention, to explain what happened, but he was too frantic and totally focused on the search.

Billy returned. Bobby was nowhere to be found on the planet. Thousands of souls joined the search. Most did not demonstrate Stevens's grief, but Jimee saw that when souls zoomed close to Stevens, they absorbed his grief, magnified it, and projected it onto others. Many more souls joined the search. The universe soon reverberated with millions of sad souls zooming in search of Bobby. Jimee sensed a small cluster of thirty souls following closely behind Stevens that were Bobby's friends from the planet.

Why hasn't Bobby made more friends since transferring? Jimee wondered. Time wasn't a concept, but Jimee knew ages had passed since the transfer to the Great Advance, maybe billions of years. *Bobby should have thousands of close friends in the universe by now,* she thought.

The search raged on. Jimee felt the souls' grief transform to fear. Bobby's disappearance made them afraid. They believed they would exist forever, so what had happened? If Bobby was gone, they were no longer safe.

Jimee pulled back to a remote corner of the universe to think. The universe didn't have corners, but she could think better if she pretended her physical self existed somewhere. From her pretend corner, she observed the zooming chaos. Stevens and dozens of Bobby's friends raced around the universe, desperately looking for him. Their wild angst affected the particles, creating sparks between the particles wherever the souls overlapped. The sparks weren't bright flashes. They were black. The sparks weren't hot. They were icy cold.

Millions more souls arrived, desperate to understand what happened to Bobby, afraid it might happen to them. Millions didn't come. Too afraid, they stayed away, remaining clustered around planets, lonely and sad.

Hovering by herself in the distance, Jimee saw Billy and noticed he wasn't afraid or sad. She guessed that he, like her, had long ago learned to understand loneliness when he was physical on their planet. Billy zoomed from one group of souls to another, trying to help them feel better, telling them not to be afraid.

Jimee's thoughts returned to Bobby. Why had he made so few new friends since transferring to the Great Advance? From her corner of the universe, she extended herself into the chaos. Whenever one of Bobby's friends was near, she reached out to talk and ask questions about Bobby and their friendship. After speaking to the three of his close friends, Jimee had to take a break. The sadness was overwhelming and depressing. Talking to a soul in such terrible grief made her weak and unable to think. Worse, she hadn't learned anything that would help her understand, only that Bobby and his friends liked to roam the universe, tell stories, play jokes on each other, and play games together. Their favorite game to play was pickle. She knew pickle was a game where two teammates played catch while guarding two bases, and a third player in the middle tried to get to a base without being tagged.

Souls can't play pickle, she thought. *How could pickle be their favorite game? Wait, are all of Bobby's friends from his baseball team? Has he made no new friends in the Great Advance?*

Jimee again extended into the searching mass of souls and talked to ten of Bobby's friends before withdrawing to her corner to rest. She'd learned nothing more about why he had made no new friends in the Great Advance.

Without regard for time or space, Stevens and millions of souls searched on and on, their intensity and determination unrelenting, reinforcing grief, fueling fear. The chaos escalated until Jimee couldn't tell one soul from another. Jimee withdrew further back into her corner.

Suddenly, Stevens zoomed close. Jimee felt his anguish, icy and black, inflaming the others. Right behind Stevens,

Bobby's friends followed, feeding on the wake of Stevens's grief-stricken frenzy. Keeping a safe distance, Jimee tried to engage Bobby's friends as they zoomed by.

"Bobby, Bobby!" they wailed. "Come play with us, Bobby!" Jimee couldn't get their attention. "Bobby, oh Bobby, this isn't funny. Come out now. Let's go play like we used to! Come out Bobby. Let's play pickle!"

Jimee reached out again, touching one, then another, to no effect. The souls ignored her, consumed by their angst.

"Pickle, Bobby, pickle!" Bobby's friends yelled in unison. "Let's play pickle!"

Needing to learn more and throwing caution aside, Jimee raced to join Bobby's friends trailing behind an anguished Stevens. Positioning herself right behind Stevens, Jimee shot into the spiritual essence of Bobby's friends and got their attention at last.

"Did you all know Bobby?" Jimee asked the boy souls.

"Yes, Bobby was our friend."

"Did all of you play catch with Bobby?"

"Yes," they answered. If Bobby and his friends had spent the last millions of years clustered around planets, longing for physical connections they no longer had, maybe that explained why they had made no new friends in the Great Advance. Jimee asked one more question.

"Where did you play catch with Bobby?"

"We played catch when we were on the planet with Bobby. Come back, Bobby! Let's play pickle again."

Certain now, and afraid for the first time since being in the Great Advance, Jimee surged ahead to catch Stevens, but he was too grief-stricken to acknowledge her.

To get his attention, Jimee did something crazy. She extended directly into his soul. The experience was horrible. Stevens's fear and sadness had morphed into something ugly and vile. She had to stop him.

Jimee extended further into Stevens's consciousness and

felt a piercing pain. A sharp speck of icy-black abomination was growing within Stevens.

"It's Jimee. You must stop. I know what is happening to everyone. I think I know what happened to Bobby!"

Abruptly, Stevens stopped. "Tell me, Jimee, where is my son?" he cried.

Before she could answer, Bobby's friends, rampaging full speed, crashed into them. The result was a tumultuous, writhing, mishmash of tortured, anguished, grieving souls. Following close behind, millions more terrified, wailing souls, no longer driven by Stevens's search for Bobby but consumed by a darker, colder, icy-black madness, smashed into Stevens, Jimee, and Bobby's thirty friends.

What happened next, even Jimee, for all her genius of observation, could not be sure. In the center of the mishmash of the terrified pileup of stampeding souls, from deep inside Stevens, the icy-black abominable speck emerged and shot outward into the universe.

Conceived of love, overcome with grief, and fed by fear, the speck sliced through the particle fabric of the universe, creating a large gash. An instant later, the piled-up, terrified energy from millions of following souls entered the gash. Torn by the icy-black speck and drenched with the fear of millions of piled-up souls, the particle fabric stilled, leaving not a single particle vibrating. Jimee feared the fabric was dead. But then the fabric shuddered and convulsed back to life, hurling a massive icy-black wave from the gash.

Jimee saw the birth of the icy-black wave and turned to Stevens. He seemed better, but neither Stevens nor any other souls had noticed the gash and the wave. Jimee asked Stevens to talk in private, but he only wanted to talk to the boys, not to Jimee.

"You were Bobby's friends?" asked Stevens.

"We were on Bobby's baseball team," said a boy.

"We played together all the time," said another.

"We even played at your house," said another.

Jimee realized the boys had slowly separated into two groups. Their separation wasn't in space but in their interaction with Stevens. Only half the boys engaged. The other half remained silent. Stevens noticed too. Jimee felt Stevens focus on one of the silent boys.

"Were you on Bobby's team?" Stevens asked the boy.

"No, but I was Bobby's friend."

"So was I."

"And me."

"Me too."

The separation had become more apparent. The two groups now clustered together in fabric space. Jimee understood why, and it scared her. Stevens continued asking questions.

"You boys belong to two groups then? Two teams?" Stevens asked.

"Bobby played on our team. Bobby was our friend," said the boy who had been at Stevens's house.

"Bobby was our friend too," said a boy from the quiet group, the other team.

"How did you get to know Bobby if you didn't play on his team?" asked Stevens. "Did you become friends after arriving in the Great Advance?"

"We played against Bobby's team," the boy answered.

Jimee's fear increased. The two groups of boys were from two different teams on their planet, and they hadn't become friends with each other, despite being together in the Great Advance for millions of years. How had the other team become friends with Bobby, and only Bobby? How was Stevens connected to one of the boys on the other team, but not to the others?

Focusing on the boy, Stevens asked, "Were you the pitcher who put Bobby in the pickle?"

"I was," replied the boy.

Jimee understood how Stevens was connected to the pitcher. Pickle was a game of intense connection between the runner and the base defenders, between one player and many players on the opposing team.

"I was a catcher," said another boy.

"I played first base."

"I played third base."

Remembering Bobby, the boys laughed and told stories of the great game of pickle that day. Jimee stayed back, watching Stevens and the boys on each team.

For Stevens, it was a celebration of Bobby, and he basked in the memories. For the boys, it was an escape from their loneliness since transferring to the Great Advance, a time to laugh again and feel happy. For Jimee, the recollections were another piece of the puzzle, and another reason to be afraid. The boys had kept their friends from the planet but had made no new friends in the Great Advance.

Other souls joined, friends from Bobby's school, friends from the baseball teams, friends of friends, thousands of souls. The boys retold the story of the pickle game. More lonely souls arrived. Millions of souls surrounded the boys and Stevens, crowding in close to hear the story. It was like soup, a soul soup. Jimee grinned, realizing she too was caught up in the wonder of the joyous celebration. She moved farther back and increased her focus on the boys, Stevens, and the slush of souls.

Three centers had formed, the two teams and Stevens. Densely packed souls surrounded each center, listening to the story, laughing together. Why so many? Why had the group grown to include souls who didn't even know Bobby? They were talking, forming connections with their telling and retelling of stories. Jimee sensed souls who didn't know anyone coming to participate. Thousands or millions of years elapsed, she couldn't tell. Souls existed in the instant and eternity, with no reference to anything physical, no attachment to anything real, except for Bobby. Bobby's disappearance was real and had become a connecting anchor for the souls. For Stevens, the two teams, and Bobby's close friends, the gathering was a celebration of Bobby, but for the other souls, the joyous discourse was an opportunity to connect and feel happy. Jimee worried because a death shouldn't make a soul feel connected and happy. If feeling happy required death, more death would naturally follow.

In the distance, Jimee saw the gash healing into an ugly icy-black scar. The massive icy-black wave continued surging from the scar and rolling out into the universe.

Jimee wanted to talk with Stevens, alone. She channeled her thoughts through the mass to Stevens, but just as she was about to get his attention, things changed again.

"Have you been back?" Stevens asked the pitcher.

"All the time," the pitcher replied. "After we transferred, we explored everything and played everywhere, but now that's where we go."

"Is that where you were when you heard about Bobby?"

"Yes, Bobby used to come too. It was Bobby's favorite place."

"Let's go there now."

Stevens and the boys from the two baseball teams returned to their home planet where they had once played baseball with Bobby, leaving the millions of souls who had come to hear the stories hovering in space. Their communication dwindled about Bobby.

The souls dispersed to various planets throughout the universe, joining clusters that had not joined the search for Bobby. Careful not to be alone, Jimee followed at the farthest distance she felt safe. Watching the souls arrive at some of the planets, she realized something had changed. The souls became unusually excited.

Focusing on only those planets, Jimee learned the source of excitement. Some planets had evolved sentient life!

The next moment a chill overtook her. She'd drifted near the gash created by Stevens's icy-black speck, now a grotesque, pitch-black scar. The particles in the scar were cold, ugly, and mutated. Jimee looked at the icy-black wave. It was massive.

She rushed to catch-up with Stevens and the boys, feeling anxious because she hadn't returned to her planet in thousands or millions of years. Had sentient life newly evolved there too? What form would it take? Arriving, she saw a forest where Stevens's house and deck had been. She sensed no sentient life. The sunrises were still beautiful, but she detected nothing within them.

Jimee found the boys' souls hovering above and extending into the depths of a large swampland that stretched for miles in every direction. This was where they had once played baseball, where Stevens had taken Bobby to play catch, and where Bobby's famous game of pickle had occurred.

Stevens and the boys were no longer laughing and telling stories. Jimee felt sadness and didn't like it, so she backed away. She hovered above millions of lonely souls who surrounded the planet. She sensed them yearning for their physical lives from long ago. Cautiously, she extended into groups who yearned the strongest. Most were families clustering around locations that had been their homes.

The planet's surface slowly changed, indicating thousands of years were passing. The swampland began to dry. Despite the passage of time, Stevens and the boys remained hovering in the same spot as before, sometimes silent, sometimes arguing. All had grown sadder.

No longer distracted by Stevens, Jimee scanned the nearby galaxies, curious about the sentient life she'd sensed before.

She zoomed to a planet where she sensed the greatest abundance of sentient life. Careful to shield her soul, she extended into a thick cluster of other souls. Unlike clusters she'd previously observed, these souls weren't just yearning for the physical existence they'd lost but were actively attempting to project themselves into the life. She zoomed closer and understood why. The sentient life was unmistakably human, just like people on her home planet! How was that possible?

Jimee remembered the history of her home planet. As a girl, she had learned how people evolved from simple life-forms living in water to living on land. The people advanced, formed societies, and developed technology that harnessed the resources of their world. The people on this planet were just beginning to evolve, still living in small groups, scavenging and hunting for food. She understood that at each stage of evolution, millions of factors conspired for humanity on her home planet to evolve as it had. How had life on this planet evolved in exactly the same way?

Jimee descended to have a closer look.

26
BRILL

BRILL COULDN'T CRY. She wished she could, she felt sad enough. She remembered crying, her eyes watering, her nose running, and her breath coming in gasps. She remembered loving her family and feeling happy, but she hadn't been happy in a long time. When the insanity had hit, no one saw it coming. Now, thousands of years later, Brill was beginning to understand what had murdered every single person on her planet.

Since the beginning of recorded history, people had flourished. Men, women, and children, everyone everywhere on the planet displayed generosity, cooperation, and love for one another. Everything had been wonderful. Everyone loved everyone.

Extraordinary advances in medicine, technology, agriculture, government, and education, and the never-ending wondrous evolution of the physical body had created a society of people at peace. Kindness was all they knew. So, when the insanity arrived, they didn't have a chance.

The insanity started with the crowds, initially in mega stadiums where a hundred thousand people gathered to watch sporting events and concerts and millions more from all over the planet watched live video that was beamed into their homes. Cheers of appreciation began giving way to ambivalence, then irritated silence. Then came jeers and insults.

The insanity spread to small groups next. In the beginning, people talked as if the insanity was something happening far away and didn't involve them. People didn't want to believe the stories or were too ashamed because it had happened to them. When the insanity suddenly exploded and spread out of control, the whole world saw it. Everyone was terrified. Then everyone got angry. Then the killing started.

Brill screamed, but she was a soul, so there was no sound.

A LITTLE GIRL sang in celebration at the worldwide annual games. Her voice was beautiful. She was the kind of wonder seen once in a century, possessing innocence, youth, and extraordinary talent. At the inauguration of the games, in front of the whole world, she sang so beautifully that she epitomized everything wonderful the planet had become.

The little girl usually sang for her baby brother, not when he was awake, but when he was asleep. She imagined her songs floating in her brother's dreams and that he sang along with her. On this day, the little girl and her beautiful singing became a senseless catalyzing event.

The little girl sang her song, mesmerizing the world by the soft beauty of her voice. Then she stopped. She had forgotten the words. She was nervous, but only a little. She had forgotten words before and knew if she closed her eyes and relaxed, she would remember, and the whole world would cheer for her. But this time was different. With the cameras zoomed in, projecting her pretty face to the whole world, someone booed, and then another, and another.

The little girl covered her face and cried. The stadium began to vibrate from the booing. The little girl thought of her baby brother. She would sing for him. Her hands fell from her face, and her shoulders straightened. She leaned back and took a deep breath. Her eyes looked straight into the camera. The crowd became silent.

The girl leaned toward the microphone. Her lips parted as she started to sing, but before she sang the first word, a large bottle was thrown. The bottle smashed into the child's face. Blood spurted everywhere.

In that moment, the evil that had washed over the planet exploded, penetrating deep into every person watching the little girl sing.

An entire world, once defined by love and kindness, transformed to hatred and cruelty. Unstoppable insanity spread, causing riots, murder, and the extinction of an entire race.

27
LIFE PROBES

Sad, floating aimlessly, unable to cry, Brill remembered her loving husband and her two wonderful, beautiful, amazing children.

Desperate to save her family, she worked day and night to create a complete synaptic map of a person's brain. On the very day the little girl sang her final song, Brill made a breakthrough.

As a scientist, Brill was quick to recognize the coming collapse of society. Something perverse, angry, and evil had infected their world. Brill and her colleagues might have eventually understood the sickness and even developed a cure, but there wasn't enough time. Millions of people died as the savagery increased. Within a few years, all social order completely collapsed. Something had transformed the people into monsters. Love became hate. Kindness became cruelty. Everyone was affected, including Brill.

Brill saw the anger within herself, her family, and her colleagues. The hate spread like a wave, and more easily through groups. So Brill kept her family isolated, pulling her children out of school, staying home, and avoiding all gatherings. To stay sane and focused on her work, Brill further isolated herself, even from her colleagues and family. She devised a protocol of communication using written unemotional messages to collaborate with her colleagues without succumbing to the evil contagion infecting their minds. At the insistence of her husband, she allowed short video talks every few days, but she programmed the system to detect and terminate any calls containing anger. The calls became shorter and shorter.

At first, Brill considered space travel an option to escape. Generations before Brill was born, people had traveled into space. The first ships were small, only allowing a few dozen astronauts to explore a nearby moon or planet. Driven by scientific curiosity, and the potential for discovering extraterrestrial life, the space program reached deeper into space. Larger and faster ships were built to move the science forward.

As a little girl in grade school, Brill had been fascinated by stories about space scientists from the past. She read scientific journals about spaceships and discoveries of new planets. The space scientists were Brill's heroes. By the time Brill became a scientist, spaceships flew faster than light and traveled great distances. Scientists searched for planets with life or that might one day support life.

On planets that might one day support life, scientists left special synaptic probes called Life Probes. If a Life Probe detected life, it would transmit instantly back to Brill's planet using the particle-network fabric, an instantaneous networking capability inherent to the universe that Brill's people had discovered.

A scientist, after being selected to observe a planet, had his or her synaptic pattern matched to the synaptic transmitter of a planet's Life Probe. Life could take many millennia to develop, so generation after generation of scientists were connected to a planet's Life Probes. Young scientists competed for the honor of being new synaptic matches. Years of waiting and observing did not matter, because society was perfect and would exist forever. Someday, a distant planet would grow life, a scientist would hear the life through the Life Probe's synaptic sensor, and Brill's people would arrive to say hello.

As chief scientist for her planet, Brill had Life Probes on many remote planets assigned to her synaptic pattern. None had detected life, but Brill dreamed that one day she might hear the sound of alien life, proving her planet wasn't alone in the universe.

None of that mattered now. Something evil was killing everyone. To survive required escaping whatever was infecting the planet. Brill readied spaceships for escape but viewed the spaceships as a false remedy. Something was infecting people's brains, making people evil. It would be futile to escape with her family in a spaceship if whatever was infecting their brains on the planet was also in space. If their brains were already infected, the key to survival was to escape their brains and live as souls in the fabric of the universe. As a scientist, Brill knew of many forms of energy that existed beyond the physical, so why not the soul?

Having created a synaptic map of the brain, Brill believed she could extract the essence of a sentient person from the confines of their brain. Once extracted, the soul could evade the murderous insanity that had overtaken her planet.

Convinced of her strategy, Brill had directed her entire focus to the comprehensive synaptic correlation between the soul and the brain. Within a few years after isolating her colleagues and family, she completed the correlation to achieve the exact sequencing necessary to separate a soul from its brain. After modifying one of the synaptic interfaces designed to monitor life on planets, Brill could now extract the soul to escape her planet's madness. The implications of what life would be like as a soul were unknown, but Brill needed to save her family, friends, colleagues, and as many people as possible, before the collapse of her world.

In small doses, so as not to go mad herself, Brill listened to news broadcasts filled with hate. She could almost feel evil permeating her brain. Mass hysteria had overtaken her city. Bands of killers were roaming her neighborhood. Brill's synaptic correlation breakthrough had been just in time. She and her colleagues worked feverishly to complete the system.

28

HAPPY MEMORIES

SAD, floating aimlessly, unable to cry, Brill remembered she'd found a way to slow the sickness using happy family memories recorded before evil hit the planet. Remembering her family, Brill smiled with her thoughts. She couldn't smile physically, she had no mouth.

"LOOK AT YOUR SLATE, honey. I've created something that will help us. Hurry, before one of us gets angry and the system disconnects us." Brill had remotely enabled her husband's slate. All he had to do was look at it. He didn't.

"Who cares about a stupid slate? You've been locked in your lab for months," he replied.

"Honey . . ."

"When can we all be together again?" he demanded. "The kids are going crazy. When can they go back to school?"

Brill knew the schools had been destroyed. She hadn't told Jay yet.

"Soon, honey," replied Brill, suppressing anger. "We have to stay separated until I figure out how we can escape the sickness, or we'll hurt each other. The slate, honey. Can you look at it?"

"How do I know you're really working? Who else is down there with you? Karl's with you, isn't he?"

"I'm alone, Jay. My colleagues are upstairs with you but locked inside private labs for safety. Only you and the twins are physically together," said Brill.

"Liar," he said.

The system lights flashed, a warning that the video would disconnect soon. Brill had programmed the system to turn off upon sensing anger. First, they'd lose video, then audio.

"Jay, we have to be calm." She was tired of being the strong one. Seconds passed.

"I am looking at the slate! It's not working!" he said.

"Try blinking," she said, closing her eyes to calm herself.

"I am blinking! There's something wrong with the damn thing!"

Brill imagined breaking the memory slate over Jay's big fat head. "Forget blinking, Jay. Just touch the image of me with your finger." She heard a thumping sound. He had poked the slate, probably right smack on her nose. The slate began playing a scene from their wedding. A song played in the background.

"Oh Brill, honey," said Jay. "You're the best."

"You remember that song?" Brill asked.

"Of course, that's our family song now."

"You were so handsome," Brill said. "Look, can you see the twins?"

"What? Nikky and Nathan weren't born yet."

"Then why'd you sing that song to my belly that night?" asked Brill, laughing.

"You're sweet."

"You're sexy."

Abruptly, Jay's tone changed. "Brill, the kids fought today. Their fights are getting worse."

Her anger rose. Nikky and Nathan were ingrates. Fighting, even normal sibling bickering, made the sickness worse. How many times did they have to be told?

"Nikky hurt Nathan," continued Jay. "Nathan said he's going to kill her while she's sleeping."

"Keep them apart, honey," Brill said with a sigh.

"I'm not an idiot!" Jay screamed.

"Honey, please, touch the next image," said Brill.

The video faded. Another emerged in its place, of a classroom of twenty small children, four to six years old.

"It's Nikky and Nathan's preschool," said Brill.

"This memory slate idea is fun," Jay said. "We started the children in school so early. They were barely four years old. All the other children were five or six."

"Watch, this scene is amazing," said Brill. "I found it by accident. You won't remember it, because neither of us were there. Zoom in on the child sitting in the far corner."

Jay zoomed in. "Is that Nikky? It is. She's crying. Look, her shirt is torn. Oh, Brill, that's when she broke her arm. She's all by herself. No one noticed."

"Watch Nathan."

Jay zoomed back until he could see Nathan standing in the center of the room, trying to get the attention of his teachers, who were in the midst of a loud and energetic game with the rest of the class. The teachers thought Nathan calling for them was just part of the fun. They didn't realize he was asking for help. The game was loud, so Jay turned the volume down on his slate. Nathan gave up, walked through the group to the water fountain, filled a small cup with water, and walked back to Nikky's corner. He gave Nikky the water as she held her broken arm in her lap.

"Zoom in," said Brill. "Turn the volume back up too."

"It hurts," said Nikky. Nathan looked around and saw a blanket and a pillow tucked inside a cubby. He put the blanket over Nikky's legs and rested her broken arm on the pillow. He wiped tears from her cheek with the blanket.

"It will be okay, Nikky," said Nathan, looking around the room.

All the other children were in the center, playing the game. There were two other boys who looked as young as Nathan and Nikky. They were having fun too, but the exuberance and size of the older children had them on the outside of the group. Nathan walked over to each boy, took them by the hand, and walked them over to Nikky. He sat down in front of Nikky, and the two boys sat down next to him, forming a semicircle in front of her.

"Listen closely, honey," said Brill.

Nathan started singing, his voice barely discernible amid the noise of the children playing. Their son held hands with the two boys, who joined his singing. They didn't know the words, so they just hummed along.

"Hey, that's our family song, from our wedding!" said Jay.

One by one, other children joined until the entire class sang along. Finally, the teachers realized Nikky was hurt and rushed to her side.

"They really do love each other," said Jay.

The video faded. A new scene appeared. Nikky stood alone on a stage.

"Hey, you went to the next one," said Brill.

"I remember this," said Jay. "It's Nikky's synaptics project where she accidentally flew her toy spaceships into the sun."

"No, I don't think that'd be a good memory for Nikky right now," said Brill, laughing. "It's Nikky's first-grade science competition."

Jay zoomed out. In the audience were students, teachers, and parents. A panel of judges sat directly in front of the stage. Nikky began her report.

"My mother's a scientist. She runs the Life Probes program to detect life in the universe. Life Probes are sensors that sense life on distant planets. The instant life evolves on a distant planet, scientists can observe its evolution using messages sent by the Life Probes."

"Nikky, has life been discovered yet?" asked a judge.

"No, but my mother says it's only a matter of time, especially as we add more planets."

"How far away are the planets?" asked another judge.

"Really super far. Trillions of light years far, or something like that," said Nikky.

"If the planets are so far away, how can we sense life instantly?"

"The universe does it, using a fabric-entropy-time loop."

"What's that?"

"I don't know, silly. I'm just a first grader."

The audience burst into laughter. Brill heard Jay's laughter boom through her slate.

"Hi, Mommy," her daughter said through Jay's interface. Jay paused the video.

"Hi, Nikky," said Brill. "I miss you, honey."

"I know now, Mommy."

"Know what, honey?"

"About the fabric-entropy-time loop, and how it lets us sense life instantly, even on planets that are far away."

"Really? Tell me."

"Pretend like Nathan and I are exactly ten years old."

"You are ten years old," said Brill.

Nikky furrowed her brow. "Mommy."

"Sorry."

"Nathan and I are ten years old, and we're standing at opposite ends of a room. I need to tell him a secret, but I can't unless we are right next to each other."

"Okay," said Brill, nodding.

"First, I start walking toward him."

"How far apart are you and Nathan?"

"Mommy, it doesn't matter. That's the point."

"Okay, sorry."

"I start walking toward Nathan. As I'm walking, I'm getting younger. I become nine years old. Then eight, then seven. I keep walking and keep getting younger. He finally sees me when I'm like four years old. When he sees me, I start getting older instead of younger. I'm still not next to him, so I can't tell him the secret yet. I keep walking. I go from four years old, to five, then six, then seven. When I get next to Nathan, I'm exactly ten years old again. When I tell Nathan my secret, it's like no time has passed. That's what the time loop means in fabric-entropy-time loop. Starting and stopping in the same place."

Brill beamed. "Wow, that's exactly right, honey!"

"What happens if Nathan doesn't see you?" asked Jay.

"That's funny. I guess I keep getting younger," said Nikky, giggling.

"That's exactly right, Nikky. You'd keep going backward in time, forever and ever," said Brill.

"What makes you get younger and older?" asked Jay.

"I don't know. Karl hasn't taught me that yet," said Nikky.

"What!" yelled Jay. "Go to your room!" Brill heard Nikky crying, then a door slam.

"You lied about Karl," said Jay.

"Jay, you can't let Nikky and Nathan be together when Nikky's upset," said Brill.

Suddenly, Brill heard a loud crashing sound.

"I'm going to kill you!" Nikky yelled.

"No, stop! Argh!" Nathan screamed.

"Jay, hurry, stop them!" shouted Brill. She heard Jay's slate clang to the floor and his footsteps.

"Nikky, get away from him!" he shouted. "Nathan, are you okay? Brill, can you hear me? Nathan's hurt!"

"I'm here, Jay. What happened?" shouted Brill, her anger surging.

"Nikky tried to break my arm, Daddy," cried Nathan.

"Nikky, stop fighting!" shouted Brill, running to the elevator. "I'm coming up!"

"Stay there, Brill. Nathan's arm is okay."

Brill stopped. She heard Nikky and Nathan crying, then a shuffling sound that she knew was Jay picking up his slate. She shook from anger. She felt sick. Jay's voice, with a hint of fun, brought her back.

"Brill, look at your slate," he said.

She looked. He'd zoomed in on Nikky, replaying the last few seconds.

"I don't know, silly. I'm just a first grader."

Brill laughed. The world had gone insane, but one thing was still true. "You're the best husband and dad in the world," she said.

That night, Brill programmed her family's memory slates with hundreds of old memories. Whenever they got angry or frustrated, Brill, Jay, Nathan, and Nikky watched their slates. Brill made slates for her colleagues too.

They made great progress on the research, though they didn't have much time. The rioting was closer to home. The calming effect of the memory slates enabled Brill and her colleagues to increase their focus on the development and testing of the synaptic transfer system. It was almost ready.

29

DADDY, IS THAT YOU?

SAD, floating aimlessly, angry, unable to cry, Brill remembered Jay's voice yelling over the speakers in the lab.

"BRILL! THEY'RE AT THE DOOR!" Jay screamed.

"Grab the kids. Meet me at the elevator!" she yelled, hearing Nikky crying in the background.

"Daddy, I'm scared."

The walls and doors had been reinforced, but Brill knew the house would eventually collapse under the force of the mob. A loud crashing sound and glass breaking grabbed her attention. She had routed all the microphones throughout the house to the speakers in her lab but couldn't determine the origins of the sounds. Brill pushed the elevator button.

"Mommy, is that you?"

"Yes, it's me, honey."

"At the door? Mommy, is that you banging on the door?"

"No, I'm on the elevator. Hurry, hide where we said. I'm coming!"

An explosion shook the house. The speakers went silent. Another explosion, then gunfire, then silence. The elevator doors opened. Empty. Laughter outside in the street. Brill darted from the elevator. Smoke stung her eyes. Four colleagues lay dead near the entrance, blown apart from the blast. They had tried to stop the attackers at the door. Brill ran down the hallway. Nikky's room was closest.

Jay, Nikky, and Nathan were huddled together in the corner of Nikky's room, not moving, arms wrapped around each other. They had survived the explosion but not the clubs. The murderers were nearby. She could still hear them outside.

Brill adjusted her beautiful Jay to a more comfortable position embracing their children, then adjusted Nikky and Nathan to hold hands. She imagined them singing their family song.

"Love you," she whispered.

She collapsed to the floor, her back against the wall, and wept uncontrollably until she fell asleep. When she woke the next morning, the house was quiet, the streets empty. Alone and numb with grief, she returned to her laboratory.

"No more testing," she said.

Brill readied the transfer system and strapped the synaptic helmet onto her head, configuring the interface for a complete transfer. She reached to engage the transfer switch, but stopped. The tears might interfere with the helmet sensors. Wiping her face, Brill scanned her lab one last time. She saw the synaptic system that controlled the toy spaceships Nikky had flown for her science project. She smiled, remembering Nikky flying her toy spaceships into the sun. The memory reminded Brill of the fleet of interstellar spaceships. Maybe she'd need them someday, if only to remember her daughter.

Blinking away tears, Brill took off her synaptic helmet, walked across the lab, and connected the synaptic interface system to the control panels of the planet's fleet of interstellar spaceships. Returning to the transfer system, she put the helmet back on, and engaged the transfer.

Brill would never cry tears again.

30
FABRIC PHYSICS

JIMEE ARRIVED at the surface of a planet that had people. She saw that groups of people and families attracted the largest clusters of souls.

She reasoned people would feel the souls in some way, but they did not seem affected. Intimate interactions between people excited souls—families talking, lovers loving, children playing. Inexplicably, all engaged in social relationships that had previously existed on her home planet! How could this be? Not only had the life on the planet evolved into the same human form as life had evolved on her own planet, but the people's social and cultural behavior seemed to emulate that of her home too.

Jimee studied sunrises all around the planet. There were no patterns, but she sensed something wonderful. Basking in one sunrise, a mother and two little girls played beside a pond, giggling together. She zoomed closer to investigate.

The air was warm, a lively, stimulating kind of warmth that made the skin shiver as if at some hidden pleasure. Birds were singing. Every few minutes a fish would splash, making the two little girls giggle and laugh. Something in the splash or the laughing heightened excitement in the watching souls.

Jimee focused on the particles near the mother and her two

girls and waited. Another fish splashed and the girls giggled again. At the same time, Jimee saw something new in the particles and sensed a strange happening within and above the pond.

A swarm of bugs hovered above the pond, and a school of fish swam below the surface. She waited for the next splash. Suddenly, about ten feet above the pond in the middle of the swarm, the particles sizzled. A bug broke from the swarm and dove toward the pond. As it reached the water's surface, the bug zigzagged, catching the attention of a fish.

The fish broke the surface, mouth open. The angle was wrong. The fish had miscalculated. The fly was going too slow. The fish was going to miss. Particles sizzled again. The fly sped up. Gulp. The fish caught the bug.

The particles returned to their normal, harmonic vibrating pattern. The fish disappeared back into the water with a small splash. The souls buzzed with excitement and drew closer. The two little girls laughed with pure joy. Jimee would have been breathless had she been able to breathe.

The mother began laughing too, making the girls laugh even harder. Then Jimee sensed something else new, this time in the particles between the mother and daughters and inside their brains.

Between the mother and daughters, the particles aligned, forming tunnels. Inside their brains, the particles vibrated together, in perfect harmony with the particles in the tunnel. The mother and her little girls laughed together for three or four seconds, as the stream of particles between them glowed bright and warm. When the laughter subsided, the particles in the stream subsided and gradually returned to their normal state. The cycle happened over and over. The bug, the fish, the laughter, and the glowing, excited, loving connection within the particle fabric between the mother and her daughters.

Jimee now understood that the universe wasn't a passive expanse. Through energy embedded within the particle fabric, the universe was an active participant in the connectedness and love between people.

Like the other souls, Jimee felt drawn to the mother and her daughters. She couldn't stop watching. The souls surged forward with each episode of bug, fish, and laughter, trying to feel the connectedness the mother and daughters felt. Eventually, the little girls became distracted by other things. They played on the shore while the mother lay on the grass. Basking in the sun, she fell asleep.

When the mother fell asleep, Jimee noticed the souls immediately shift from the mother and her two girls to just the two girls, which made sense, but Jimee suspected there was something important about why souls completely ignored a sleeping person.

The mother smiled. Jimee imagined the mother was dreaming about her daughters. She extended into the sleeping mother, eager to experience the joy of her dream, but found that the mother's brain had formed an impenetrable wall, rendering her mind completely inaccessible.

While sleeping, the mother's presence was detectable to Jimee but not her thoughts or dreams.

Jimee was about to investigate further when, yet again, something new happened. The two girls were playing together when the smallest of the two began laughing excitedly, lost her balance, and tipped over. The pond was shallow, and she easily pushed herself up to a sitting position, but the water was cold, and she was muddy and soaking wet. She stopped laughing.

Sound asleep, the mother didn't wake. The wet, muddy little girl's face scrunched up. The older sister giggled at her little sister's face. As the little sister began to cry, the particles about her shifted to form a halo radiating from her head, not the warm glow between the mother and her daughters while laughing at the fish. Instead, the particles created a cold, dark halo emanating from the little girl's brain and streamed toward her older sister.

The next instant, the normal, warm particles between the girls intensified, strengthening their vibration and pushing back the cold, dark particles streaming from the little girl until they vanished.

The little girl stopped crying and laughed again. The girls had discovered a new game, throwing dirt and mud at each other. They were sitting in dirt softened by the water at the edge of the pond, so it was easy for their little hands to scoop up fistfuls of dripping wet mud to throw at one another. With each scoop, water ran into a fresh hole left by their hands, readying the soil for the next scoop. Both girls' throws were bad. They almost always missed. They giggled each time one of them got a direct hit. Mud flew between them. Particles glowed warm and excited between them. It was a spectacle of pure fun. Jimee felt irresistibly drawn into the joyous pleasure.

Excited, Jimee realized she'd just discovered the answer to the happy versus sad question that she'd been seeking. The fabric of the universe naturally connected people, actively encouraged happiness, and vigorously rejected sadness.

She observed the clustering souls, hovering closer, enveloping the two girls. The souls wanted to be part of life again. The attraction of love and life was irresistible.

The girls, absorbed in their mud battle, squealed with laughter, waking their mother. Still drowsy from the warm morning sun, the mother blinked the sleep from her eyes and sat up. With all her powers of observation, Jimee couldn't have imagined what happened next.

One of the little girls reached into the soft soil to grab another fistful of cold, wet mud. As she leaned over, her fingers grabbed a mud-covered rock by mistake. Laughing at the fun of it all, the little girl's arm jerked back to throw the mud at her sister. Whatever concern Jimee had about the rock vanished when she saw the little girl's windup. The rock was certain to miss the girl's sister. It flew from her hand, sending mud flying as it spun through the air.

Jimee gasped and futilely extended to block the rock, but it passed through her and smacked the mother on the forehead.

The mother cried out in pain. Blood dripped down her face and between her fingers as she held her hand against the cut. The girls screamed. Tears streamed down their muddy faces. Jimee and the closely hovering souls zoomed back.

Everything happened so fast, Jimee almost missed what actually happened within the particle fabric. It wasn't the mother's scream or her blood that caused the girls to cry. When the girls were having fun in the mud, a warm glow of particles surrounded them. When the rock hit their mother, cutting her forehead, the particles around the mother went out of phase, vibrated violently, and emitted an icy-black stream of energy. The sinister stream surged from the mother toward the two girls, entered their brains, and overcame their joy, replacing it with fear and confusion. Only then, the mother screamed. Jimee realized it wasn't the mother's scream that had frightened the girls, but the new icy-black energy before the scream.

The next instant, everything reversed. The mother's anger ended. She cried and scooped up her girls and pulled them against her chest, soothing them. They all cried together. Then they were quiet, holding on to each other. The mother looked down at her oldest daughter, smiled, and drew a little heart in the mud on her cheek. The youngest daughter reached over and tried to draw a heart on her sister's other cheek, smearing the mud-tear mixture all over her sister's face.

Still holding her daughters tight, the mother laughed, and the children laughed too. One of the girls looked at the cut on her mother's forehead and reached up and touched it, making the tip of her finger red with blood. Then she took her blood-tipped finger and touched the end of her sister's nose, making it red. The fear and pain were gone, vanquished by laughter and love.

Jimee realized she had witnessed the universe actively managing human relationships, extinguishing not only sadness but also anger and fear. She had discovered something more complex than particles, more exciting than energy, more universal than a fabric that connected everything and everyone.

Jimee thought back to first time she'd sensed vibrations, while watching Bobby and his father play catch, and when Mikey and Angel made love. The surges and waves had encouraged Bobby's dancing on the railing. The vibrating particles and the fabric they formed connected people.

Jimee thought about the bugs. How were the bugs involved? Bugs had entertained the girls. A bug had saved Bobby and had tried to save Stevens.

The icy-black presented another question. If Jimee had not spent thousands of years studying particles all over the universe, she might not have seen the dark energy form deep in the mother's brain or the white-hot counterattack that vanquished it.

Jimee replayed in her mind what she had observed. The burst of icy-black energy from the mother's brain had spread to her children, whose brains absorbed the energy, amplified it, then spewed icy-black into the particle fabric around them. Amplified, the icy-black energy spewing from mother and daughters assimilated every particle in its path.

Next, Jimee had seen the universe rise up and fight back. Just beyond the edge of the icy-black spewing from the mother and her daughters, warm particles rose in giant waves, vibrated vigorously, harmonically, fiercely, creating a white-hot, fiery passion. The white-hot waves attacked the icy-black, beating down the out-of-phase particles and transforming them back to their normal loving state. The effect on the mother and daughters was instantaneous. Hit by the white-hot wave, their crying stopped. They held each other and became a loving family again.

Jimee trembled with excitement. She now understood how the connectedness of people and the particle fabric of the universe were related, and that the particle fabric actively promoted positive connections between people, specifically between the brains of each person.

The fabric of the universe was an active participant with a deliberate, amazing, wonderful energy. This energy encouraged positive connections between people based on love and kindness, and vigorously fought fear and sadness. Jimee now understood why people on her home planet could not remain afraid, angry, or sad. The universe itself was a creator of love and happiness and possessed a white-hot immune system to fight fear and anger.

Jimee contemplated what her new understanding meant about the nature of people. People were kind and caring, not because *people* were inherently good, but because the *universe* was. The fabric of the universe propagated love. The fabric extinguished feelings of fear, anger, and sadness.

Jimee shivered with unease. If love wasn't an invention of people but an energy built into the fabric of the universe, then people had only evolved to learn how to harness love. Brains absorbed, amplified, and retransmitted love, making everyone stronger. Because love was energy, love could be mutated. Once mutated, icy-black energy attacked light. If not for the universe vanquishing the icy-black, people who naturally absorbed and amplified love would naturally absorb and amplify hate.

People were innately neither good nor evil. The universe made people good or evil with a built-in immune system to control the potential for evil.

Something else was also at work—and still a mystery. The sunrise was a clue. Something lay beyond the sunrise and the particles. Something was communicating, maybe controlling things. Something had tried to warn Stevens about the Great Advance.

Jimee left to find Stevens, who she hoped would still be at their home planet. While zooming through space, she thought of her own physical existence, remembering that she hadn't seemed to participate in the universe's balancing of happy and sad. Why? She knew her brain had been different from others. Maybe that was why. Billy, the attendant, had seemed different too.

She remembered her experiment with Eugene, who'd accidentally caused the death of her mother. Jimee had become angry and wanted to hurt Eugene, and the white-hot didn't stop her. Somehow, the confrontation had ended peacefully. She hypothesized that the white-hot had helped by influencing Eugene, not by influencing her.

Fortunately, people everywhere have the universe on their side, she thought. *A person can be angry and afraid, but only for a moment, thanks to the overwhelming strength and goodness of the particle fabric.*

Then Jimee remembered the massive icy-black wave.

31

BUG BITES

"Jimee, there's something going on at our planet," said Billy.

"What is it?" she asked.

"Something's wrong with Stevens."

"What's wrong?"

"I don't know, but he's upset and scaring the souls."

"He's been sad for thousands of years, since Bobby disappeared," Jimee said.

"I know, but not like this. Stevens can do things. He's affecting the planet. You need to come and see."

Jimee and Billy raced to Stevens. On the way, Jimee sensed sentient life on hundreds of other planets, all of it human! How could that be? Several planets had advanced civilizations. Zooming to keep up with Billy, Jimee almost failed to see the spaceships.

"Wait! Stop!" she shouted. Hundreds of galaxies and thousands of planets surrounded her and Billy.

"What?" asked Billy.

"Shh, listen."

"Spaceships?"

"No, something else." She'd heard a sound that she had never forgotten. Where was it coming from?

"We need to help Stevens! We need to go," urged Billy.

"There. Follow me," Jimee persisted.

They zoomed to a planet with a vast population. Jimee extended through the planet's atmosphere to its surface. She touched everything and everyone on and around the planet all at once.

"Jimee, what are you doing?".

"These people have evolved just like we did," she said. "Happy, content, loving, supportive. Advanced technology, space travel, and no disease, like on our planet. The odds of that are incalculable. Well, by most."

"That's how a lot of the planets are now," said Billy. "Not the no-disease part, or the space-travel part, but they have lots of nice people. Our home planet is like that now too."

"Over here," said Jimee, hovering over a large building. "Follow me inside."

They seeped into the building together. There were tens of thousands of people inside, working in harmony with perfect teamwork. Jimee felt sadness, not from the people in the building, but from Billy.

"You recognize what they're doing?" she asked.

"I think so."

"They are almost ready. They will be joining us soon. They are finalizing their own version of the Great Advance."

Jimee felt Billy's essence stiffen.

"Can we warn them?" he asked.

Jimee froze, remembering the warning she'd sensed in Stevens's journal. "You're right, we need to go," she said. "Stevens needs our help."

WHEN THEY ARRIVED above their home planet, Jimee saw how long it had been since she left Stevens and Bobby's baseball team hovering in grief around the lifeless planet. She'd been wrong about time. Millions of years had passed, not thousands.

The planet now teemed with newly evolved life: animal, aquatic, insect, and still a mystery, human life—physically, culturally, and socially evolved exactly as it had been before the Great Advance.

"Was it like this when you left to find me?" Jimee asked.

"Yes, except there's more of everything now, more people, especially," said Billy. "Look, they've built ships to cross the seas! Just like the explorers in my history books!"

Jimee found Stevens and the boys on the other side of the planet, still hovering above the field where Bobby and the boys used to play baseball. The swamp was now a small town.

Jimee sensed something different about the town. She had observed hundreds of planets. Universally, whenever people became angry, hurt, or frustrated, icy-black would burst outward and be extinguished by an overpowering white-hot from the fabric of the universe. Now, she sensed the same white-hot counterattacks in this town, except the phenomena happened continuously and to everyone. The people experienced thousands and thousands of explosions of the icy-black, more than on any planet Jimee had seen.

Jimee descended toward the town. Stevens's essence was concentrated exactly over Bobby's old baseball field. The site had become a neighborhood of houses. Jimee saw Stevens directing the bugs, making them fly this way or that way, causing them to swarm, guiding them to dive into water and drown, or making them fly so high they died of oxygen starvation.

"Look at what Stevens is doing to the people," said Billy.

To Jimee's horror, and to the delight of millions of souls, Stevens was directing bugs to bite the bare skin of people. Exclamations of pain and anger followed explosions of icy-black from their brains. The white-hot from the fabric was ever present, instantly rising up and extinguishing the icy-black.

"Jimee, this is what Stevens was doing when I left to find you," said Billy. "Look at all the souls hovering around the people. At first, the souls were scared when Stevens made the bugs bite people, but now they like it. Why is Stevens hurting the people? Why do the souls like watching?"

Jimee tried to talk to Stevens without success. He was focused entirely on controlling millions of bugs, extending a tiny sliver of his essence into each one, guiding its flight, timing its bite. Jimee thought of the bug on the deck that had saved Bobby, the bug on the steps that had tried to save Stevens, and the bugs on the pond making the little girls laugh. All the bugs seemed to be helping people. Who or what had controlled those bugs?

"Sometimes Stevens calls out for Bobby," said Billy, reminding Jimee of the last time Stevens had seen Bobby on the planet. Mortally injured from his fall off the porch, Stevens couldn't hold his head up as he struggled to look at his son. Only when Billy had taped Stevens's head to the back of the transfer chair could the synaptic cables be attached.

That's when something happened to Stevens, thought Jimee. *It has to do with the bug mist and the tape.*

"Billy, in your Great Advance training, did they say what would happen if a bug transferred with a person?"

"No, but the mist was specifically designed to kill bugs," said Billy.

"I think a bug transferred with Stevens."

"How?"

"The tape we used to hold his head protected the bug from the mist."

Jimee and Billy watched Stevens tormenting the towns-people. Those whom Stevens directed the bugs to bite lived in the homes directly over the millions-of-years-old baseball field. Stevens wasn't seriously hurting people, but he was making their lives unbearable with constant bug bites. Gnats, so small they could hardly be seen, were made to whir in their ears. The farther away people were from where the field used to be, the less Stevens bothered them. People nearest the field put their homes up for sale and moved away. If a new family moved in, Stevens's bugs harassed them too.

"Billy, when I was away, where did you watch this from?" asked Jimee.

"From up here, maybe a little farther away," he replied.

"You never joined the souls at the surface?"

"A few times, to check on my mother. She's lonely, so I help her."

Years passed. Families moved out and no one moved in. The homes directly atop the old baseball field became abandoned. Souls enjoyed hovering near tormented people, often clustering around a person who was not being bitten to show Stevens where to send the bugs.

"You don't get lonely?" asked Jimee, realizing she herself never felt lonely, probably because she'd become accustomed to being alone while physical, before the Great Advance.

"No, why would I get lonely?" Billy asked.

Construction crews came and tore down the homes. Stevens's bugs left the construction crews alone. New crews arrived to build a shopping center. Stevens reacted immediately. The bugs attacked the crews with intensity. The construction project was abandoned. Years later, another construction company began clearing the land to make way for large fields. They brought large fences and signs. Jimee felt Stevens grow happy. Stevens had been using the bugs to clear the area for baseball fields! Trucks brought concrete and began laying down long strips of pavement. It was obvious they were building an airport.

"You don't miss people?" asked Jimee.

"I don't think so," said Billy.

Stevens became angry and sicced the bugs on the

construction workers. For the first time, he actually scared and hurt the people. Billy tried to intervene, but Stevens ignored him. The construction disappeared, leaving signs to warn people away from the area. Decades passed. The fields became overgrown with weeds. People remembered bugs biting anyone who tried to build on the land, so the land remained untouched in the middle of a thriving, growing, vibrant city. Millions of souls continuously hovered above the people.

"Billy, did you ever get sad or angry before the Great Advance?" asked Jimee.

"Not angry, but sad."

"How long were you sad?" asked Jimee.

"Three years, I think. From when my mother transferred until I transferred."

"The sadness never went away that whole time?"

"No," replied Billy.

One day, a small boy snuck under the fence and onto the fields. The grass was thick and tall, so no one from the town noticed him. He had a baseball in his right hand and a glove on his left. As he walked, he played catch with himself, throwing the ball repeatedly into the worn and oiled leather pocket of his glove, relishing the thwacking sound.

"That boy loves baseball," said Jimee. "Billy, how is it possible that these people love baseball, the same exact game our people played before we transferred?"

"It's a fun game," said Billy.

"Really? Standing in a field, sitting on a bench?"

"Baseball's more than just standing and sitting," said Billy. "I played a few times, right field. Maybe someday we'll play on the same team."

"How?"

"Somehow," said Billy.

In the center of the field near a small pond, the boy began throwing the ball high into the air and catching it, pretending to be in the outfield catching a game-winning pop fly. Stevens stilled, watching the little boy. For the first time since Jimee and Billy returned to the planet, the bugs no longer bit anyone. The boy closed his eyes.

"Championship game," he whispered. "Bottom of the ninth. Bases loaded."

"Jimee, look at the bugs," said Billy. Millions of insects hovered above the boy. Stevens had shaped them in a large circle, like an audience in a stadium. The boy opened his eyes and shouted.

"SMACK! Home run!" The bugs buzzed wildly. The boy threw the ball high in the air.

"Game over!" shouted the boy. The ball came down, splashing into the middle of the pond. The best player in baseball history became a little boy who had lost his ball. Undaunted, the boy removed his shoes and walked into the pond. He was careful, and the water wasn't cold. Jimee sensed his confidence grow as he waded toward the center. There was a drop-off. The boy would fall off the edge and perhaps drown. Heartfelt concern from millions of souls enveloped the boy, warning him, to no effect. He took another step.

Suddenly, the circle of bugs rushed downward, forming a buzzing blockade between the boy and the drop-off. Frightened by the bugs, the boy ran out of the pond, through the field, under the fence, and back to the safety of his parents. Jimee looked at Stevens. She finally had his attention.

"I know what happened to Bobby," she said.

"Tell me," Stevens said.

Jimee hesitated, unsure where to begin. "When you and I were with Bobby—"

"No, Jimee, not like that. Show me," said Stevens, opening his mind, inviting Jimee to blend with his essence, to overlap their thoughts and memories until they became one.

"You too, Billy," said Stevens.

Three souls blended and became one. Jimee presented her explanation.

"You and I were hovering in remote space, far from the planet and any other souls. When Bobby arrived and shocked us, we reacted involuntarily and shot away. We left Bobby abandoned in empty space, utterly alone in the complete blackness of nothingness."

"Bobby's time alone could not have lasted more than an instant, but to a soul, time is meaningless. An eternity is an instant. An instant is an eternity.

"Without a body to hug, or brain to embody. Without a heart to break, or tears to cry. Without love or hope or nearby thoughts from another soul, Bobby, in that eternity of an instant, died."

Jimee then presented another thought, about what would have happened to her and Stevens if Billy hadn't arrived.

"The physical mind reacts instantly to shock with fear, pain, or flight. The floating mind has no DNA to provide instinct, no subconscious to ready reaction. When you and I were unexpectedly exposed to Bobby's pain, and then he vanished, our minds were so shocked, so unprepared, that for a moment we had no thoughts. A soul without thoughts and without a brain to contain it fades to nothing. If not for Billy, we would have died too."

Jimee, Stevens, and Billy deblended. They became three again. Stevens was still. Jimee struggled for words to comfort him.

"Welcome back," said Billy.

32

DISCONNECTED

JIMEE, Stevens, and Billy hovered above their home planet, supporting Stevens as he fully regained his state of mind. Years passed. The boy Stevens had saved grew up, became a father, and began playing catch with his son. Fully himself again, Stevens turned to Billy.

"How's your mother?" he asked.

"I think she should be with us," replied Billy.

"I know what happened to the universe, and to souls," said Jimee.

"Let's get Anna first," said Stevens.

Jimee extended and found Billy's mother, Anna, at a distant planet amid a small group of souls. To talk privately, Jimee, Stevens, Billy, and Anna moved away from the planet into a remote region of space.

Jimee told them she had made many discoveries about the universe. She described particles and vibrations, and how vibrations carried different types of energy from one particle to another.

"One energy is warm, light, and soothing, and is inherent in all particles. Another energy is icy and black. The icy-black energy makes people angry and afraid. When the icy-black energy occurs, the light, warm particles respond and create white-hot energy. The white-hot energy extinguishes the icy-black energy, eliminating peoples' anger and fear."

"How do you know this?" asked Stevens.

"I sense things," replied Jimee. "The things that you barely feel, I can see." Looking at Billy's mother, Jimee continued. "On the planet where I found you, why did you and the other souls surge into people when they laughed or loved?"

"We wanted to feel their happiness like we did before the Great Advance," said Anna, "but we couldn't, unless we hovered so close that we overlapped with them. Even then, we could barely feel their happiness."

Jimee scanned the area to be certain no other souls were listening. "I can see the energy that you were trying to feel. It's a warm light that surrounds people and connects them. The connection between people is amplified by tiny particles within the fabric of the universe." She hesitated, knowing what she had to say next would upset her companions.

"The particles interlink, making a kind of fabric across the universe. The fabric then connects to the synapses in peoples' brains. The connections stream energy between people, from brain to brain, through the particle fabric of the universe," Jimee said.

"You can see inside a brain?" asked Anna.

"You can see connections form, brain to brain?" asked Stevens.

"I believe that's what I'm seeing," replied Jimee. "I see the energy being carried by the particles from one brain to another. All people are subconsciously connected by the light, warm energy of the particle fabric, all the time."

"Can particles transmit different feelings?" asked Anna.

"Yes. Connections between particles are how people feel empathy for one another. That's why people feel a sense of belonging."

"But we don't have brains," said Anna quietly.

"Not anymore. Not since we transferred," said Jimee.

"Brains are synaptic organs that enable people to connect with one another via the fabric." She sensed Stevens realizing the truth and becoming upset.

"That's why Anna and the souls couldn't feel the peoples' happiness?" he asked.

"I think so," replied Jimee, knowing so.

"Unless we overlapped with their brains?" asked Anna, nearly shouting her question. Billy wrapped his essence around his mother.

Jimee waited for Anna to calm, then answered. "Overlapping with a person's brain might allow souls to participate in that person's connections, maybe a little."

An onslaught of Stevens's distress startled Jimee. In anguish, his mind was wide open. She sensed him remembering William's letter about Anna's lab mishap and his warning about the Great Advance. She saw Anna and Billy staring at Stevens. Anna seemed shocked, Billy concerned.

"Jimee, the people I tormented with bugs . . ." said Stevens, his thoughts shaking. "They were experiencing pain, not happiness, but the souls enjoyed it."

"That concerns me," Jimee said gravely.

The four souls hovered, absorbing Jimee's explanation. Time passed. They were so remote and distant from any physical reference that Jimee couldn't tell if a year or a million years went by. Anna seemed angry at Stevens, Jimee knew, because of William's letter. Billy broke the silence.

"Jimee, that can't be right," he said. "Souls can still connect. We still connect. We connect by communicating with each other through what we say and think. People connect by communicating too."

"Yes, Billy, but it's not the same thing," said Jimee.

"Why not?" he asked.

"We can connect to each other by communicating, but communicating has significant disadvantages compared to when we had brains and were constantly connected by the particle fabric."

"Like what?" asked Billy.

Realizing her answer was long and complex, Jimee asked Billy, Anna, and Stevens for permission to violate their privacy and blend thoughts so she could more effectively answer Billy's question. Billy and Stevens agreed. Anna didn't answer.

"Are you okay, Mother?" asked Billy.

Jimee and Stevens waited. Some years later, Anna told Billy she was okay and willing to blend. The four souls intertwined essences until their thoughts and memories became one.

Jimee explained in a prepackaged thought. "Communication exists only while we are consciously trying to communicate, which is a small percentage of time. Connections via the fabric exist continuously. Communication is based on language, which can be inadequate and result in misunderstandings. Communication typically consists of short conversations about specific topics, especially among strangers, and so requires effort, patience, and trust to create empathy and understanding between two people. In contrast, being connected across the particle fabric via the brain's synaptic interface creates a continuous, never-ending, subconscious empathy between everyone's essences. Before, we didn't need communication to be connected. Now, without our brains, communication is all we have. Upon transferring to the Great Advance, souls weren't skilled at using communication to form connections. Thus, souls didn't create new relationships, they merely maintained the relationships they once had. So, Billy is correct. Communication can create connections between us but requires more time and effort from both sides. And if either side stops communicating, or doesn't genuinely communicate, we quickly become disconnected."

Suddenly, Anna's thoughts drowned out Jimee's. Anna had accessed Stevens's memories about William's letter.

My dearest Rob . . . The truth about the lab mishap . . . I write this letter to tell you the truth . . . You were right, Rob, when you said the Great Advance kissed our Billy and made him special . . . Since then, I have learned how Anna's mishap in the laboratory of the Great Advance changed Billy . . . The Great Advance took Billy's connectedness. Billy doesn't belong . . . ONCE TRANSFERRED, WILL THE GREAT ADVANCE TAKE FROM OTHERS WHAT IT TOOK FROM BILLY?

Jimee regained control of the blending and one-by-one disentangled Stevens, Anna, and Billy from the blend.

Jimee sensed her companions. Stevens was devastated. Anna was furious. Billy tried to comfort each. Jimee waited for what she believed was a short time for them to regain themselves, then decided proximity to people and fellow souls might help. She led the group back to the planet where she had found Billy's mother among the souls watching the people. Hovering above, they watched families love and support each other while souls overlapped with the people, trying to participate in their connections.

"Jimee, is there more?" asked Billy, holding his mother.

"Yes. I think when souls first transferred to the Great Advance, they were fine for a time. Souls felt happy, liberated, and enjoyed exploring the universe while debating intellectual and philosophical questions. As time went on, however, the souls began to miss connecting. Souls missed the sense of belonging to something bigger than themselves and wanted to be part of humanity again." She paused, sensing Anna's anger toward Stevens increasing.

"Mother, everything will be okay," said Billy, wrapping tightly around his mother again. "Tell us, Jimee" he said.

Jimee directed their attention back to the souls on the planet and continued. "Look at them. The souls are desperate to get back what they once had. Since Bobby's death, they know connecting is about survival. Souls need to belong to something to live."

"We exist together, but alone?" muttered Stevens. "We are in the universe, but are not part of it?"

Jimee searched her mind for a way to answer without upsetting Stevens. She found none. "Yes," she said.

Stevens's thoughts blasted the group. He had not led a Great Advance, he had led humanity to its doom.

"Yes, and no," said Jimee. "Since the Great Advance, humanity seems to have spread throughout the universe. I think I know why."

"Will we die, Jimee?" Stevens asked. "If we need to connect to survive, and we can't, will everyone that transferred die?"

"I don't know," said Jimee.

"I know," said Billy, still wrapped around his mother. "We can stay alive by being together and helping each other, communicating constantly."

Jimee looked at Billy and remembered his unusual strength at the transfer station, how he'd hovered high above planets, not descending to the surface with the others, and that he'd remained sad after his mother transferred, unaffected by the fabric's white-hot response.

"I'm sorry, Billy," said Stevens, looking into space.

"You should be," said Anna accusingly.

"Mother?" asked Billy.

Anna bristled at Stevens. "William figured out what really happened the day I went to the lab to tell him I was pregnant. He warned you about the Great Advance, and you did nothing!"

Stevens cried out in anguish at the enormity of his mistake. Billy zoomed to comfort Stevens but had no effect. Stevens's grief intensified, unabated.

"Mother, help," said Billy.

Jimee zoomed to help, enveloping Stevens and Billy. Anna didn't move.

"Mother," pleaded Billy. "Stevens needs us."

Sobbing, Anna joined Billy and Jimee. Mother and son blended with Stevens, forgave him, and assured him everything would be okay.

While helping comfort Stevens, Jimee sensed a perturbation in the fabric. Scanning, she saw an extra-black blackness in the distance. Jimee recognized the icy-black wave from eons ago when Stevens lost Bobby. The wave, bigger, blacker, and icier, was spreading. She quietly separated from the group and zoomed toward the wave, immediately feeling cold. Then she observed something she hadn't noticed before. The particles behind the wave's path were blackened and burnt, like the aftermath of a fire. The icy-black wave was blackening the fabric of the universe. Alarmed, Jimee looked back at Billy, Anna, and Stevens. They were looking the other direction.

"Jimee, what's that bright thing way over there?" asked Billy. "What's that great big ball of light?"

33

SPEEDY

BRILL WANDERED AIMLESSLY IN SPACE. Her grief prevented her from experiencing any sense of wonder or exhilaration at her new existence, but she soon learned she was not alone. The universe was filled with other souls. Despite extensive space travel and deep space probes, Brill's planet had never encountered sentient life. Confused, she wondered where the souls came from and how they could all be of human origin.

Keeping her distance, Brill observed the souls and learned that many shared the same home planet and had transferred in a project called the Great Advance. Their frenetic hovering among people scared her. She moved farther and farther out into empty space, as far as she could, until she felt herself fading into nothingness. She realized being completely alone was dangerous.

Brill pushed the limits of how far away from other souls she could safely drift, learning to maintain her strength at greater and greater distances. Soon she discovered a trick that created more distance. If she spread out, leaving only a thinned part of herself extended near other souls, she could survive farther out. She became adept at manipulating her essence, spreading, thinning, and compressing.

From her far-off solitary place, she witnessed many souls

die. They'd float upward, drifting away from the planets and each other, deep into remote space. Most became afraid and reversed back toward the company and safety of other souls, but it was often too late. Sometimes she sensed a fading soul's last gasp.

While wandering, she came upon a family of souls, a mother, father, and two children, floating together, their spiritual energy tightly intertwined. She sensed they were desperately trying to regain the human connection they once had. The little boy was crying and pleading with his mother.

"Please, Mommy, hold me like you used to. Cuddle me."

"Jax, you know we can't cuddle, honey, not anymore, but I'm wrapped all around you. Jen is around you too. Try to pretend you can feel me."

The father encircled his family. "Nora, maybe if we try blending our thoughts again?"

The little boy continued to beg. "Hold me. Please, hold me."

"No honey, Jen's memory of the dogs at the lake scares Jax."

Jen began to cry.

Brill saw Nora extend a thread of her essence. The father did the same. The two threads interleaved, away from the children. Brill realized they intended to talk privately.

"Ken . . ." said Nora, her voice trailing off.

Brill was too far away to hear the remainder of the conversation. Ken and Nora retracted their threads back to their family center, then interleaved each of their essences with one another and each child until the entire family was tightly bound into a spiritual bundle. The mother and father kissed each child. While the whole family kissed, the father accelerated the family bundle into remote space.

To Brill's astonishment, the family zoomed straight at her. She had been a soul for long enough to know the family wouldn't crash into her, and there was no risk of accidentally blending without her permission.

Nonetheless, Brill reacted instinctively to avoid a collision with the barreling family. She shot backward, zooming faster through space than she'd ever zoomed before. The family would have overtaken Brill and run right through her, but suddenly the father and mother disentangled and spun, throwing each family member in a different direction. Apart, alone, and terrified, all four faded to nothingness. Then Brill felt her own terror, realizing that she'd shot far beyond the limit for her own survival. She prepared to die.

The next instant, a wonderful warmth she hadn't felt since long ago on her own planet, before the insanity, washed over her. She wasn't alone. She'd flung herself near a large planet in a remote region of the universe.

Brill soaked up the wonderful bliss. The planet was densely populated, with over a hundred billion people, everyone living in a perfect state of harmony.

Humans, like on my planet, she thought, her scientific mind calculating the improbability of that.

Keeping her distance, she imagined her eyes were closed as she floated around the planet. She detected only a few souls hovering among the living people. That made sense because the planet was so remote. She drifted, soaking in the loving goodness.

"Hey, miss, can you help me?"

Brill startled awake and recoiled. She had always kept her distance from other souls and had never been approached by one before.

"Miss, I'm afraid. Can you help me find my father?" asked a little boy.

The boy reminded Brill of her own children, Nikky and Nathan. She draped her essence around the boy to comfort him and scanned for the boy's father.

A soul raced toward them from the far side of the planet.

"Speedy, are you okay? Where have you been? Your mother and sister are worried sick!" said the father.

"I got lost, Father. I'm sorry. This woman saved me," replied the boy.

Brill disentangled her embrace from the boy, and the father's essence enveloped him.

"Ma'am, I'm sorry about that," the father said to Brill. "Thank you so much for helping my boy."

"She saved me, Father!" Speedy said, forgetting how afraid he'd been only a few moments before.

"Thank you, again, ma'am. My son gets excited. Speedy has been high energy since the day he was born. That's why we call him Speedy."

"You're welcome," she replied. It was the first time she'd spoken since becoming a soul. Talking felt good.

"What's your name, miss?" asked Speedy.

"My name is Brill."

"What are you doing over here?" asked the father. "Don't get me wrong, I'm glad you were here, but I think maybe we're all supposed to meet on the other side of the planet. Are you coming?"

Brill realized the father thought she was a soul from the massive planet. "You go on ahead. I will come soon."

"Thank you for saving me, Miss Brill!" shouted Speedy as he and his father zoomed away.

Brill watched them leave. When they were far enough away, she rose high above the planet to see where they were going. The two zoomed to the other side of the planet and joined a group of souls that included other families. Speedy was living up to his name, zooming about and having a great time. The father laughed at his son's antics. Brill focused on the planet.

The hundred billion people lived everywhere, on land in structures so high they penetrated the atmosphere, at sea in floating cities anchored to the ocean floor, and in large space stations orbiting the planet. As a scientist, Brill was impressed by what these people had accomplished. One of the space complexes orbited past the area where the father and son had gone, drawing Brill's attention back to the group.

Are there more souls now? she wondered. *There seem to be more souls in the group.* The group of souls was twice what it had been only hours or maybe days ago. Brill realized she'd lost track of time. Years had passed. The number of souls was now increasing exponentially.

Brill watched, impressed by the peoples' soul-transfer program. The people were perfectly organized. They had placed thousands of synaptic transfer stations throughout their world and on space stations orbiting the planet. The transfer stations worked flawlessly, and the whole program seemed to be executing perfectly. The people were enthusiastic and excited about transferring. The scientists seemed to have thought of everything, including providing uninterrupted medical, health, safety, and education services to the population. Thousands of robots maintained the planet's infrastructure.

As people arrived in the spiritual domain, they were met by a specially trained welcoming group that immediately encircled the newly transferred souls to minimize disorientation. There was no fear of the kind Brill had experienced after her transfer. She examined the planet's technology. It was nothing short of amazing.

The transferred souls now numbered in the billions. Brill sensed Speedy playing among a group of a few million child souls. The energetic boy darted among the children, who laughed and tried to follow. Old and young souls danced among the stars, playing games of tag and hide-and-seek. It was like a dream come true for the new souls, a dream that Brill knew must have taken thousands of years to unlock. The new souls felt only joy and happiness.

Brill wondered what had sickened and killed all her people while this planet prevailed.

When the transfers were over, she scanned the planet and the space stations. Every last person had transferred. Only plants, animals, fish, and insects remained. A hundred billion souls hovered in a loving, joyous group on the other side of the planet.

Careful to not intrude, Brill extended a thin thread of her essence into the group. She estimated more than one hundred billion souls. All seemed excited to begin the next phase of their evolution, to expand their enlightenment as a people. The souls hovered closely together, creating a massive ball of light as they departed the planet.

Knowing she couldn't survive if left completely and totally alone, Brill followed.

34

YOU'RE ONE OF US NOW

JIMEE STUDIED the ball of light Billy was pointing at.

"That ball's massive," said Stevens.

"And bright," said Anna.

"Stay here. I'll be right back," said Jimee.

Stevens, Billy, and Anna watched Jimee approach the ball, stretching herself to avoid being detected.

"Is that a child speeding around out front?" asked Anna.

"That kid's fast," said Billy.

An instant later, Jimee was back.

"There must be a hundred million of them," said Stevens.

"One hundred billion three hundred million seven hundred and seventy-two thousand four hundred and twenty-seven," said Jimee.

The ball of light was a spectacle impossible to imagine. Billions of souls were packed tightly into the massive, humming ball, rolling through the universe. Happy, joyful spirits danced and sang. Children zoomed around the outer perimeter, darting this way and that, playing games of tag. Intellectuals gathered in groups of ten or twenty million, debating and discussing. The ball of light shimmered with the energy of one hundred billion souls, all happy and in love with their new freedom to grow and learn.

"They're headed straight for that planet," said Stevens.

The four friends watched the massive ball slow as it approached the planet. The ball stopped for a few minutes as if deciding what to do next, then began moving again, continuing toward the planet until the ball's outer edge touched the planet. The effect was electrifying. The people on the planet began to pulsate as the ball of light enveloped their world, drenching them with pulses of spiritual warmth. The people, already good, kind, and loving, became even more so.

Remembering that souls hadn't seemed to affect the mother and her two little children at the pond, Jimee focused on the particles making up the fabric of the universe. Somehow, the incredible density of the one hundred billion loving souls in the ball of light energized the particles, despite the souls no longer having brains providing connections to the fabric. In turn, the particles were energizing the people. Souls did affect particles, and therefore people! At least, one hundred billion souls all in loving harmony could!

Jimee recalled her theory about how humanity had spread throughout the universe after the Great Advance, influencing all life to be physically and culturally the same as on her home planet. *Not a theory, a fact*, she thought.

The ball of a hundred billion souls passed through the planet, moving with joyful slowness, leaving ripples of positive energy in its wake. When it was exactly at the planet's center, the ball paused long enough to expand its diameter to match the planet's. For a moment, the ball and planet were one, a mix of blissfully happy people and souls.

Jimee became so mesmerized by the ball of light, she failed to notice the sad and lonely soul following the ball.

FOLLOWING behind the hundred billion souls, Brill noticed a group of four souls watching the ball approach. When one zoomed to investigate, Brill hid by thinning and moving into the ball's outer edge, effectively concealing her essence within the loving warmth of millions of other souls.

After the one soul returned to the small group, Brill moved closer to learn about the four souls as they watched the ball envelope the planet. Sensing their friendship, she realized how lonely she had become.

As a trained scientist, Brill knew the soul named Jimee was commingling herself with the universe somehow, studying something deep within the universe's fabric. Brill's curiosity and loneliness overcame her caution. She zoomed to Jimee and her friends, who were so enamored with the ball that Brill had to speak to get their attention.

"Hello," she said, startling all four.

"Hello," replied Billy. "This is my mother, Anna, and these two are Jimee and Stevens. We're friends."

"Hi," said Anna.

"Why aren't you with the others?" asked Stevens.

"I'm not from their planet," replied Brill.

"Did they kick you out?" asked Billy.

"Billy!" exclaimed his mother.

For the first time since her transfer, Brill laughed. It felt good, and she let the sensation linger as the laughter flowed through her entire essence. She decided she liked this soul, Billy.

"It's okay," she said.

"Where are you from? Why are you following the ball of souls?" asked Stevens, motioning toward the planet still encircled by the hundred billion happy souls.

Brill looked at Billy and then into distant space. "Over there is my planet."

"Why are you all by yourself?" asked Billy.

"I'm the only one left," she answered. She sensed Jimee probing her.

"Why?" asked Billy.

Brill tried to contain her sadness. Except for Speedy and his father, these were the only souls she had spoken to. She had been lonely for hundreds or thousands or maybe millions of years. She liked Billy and his mother. Jimee and Stevens seemed okay too.

Brill realized she was the only being in the universe who recalled her planet and family. She wanted them to be remembered, so she answered Billy's question by telling him about her people and what had happened to them.

"Over thousands of years, my people achieved vast intellectual and cultural enlightenment. We journeyed and sacrificed, but supported each other and worked together. We cured disease. We built great spaceships and traveled to distant planets. Whatever we aspired to achieve, we united and accomplished." Brill spoke for a long time about her planet. As she spoke, her thoughts grew increasingly quiet, then she stopped, her essence shaking in sadness.

Billy moved closer. "Don't be sad."

"What's your name, ma'am?" asked Stevens.

"My name is Brill."

Billy moved still closer and wrapped his essence around Brill. "You aren't all by yourself anymore," he said.

"Can you tell us what happened to your people?" asked Stevens.

Brill looked at Billy, thanked him, and continued her story. "I was a scientist in charge of technological development. Long before I was born, my people built spaceships to explore other worlds. We also discovered synaptics and particle space and combined the two discoveries to build an instantaneous communications network connecting the whole planet. We used the technologies to communicate with spaceships and distant planets that we studied."

"Who were you communicating with on distant planets?" asked Stevens.

"No one. We were hoping to discover life, but we never did," answered Brill.

"What do you mean by 'particle space'?" asked Jimee.

Brill was in her element now and pleased by their interest. "We discovered the universe is made up of infinitesimal particles, all interconnected, essentially creating a fabric spanning the entire universe. We learned that the fabric connects everything. Synaptic energy exists within the fabric like electricity exists in an electrical grid. We also discovered that the energy within our minds connects to the fabric and can live in it.

"We called the fabric 'particle space.' I was in charge of the particle space program involving thousands of scientists. We created a network of instantaneous communication, billions of times faster than any network before, and developed the capability to connect our brains to it. We even developed the ability to see into the fabric with our minds. When the discoveries were first made, we became so excited that we formed a new goal—to transfer the mind of a person into particle space."

Brill sensed the four of them tense. She wondered if they knew anything about the insanity that destroyed her people. Suppressing suspicion, Brill continued.

"Unlike the people in the ball of light—I mean, those hundred billion souls—after centuries of debate, our people never gained consensus to transfer ourselves into particle space. By the time I became chief scientist, science had shifted away from transferring minds into the fabric. Instead, we used the knowledge for a more practical purpose, instantaneous communication."

"Instantaneous communication, how?" Jimee asked.

Brill didn't hear Jimee's question. She was transfixed by the planet, still enveloped by the hundred billion souls. "I watched them transfer. I arrived just after they had begun. Their planet was many times more advanced than mine. I watched them transfer billions of their people. Every one of

233

them was content, excited, and couldn't wait to transfer. They were tens of thousands of years more advanced than my planet."

"We debated on our planet too," said Billy. "All the way to the end. Many people chose not to transfer."

"On my planet, everything was fine, everyone was happy, then something terrible happened," continued Brill. "Everyone on my planet got sick, every single person, all at once. We went insane and murdered ourselves."

"You didn't have doctors?" asked Billy.

"It wasn't that kind of sickness, Billy. The sickness was in our minds. Our minds had never been sick before, so our doctors didn't have a cure. Our scientists tried to help. I tried. People became irritated about things that had never bothered them before. Arguments and fights ensued. It was worse in groups. The mind sickness spread from one person to another, multiplying. People went insane, fighting, killing . . ."

"Everyone? All at once? You mean every person on the planet?" asked Jimee.

"All of us, some more quickly than others. Me too, and my husband and children. Yes, everyone."

"You had kids?" asked Billy.

"Yes," she said. "I realized my family would be safer, unable to fight and hurt each other, if we stayed apart. Whatever was making us sick was stronger when we were together. I separated my kids in their rooms, my husband upstairs, and I worked downstairs in the lab. Separating worked. Then one night, a crazy mob broke into the house and murdered my family. I heard my children screaming for help, but I was downstairs and couldn't get to them in time. Sick with grief and all alone, I connected myself to a transfer system in my lab and threw the switch. From particle space, I watched the last of my people go completely insane and kill themselves. My people are gone. My husband and kids are gone. I'm the only one left." Brill stilled, fighting off sadness.

"You're one of us now," said Billy.

"How did you transfer, if your people agreed to never make a transfer system?" asked Anna.

"We had the base technology. For research purposes, we had developed everything except an actual transfer system. Once I realized the sickness was in peoples' brains, my colleagues and I began building a transfer system to escape our brains."

"Look, something's happening!" said Billy.

The massive ball of a hundred billion souls, packed together in a giant glowing ball of light, began to move. It was a surreal sight, two enormous round objects, one a planet full of kind, loving people, and the other a hundred billion happy, joyous souls. The massive ball of a hundred billion souls separated from the planet and rolled off into the distance.

"Should we follow them?" asked Stevens.

"Brill, if it's okay with you, I'd like to go to your planet," said Jimee. "Together we might learn what happened to your people."

Brill hesitated. She'd never been back.

"Don't worry, Brill. We'll be right beside you," said Billy.

35

ENTROPY LOOP

Brill led the four friends to her planet.

As they traveled, Billy addressed her. "You didn't answer Jimee's question."

Brill stopped and waited for Jimee, Stevens, Anna, and Billy to gather around her. "What question?"

"About instantaneousness," said Billy. "I think that means fast."

Brill looked at Jimee.

"You said you used the fabric for an instantaneous communication network," said Jimee.

Brill understood. "Ahh, we also installed Life Probes on distant planets in order to detect life the instant it evolved," she explained.

"Did you detect life?" asked Jimee.

"No, but we'd only been searching for a few hundred years."

"Instantaneous means fast, right?" asked Anna.

"Not just fast, instantly, with no delay at all," said Brill.

"How?" asked Billy.

Brill remembered Nikky's explanation for her science competition and modified it for retelling her friends.

"Billy, pretend you and I are physical. You want to tell me

a secret, but we're on opposite sides of a room. You can't tell me the secret unless we are right next to each other."

"Okay," said Billy.

"You start walking toward me. As you walk, you magically start getting younger."

"How?" asked Billy.

"Just pretend for now," said Brill.

"Okay."

"How old were you when you transferred?" she asked.

"One," said Billy.

"He was twenty-two," said Anna.

"I'm pretending, Mother," said Billy.

Brill continued. "Okay, pretend you're still twenty-two. As you walk toward me, you get younger. You become twenty-one, then twenty, then nineteen. You keep walking. You become eighteen, then seventeen, then sixteen. Finally, I see you approaching. By then, you're fifteen years old. When I see you, the magic instantly reverses, and you start getting older instead of younger. You aren't next to me yet, so you can't tell me your secret. As you keep walking, you begin aging, from fifteen to sixteen to seventeen. When you reach me, you're exactly twenty-two years old again. When you finally tell me your secret, it's like no time has passed."

"That is magic!" said Billy.

"In space-time, that's magic," said Brill, laughing. "But in fabric-time, that's physics."

"What do you mean by space-time and fabric-time?" asked Jimee.

Brill looked at Stevens. "Your Great Advance scientists understood," she said.

"Stevens isn't a scientist. My father was though," said Billy.

Brill began the explanation. "There are two kinds of time in the universe, space-time and fabric-time.

"Space-time is where things exist, like books, toys, and

people. Things take time to travel through space, that's why it's called space-time. The fastest things can travel is the speed of light, although on our planet, we learned how to go faster than the speed of light with some things, like with our spaceships.

"Fabric-time is what connects us. A particle fabric that stretches throughout the whole universe connected all life. The fabric manipulates time to make connections instantaneous."

"After transferring, we lost the ability to keep track of time," said Jimee. "Is that because of fabric-time?"

"Yes," Brill said. "As souls, we exist in the fabric, so unless we are near a space-time reference, like a planet or a star, we can't tell time. Life Probes exist in space-time, but we designed them to transmit instantaneously via built-in synaptic portals that inject their signals into the fabric."

"Like magic!" said Billy.

"How does the fabric actually manipulate time?" asked Jimee.

"That's where it gets a little complicated," said Brill. "A fundamental law of the universe is that entropy—"

"What's entropy?" interrupted Billy.

"Entropy is a fancy word for the randomness of the universe."

"Oh," said Billy.

"A fundamental law of the universe is that entropy increases with time. Because the fabric of the universe is made up of interconnected particles, the fabric can affect time by manipulating the entropy, or randomness, of its particles. If the fabric decreases the randomness of its particles, time goes backward. If the fabric increases the randomness of its particles, time accelerates. The fabric makes connections instantaneous by doing both, which creates an entropy loop in the specific particles that lie in the path between a sender and receiver."

"What's an entropy loop?" asked Billy.

Brill sensed Jimee, Stevens, and Anna had the same question. "An entropy loop works like this. When the sender initiates a connection, the fabric starts the loop by reducing the entropy in the particles making up the connection. This decrease in entropy results in the connection going backward in time, like when Billy was getting younger. A receiver is required for the fabric to reverse the loop. When a receiver acknowledges the connection, the fabric reverses and focuses the entire signal toward the receiver while increasing the entropy, accelerating time until the loop is closed. That's like when Billy was getting older. Because the loop begins and ends at exactly the same point, the connection is sent and received at exactly the same time, no matter how far apart the connection."

"Why doesn't the fabric just leave entropy fixed for each connection, unchanging, thus stopping time for the duration of the connection?" asked Stevens.

"That's a property of the fabric," replied Brill. "Connections only exist within the fabric when entropy is changing. If entropy wasn't changing, there'd be no energy between the particles to maintain the connection."

"Like if I wasn't walking toward you to tell you a secret, I wouldn't be moving," said Billy.

"Yes, like that," said Brill.

"What if there's a sender, but no receiver?" asked Anna.

Brill started to answer, but Jimee interjected.

"If there's no receiver, the message won't get reversed. The fabric would transmit the message back in time forever and ever."

"Correct," said Brill.

"Who would send a message to no one?" asked Billy.

36

TIDAL WAVE

BRILL RESUMED LEADING the four friends to her planet. As they traveled, she questioned Jimee.

"You seemed to understand particle space," she said.

"Jimee knows everything about particle space," said Billy. "Jimee can even see super small things."

"You can see particles?" Brill asked.

"When I'm still or moving slowly," Jimee replied.

"We're getting closer to my planet. Soon, space will become colder and darker," Brill said, slowing down. "I'd like to know what you observe about the particles."

She moved slowly but steadily ahead, the others following. After reaching the darker, colder space, Brill stopped and looked expectantly at Jimee, who was already analyzing the particles.

"It's colder here," said Stevens.

"Colder and blacker," said Anna, shivering. "I don't like it."

"What caused the change?" asked Billy.

"I don't know, Billy, but I think whatever caused the change also killed my planet," said Brill. "Jimee, can you determine anything from the particles?"

"Yes, I think I understand," replied Jimee. "The particles

are blackened and icy cold. Let's go to your planet, so I can be sure. Lead the way, Brill, quickly. I don't like it here either."

Brill zoomed the remainder of the way to her home planet. She had not been back in thousands, maybe millions of years. Immediately obvious were the bugs swarming in thick black clouds, all around the planet. Signs of a great civilization were everywhere. Once beautiful cities lay empty. Shiny buildings reached into the sky. Enormous ships were docked at empty ports. Space stations silently circled the planet. The great windows of the space stations were the only hint at the wonder and awe people once experienced gazing down at the beauty of their planet.

"It's a beautiful planet," said Anna.

The four of them hovered over the planet while Jimee orbited, analyzing particles, shifting each orbit longitudinally in order to scan the entire surface.

After scanning all around the planet, Jimee continued circling, increasing her distance from the planet each rotation.

"I can hardly see her," said Anna.

"Maybe we should move farther out?" said Brill, worrying about Jimee becoming separated in remote space and disappearing.

"She'll be back," said Billy.

A second later, Jimee reappeared.

"Why'd you go so far out?" asked Stevens.

"It was the only way to be sure," replied Jimee. "I think I know what happened to Brill's people."

Brill tensed, waiting for her to continue.

"We did it," Jimee said, looking at Stevens. "I'm sorry, Brill. We killed your family and everyone on your planet."

"What do you mean, we killed everyone?" asked Stevens.

Brill waited for Jimee to continue, knowing that only something in particle space could have infected all the minds on her planet at once. She remembered how the four friends had reacted to the part of her story about particle space and transferring minds.

"I think we may have doomed everyone else in the universe too," said Jimee. "It happened after Bobby died. At first, we believed Bobby was missing, so we searched for him. Stevens, you and the boys from Bobby's baseball team searched for Bobby together, remember?"

Brill remembered searching for her family.

"I remember," Stevens said.

"You were overwhelmed by sadness," said Jimee. "You and the boys searched the universe looking for Bobby. Others who loved him joined, then thousands more followed. Your grief became anguish and then pain. You screamed for Bobby, and more souls joined. Pain led to fear and anger. Millions more souls joined, afraid that if Bobby could vanish, so could they. Millions of screaming, agonized souls raced through the universe searching for your son."

"I remember. I went crazy looking for him," whispered Stevens.

Brill remembered wanting revenge on the murderers who killed her family.

"Not just you," said Jimee. "You and the boys and the others. I followed you, watching the fabric of the universe stretch and strain. The fabric held, but tiny rips formed. The rips healed. I saw the fabric heal itself." Jimee stopped and pointed out into the distance.

Brill didn't look. She understood what had happened to her people. She sensed Billy move near her. "Thanks, Billy, I'm okay," she said.

"You stopped over there, Stevens," continued Jimee. "By then, you had millions of frightened souls following you. All of a sudden, without warning, you stopped. Your anguish and the pent-up fear of the souls behind you created a massive pile-up, tearing the fabric of the universe and unleashing a tidal wave of icy-black energy. The tidal wave headed straight at Brill's planet."

Jimee stopped. The friends hovered in silence. Brill sensed each friend struggling to accept what had happened.

"Jimee, what do you sense in the particles?" asked Brill.

"Particles hit by the wave have mutated," replied Jimee.

"Mutated, what does that mean?" asked Anna.

"Permanently changed," she replied. "The wave changed the particles to now vibrate at different frequencies and phases, similar to the different levels of fear and anguish with each soul following Stevens."

"What does that mean?" asked Anna again.

"It means the universe isn't intrinsically good anymore, at least not where it was torn, and not anywhere the wave hit," said Brill.

"What?" asked Billy.

"Wherever the wave traveled, the universe was good before and it's bad now?" asked Stevens.

"Not just bad, evil," said Brill.

"Something like that," said Jimee. "Maybe not evil on its own, but the mutated particles amplify fear and hate, and suppress love and kindness. Exactly the opposite of the way the particles worked prior to the wave."

Jimee described the mother and her two children at the pond. She told them she had observed that whenever a living person was upset, hurt or afraid, icy-black energy was released. The particles in the fabric responded with a hot, light energy that quenched the cold, dark energy and returned the fabric to good.

Brill offered a medical analogy. "What Jimee means is that before the hate wave, the particles in the fabric of the universe functioned like an immune system. The particles attacked and stopped icy-black energy from spreading through the fabric. Now the particles are damaged, and the immune system no longer works. Good no longer overcomes evil."

"If you two are right, people have had help being kind and good. Now people are on their own," said Anna.

Jimee agreed. "Not only that, people hit by the hate wave are no longer continuously connected by the fabric. Particles that used to vibrate in sync with the synaptic connections in peoples' brains now vibrate at millions of different frequencies, making the connection between the fabric and the brain intermittent, or breaking the connection entirely."

"Jimee, are you saying that after being hit by the hate wave, communication is peoples' only means of connection? Like souls? Like us?" asked Stevens.

"Yes, if I'm right," said Jimee. "We left our brains when we transferred to the Great Advance, causing us, as souls, to lose most of our connection to the fabric, but people remained fully connected. Now, because the hate wave mutates the fabric, any people in the path of the hate wave will also become disconnected."

"Souls haven't handled being disconnected very well," said Anna quietly.

"So, we were never good?" asked Billy.

"I think you were good, Billy," said Brill. "My people were good too, but we weren't good because people are inherently good. People are just people, capable of being good and bad. The particles in the fabric of the universe helped us be good most of the time."

"And now the universe is the opposite?" asked Billy. "It makes people bad?"

"Yes, Billy, I think so," said Jimee. "Brill, I think the wave killed your planet. When the wave hit, your people no longer had help being good, and they all became disconnected at the same time. Worse, the wave had just formed and was at full strength. It hit your people so hard and fast that they couldn't adapt."

Brill now understood. "The wave soaked my planet in hate. We didn't have a chance."

"What about all the people in the ball of light?" asked Billy.

"It was still warm there," said Brill. "The wave hadn't hit their planet, yet."

"I'm cold," said Anna, her essence shivering.

"Where is the wave going now?" asked Billy.

"Everywhere," said Jimee.

Without a word, Billy zoomed in the direction of the strongest part of the hate wave.

"Where are you going?" asked Anna.

Billy stopped and looked back. "People hit by the hate wave will need our help," he said before zooming off again.

His mother, Jimee, Brill, and Stevens followed. After zooming past dozens of decimated planets, they passed by an entire solar system that seemed to be thriving. Jimee and Brill zoomed to catch up with Billy.

"Billy, we'd like to study these planets," said Brill.

"They don't need our help," he said, increasing his speed.

"Billy, after being hit by the hate wave, they not only survived, but seem to possess advanced technology. Even from this distance, I sense thousands of spaceships and millions of robots," said Jimee.

Billy stopped. Stevens and Anna caught up.

"Did you see those spaceships? Those planets seem to be doing fine," said Stevens. "Of course, they weren't in the direct path of the hate wave."

"Unlike my planet, they didn't take a direct hit," said Brill.

"Maybe the hate wave isn't as bad as we thought if people aren't directly in its path," said Anna.

"Let's investigate," said Jimee.

Brill nodded. The two began zooming toward the robot planet.

"Stop!" said Billy. Jimee and Brill stopped. Billy zoomed right up to them. "You two want to study robots instead of finding people who might need our help?"

"Billy!" said Anna.

"We might learn something to help others survive," said Jimee.

"Billy's right," said Brill. "I admit, the robots fascinated me. Jimee, we can always return to study their science later."

Jimee quickly extended a thread of herself toward the solar system. She sensed extensive infrastructure on each planet, and many people, including children and families, but the planets were still too far away to sense anything about their peoples' states of mind. She retracted her essence. Billy and Brill were right. These people had survived and were likely thriving. Other people might actually need help. Studying the robot planet would have to wait.

"Billy, lead the way," said Jimee.

37

ROBOT PLANET

RAMIEN LOVED PLAYING WITH ELLE, but on this morning, he was afraid. He'd just turned five, and the night before, his parents had told him that tomorrow he'd begin training to fight and kill murderous robots called Synmen. They explained how killing Synmen would allow everyone to leave the cavern and save their planet.

But he was also sad. He and Elle had played together every day for as long as he could remember, but soon, because of his training, they'd be apart most of the day.

Sitting on one of the remaining patches of artificial grass, he waited for Elle to come out and play. Toys lay scattered across the yard from the day before. High above, a light flickered on, signaling the start of the day. Elle and her mother emerged from their home. Ramien waved but didn't call out. Constant pounding from the nearby cavern walls made conversation impossible unless people were right next to each other.

Elle ran to Ramien, and her mother followed. "Guess what I have," Elle said, holding up her hand, clutching something in her fist. Ramien shrugged. "Guess!"

"Shh, Elle, it's a secret," said her mother. "Ramien, what's wrong?"

"My mommy and daddy said the pounding is Synmen trying to break in and kill us."

"That's right," said Elle's mother, patting Ramien lightly on his head. "We live underground to escape the Synmen. You have to start training soon?"

Ramien nodded sullenly. "Tomorrow."

"I'm sorry, Ramien," said Elle's mother.

"I can go to work with my mommy tomorrow too, cleaning and cooking for the scientists," said Elle.

Ramien sniffed. "I don't want to kill people," he muttered under his breath.

"Not real people. Synmen," said Elle's mother.

"What are Synmen?" asked Elle.

"Ramien, did your parents explain the difference? Synmen aren't real people. They attacked our planet, tortured and killed almost everyone, and forced us underground. That was hundreds of years ago. We've lived in this cavern ever since."

"Why, Mommy?" asked Elle.

"No one knows," Elle's mother replied, patting the two children on the head.

She left for work, reminding Elle and Ramien to pick up their toys before she returned. Elle sat down facing Ramien and scooted close so he could hear her talk softly over the pounding.

"Don't be sad, Ramien," she whispered. "Look what I have." She held out her hand and opened her fist, exposing a large red strawberry.

"Only scientists get strawberries, not tourists," said Ramien, shaking his head.

Elle held the strawberry out until it touched his lips. He leaned away, his hands pushing into the rough, threadbare turf of the underground cavern.

"My parents might see," he said, glancing over his shoulder at his home, a small house behind them, one of thousands clustered closely together. Elle lived in the house next door. In contrast to their small, rundown homes, across the street stood a massive, shiny black building, so long the ends faded into the distance, and so tall its roof seemed to touch the cavern ceiling thousands of feet above.

"My mommy got this one for us," said Elle. "Her scientist boss gave it to her. She can get us cherries too." She slid to Ramien's side, and her arm touched his. "Smell it, Ramien," she said, giggling and touching his nose with the strawberry. "My turn. Yummy!"

Ramien opened his eyes and saw her sniffing the strawberry. He suddenly felt less afraid.

"Your turn," she said, passing him the strawberry. "Eat the tip, just a teeny, tiny bit.

Ramien took a nibble. Elle laughed. He handed her the strawberry, barely nicked by his teeth.

She took a nibble too. "A billion teeny, tiny bits. We'll make it last." Back and forth, they passed the strawberry.

"Strawberries and cherries," said Ramien, before each bite.

"Best-friend berries," said Elle.

Bit by tiny bit, Ramien and Elle ate the strawberry, until Elle held a single tiny bit between her fingers. Ramien looked away. Elle scooted closer.

"Elle, I can't play with you anymore."

"Why?"

"My daddy said it's not allowed once I start training." A tear trickled down his cheek. He felt Elle dab the tear with the tiny bit of strawberry.

"Look, Ramien," she said.

He looked at her and felt a soft warmth swell deep inside him.

"Best-friend berries," she said, putting the tiny bit of strawberry in her mouth. Her cheeks swelled as she pretended it was a whole strawberry.

Ramien laughed. He realized he was no longer afraid. They lay back in the grass. Ramien took her hand.

"Strawberries and cherries, best-friend berries," they sang.

Suddenly, the pounding stopped. Ramien and Elle froze. All their lives, the pounding had been present. Ramien's parents burst from their home and ran toward the children, brandishing heavy weapons. Men and women ran from houses all over the community, also armed. Each took up defensive positions.

A group of scientists emerged from the shiny black building, ran partway toward Elle and Ramien, then stopped at a fence around the building's perimeter. The fence had no gate. The scientists pointed at Elle and Ramien excitedly.

"Why are they pointing at you two?" Ramien's mother asked. The next instant, speakers placed throughout the tourist area boomed.

"Stand down. The cavern walls are not breached. Stand down."

"What are scientists doing inside a building near the tourist area?" asked Ramien's father.

"My mommy said it's for experiments," said Elle.

"What kind of experiments?" asked the father.

The pounding resumed.

38

CHIEF SCIENTIST FRED

ELLE LOVED PLAYING WITH RAMIEN. It was the day after the pounding had stopped and their first day apart. Ramien had begun training, and she'd joined her mother, helping to serve the scientists. Scientists questioned Elle about what she'd been doing when the pounding stopped. She told them about Ramien and the strawberries and cherries.

Elle thought of Ramien all day long. She was happy when the scientists told her mother that from now on, they could leave in the middle of the afternoon, and even gave Elle a bag of strawberries and cherries.

"Maybe Ramien will be home early too," said Elle to her mother on the walk home.

"I'm sorry, but Ramien won't be home until late from now on," her mother replied.

"The scientist man said the strawberries and cherries are for Ramien too," said Elle.

"Which scientist told you that?"

"Mr. Fred, the scientist you work for, Mommy."

"How does Mr. Fred know you and Ramien like strawberries?"

"The scientists asked me what Ramien and I were doing when the pounding stopped," said Elle.

All the way home, Elle thought about playing with Ramien. She squealed in excitement when she saw him sitting on the grass where they usually played, toys scattered all around him. He wore all black. Elle ran the last distance and sat down opposite him, like she always did. The pounding from the cavern walls was as loud as ever.

Ramien grinned broadly and pointed at his feet. "I got new boots."

"They're shiny, like that big black building," Elle said. "What's that thing on your leg?"

He pulled a knife partway from a sheath strapped to his thigh. Elle saw the blade glisten, as if alive. Quickly, Ramien pushed it back.

"I'm not allowed to take it out," he said.

"Is it real?" she asked.

"My trainer said it's made of special metal. Scientists designed it to kill Synmen."

"Hi, Ramien," said Elle's mother, approaching.

"Mommy, I want a uniform and new boots. Not black though, pink!" said Elle.

"Ramien, you're so handsome," said her mother. She bent over and kissed him on the cheek, then took Elle's hand. "Elle, come inside. Ramien can't play. Once boys start training, they can't play anymore."

"I can play," said Ramien. "I'm supposed to. It's part of my training."

"That's strange. Your trainer said that?" Elle's mother asked.

Ramien nodded.

"Yay!" said Elle.

Admonishing the two children to stay in the front yard, and Ramien to keep the knife in its sheath, Elle's mother went inside. Alone with Ramien, Elle reached into the bag the scientist gave her.

"Guess what I have," she said excitedly.

"Strawberries and cherries!" said Ramien.

Elle laughed. "A whole bag of them!" She reached in and pulled out a strawberry. The next instant, she heard a thwack.

"Ow!" Ramien yelped, grabbing his forehead as a small rock bounced off his leg. Groaning, he fell over and lay on the grass.

Elle scooted over and laid his head on her lap. "Don't cry, Ramien," she said, petting his head and looking all around for who threw the rock. The streets were empty.

"Let me see." She pulled his hands away, exposing a swollen red bump on his forehead. Slowly, Ramien sat up, touching the bump. He looked at Elle and started crying again. Elle wanted more than anything in the world to make Ramien feel better. She reached into her bag, pulled out a strawberry, took a bite, and handed it to him.

"Best-friend berries," she said.

He ate the whole berry in one big bite. "Best-friend berries," he said, grinning, juice running down his chin.

The pounding stopped. Seconds later, it resumed. Elle giggled and reached into her bag for another strawberry.

———

THE NEXT MORNING, Elle went to work with her mother, and Ramien went with his parents to training. Scientist Fred gave Elle another bag of strawberries and cherries. When Elle arrived home, Ramien was waiting in the front yard. The children laughed and played and ate berries until a sudden wind came up and blew debris into Ramien's eye, causing him to cry out in pain. Again, Elle comforted her best friend.

"Best-friend berries," they sang. The pounding momentarily stopped.

Every day, Elle and Ramien played together when Elle got home. Each time, an accident happened causing Ramien sudden pain, a falling tree branch, a sharp object inside a toy, another thrown rock. Each time, Elle's love made Ramien's pain and fear disappear.

"Best-friend berries," they'd sing, and the pounding would always briefly stop.

One day, when Elle arrived home to find Ramien waiting for her, she saw that he'd been crying. She sat down three feet away so he wouldn't be afraid.

"We can't play anymore," she said. "I don't want you to get hurt again."

"We have to," he said, trembling.

"Why?"

"My trainer said so."

"I have an idea. Wait here, I'll be right back."

Elle ran inside her home to get a blanket. They'd eat best-friend berries and play underneath the blanket. The blanket would protect him. When she returned, he was gone. She walked to his house and knocked. No answer. She returned to the yard, sat down, and waited. An hour passed, then two. The pounding seemed louder than ever.

She picked up all the toys and stacked them in neat piles. Then she set the bag of strawberries and cherries on the ground in case Ramien returned, and went inside.

39

FITZ

THE NEXT MORNING, Elle and her mother left for work. The pounding had grown even louder than the day before. Elle saw the bag of berries still lying on the ground exactly where she'd left them. They went to Ramien's house. No one was home. On the way to work, Elle's mother asked people if they'd seen Ramien. No one had.

Upon their arrival at her mother's work, they were greeted by Mr. Fred, the scientist that Elle's mother worked for. At his side was a boy who seemed a few years older than Elle.

"Good morning," said Mr. Fred cheerfully. "Elle, this is my son, Fitz. You are welcome to play with him and his friends today, if your mother says it's okay." Elle looked excitedly at her mother. Everyone knew that scientists' children were special. They learned to read and write and became scientists or leaders of the community. Tourist children were taught to fight or serve scientists and were never allowed to interact with scientists' children.

"Can I, Mommy?" asked Elle, sensing her mother's hesitation.

Mr. Fred winked at Elle. "Elle's going to learn about science and meet a lot of new friends," he said.

"Mommy?" pleaded Elle.

"Are you sure it's okay?" asked Elle's mother.

Mr. Fred laughed good-naturedly. "I'm in charge, so I'm pretty sure. Fitz, you make sure everyone treats Elle just like she's a scientist's child, understood?"

"Yes, Father," said Fitz, taking Elle's hand.

"You two better get going. You don't want to be late," said Mr. Fred.

"Late for what?" asked Elle's mother.

WHAT LITTLE NERVOUSNESS Elle had because of her mother's hesitation vanished when Fitz smiled, gently took her hand, and led her down the hallway to a large room full of toys but no other children.

"Where are the other children?" asked Elle.

"A special place," said Fitz, lowering his voice. "I'll take you there if you promise not to tell. You can't tell tourists, including your mother."

Excited to be invited to a special play area, Elle agreed. Fitz took her hand again.

"I'm glad you can play with us," he said.

She smiled. She couldn't wait to tell Ramien about her new friend. "What's in the special room?"

"You'll see. We have to hurry, or we'll miss the show," said Fitz.

Elle followed Fitz out of the room, down a long hallway, up stairways, around corners, into elevators, and across a final, long hallway high up in the cavern's ceiling. She could see the entire cavern below. They walked and ran, passing many scientists along the way. All smiled warmly at the two children. Elle felt happy to have a new friend and couldn't wait to reach the special place. A moment later Fitz stopped.

"Look, Elle, that's the tourist area where you live," he said, pointing down toward a vast area of the cavern.

Elle realized she was now inside the shiny black building near where she lived. She looked out at the dirty brown roofs of thousands of tourist homes. Even inside the building, the pounding seemed loud. She imagined how loud the pounding must be on the outside.

"Lab rats," said Fitz, under his breath. Elle sensed the cruelty in his voice.

"What's a lab rat?" she asked.

"Nothing, I'm sorry," he replied, his voice again gentle and reassuring.

"I want to go back," she said.

The elevator door opened. Fitz stepped inside. "C'mon, Elle," he urged. "Almost there, right through this elevator. Everyone's waiting for us in the special room, just below. Then, we can go back if you still want to."

Elle stepped into the elevator. The doors swished closed. Fitz was smiling. Everything would be okay. The door opened. Fitz took her hand and led her into the room.

The room was a large viewing area with windows all around. A dozen children were lined up on one side, looking out the window. They turned and looked at Fitz and Elle, then turned back to what they were looking at.

On the opposite side, Elle saw the tourist area as before, only now the viewing area was lower, so she could see details. She'd never seen her home from above before and wondered if Ramien had returned. Excited, she ran to the window and looked out.

She recognized her house and the front yard where she and Ramien had lain on the grass, holding hands, singing and laughing and chanting "best-friend berries." She saw her toys in the front yard, neatly stacked. The bag of strawberries lay untouched, exactly where she'd left it.

Fitz called to her. "Elle, come over to this side."

She turned to Fitz, who was with the other children on the other side of the room, his arm waving, encouraging her to join them. The other children were laughing and cheering, looking through the windows of the viewing room at whatever was on the other side. Elle walked to their side, curious about what excited them. Fitz moved aside to make space for her at the window. His gesture made her feel welcome. She stepped to the window and looked down into a large room that seemed to take up the entire interior of the building.

Elle saw a long, winding line of people, all tourists. Some she recognized from her neighborhood. On each side of the line stood large, square-headed, mean-looking men. To Elle, they looked like beasts. The line of tourists wound all around the room, stretching end to end, zigzagging left and right, finally ending in the center of the room. Elle gasped. At the end of the line stood a little boy dressed in black. Ramien!

All at once, every square-headed beast man turned and looked up at the window, straight at Elle.

With his eyes fixed on Elle, a beast-man grabbed Ramien's head. The man's long fingers draped down, all the way over Ramien's forehead and face. The beast-man laughed and pushed his fingers into Ramien's eyes. The children laughed and cheered. Elle stepped back. Fitz shoved her forward against the glass.

"You're supposed to watch," he said. "How else you gonna learn about lab rats?"

Ramien flailed, his small hands grabbing at the fingers that squeezed his skull. The beast-man laughed, then shrieked, a long, piercing scream. Every beast-man in the room shrieked. On each side of Elle, children flailed their arms, pretending to be Ramien. Others shrieked and laughed, pretending to be beast-men.

The beast-man lifted Ramien up by the head. His arms and legs swung spasmodically, twitched, then stilled.

"Don't worry, Elle," said Fitz, laughing. "Synmen usually kill by whirling." Elle remembered Ramien telling her he'd been training to kill Synmen.

"That's a Synman?" she asked weakly.

Suddenly, Synmen throughout the room grabbed tourists from the line. One whirled a tourist straight at Elle. He smashed into the thick protective glass. All the Synmen began whirling tourists at Elle. Body after body mashed into the window, inches from Elle's face. Elle tried to back away, but Fitz pushed her face into the window. Bloody mush dripped down the window.

"Uh-oh," said Fitz, laughing. "Look at your boyfriend."

The Synman squeezing Ramien's head looked up at where Elle stood behind the gore-smeared window and smiled. Its fingers pushed slowly into Ramien's eyes. Elle felt Ramien's pain. She felt his legs twitch. She heard their song.

"Strawberries and cherries, best-friend berries."

The Synman lifted Ramien above its head.

"Here comes the whirl," said Fitz, shoving Elle's face even harder against the window.

Elle felt something swell inside her, something white hot, her love for Ramien, and something icy-black, her hate for Synmen, scientists, Fitz, and the children all around her. She screamed. A swell of white-hot and icy-black surged forth.

The pounding stopped. All the Synmen collapsed. Ramien dropped to the ground and scrambled away. Elle stood rigid, motionless, peering through the gore.

Men in white coats pulling a gurney rushed into the room. They grabbed Elle and strapped her to the bed, so tightly her wrists and ankles hurt. Chief Scientist Fred entered the room.

"Shh! Listen!" he commanded. Everyone in the room froze. The pounding was gone. Only Elle's sobs could be heard.

"Good work, Fitz," said Chief Scientist Fred. "You're going to be a great scientist one day."

40

BEACHES AND BUGS

BILLY ZOOMED in the direction of the strongest part of the hate wave.

"Look for a planet with life," he said to Jimee, Brill, Stevens, and his mother. "If it has people, they might need our help."

Before long, maybe a hundred, maybe a thousand years, the friends arrived at a planet teeming with life. Clusters of souls hovered around the planet. Brill, Stevens, Billy, and Anna hovered high above, waiting for Jimee, who trailed behind studying the particles damaged by the wave. When Jimee caught up, all five descended to the planet, Billy in the lead. Swarms of bugs blanketed the land.

"I don't understand," said Brill. "I studied thousands of planets when I led our space program. People should have evolved on this one by now."

"There're no animals either, not a single animal of any kind," said Stevens.

"There are fish. The oceans have billions of fish," said Anna.

"Good, then there will soon be animals," said Brill. "Watch the beaches."

The five souls extended, watching hundreds of beaches all around the planet. Years passed.

"What are we looking for?" asked Billy restlessly.

"There, Billy. Coming out of the water! See that? Over here too!" Brill exclaimed.

Billy watched in awe. On beaches all over the planet, fish were crawling out of the ocean onto land. They used their fins to push themselves across the sand. Some burrowed into the sand, while others with bigger fins moved farther inland.

"The fish are evolving, aren't they, Brill?" asked Billy excitedly.

"Are we seeing fish change into animals?" asked Anna.

"We're witnessing evolution," Brill replied. "Still, it doesn't make sense. Why is this planet evolving so late? Why are there so many—"

"Bugs," Stevens interjected. "Look, here they come."

Swarms of insects descended on the crawling fish, biting, stinging, and leaving any fish that dared to venture from the sea lying dead on the sand. A large cluster of souls accompanied the bugs, acting as frenetically as the insects were.

"Oh no!" said Billy.

"What are those souls doing?" asked Anna.

"They seem to be agitating the bugs," said Jimee.

"I think I know what happened," said Brill. "There used to be animals on the planet, but the insects killed them off when the hate wave hit the planet."

"There might have been people as well," said Jimee, eyeing the souls. "People who were recently evolved and living in harmony, but too primitive to have homes to evade the bugs."

"The bugs are killing anything that moves. Evolution doesn't have a chance," said Brill.

"Those souls seem to be enjoying the bug attacks," said Stevens.

"Help me save the fish!" yelled Billy, zooming into a

massive swarm of insects that had attacked a group of fish crawling onto the sand. After a moment, he called back, "These fish are all dead!"

The insects swarmed furiously, stinging and biting dead carcasses in a buzzing rage. Billy saw a fish a mile down the beach just as it began crawling out of the sea.

"There's another one!" he yelled. The huge fish, now entirely out of the water, attracted the attention of the angry swarm of bugs.

Billy zoomed toward the bugs, concentrated his essence, and swatted himself back and forth through the bugs. Unaffected, the swarm raced toward its prey.

"Help me!" shouted Billy.

Jimee, Anna, and Brill zoomed to join him but could only watch helplessly as the swarm descended on the fish. The fish was doomed. But just as the insects were about to attack, they reversed course and flew away. The fish resumed crawling onto the land in perfect safety. Billy was ecstatic.

"We did it!" he shouted.

No one spoke. Billy looked at his friends. His mother shared his joy. Stevens was controlling the bugs, as he had at their home planet. Jimee was studying the bugs and the frenzied souls among them. Brill seemed ill at ease.

"What's wrong?" asked Billy.

"You transferred with bugs?" asked Brill.

"Stevens did," replied Jimee, still studying the bugs. "It was an accident."

"What? How?" asked Stevens.

"I don't understand?" asked Anna.

"Mother, remember when you were transferred, there was a mist? The mist was for killing bugs before you transferred," said Billy.

"Why? What happens if a bug transfers?" asked Anna.

"Nothing. Bugs die when they transfer," replied Brill. "Unless a bug transfers with a person. Didn't you have a sensor system to ensure the mist killed all the bugs, to guarantee none transferred? That should have been one of the first things your scientists figured out."

The fish had crawled up the beach and disappeared into a tall grassy marsh. Hundreds more fish crawled out of the sea. Stevens kept the bugs away from the crawling fish, but they returned, accompanied by even more souls. A large, angry black wall formed where Stevens held the bugs back.

"There was mist when I transferred. I'm certain I remember the mist," said Stevens. The black bug wall buzzed with anger, fighting his hold on them. Stevens continued. "I remember I looked at Bobby, and then I couldn't see him because of the mist. Then I transferred."

"It's complicated, but I can explain," said Jimee.

"Please do," said Brill.

Eyeing the souls among the bugs, Jimee said, "Remember the notion of people being connected to the universe, the fact that the connection is active, and the theory that—"

"Can we do that blending thing?" asked Billy.

Anna, Stevens, and Brill nodded in agreement.

Jimee opened her mind. The five souls blended, their thoughts and memories became one, and Jimee reminded them that people not yet hit by the hate wave were connected to the fabric of the universe. She theorized that bugs might also be connected to the fabric. Jimee speculated that bugs might even be a type of super large particle facilitating an active connection between the fabric and life, which might explain why bugs were so pervasive, evolving before animals and humans. She replayed the bug saving Bobby from falling to his death, the bug trying but failing to save Stevens from tripping down the stairs, and the bug stuck to the tape after Billy secured Stevens's head to the back of the transfer chair.

"The bug must have been alive when Stevens transferred. That's why Stevens can control them," said Jimee.

"Stevens can even make bugs bite people," Billy added.

"What?" asked Anna.

"I can explain that too," said Jimee.

"Please do."

Jimee revealed that when Stevens had been mad with grief, he'd made bugs bite people who ventured onto Bobby's baseball field, and he'd also used bugs to save a boy from drowning. Jimee described the bugs that entertained the little girls by synchronizing with a fish. She then presented herself sitting on Stevens's deck, and said, "I also have a theory about bugs and sunrises."

Billy offered, "Maybe the fish are somehow connected too."

"Maybe every living thing is connected," Anna said.

"*Was* connected, not anymore," Brill added.

"I can't hold these bugs much longer," said Stevens, straining against the weight of millions of raging insects fighting to attack the crawling fish.

Still blended, the friends watched thousands of fish cross the beach and arrive safely at the marsh.

"Stevens, you're fighting more than angry bugs," Jimee said. "I think those souls are directing the bugs to kill the fish."

"What?" they all asked.

"How is that possible if Stevens was the only one who transferred with a bug?" asked Brill.

"I don't know," said Jimee.

The bug wall inched forward. Stevens pushed them back.

"Maybe all those souls transferred with bugs too," said Anna.

"Maybe, but if so, how?" asked Jimee.

"Every single Great Advance transfer went perfect, except for the last day," said Stevens, his voice shaking from the strain of holding back the swarm.

"Stevens, you're a hero," said Billy.

"He'll have to hold back the bugs for millions of years for

the evolutionary process to have a chance. We'll leave the planet before that, so the fish are doomed," said Jimee.

Billy's sadness overwhelmed the blending. He separated, followed by Jimee and the others.

"I'm sorry, Billy," said Jimee.

"On my planet, after the wave hit, bugs formed angry swarms like this," said Brill. "If the hate wave disconnected bugs from the fabric, maybe that's why they're angry. Like souls, they swarm together but still feel isolated, no longer part of the universe. Jimee, before we deblended, were you about to tell us another theory?"

Jimee nodded and glanced at Stevens.

"I can hold the bugs for a while longer," he said.

Jimee continued. "I was about to present my theory about sunrises and bugs. Our blending was interrupted, so maybe you didn't absorb it."

"I did," said Brill. "You revealed the patterns in the sunrises and that something in the sunrises might have controlled the bugs through the fabric."

Jimee nodded. "If the bugs have lost their connection to the fabric, then whatever was in the sunrise has lost its connection to the bugs," she said.

"That could explain the swarms. Like clusters of souls, bugs might be trying to regain their connection," said Brill.

Billy sensed Stevens straining to contain the bugs. He enveloped Stevens, searching for a way to help.

"There's one more thing," said Jimee. "Stevens, on your deck that last afternoon, I read your journal while you were in the house. You had described the sunrises each morning. Do you remember?"

"Yes," he said. "They were beautiful."

"On the last morning, you recorded the sunrise with a synaptic imager. I found a message within the recording."

"What was the message?" asked Billy.

The pitch-black wall of bugs roared with anger. Billions

now, egged on by millions of souls, edged closer to the fish. Billy blended with Stevens, hoping his thoughts would make Stevens stronger. Anna, Jimee, and Brill joined the blending. Jimee recalled the message. The bugs broke through. Blended as one, the friends absorbed the message.

STAY AWAY OR DIE!

41

THE ROCK AND THE GIRL

CLUSTERED TOGETHER IN A TIGHT GROUP, the friends left the planet, passing thousands of souls rushing in the opposite direction, many screaming insults. Jimee extended into several clusters.

"Those souls aren't from the ball of light and aren't from the Great Advance," she said. "However, they do seem to be coming from our home planet."

"I don't understand," said Stevens.

"Neither do I," said Jimee, but she had a theory. She hoped it wasn't true.

TRACKING THE HATE WAVE, they stopped occasionally so Jimee could study the mutated particles.

They had been following the hate wave for weeks, or years, when they came upon another planet teeming with life.

"That planet is flourishing with people," said Jimee.

"They have no technology, and most live in small villages," said Brill.

"Millions of souls are here too," said Anna.

Jimee extended into a soul cluster.

"Any from the big white ball of souls?" asked Billy.

"This cluster is from the Great Advance," said Jimee.

"What about those souls?" asked Brill, motioning toward a cluster hovering above a village. The five friends descended toward the village.

"These souls seem malicious, more like the ones we encountered on the fish planet," said Brill, zooming higher and a short distance to the side of the village, out of the way of the souls. "Until we know more, let's stay out of their way and observe from a distance."

"How did these people survive the hate wave when Brill's people didn't?" asked Stevens.

"I think I can check without attracting attention," Jimee said, thinning and extending a wisp of herself into the village and wafting among the people.

"Jets of icy-black shoot between people and between particles," she reported. "I also see many white-hot jets of warmth."

"Is the white-hot coming from the particle fabric?" asked Brill.

"No, the fabric is mutated. The white-hot comes directly from the people," replied Jimee. "The souls are entirely focused on the people. I think it's okay to get closer."

"Besides calling us names, what could the souls do to us anyway?" asked Billy.

"Everyone, stay together," said Brill.

The friends descended to hover directly above the people. It was early morning, and they were just waking up. Thousands of souls intermixed with them.

"The souls appear angry," said Stevens. "They rush to anyone who is waking up."

"The people seem okay," said Anna.

"Jimee, what can you sense?" asked Brill.

"The souls are excited by spurts of icy-black and white-hot coming from people as they awake. No energy, neither icy-

black nor white-hot, comes from villagers who are still asleep."
Jimee remembered being blocked from entering the brain of
the sleeping mother while her daughters played beside a pond.

"The brain must seal itself off to guarantee a good night's
sleep," said Brill.

"Fortunately," said Anna. "Look at those crazy souls trying
to blend with those people. It's like they're trying to scare
them. Can you imagine the nightmares?"

"What do you mean, Mother?" asked Billy.

Anna motioned toward a thick cluster of angry souls
rushing toward a person who had just awoken. "What if those
souls could get inside a sleeping person's brain? The nightmares they'd give a person would be terrifying."

The people worked to support the village, gathering, hunting, fishing, and farming. There were angry bugs, and some
souls made bugs sting people, but the people had learned to
protect themselves. They even caught and ate bugs for food.

Brill estimated the people had evolved over the last ten or
twenty thousand years. Based on their intelligence and
mastery of tools, they would soon discover electricity, invent
flying machines, and eventually discover space travel.

The friends watched the people for several days. Children
played, laughing, throwing stones, and chasing each other.
Everything seemed normal.

"They've learned to be good people without help from the
universe," said Stevens.

"Maybe not all good. Look over here," said Brill, pointing
toward two men arguing by a creek at the edge of the village.
Souls hovered around the two men, egging them on.

The argument turned into a vicious fight. Jimee, Stevens,
Billy, and Anna, having never seen people fight before, were
horrified. The men were beating each with their fists and feet.
One man bit the other man's face.

"After the hate wave, my people fought like this," said Brill.

The men fought on. Unable to help, the friends watched

in shocked silence and were relieved when people from the village ran toward the fight.

"Good, they will stop the fight. Wait, what are they doing?" asked Billy.

The villagers surrounded the two men and cheered them on. Young boys and girls were moved up front or lifted onto shoulders so they could see too.

"Jimee, what's happening to the particles now?" asked Brill.

Jimee described icy-black jets shooting between the two men and radiating out into the crowd, only to be absorbed, amplified, and shot back toward the fighters. Souls attempted to interact with the icy-black jets.

Stevens drifted closer. He extended a thin tendril of his essence into the fight. "Ugh! Those aren't men. They're boys, my son Mikey's age!" he said.

The fight was over within minutes. One boy had been thrown onto his back and hit his head on the ground. Exhausted, barely able to move, he lay still while the other boy attacked, smashing his fists into the fallen boy's face. The crowd erupted as the victor raised his hands in triumph, clutching a gouged-out eyeball in each hand. He dropped the eyeballs onto the mutilated boy and staggered back to the village.

The people returned to whatever they had been doing before the fight as if nothing had happened. A dozen children remained behind. They sat on the defeated boy's arms, holding him down, pretending to care for the boy by putting his eyeballs back into his bloody sockets, then pulling the eyes out again. The children took turns at first, then fought over the eyeballs, crushing them. The game was over, so the children returned to the village.

The beaten blind boy lay alone beside the creek. The friends hovered over the boy in horrified shock. The boy began making small wheezing sounds. Bugs, directed by souls, crawled into his eye sockets.

"Those souls are sick," said Anna.

Jimee agreed. "We need to find out more about them."

"Brill, is this what happened on your planet?" asked Stevens.

"Yes and no," answered Brill. "During this fight, the madness spread into the crowd, but the people didn't start fighting themselves. On my planet, the crowd made fights worse by joining in, killing one another, often killing the original fighters. Here, the crowd only cheered."

As Brill was speaking, an old lady walked down to the creek where the boy lay. She squatted over the boy and spat in his face. Then she walked back to the village.

"I sensed particles around her the whole time," said Jimee. "The particles are mutated-normal. By that, I mean the particles weren't radiating icy-black toward the woman. She wasn't radiating icy-black either. That woman was not mad, angry, or insane."

"Just cruel," said Stevens.

"They've learned to live without the universe's help to be good, but there's nothing to stop them from being cruel," said Brill.

"That's not living," said Billy.

The friends watched the people into the evening. Everything was peaceful. Everyone seemed to go on with their lives, but the five souls were unsettled. After everyone had gone to sleep, some souls noticed the friends and heckled them.

To avoid a confrontation, the friends moved to the other side of the planet where souls were distracted because the population was awake. Anna wanted to leave the planet and zoom to someplace warm, not yet mutated by the hate wave, but agreed to stay longer to learn more about the sick, angry souls, and how the hate wave was mutating the particle fabric of the universe and affecting people.

The friends found another group of people, similar in size to the group they had just left, but with an even greater concentration of souls mingling among them. Watching from above, the friends zoomed higher when the people slept to avoid being bullied by frustrated souls.

The people seemed more peaceful than those on the other side of the planet, but they had confusing customs. Each morning, they walked across a field and up a steep hill to a large rock where they got down on their knees and looked at it.

"What's so important about that rock?" asked Billy.

The five friends descended to the rock. Jimee focused on the particles, then looked at Brill, who had also extended a sliver of herself into the rock.

"If you can sense things, I should be able to as well," Brill said.

"I want to try," said Billy.

Anna and Stevens joined too, and all five extended into the rock.

"Do you sense anything?" Brill asked Jimee.

"No, the particles are normal," replied Jimee. "I mean, mutated-normal. It's just a rock." Jimee sensed Brill, Stevens, Billy, and Anna knowingly glance at each other. "What?" she asked.

"What's the good of all your observational powers if you can't see what's right in front of you?" asked Brill, grinning. "It's not just a rock. Look at the people and the rock."

Jimee embedded herself deeper, spreading herself throughout the rock. The other four retracted and hovered just above.

"I sense two large cracks," she said. "It'll break apart soon, in three or four hundred years, but it's just a rock, nothing more."

"I see it," said Anna.

"Me too," said Stevens.

"I do too," said Billy.

Jimee retracted from the rock. "None of you are even sensing anything," she said.

"Don't look at the particles. Just look at the rock," said Stevens.

"Oh, I see now," said Jimee.

The rock was the shape of a big head with holes carved out for the eyes, nose, and mouth. The eyes seemed to look directly down at the people, who looked back.

"Jimee, do you sense icy-black or white-hot between the people?" asked Brill.

Jimee extended among the people directly in line with the rock's eyes. "It's strange, like they are all searching for something. The energy from each person's brain is reaching out to the rock."

"To find what?" asked Stevens.

"I don't know."

"The rock seems to help them feel better, somehow," said Billy.

The friends remained on the planet to learn why the people knelt before the rock. Soon, the friends began feeling a hypnotic attraction, not to the rock, but to the people while they knelt before it. One day, the entire village came. With the whole village kneeling, the hypnotic effect on the five friends and other hovering souls intensified.

An older man stood and began chanting. Everyone else remained kneeling and began chanting with the older man. The hypnotic vibes felt wonderful. Thousands more souls arrived.

"Look at how many souls are arriving just in time," said Brill. "It's like they already know what's going to happen."

The older man raised his arms up high and toward the rock. Still chanting, he turned back toward the crowd and took the hand of a little girl. She was about five years old and wore a white dress. The man led her toward the rock, looking up into the rock's carved eyes. The chanting intensified. Thousands of souls joined in, including Anna. Billy enveloped his mother, quieting her.

The older man reached into his clothing, withdrew a knife, and pulled the blade across the front of the child's neck, slicing her throat wide open. Blood gushed down the front of her white dress. She gurgled, reached for her neck, and fell forward. The man caught her and laid her down at the base of the rock. The girl twitched and went still. The people stopped chanting, stood up, walked down the hill to their village, and returned to their daily routine.

Hovering tightly together, the friends rose to a position a few hundred feet above the village. Some souls had followed the people back to the village, but many souls remained.

"What are the souls still doing at the rock?" asked Stevens.

Jimee descended and returned a second later. "Chanting," she said.

"Let's go," Anna said, shivering.

"I agree," said Brill, moving away from the planet.

"Me too," said Billy, following.

"Wait, what are the souls chanting?" asked Stevens.

Jimee extended into the souls, then retracted and joined her friends.

"Kill more girls. Kill more girls," she said.

42

USURPED

CLUSTERED TOGETHER, the friends followed the hate wave, not to explore planets but to get ahead of it to someplace warm. They passed by many advanced planets with dead or dying populations, and many primitive planets thriving with people. All planets with human life were thick with souls. As Jimee scanned each planet, she reported what she sensed to her friends.

"Why are only primitive people surviving?" asked Billy.

"I have a theory about that," said Brill. "Advanced planets are less capable of surviving the hate wave than primitive planets, because advanced civilizations have existed longer, and have evolved to become more dependent on the goodness in the fabric. The less advanced a culture is, the less dependent they've become on the fabric," she speculated.

"Makes sense," said Jimee. "Primitive life has largely evolved within the mutated fabric, so it has minimal need to adapt. But advanced life has already evolved, so it has difficulty adapting."

"What about the rock?" asked Stevens.

"The rock is a mystery," replied Brill. "Let's look for a planet where life is evolving from its primordial form. I believe the culture will hardly notice being hit by the hate wave."

Jimee agreed. "Life that evolves after the hate wave hits might thrive in the mutated fabric, growing even stronger."

"Our home planet is directly ahead," said Stevens. "It took a direct hit from the hate wave."

The five friends approached in silence.

"Our planet had good people when I was last here," said Anna.

"Was there an advanced culture?" asked Brill.

"Not technologically, but the people were civilized and socially sophisticated," said Jimee. "They had discovered electricity. The planet had cities, art, politics, and sports."

"And baseball," said Billy.

"Doesn't it seem strange that all sentient life in the universe is human?" asked Brill.

"What do you mean?" asked Anna.

"Not only is all intelligent life human, but it also has the same cultural preferences, including baseball."

"That is strange," said Stevens.

"It makes sense. It's a fun game," said Billy.

"Scientifically, it makes no sense," said Brill.

"It makes sense," said Jimee.

Billy nodded, grinning broadly. Jimee explained.

"Prior to the Great Advance, we believed we were the only sentient life in the universe. When we transferred, we verified that by zooming everywhere in the universe. Primitive life existed, but we found no sentient life. Soon, we missed our human existence. We began concentrating around planets with emerging life, yearning for our previous physical lives. Energy from our spiritual essence excited the particle fabric, which excited the emerging life, stimulating evolution."

Brill interrupted. "Thus, shaping all evolution throughout the entire universe toward humanity."

Jimee continued. "After humans evolved, souls became even more lonely, desperate to be physical again, hovering around the humans, trying to experience the lives the humans were living. The particle fabric absorbed this energy too."

Brill interrupted again. "Imprinting the social and cultural template of the souls from your planet onto humanity everywhere in the universe."

"Yes," said Jimee.

Brill continued. "So, to summarize, the Great Advance transferred everyone on your planet, the only humans in the universe, effectively wiping out humanity. Then human souls from the Great Advance roamed the universe, molding all future life in humanity's own image, usurping natural evolution that would have created a diversity of sentient life, and spreading humanity in the sole image of your home planet throughout the universe."

"Wow," said Billy.

"That's not all," said Brill. "Then those same human souls mutated the universe, dooming all sentient life, which had already been preempted by humanity, to an existence of hate and cruelty."

No one spoke. After an unknown amount of time, Brill motioned toward Jimee, Stevens, Billy, and Anna's home planet. Thousands of souls zoomed from the planet, going in all directions. Many shrieked wildly.

"Something strange is happening," she said.

"I understand what you said about humanity and the universe," said Billy.

"Not that, Billy. I mean right now, on your home planet. Jimee, can you determine how long since the hate wave hit?"

"I can't measure time anymore," answered Jimee, extending herself into the fabric. "Maybe a few thousand years."

"Long enough to see how the people adapted, if at all," said Brill.

"I hope they haven't all killed themselves," said Billy.

"Let's go find out," said Jimee.

43

IDIOTS

IT WAS GOING to be a good morning. No, a great morning. No, an absolutely unbelievable morning. It was another of his very ridiculously fabulous mornings. How many super fantastic mornings he'd had, Howard didn't know. *Whoosh poof.* Howard had been having mornings like this for a long time.

Howard remembered his excitement when he'd first learned about the killers. The idiots had been killing since probably the day they were born. Psycho idiots. Probably killed their mothers right after. The stories that had come out during their trials were crazy. "A" students had killed their teachers. Star athletes killed their coaches. Babies, kids, old people, sick people, all killed by the sicko idiots. Howard grinned, imagining. The sickos probably even killed dead people who they'd dug up and pretended to kill again.

How'd they get away with killing for so long? That's what everyone wanted to know. Idiot police didn't know. Idiot judges found out during the trials that the maniacs had help. At first, it was thought only dozens of crazies were involved. During the trials, it was discovered there were thousands of sickos, including the idiot police. That's how the bastards got away with it for so long. Not anymore! Psycho, sicko, maniacs. Howard chuckled. Today would be fun. Every day was fun.

The news always said that all the sickos had been caught. Don't worry, it was now safe, said the news. All five hundred thirty-four thousand six hundred sixty-nine murdering maniacs had been captured and put behind bars. Howard laughed. Every day, the news announced all sickos had been caught, don't worry, you are now safe. Every day, the news was wrong. More sicko idiots meant more fun. Howard loved the news.

According to the news, the idiot police used a super-top-secret brain-testing machine to prove the maniacs were guilty. Once, they'd tested Howard, and that had made him nervous. Howard knew he wasn't a killer. Well, maybe he was, but killing was his job, his duty to society. Someone had to do it. How else would the murdering idiots get killed?

The sickos had been tried, found guilty, and sentenced to die by means of Howard. On this wonderful, amazing day, Howard was going to do what he loved, what he was trained to do, what he'd been doing for years—throw the switch. *Whoosh poof.* The idiot killers would be gone. Howard thought of the chairs. The chairs were beauties, but to be the best whoosh poofer took skill and passion. Howard was the best whoosh poofer of all the executioners.

Before the chairs, executions were carried out in numerous ways, determined by a vote of the people. The only people who didn't vote were the killers being voted on. Many people voted to shoot, boil, hang, or chop off the killers' heads. Idiots. They didn't understand the chairs. Howard understood the chairs. Woe to the sicko idiot Howard strapped into a chair.

There were one hundred and three chairs in Howard's building. New chairs were being found all the time. Howard knew of at least three other whoosh-poofing stations.

He grinned, remembering the story about how the chairs were found. A construction crew had been digging and excavated a building with fifty chairs inside. The building was a story all by itself. It was airtight and strong. The construction company couldn't break it open for months. They made special tools to bash it apart. The stupid idiots smashed half the chairs in the process. They found more buildings later and were more careful.

The story about the first chair was funny. After breaking open the building, the construction company had put the chairs in a warehouse somewhere. Then someone had sat in a chair, put the helmet contraption on, and pulled the switch. *Whoosh poof*, the idiot was gone. Howard always laughed thinking about it. The switch was located in the back and was hard to reach, but the idiot still found it. Five or six idiots got whoosh poofed before the powers that be figured out the real purpose for the chairs: killing sicko idiot psychos.

Some people are just lucky, thought Howard. He wished he'd been alive when the first psychos were whoosh poofed. If so, maybe he'd be called the father of whoosh poofing. Maybe he'd even be on the news, commenting gravely, assuring people not to worry, that the father of whoosh poofing was keeping them safe.

Howard's first whoosh-poofing victim was a bad man. The idiot didn't seem that bad to Howard, but no one seemed bad when they got to Howard. A bunch of higher-ups attended Howard's first execution by chair. They lined up on a piece of tape that Howard had placed across the floor to look more official. Howard took his job seriously, but he hated higher-ups. The room was hot, humid, smelly, and buggy, dense with flies, gnats, bees, crawling things of all kinds. The idiot higher-ups were miserable but tried to look official. Howard liked the heat and loved the bugs. With the higher-ups watching, he behaved professionally. Professionals were careful, methodical, and took time to do things right.

Howard wrinkled his forehead as he positioned the bad man in the chair, making it seem difficult to get the straps just right. He looked gravely at the helmet contraption before placing it on the bad man, making a show of adjusting to the left, then to the right. Howard suppressed a smile, watching the idiot sweat like a pig. Bugs covered the man's face, sticking to his sweat. Howard touched the helmet as if adjusting it. As if moving the helmet even mattered. He made the process look official as hell.

Howard's idiot boss stood with the higher-ups, feet planted on the tape, right in the middle, looking official. Howard daydreamed about whoosh poofing his boss all the time. He waited for the idiot's nod, then grim-faced and official-like, Howard pulled the switch.

Whoosh poof.

The bad man was gone. That had been the first execution. Now, decades later, Howard still had one hundred and three chairs, a dedicated team of fellow executioners, and a wonderful life. The morning was gonna be great. Howard hadn't done the math, but he estimated that by whoosh poofing one hundred and three people at once, he and his team had been executing six hundred people an hour, or six thousand a day. He laughed, considering there were hundreds of additional chairs in other whoosh-poofing stations. That meant gazillions of crazy, psycho, idiots had been whoosh poofed to wherever they went, which of course was nowhere.

Vaporizing psycho killer idiots is my kind of fun, thought Howard.

44

OLD GRAY CONCRETE BUILDING

JIMEE ANXIOUSLY SCANNED her home planet, sensing the same worry and trepidation in Stevens, Billy, and Anna. Hundreds of millions of souls clustered around the planet. Millions seemed to be leaving, zooming away in all directions.

"Where are they going?" asked Anna.

"There're almost ten billion people," said Brill.

Jimee had already counted. "Nine billion nine hundred nineteen million two hundred eighty—"

Billy interrupted. "They've done well!"

"Let's go to the baseball field first," said Stevens. "I spent hundreds of years there, so we should be able to learn the most about what has happened since."

"Something doesn't feel right," said Jimee, eyeing a large cluster of souls. "Stay together."

Stevens led the way. Where the baseball field had once been, there was now a large, old gray concrete building. The surrounding land was unkempt, thick with weeds. A few souls hovered outside the building. Countless more clustered inside.

"What's that sound? Are those souls shrieking?" asked Anna.

"There must be people inside," said Stevens.

"Nine hundred forty-seven," said Jimee.

Brill extended a thin sliver inside. "I count eight hundred forty-four," she said. "Ugh, something horrible is happening!"

"Wait here," said Jimee, extending herself into the building.

Angry swarms of bugs roamed throughout. Intense waves of icy-black surged from everyone inside, pulsing across the interior space, amplified and re-amplified by each person. Twenty-three emitted mutated-normal particles, but they too were affected by the icy-black surges—and, strangely, seemed to enjoy them immensely. Jimee recounted the people in the building before returning to the group.

"There are eight hundred and twenty-one people in cages, all emitting the strongest surges of icy-black particles I've ever seen. They are all insane. Twenty-three people seem different, and they aren't in the cages," she reported.

"Different how?" asked Brill.

"They're less insane, or more," said Jimee, "and they're wearing protective suits."

"That's a total of eight hundred forty-four, so Brill was right," said Stevens.

"I think we were both right," Brill said. "I count only seven hundred forty-one people now."

Jimee poked into the building and back. "Seven hundred eighteen in cages, same twenty-three in suits," she said. "Brill's right, only seven hundred forty-one people now."

"That's one hundred three fewer people each time," said Stevens.

"What's happening?" asked Billy.

"Let's go inside and find out," said Brill.

"Stay together, match my movements as I spread throughout the building," said Jimee.

She entered the building and spread her essence from wall to wall, slowly, to fully sense what was happening. She felt her friends retch at the sickening evil. Steel cages held the meanest, cruelest, most hateful people imaginable. In another room was a long row of chairs. Anna concentrated her essence around one.

"Oh no!" she exclaimed. "These are transfer chairs from the Great Advance!"

"One hundred three chairs to be exact," said Brill. The chairs were lined up side by side. Bugs attacked everything, including each other, feeding on the filth lining the chairs. Cutting through the icy-black, Jimee sensed a surge of anger from Brill.

"How did this happen?" Brill demanded. "After the Great Advance, you left the chairs intact? You didn't destroy them?"

The door opened. A man wearing a protective suit walked in. Chuckling, he walked to the side of the room opposite the chairs and opened a large door. Naked, screaming men from the cages were herded into the room by more men wearing protective suits and wielding electric-shock batons and baseball bats.

"One hundred three naked men, one per chair," said Jimee, "and twenty-two more men in protective suits."

Angry, burrowing, biting bugs covered the men from head to toe. Souls egged the bugs on. Some actively controlled the bugs. One by one, each naked man was dragged and bound to a chair by one of the twenty-two men.

The chuckling man followed behind, fastening each naked man's head into a helmet attached to the chair. He repeated the process until all one hundred three chairs held a naked, screaming, bug-covered man.

The twenty-two men in the protective suits left the room, closing the door behind them. The chuckling man remained. He walked to the chair at the end of the row and stood, watching. The man in the last chair squirmed in agony as thousands of angry bugs feasted on his flesh, burrowing deep into the warm, bloody mush of his body.

"He's still alive," said Anna.

"The man in the suit is going to pull the switch," said Billy.

"Whoosh poof," said the man.

The machine emitted a *whoosh* hissing sound, followed by a shorter *poof* sound. The bug-covered man in the chair vanished. The man in the protective suit chuckled and moved to the next chair. The naked man strapped to it was quiet, his eyes and mouth squeezed shut.

"Scream," said the chuckling man, slapping the naked man's face.

The captive shook his head. The chuckling man pulled a large knife from a sheathe at his waist and jammed it into the naked man's thigh. The captive screamed, his mouth wide open. Hundreds of bugs swarmed in.

"Whoosh poof," the man said again, laughing.

Jimee, Stevens, Billy, and Anna stared at the empty chair. The *whoosh-poof* sound came with no accompanying mist to kill the bugs. Jimee knew the mist came from tanks attached to each chair. She scanned the tanks. Most were empty, all would be soon. Thousands of bugs were being transferred with each person.

"These people still use electricity. How'd they figure out how to operate the chairs?" demanded Brill.

Jimee had already extended a sliver of herself around the planet, seeking to answer Brill's question, when Billy answered.

"We learned that the chairs have perpetual energy generators. So, if the power grid failed during the Great Advance, the chairs would still work."

Brill looked at Billy, quizzically.

"I learned that in training," said Billy.

Stevens pointed to the perpetual energy generator beneath each chair. "We didn't want to leave people stranded," he said.

"Well, it worked," said Brill sarcastically.

45

RUN!

JIMEE LED the friends out of the building and high above the planet. They watched wave after wave of vicious, insane souls transfer into space. Some returned to the planet, seeking vengeance, amplifying icy-black fear and hate, their terrified screams now savage shrieks. Others zoomed away, howling furiously.

With each batch of one hundred three transfers from the old gray concrete building, the five friends gathered closer together, intertwining their essences into a glowing ball of mutually reinforcing strength and support.

"Jimee, Brill, look at the other side of the planet," said Billy. "There's another building transferring people in addition to the one we saw."

"Three more," said Jimee.

"These people survived the hate wave, but it made them sick, and they're transferring the sickest," said Brill.

"Millions and millions of cruel, sick souls," said Stevens.

"Not souls, demons," said Billy.

Suddenly, Jimee screamed, and not from fear but from a searing burning pain. Anna screamed next. Then Billy, Brill, and Stevens.

Jimee heard shrieks of laughter and realized they were

being attacked by the insane transferred souls. Although small and compressed, their glowing ball of white essence in an icy-black universe wasn't hard to detect. The evil souls dived at the light, penetrating their soul-ball refuge, shooting cold, dark, searing pain into each friend. With each cry of pain, the evil souls shrieked with sadistic glee.

"Jimee, Billy!" yelled Brill, "We have to run!"

"Run where?" yelled Anna.

"To the front of the hate wave where it's warm and light! The demons might not follow," yelled Brill.

"Stay together! Wrap around each other to strengthen our ball!" yelled Jimee.

Anna wrapped her essence around Billy, Brill wrapped around Anna, Stevens wrapped around Brill, and Jimee enveloped them all. From the outside of their supportive ball, Jimee charted their path. Careful to zoom at the same speed to maintain their ball, the friends raced to overtake the hate wave. Millions of the evil demon souls chased the ball of friends across the universe.

Through galaxy after galaxy, from solar system to solar system, past planet after planet, the friends zoomed. Most of the planets were cold and forbidding, unable to sustain life. Other planets, rich with life, had been traumatized by the hate wave. One planet was experiencing massive explosions, destroying itself in a world-wide war. Anna convulsed, causing a slowdown. Demons shot into the friends, scoring direct hits of searing pain.

"Don't look," Jimee shouted. "I will describe what I sense!"

On another planet, devastating plagues raged. Suppressing her screams, Jimee relayed everything she sensed.

"All these planets were hit by the hate wave," she yelled.

An entire planet seemed to be on fire. The sky burned, the oceans boiled. On another, hundreds of spaceships loaded with people flew straight into the sun. The icy-black of the particle fabric suddenly thickened.

"The crest must be near," Jimee yelled. "If we get beyond the crest of the hate wave to the other side, we might have a chance."

Millions more shrieking souls joined the chase. Jimee sensed the terror in her friends as their ball began to unravel. She squeezed the friends together, so tightly she could no longer distinguish one from another.

"There, up ahead. I see a shimmer. Do you see it?" she yelled.

Stevens screamed. Billy cried out in pain. Jimee increased her focus as their soul-ball kept unraveling. She squeezed, tightening their embrace again. The friends came back together. She accelerated straight at the shimmer.

"Not far, stay together!" she yelled.

"There's a wall of evil souls at the crest!" yelled Brill.

"Faster, blast through!" shouted Jimee.

The friends slammed into the wall. Shrieking demons sliced into their ball. Anna screamed. A dive-bombing demon tore through Brill, separating a thread of her essence from the group. Stevens reached out and pulled the separated thread back to Brill.

Jimee saw the crest of the hate wave. They might make it. A ten-pack of dive-bombing demons slammed into their ball. Direct hit. All ten demons exploded from the inside out. Layers unraveled. Threads trailed.

Jimee surged toward the crest, holding on to her friends with all her might.

46
YOU LIVE IN A SPACESHIP?

DISORIENTED, Jimee fought to regain her bearings.

Their ball had unraveled completely just before tumbling wildly over the crest of the hate wave. After being in the icy-black for so long, Jimee shivered reflexively in the soothing, warm light. She looked back, hoping the shrieking demons wouldn't follow. Thousands were now streaking through space, intending to cross the crest.

"Regroup, here they come!" she yelled.

Hateful demons shot across the crest, plunging from the icy-black into the warm light. The fabric of the pure and good universe responded instantly, unleashing a massive rebuttal to the evil. There was nowhere to run. Pitch-black became bright white. Icy-cold became molten hot. Hateful shrieks became confused whimpers. All became quiet. The fiery-hot mass that had been demons returned to a soft, warm light. No more demons attempted to cross the hate wave.

"Look, the demon souls have learned not to cross the wave," said Billy.

"They know to follow the crest, though," said Brill, staring at the thousands of demon souls surfing the icy-black crest of the hate wave, shrieking and laughing hysterically.

"We escaped," said Billy. "Why are they laughing?"

Jimee and Brill scanned the crest of the hate wave. Demons pointed hateful tendrils at Billy, still laughing. Billy edged toward the wave, confused. Stevens stayed at Billy's side.

"I think they're laughing at you," said Stevens.

"The crest of the hate wave spans endlessly," said Brill. "There's no way around it."

The hate wave rolled closer, forcing all four to retreat.

"Stay back," said Jimee.

Millions of evil souls now amassed against the crest of the wave. All seemed to be mocking Billy.

"Why are they laughing at me?" he asked.

"Keep moving," said Jimee, zooming back a short distance so they could talk uninterrupted by the gleeful shrieks. Brill and Stevens joined her.

Billy remained near the crest. "Hey, where's . . . what's that?" he asked.

Behind the crest, behind the mass of shrieking demon souls, Jimee saw a black spot where stars should have been. Stars twinkled around the spot, but within it was only pitch-black. Jimee imagined how icy cold the black spot must be. She extended a sliver of her essence to investigate, stopping at the crest of the hate wave. The black spot moved. Demon souls raced to get out of its way. Jimee froze. Sensing the black spot sensing her, she slowly retracted her essence from the crest.

"Move back, everyone," she whispered. She doubted the black spot could hear her, but there was no way to know for sure.

"What is it?" asked Stevens.

"I don't know. Stay together and keep moving back."

"Wait! That's my mother!" yelled Billy, pointing across the crest again.

Pieces of Anna floated across the icy-blackness. The black spot held what remained of her, struggling and screaming, while demons ripped her apart. Anna stopped struggling. The black spot let her go. Shredded into billions of pieces, Billy's mother drifted aimlessly into space and disappeared into the icy-black. Billy rushed the crest. Brill and Stevens raced to stop him. Jimee focused on the black spot. For a moment, she sensed an innocent little girl, then felt pure hate.

The black spot motioned, sending demons into a shrieking frenzy, dancing around blackened fragments of Billy's mother, pretending to hug and kiss each fragment.

Billy would have crossed the crest but for Brill and Stevens blending with him. Jimee joined, and memories merged. A little boy, Nathan, comforted his twin sister, Nikky, with a song. Brill began singing the song to Billy. Jimee and Stevens sang too. Billy wept uncontrollably.

Inches away, millions of evil souls shrieked. Some darted across the crest. The white-hot sizzled, forcing the demons back. Jimee felt the agony of Billy, the heartache of Brill, and the remorse of Stevens. The friends sang together. Hundreds of years passed. Jimee kept watch, moving steadily, staying just ahead of the advancing wave.

"I'm okay now. Thank you," Billy said, separating. Demons shrieked furiously on the other side. Billy ignored them. Jimee sensed his unusual strength had returned.

"Those were good songs," said Billy.

"Sung for a friend," Brill said.

Billy smiled. "Sung by friends."

Demons at the crest went berserk. Sparks flew as some tried to cross.

"There's a planet over there," said Brill. "Let's go to the other side, out of sight of the wave."

The friends zoomed toward the planet. Safely behind the planet, Jimee wanted to discuss the black spot but was unsure how to begin without upsetting Billy.

"What was that blackness that killed my mother?" demanded Billy.

"Whatever it is, it's tracking us," said Jimee.

"It's in command of the demons too," said Brill.

"Did that black thing follow us here from our home planet?" asked Stevens.

"I think it joined the chase along the way," answered Jimee.

"What do we do now?" asked Billy.

Jimee didn't know. She looked back at the hate wave. It was coming and would overtake them eventually, even if they ran. Ultimately, the entire warm, light universe would be corrupted and mutated into icy-black. Jimee sensed the fabric's immune system work to brighten the increasing gloom of the group, despite them being disconnected souls. The warm light began to cool, so depressed was the friends' collective state of mind. Suddenly, Jimee felt a new presence.

"Hello," said a voice.

Jimee had heard stories of people relaxing, napping on a beach or listening to music, and being surprised so suddenly the person would age ten years in a single nanosecond. Upon hearing the voice, her first thought was to be thankful they were no longer physical. If so, they would surely have died of old age from the shock.

"Hello," said the voice again.

Billy came to his senses first. "Hello," he said. "Who are you?"

Jimee scanned all around. She felt Brill scanning too.

"Nice to meet all four of you," said the voice.

"Where are you?" asked Stevens.

Jimee had already deduced the answer to Stevens's question. She'd sensed the voice within the fabric as if it came from a soul hovering among them. Since no other soul was hovering nearby, it had to be projecting from somewhere else. Jimee connected with Brill, who had three theories. The voice could be coming from a demon behind the crest, or from the black spot, or maybe from the planet.

Jimee extended around the planet, then rejoined her friends. "The voice is coming from a man on the planet," she announced.

"You're physical?" Stevens asked the voice.

"How can you talk to us?" asked Billy.

"He has a synaptic interface," said Jimee. "He's using the interface as a portal."

"Do you need help?" asked Billy.

"I do. In return, maybe I can help you," replied the voice.

"How can we help you?" asked Jimee, truly at a loss how she could help a stranded person.

"My spaceship is damaged."

"We will definitely help you," Billy said to the man, then addressed Jimee, Stevens, and Brill. "How can we help him?"

"First, we need to learn more about his situation and how he got here," answered Jimee, descending.

The friends followed her to a small spaceship buried halfway into a hill and found a young man inside, connected to a synaptic portal.

"What happened to your ship?" Jimee asked.

"Wow. You live in a spaceship," said Billy.

"More like a ground ship now," said the man, then more seriously, "You want to know about the black spot."

"How do you know about the black spot?" asked Jimee immediately.

"Billy, I'm sorry about your mother," said the man.

"That happened hundreds of years ago," said Brill. "How can you possibly know what happened to Billy's mother?"

"I will tell you, but it's a long story," the man replied.

"Our only constraint is a hate wave, demons, and a murderous black spot that will overtake us in a few hundred thousand years," said Jimee.

The man turned a dial on his synaptic portal, extending his essence directly toward the black spot. Jimee sensed sadness overwhelm him. He retracted his essence back to the planet.

"Then I better get started," he said quietly. "Billy, as you noted, I live in this spaceship. I look through this portal to see who might be coming and whether they intend to help me or hurt me."

"Who would want to hurt you?" asked Billy.

PART THREE

SYNMEN

47

ROBOTS

BEFORE I TELL you about myself, I must tell you about my planet.

My people were enlightened, cultured in art, literature, science, and technology, and were driven by a passion for exploration and discovery. After millennia of advancement, our home world became fully known to us, so we built spaceships and traveled to all the planets in our solar system.

Of the eleven planets in our solar system, we colonized four. Six other less hospitable planets we used for deep space research. On these, scientists built enormous ships and traveled to distant planets farther and farther from our home system. After thousands of years of exploration, we reached the limit of our discovery because spaceships could only travel so far piloted by humans who could only live so long.

What followed was an age of beauty. We continued to advance as a people, not by discovery of the universe but by living in harmony with one another. Love and happiness united us. Thousands of ships flew continuously between the planets, transporting families and friends. Each of the five populated planets emphasized a specific kind of beauty— music, literature, nature, architecture, and the human mind.

Then scientists made a discovery that changed our society

forever—how to connect our minds to robots using synaptic interfaces. The breakthrough enabled people to literally feel the robots and control them using only their minds.

Every aspect of society adopted this new technology, from the mundane in the home, such as children's toys or kitchen appliances, to the exotic in deep space. Scientists built new ultra-long-range spaceships with synaptic interfaces to explore deep space from the safety of our home planet. New synaptic robots were built to study the deepest seas, the most violent volcanoes, the center of our planet, even the center of the sun. Finally, microscopic synaptic interfaces implanted in our bodies revolutionized our understanding of human physiology.

This last discovery led to the invention of a new generation of synaptic robots designed to replicate a human body.

These new robots were designed to be physiologically identical to humans to enable them to freely move about in our society using existing infrastructure, except for one important difference. Scientists constructed the new robots using the most advanced materials known. Every muscle was stronger, every nerve more sensitive, every bone unbreakable.

The new robots were called Synmen. They were so sophisticated that each Synman became an extension of the person connected to it through its portal. Because Synmen were physiologically identical to humans, doctors trained to heal humans could repair damaged Synmen. However, Synmen were built to be so strong they never suffered injuries. They were controlled by people using synaptic portals, much like the one I'm using to tell you this story.

The prototypes were sexless but bulky, so they looked like men. I think being based on synaptic technology and looking like men was why they were named Synmen. As manufactured, all of them shared a common boxy look. Experienced controllers could reshape the bone and muscle structure of each, however, maintaining any form other than the standard boxy shape required immense skill and constant mental focus. Most controllers left their Synmen looking the same as originally manufactured. Synmen became deeply integrated into our society, for work and play. The robots kept people safe by doing jobs that were dangerous. Teams of Synmen provided entertainment by playing sports and performing incredible acrobatics. We even developed new sports with special versions of Synmen that could fly. Our society became so comfortable with the robots that we accepted them as if they were actually the people controlling them.

As amazing as Synmen were in everyday use, the advances the technology brought to our space program were extraordinary. Impervious to the inhospitable conditions of space, ageless, and controlled by human hosts, Synmen made the entire galaxy our home.

48

TWITCHES

Eventually, Synmen began experiencing two problems that scientists didn't figure out for a long time.

First, people began to hear noise in the portal interfaces used to control their robots. Scientists couldn't find the source of the noise. Because it didn't occur all the time and didn't affect the operation of the Synmen, people continued to use them.

The second problem was twitching. Ten or twenty years after the noises began, the Synmen began twitching unexpectedly, making small jerks like nervous tics. Subtle at first, the person controlling the Synman rarely noticed it. However, when the tics began happening more frequently, scientists knew something was wrong. Why should a finger jerk, a leg twitch, or an eye blink? The nervous systems of the Synmen were controlled by people's minds through synaptic portals. Scientists worried something was interfering with the Synmen's nervous systems. Further confounding scientists, when people disconnected from their Synmen, the twitching continued. As with the mysterious noise, scientists were unable to figure out what was happening.

Accidents started happening. Small at first, unimportant. However, something as insignificant as a Synman's hand twitching while holding a glass became serious if the twitch occurred while the Synman was holding a child. Some tragic accidents happened. Twitching Synmen became a public safety issue, and the problem wasn't limited to the ones on the planets. The space program operated thousands of synaptically controlled spaceships, called Synships. Minor twitches in a Synship caused sudden changes in direction or speed. Synships began crashing into each other, and into planets. Some flew into deep space never to be seen again.

Scientists were stymied. Unable to figure out what had gone wrong, they decided to disable all Synmen. All the Syn robots were taken offline, including Syn appliances, Syn toys, and Synships. Billions of the machines were stored in giant warehouses on the outlying planets. Massive Synships, too large to store, were abandoned in wide orbits around the sun. Scientists continued to study the problem, but until a solution was found, taking the Syn machines out of service protected everyone.

Sooner than people imagined, things got back to normal. Within a few years, people adapted to living without Syn technology. The biggest regret was the loss of the deep space program. Some of our deep space Synships had just detected life and were about to investigate when we called the ships back and placed them in storage.

History describes the next period as a renaissance of wonder. Except in scientific research, Syn technology came to be remembered as a blessing, an important step in the advance of civilization that led to a more wonderful world.

This belief became so accepted that hundreds of years later, when scientists discovered how to prevent the twitches, Syn technology was no longer important. So the correction was never implemented.

49

INVASION

OUT OF NOWHERE, for no reason, people turned angry and cruel. I mean everyone, everywhere, on all eleven planets. The change did not happen gradually, but all at once. One day, everyone got mad. People started fighting. Kids and parents fought. People fought over unimportant matters. Friends fought. Even bugs seemed to get angry. Then something completely unforeseen happened, something that had never happened in the history of our planet. A person intentionally killed another person.

One hundred billion people on all eleven planets heard about the first intentional killing ever. People were so stunned that everything stabilized, but not for long. New fights broke out, worse than before. Killings happened every day, too many to count.

Violence became accepted as part of society. Changes were made to control the violence. Administrators responsible for managing cities formed special organizations to provide help and support. People calmed down, at least when the helpers were present, but it wasn't long before the helpers themselves began getting hurt.

To protect themselves while controlling the violence,

helpers began fighting back. Violence escalated. Gangs formed to fight the helpers. No one felt safe.

Someone came up with the idea to use Synmen to help maintain the peace. The idea made sense because Synmen were indestructible, so no one would dare fight a Synman. The violence could be controlled, and no more helpers would be killed. Instead of patrolling the streets, helpers would control Synmen from a safe location. As naïve as the plan seems in retrospect, it worked at first. Synmen were taken out of storage, modified to eliminate the twitches and jerks, and deployed in the streets. People still got angry, fought, and didn't trust each other, but the violence stopped. Unfortunately, not for long.

Synmen began hurting people. Scientists discovered some helpers were to blame, and the offending helpers were replaced. Helpers were monitored to assure good behavior. This solved the problem, but again, only temporarily. Within a year, Synmen resumed hurting people. Helpers swore it wasn't them, that something had taken over their Synmen. Even when a helper disconnected from their portal, the Synman continued hurting people.

The brightest scientists attempted to figure out what was happening with the Synmen, but the Synmen had been decommissioned for so long, few scientists understood the technology. Once again, the Synmen were shut down. Without either Synmen or helpers to intervene, the violence intensified. Years passed. Slowly, our people adapted. With the introduction of laws, police, punishment, and prisons, people learned to feel safe despite the violence.

Then abruptly, our main planet lost contact with the outermost planet at the edge of our solar system. The planet stored billions of Synmen, Synships, and other decommissioned Syn machines.

Manned spaceships were dispatched to investigate, but we lost contact with the ships when they approached the planet.

No spaceship had been lost in hundreds of years. Losing multiple ships at once was unthinkable. Another group of ships was sent to circle the planet, not to land, but to orbit and observe. Those ships maintained continuous contact with each other and with the home planet. The ship's captains reported that everything seemed quiet on the planet. There appeared to be no signs of life, no signals calling for help, nothing. Then we lost contact with the ships.

Two days later, ten thousand Synships filled with hundreds of millions of Synmen landed on the home planet.

The Synships didn't respond to hails. Ten thousand Synships and millions of Synmen required exactly that many controllers, one per Syn machine. Populations that large existed only on three of the other ten planets. The home planet's council urgently called the three planets and discovered that all three had detected Synships approaching their planets too. Who had sent the Synships? The four major planets stayed in contact until the Synships arrived, then all communication between planets ended.

Before the Synships landed, they hovered for a few minutes. People emerged from their homes and offices to see what was happening. The Synships were massive, a few miles square. When the ships descended, they dropped without warning, crushing whatever lay beneath. Tens of millions of Synmen rushed out, shrieking with laughter.

The Synmen herded people into groups. Anyone not moving fast enough was whirled. A Synman whirled a person by grabbing an arm or leg, then whipping the person round and round before letting go. The whirled person smashed into people farther away, or into a building, or disappeared into the sky. People ran to escape the flying bodies only to be grabbed and whirled themselves. Sometimes, two Synmen stood side by side and whirled in opposite directions, not throwing but smashing the two people into each other so hard their bodies burst apart. That was just the first day.

Hiding underground in a safe area known as the cavern, scientists watched the carnage unfold. Prior to the madness, when we were a loving, open society, a vast camera network had been installed to bring everyone closer together. Scientists had installed cameras everywhere, embedding millions of microscopic cameras in buildings, trees, fences, and signs. Cameras were even sprinkled on the ground like dust. The cameras formed a continuous integrated three-dimensional image, viewable from any perspective, and not just video. Camera sensors also recorded odors and atmospheric data such as humidity, wind, temperature, and pressure.

Scientists knew that Synmen required people to operate them and that people required sleep, but these Synmen never slept. They shrieked, whirled, and killed nonstop. Scientists hypothesized that people from one of the other planets must be taking turns controlling the Synmen, somehow perfectly synchronizing the exchange of one human controller for another.

50
THE CAVERN

THOUSANDS OF YEARS before the Synman invasion, my people built the cavern to test ultrapowerful rockets for deep space exploration. Thick titanium walls enclosed the cavern to protect the people on the planet's surface in case of an accident.

After Synships were decommissioned, the cavern was repurposed to study Syn technology to discover the source of the twitches. Top scientists from each planet and their families moved into the underground laboratory, transforming it into the most respected research center in the solar system and a small but thriving community. It even had a perpetual energy system capable of providing power, as well as recycling systems providing water, food, and medicine.

The cavern became a top destination for tourists. The most popular attraction was the Syn playground scientists constructed. Under the watchful eye of scientists, and in a controlled environment, people could guest-control Synmen and engage in many exhilarating sports and activities. To protect guests from the twitches, scientists modified the Synmen to automatically shut down upon any movement that wasn't the explicit command of the controller. Tourists had fun, while allowing scientists to advance their understanding of Syn technology.

The scientists sealed the cavern when the Synmen attacked. Safely behind thick, titanium walls, those inside watched Synmen run amok, whirling and killing.

Shortly after the invasion, scientists noticed a change in the behavior of Cavern-Synmen. Within a few seconds of being enabled by a controller, a Cavern-Synman developed a mind of its own and became violent in the manner of the invading Synmen. Fortunately, scientists had installed remote-controlled disabling switches on all Cavern-Synmen.

To understand who had taken control of the Synmen, scientists built small titanium vaults, locked the Synmen in the vaults, and carefully studied the synaptic signals while control of the Synmen shifted from the scientists to someone some-where unknown. Despite observing the change of control, scientists were unable to determine the location or identity of the synaptic hijackers.

Within a few years, the cavern community began hearing the pounding from above. The invading Synmen were trying to break in. Scientists assured everyone that the Synmen would never break through because the walls were titanium and ten feet thick. Nothing, not even the largest spaceship traveling at top speed, could possibly break through.

Then scientists saw what happened at the coliseums. I think that's when the evil first got in, long before the walls came down.

51

THE COLISEUMS

WHEN THE SYNMEN first arrived on the planet surface, they herded people into camps where they were starved, beaten, tormented, and whirled.

The Synmen soon tired of the camps and built huge coliseums, not stadiums like our people had built for entertainment and sports, but huge structures that held a million people. Synmen are strong and designed for construction, but they made my people do the building. Hundreds of thousands of people died during construction. Their remains were left where they died, embedded in the superstructure. The coliseums literally wreaked of death and were so poorly constructed that entire sections would collapse during events, dropping tons of cement and thousands of screaming people onto the sections below.

Coliseum events included every bizarre spectacle the Synmen could imagine. They forced people to fight to the death and to be eaten by wild animals. The Synmen's favorite game was whirling. They'd crowd people onto the floor of the arena, then grab people from the stands and whirl them into the crowd.

As sickened as the scientists were by the games, they studied every event hoping to learn more about the Synmen.

The most remarkable thing they discovered, however, wasn't about the Synmen but about our own people. The Synmen discovered this too and became confused and afraid. Everything got worse after that.

Scientists didn't know exactly when the change in the people started, because there were dozens of coliseums operating continuously, day and night. Once scientists realized something had changed, they traced backward and found that the origin lay in the lines of people waiting to enter the coliseums.

To assure a constant supply of people for their coliseum games, Synmen forced thousands of people to stand in line outside the coliseum to take the place of people who died inside. Synmen guarded those in line and entertained themselves by pretending to be distracted, baiting people to run. People usually ran in twos or threes. Synmen gave chase, shrieking after them. The runners would be dragged back and tortured in full view of everyone in the line.

The day everything changed began like every other day. It was early morning, just before sunrise. A line of tens of thousands of people wrapped around the stadium. Every ten or fifteen minutes, someone tried to run, soliciting shrieks of glee from the Synmen.

Within the coliseum, the cool morning air was pierced by screams of terror and shrieks of glee. The intermittent thud of bodies thrown from the coliseum and landing in the field beyond the line of people increased the fear of those in line.

No one ever ran from the front of the line. People in the front walked willingly into the coliseum. Scientists didn't know why. Maybe, after being in the line for two or three days, the people had lost hope. At the front of the line, shrieking Synmen spat on people as they walked through the entrance.

A morning glow from the rising sun was peeking over the horizon when an old couple next in line to enter the coliseum suddenly walked out of line and into the field. The Synmen at the entrance, bored because no one ever ran from the entrance, shrieked excitedly, then realized the couple wasn't running. They were just walking. The couple stopped, looked toward the sunrise, and embraced.

The sunrise glowed, still far from full brilliance, yet it cast the couple's long shadow over the people in line. The people in line who had been afraid, with heads, eyes, and arms down, trying not to be noticed by a Synman for fear of being whirled, raised their heads, transfixed by what was happening. The Synman at the entrance shrieked in anger and rushed straight at the couple. The couple ignored the robot. They had just kissed, a delicate kiss, their lips barely touching when the Synman reached them. Inches from the embracing couple, it froze.

The couple looked into the eyes of the Synman. It glared back. The couple turned away and kissed again. Tears fell from the woman's eyes, down her cheek and onto her lover's chest. Everyone went quiet, including the Synmen. Even the shrieks and screams from inside the coliseum faded. There was a thud. A body from inside the coliseum had landed in the field. Then total silence. A full minute passed. There was no sound. Absolutely nothing moved. It was as if the universe had come to a complete stop.

Then the Synman grabbed the old man by his neck and the old woman by her arm and whirled them into the coliseum wall so hard their bodies stuck. Synmen up and down the line shrieked hysterically. Some people in line lowered their heads, afraid again. But not all.

A mother held her daughter and kissed her on the cheek. The nearest Synman watched, for a few seconds unable to move, then whirled them. Farther down the line, a father comforted his family. The nearest Synman seemed momentarily paralyzed before tearing them to pieces.

Scientists were ecstatic. People expressing love for one another seemed to temporarily disable Synmen, if only for a second. They had found a force that adversely affected Synmen, if only they could replicate, amplify, and weaponize it.

Experiments were designed to replicate the love scenes of the people in line. The problem was that the scenes required people and Synmen interacting together. Scientists had dozens of Synmen in the titanium vaults that could be used, but no scientist would dare enter a vault with a Synman.

Then someone thought of the tourists.

52
TOURISTS

When the Synmen invaded, scientists and tourists were trapped inside the cavern. Scientific research into Syn technology was the only hope against the Synmen and became the top priority. The cavern was automated and self-sustaining, so tourists had no purpose. Scientists got the best of everything, food, medicine, and shelter. Tourists got what was left over.

Scientists relegated tourists to the outer edges of the cavern, against the outer wall. Inner research zones, more distant from the pounding, were reserved for scientists. Some tourists offered to help the scientists with their research, but the only help the scientists accepted was for housecleaning and cooking. It wasn't long before scientists realized tourists could serve another purpose—fighting.

Originally designed by prior generations of scientists, Synmen were built to be indestructible and to self-heal if injured. Scientists believed stopping the Synmen required new technology that could destroy them when they inevitably broke into the cavern.

Although scientifically advanced, our people had never had the need for weapons. In fact, prior to the invasion of the Synmen, tools for fighting had never been designed in the entire history of my people. Now, scientists in the cavern developed special weapons to destroy the Synmen, and tourists were trained and deployed wherever the pounding was loudest.

Tourists evolved into a highly trained fighting force, obedient to their scientist leaders. Scientists staged attack scenarios using Cavern-Synmen from the cavern's vast warehouses. Many tourists were killed during the training, and others became demotivated. Scientists responded by secretly disabling Synmen during battles and allowing tourists to be victorious. Morale quickly returned.

Scientists knew, however, that after Synmen broke in, no matter how high the morale, no matter how many staged attacks the tourists won, no matter how joyous the celebrations after each win, Synmen would quickly defeat the tourists and kill everyone inside.

Then came the kissing old couple, and the love scenes between people in line that somehow had momentarily stopped Synmen.

No weapon developed by the scientists had yet affected a Synman. No tourist, no matter how disciplined and well trained, had ever fought Synmen unafraid. Yet an old couple, with one kiss, stopped a Synman and inspired love scenes between other people that did the same. What made an old couple's kiss so powerful that it could do what a trained tourist soldier could not? Finding the answer to that question consumed the scientists.

After the old couple's kiss, the pounding grew louder all around the cavern. Some walls cracked. Scientists became desperate to discover the force, emanating from love between people, that could stop Synmen.

They designed a new experiment to simulate what happened on the surface. First, a large warehouse at the outer edge of the cavern, alongside tourist homes, was reinforced with thick black titanium walls. Then kidnapped tourists were taken to the warehouse and forced to stand in long lines as if waiting to get inside the coliseum, replicating the scene where loving couples momentarily stopped Synmen. Tourists were specially chosen and placed in line such that most had no relationship with those around them. Only a select few had loving relationships.

Once the line of tourists was fully in place, disabled Cavern-Synmen were carried into the warehouse, set alongside the line of tourists, and activated. From behind a one-way window in a viewing area high above the floor, scientists recorded what happened, hoping to observe the force that had emanated from the loving couples who had somehow stopped Synmen. In the name of education, to train the next generation of scientists, classes of children also observed.

The experiments didn't last long. Tourists were grabbed, torn apart, or whirled indiscriminately. All the experiments failed, and scientists learned nothing. The children loved watching the violence and giggled when a tourist's bloody pulp stuck to a wall.

Then a scared little boy and the most beautiful girl in the world changed everything.

53
EXPERIMENTS

A WEEK after the experiments began, hundreds of tourists had been killed. Scientists worried the tourists might discover the experiments and revolt. They were about to abandon them when the Cavern-Synmen began behaving strangely.

During one experiment, the Cavern-Synmen began whirling tourists directly at the viewing area instead of tearing them apart.

Scientists assumed they themselves were the target because they observed the experiments from behind a glass wall in a viewing area. However, that didn't make sense because the glass was one-way. It was impossible for the Synmen to know the viewing area existed.

Nevertheless, scientists rotated different people in the viewing area and repeated the experiment each day, varying the times of the day. Sometimes Synmen whirled tourists against the window, and sometimes they did not.

Then, one morning before an experiment, the scientists were called to a meeting, so they conducted the experiment while the room was completely empty. Surprisingly, the Synmen whirled tourists at the window of the empty viewing area. Then, extraordinarily, the Synmen collapsed just as pounding against the cavern walls momentarily stopped, too.

Scientists ran out of the building to the side where the tourists had been thrown and saw two children playing, a little boy and a little girl. Immediately, the scientists understood. The Synmen weren't whirling victims at the viewing area, they were whirling them at the two children who played outside!

Scientists had learned the Synmen's true target, but they didn't know how to utilize the information to permanently disable the robots. Additional experiments were required. Why had the Synmen collapsed? Why did the pounding stop? Why were both temporary?

A review of the recordings of the two children playing in days previous and during the day the Synmen had collapsed revealed two differences: the boy had been sad, and the girl had just comforted him with a strawberry. Arrangements were made so that the two children would play together again the following afternoon. Each element of their interaction was replicated as closely as possible. The girl was provided strawberries, and the boy was made sad. The challenge of how to make the boy sad so that the girl would comfort him was solved by inducing minor but painful injuries to the boy. The experiments had the desired result. Each afternoon, while the two children played, the Cavern-Synmen momentarily collapsed and the pounding stopped.

Two problems quickly emerged.

The first was that after each experiment, when the pounding resumed, it was louder and more intense than before. Whatever the boy and girl were doing to anger the Cavern-Synmen in the warehouse was angering the Synmen outside who were trying to break through the cavern walls. Nanoscopic cracks were detected in some of the walls. Scientists knew they didn't have much time.

The second problem was that the little girl didn't want to play anymore. She had realized that her friend got hurt whenever they played.

A decision was made to engage a final experiment. The

boy was kidnapped, taken to the warehouse, and told to stand at the end of the line. The girl was tricked into visiting the viewing room. When the Cavern-Synmen were activated, they went berserk, whirling tourists at the girl. One grabbed the boy.

The next instant, the Synmen collapsed and didn't get up. The pounding stopped and didn't resume.

The Synmen had been defeated.

54
LOTS OF QUESTIONS

"What happened to the girl?" asked Billy.

The man hung his head. Minutes passed. Jimee sensed sadness exude from him, barely repelled by the fabric's white-hot immune system. A tear fell, then another, and another. The man disconnected from the synaptic portal, walked across the ship's bridge toward a pitch-black cube the size of a small table, grabbed a cloth from a neatly folded stack of cloths lying atop the cube, dabbed his tears, and returned the cloth. Jimee felt a sensation from the cube when the man handled the cloth. Curious, she extended herself into the cube. She noticed Brill do the same. The cube was packed with synaptic amplifiers. Brill connected with her to privately share a thought.

"That black cube is designed to blast synaptic energy into the fabric," thought Brill.

The man walked back to his synaptic portal and reconnected.

"Can you tell us what happened to the boy?" asked Stevens.

"Whatever the girl had done, whatever love or rage she'd unleashed, she completely disabled the synaptic circuitry that controlled the Synmen," he replied. "Synmen pounding on

327

the cavern's walls were disabled. Synmen on the surface were disabled. We later learned that all Synmen throughout our entire solar system had collapsed. The girl was a hero. She defeated the Synmen and saved our people."

"But what happened to her?" asked Billy.

The man didn't answer. Jimee saw him glance at the black cube. At that instant, a bolt of anger surged within his sadness.

"What happened to the boy and girl is what the remainder of my story is about," he said finally.

"We have a few questions before you continue," said Brill. "Did the human controllers feel pain when their Synmen felt pain?"

"Yes, feeling was important to properly operate Synmen," said the man, "but controllers could desensitize their Synman's nervous system to prevent any real discomfort. Also, as a safety measure, Synmen were built with a maximum pain threshold."

"Who were the controllers that took over the Synmen and attacked your people?" asked Stevens.

The man shrugged. "No offense, but I think you already know."

"Are you a scientist?" asked Billy.

"No."

"Good," said Billy. "Brill's a real scientist."

"How long have you been on this planet?" asked Brill.

"Two hundred and thirty-seven thousand years," the man replied.

"Okay," said Billy.

The man pointed at a dome lying atop his bed. "I don't understand all the science, but that dome keeps me asleep. While I am, I don't age, except maybe a minute in millions of years. Scientists designed the beds for deep space travel before Synmen were invented. I configured the bed to keep me asleep for one thousand years."

"You don't age while sleeping?" asked Billy.

"Not if I sleep with the dome down. For me, every day is one day. Every night is one thousand years. Today is my two hundred and thirty-seventh day, which is two hundred and thirty-six one-thousand-year-long nights. You can see how the dirt builds up around the ship. When I wake, I use the landing thrusters to break free. Luckily, the ship works well enough for that."

"Luckily, you haven't been completely buried yet," said Brill. "One thousand years is a long time."

The man walked over to a spider web that spanned the upper half of the doorway. A fly trapped in the web struggled to escape. Without damaging the web, he edged the fly free with his finger.

"On our planet, insects grew angry when the people did, swarming and biting. The insects here are nice," the man said.

"Ask him about the black cube and that stack of cloths on top," Jimee thought privately to Brill as the man walked back to his portal and reattached himself to the synaptic interface, presenting his mind to the friends.

"Let's hear the rest of his story first," thought Brill.

"Stevens can control bugs," said Billy. "He accidentally transferred with a bug."

"Transferred!" asked the man, suddenly upset. His thoughts raced uncontrollably, projecting his memories. Scenes of a little boy and girl sharing a strawberry pulsed from his mind, followed by an image of an old gray concrete building.

"How do you know about that building?" asked Stevens, alarmed.

"Are you the little boy?" asked Billy.

"Who's Elle?" asked Brill.

The man took a deep breath. A tear fell from his cheek. His thoughts of a bloody limbless torso staggered the friends.

"The love of my life," he said.

55
SORRY, KID

My name is Ramien. I was the little boy.

My trainer took me from my front yard and into the building next to the tourist area. I cried and begged him to let me go. My parents would be home soon, and they expected me to be there when they arrived. I was taken down long hallways and past many rooms. I could see the people through the transparent doors that glistened when we walked by. Some I recognized from my neighborhood. I wished my trainer had left me in one of those rooms.

My room was different. Instead of transparent doors, it had thick heavy doors. Dead people lay in a pile against the back wall, stacked, as if unloaded from a cart. Now I know they were Synmen. I didn't realize how cold it was until the door slammed shut behind me. I heard voices from the hallway.

"Sorry, kid, no mingling with the guinea pigs," said a voice.

"Why not put him with the others?" asked a different voice.

"Scientists' orders. The others will comfort him. He's to be as frightened as possible in the morning."

Then the lights blinked out. I stood in the pitch-black for

as long as I could before shuffling to a wall, away from the bodies. I sat down against the wall. Soon, I was shivering uncontrollably. I couldn't feel my hands. That's when I felt the warmth coming from my right. I crept along the wall toward the warmth, terrified because I knew what lay ahead.

I crawled across two bodies before reaching the pile, then climbed over three more until I found a gap and wedged myself inside. My shivering eased. I pulled an arm around me, snuggled my face against a belly. I felt warmth deep inside the belly. I took my knife and sliced the belly. Sticky warmth gushed all over me, then somehow flowed back into the belly. I felt the belly and the slice was gone. All night, I sliced the belly, again and again, keeping warm. The door opened the next morning. Scientists loaded the disabled Synmen onto a wagon and wheeled them away.

Another scientist came and took me to a large room full of people. Everyone stood in a long winding line. Alongside the line lay the disabled Synmen I had slept with. I was led into the room, forced to step over a man and woman along the way. I didn't recognize the woman; her head was smashed. The man was my father.

"That's what'll happen to you if your little girlfriend doesn't save you," said the scientist. He left me at the end of the line.

The Synmen woke, shrieking wildly. One grabbed my head. I saw Elle. Fingers poked my eyes.

Suddenly, I felt the love of my life, Elle, inside me. She sang our berry song. The Synman squeezed my head, as if to force her out. Elle grew angry. Her love, her innocence, her warmth, everything that made her glow went black, and the Synman collapsed.

56

ARE YOU HUNGRY, PIG?

I WOKE IN A SOFT, fluffy bed. A boy my age stood at my side. I could move, except for my head, which was fixed inside a helmet. Frightened, I closed my eyes, pretending I was still asleep.

"He's awake, Father," the boy said.

"I'm almost ready, Son," said a man from behind me.

I heard a hum from the helmet, then felt hundreds of needles push into my skull. The boy dangled a bag in front of my face. I recognized Elle's bag of strawberries.

"Are you hungry, pig?" the boy asked.

"Not yet, Fitz, not until I say," said the father.

The needles vibrated. Something forced my mouth open. The needles vibrated again. Suddenly, I was sitting alone in Elle's front yard, crying.

"What an idiot," said Fitz.

Elle appeared. The needles warmed. She sang our berry song.

"Now, Fitz, gently. Don't choke him," said the father.

The boy jammed a strawberry into my mouth. The needles tingled. Something made me chew. Juice trickled down my cheek. Elle laughed. Together, we sang our berry song. The needles stopped tingling. I felt happy.

"You're right, Son. They sing that song together," said the father.

Fitz leaned over me, his mouth bulging with a strawberry. He spit all over my face. I felt Elle again. She soothed me and told me to kill Fitz. She reminded me about the Syn knife strapped to my thigh. I reached for it, but it was gone. The father held up my knife.

Fitz laughed and patted me on the head. "Clone time," he said.

Nearly twenty years later, I learned what he meant.

57

SCAREDY-CATS

No ONE from the cavern had been to the surface in hundreds of years, not since the Synmen attacked. Synmen had destroyed the planet-wide camera system. Scientists didn't know what to expect and were surprised to find millions of people still alive. Most lived in misery, without food or clothing. The people looked up at the sky and rejoiced. Scientists became angry because the survivors were being disrespectful, the sky hadn't saved the people. Scientists ordered the tourist army to correct the situation.

Tourists lured survivors into the coliseums, promising them supplies and medicine. Once inside, the survivors were slaughtered. In a few months, the coliseums were filled to the brim with the bodies of former survivors. Thousands of black birds flew above the coliseums, feasting on the rotting bodies. The coliseums were declared monuments. Artists rendered beautiful paintings of the black birds, swirling and squawking above the coliseums. Scientists could now restore the planet to its previous greatness.

Then a discovery changed everything. Scientists initially believed all Synmen had been disabled throughout the solar system, not just on our home planet. After flying to the other planets, scientists discovered hundreds of millions of Synmen and tens of thousands of Synships were missing! Where had they gone? Were they coming back?

"Let the Syn scaredy-cats come back," the scientists bragged.

In the years underground since the invasion, scientists had learned much about Syn technology and had been designing a new generation of Synmen, each stronger than ten originals. Freed from the resource constraints in the cavern, scientists quickly completed the design and manufactured millions of new Synmen.

Scientists planned a surprise for the original Synmen. Upon their return, the original Synmen would find the planet fully repopulated. However, the people would actually be new Synmen. Unlike original Synmen, who had human form but could be identified by a discerning eye, new Synmen were designed to be indistinguishable from people.

New Synmen were distributed across the planet, living as humans, working, playing, and raising families. When the original Synmen arrived, the newly minted Synmen would tear them apart. It would be the perfect trap. Safely hidden in ten specially built Syn-control centers, people controlling the new Synmen would destroy every last original Synman.

"RAMIEN, I HAVE A QUESTION," said Brill. "Even if new Synmen looked like actual people, with only standard looks for the male and female, all males would look alike, and all females would look alike. Wouldn't that make the new Synmen recognizable by the returning original Synmen?"

"Scientists thought of that," replied Ramien. "Unlike original Synmen, which all had the same bulky human shape, new Synmen had three standard looks: new-male, new-female, and original. Additionally, new Synmen were designed so controllers could easily switch between the three looks, and also make thousands of minor changes, such as hair, skin, and eye color, including changes to the facial structure and posture. No new Synmen looked alike."

"Original Synmen couldn't change their looks?" asked Jimee.

"Yes, they could. However, maintaining anything but the original bulky look was extremely difficult. Only the most skilled controllers could maintain changes in the appearance of an original Synmen for more than a few minutes. Thus, all original Synmen looked the same," said Ramien.

"Tell us what happened to you and Elle after she disabled the Synmen," said Billy.

58
HERO

WHILE SCIENTISTS on the surface were building an army of new Synmen, I was kept below, held in captivity in the shiny black building, along with two hundred other tourist children whose parents had been killed in the experiments. We were given only enough food to survive.

Months passed. I longed for Elle. Often, I felt her inside my mind, singing our song. Sometimes I felt her crying, begging me to make them stop. I tried to help her, like she always did for me, but I didn't know how. I promised I'd escape and rescue her.

Then one day, we were taken from the shiny black building to a large room inside a new building still under construction, located deep beneath cavern. The chief scientist stood in the room as we were led inside, his son at his side. Throughout the room, workers installed computer stations. Adjacent to the room was a large, transparent wall that provided a view to an even larger room, containing all manner of objects and structures. Workers carried men and women into the room and laid them in rows on the floor. The chief scientist pointed to the computer stations and spoke.

"Those are new Synmen, designed to look exactly like people. You will learn to control them. Their synaptic control systems are vastly more complex than original Synmen, much more difficult to learn. Children are best at mastering the controls. A year from now, the top one hundred children will be sent to the surface to train an army of controllers. The bottom one hundred will help my son, Fitz, who I've put in charge of a new set of experiments."

I practiced every waking hour. The objects in the room were for training. Within months, my new Synman could dance blindfolded on a tightrope, balance on the tip of its nose atop a pyramid, and juggle a dozen hundred-pound weights. I mastered every look, man, woman, original, and every possible variation of size, shape, and color. I became the best of all the children. My skills were so advanced that I discovered dozens of flaws in the new Synmen, allowing scientists to perfect the design. I became a hero to the scientists. I didn't know I was already a hero to the tourists.

A year later, myself and ninety-nine others were sent to the surface. I was assigned to the head tourist, who was responsible for deploying new Synmen across the planet. Hailed as the boy who had defeated the original Synmen, and as a master of the new Synmen, they welcomed me into their family. That's where I learned about the true history of my planet, what happened to the survivors, and how to fight.

Tourists were soldiers, trained to fight Synmen if they ever broke into the cavern, but tourists had never learned to fight *using* Synmen. I was the best Syn controller but didn't know how to fight. In order to train tourists to control Synmen to fight, I had to become a fighter myself. For the next fifteen years, every morning, tourists trained me to fight. I became the best fighter of any tourist soldier in our entire army. Every afternoon, I taught tourists to control new Synmen. I trained tens of thousands. Every night, I dreamed of Elle, and we sang our song. What were they doing to her? Countless nights, I snuck out to rescue her, but the entrances to the cavern had been sealed and were heavily guarded.

One day, klaxons sounded. Deep space probes had detected the original Synmen returning. By then, the other ninety-nine trainers and I had trained hundreds of thousands of controllers all around the planet to operate the new Synmen. The cavern entrances opened, and thousands more soldiers emerged to join the fight. My fellow trainers and all the controllers were deployed to each of ten specially built Syn-control centers to defend our planet against the returning Synmen. Except me.

I snuck into the cavern to find Elle.

59

FINDING ELLE

ON THE SURFACE, I was a famous Syn trainer and the deadliest fighter in the army. Nearly everyone knew me. I couldn't go anywhere without being recognized. In the cavern, I was anonymous, just another tourist soldier. The problem was that all the tourist soldiers in the cavern were scrambling to predetermined positions. I'd made it to the scientists' headquarters when my luck ran out. Rounding a corner, I came face-to-face with five heavily armed tourists. Their sergeant slammed me against the wall.

"You aren't allowed here!" he barked. His forearm rammed into my throat, choking me.

"I'm looking for someone," I gasped.

His men laughed. Their backs were to me. I realized they weren't laughing at me.

"Look at that disgusting pig," one said.

Behind the sergeant, past the men and through an open door, I saw a young woman on the floor, crawling toward us. She wore a hospital gown, and her head was partially shaved. Wires stuck into her head and draped across her bed toward a machine. The wires went taut, stopping the girl and jerking her head back so I could see her face. I'd found my true love, Elle.

"I think she likes me," taunted a soldier, walking toward her.

The girl looked up at the soldier. Her eyes blazed with fear and hate.

"Hurry," said the sergeant. "Her scientist friends will return soon."

He was still choking me when I snapped his neck. Three soldiers stood between me and the door. My foot killed one. My fists killed the other two. The remaining soldier had bent over Elle. My knife killed him.

I ran to my true love. I held her. I cried. When I heard shouts in the hallway, I turned to get up, determined that no one would separate us again. Elle grabbed my shoulder.

"Love me, my love," she said. I let her pull me back down. Her finger touched my lips as she whispered, "Your turn."

I looked at her, confused.

"Eat the tip, just a teeny, tiny bit," she said.

I shivered.

"A billion teeny, tiny bits," she said again.

I remembered. "Strawberries and cherries." Tears streamed down my cheek. A blast hit my back, paralyzing me, knocking me forward. She caught me. Her lips kissed my ear. Hands grabbed at her. She fought, holding me tight.

"Best-friend berries," she whispered.

Something smashed my head, and I blacked out.

VOICES WOKE ME. I ached all over, and my head hurt, but I lay still, pretending to be asleep. Squinting, I saw that I lay on a small cot amid equipment in racks and on tables in the back of a room. I was in some kind of makeshift command center. A dozen men, tourist soldiers, all sat with their backs to me, about ten feet away, focused intently on the front of the room. I remembered Elle and frantically looked around. She was gone. I closed my eyes and tried to sense her, but felt nothing. Footsteps approached.

"Get him up."

A hand gently nudged my shoulder. I remained motionless.

"He's asleep, sir."

"Wake him. He needs to see this."

"Yes, sir."

A minute later, I was sitting among the soldiers watching an enormous display that covered the entire wall. Next to me sat the leader of the squad, who'd ordered me awakened. He held out his hand. I took it. His grip was strong.

"I'm Alvin," he said.

"Ramien," I said.

"We know." He motioned toward the left side of the display. "Your handiwork. I hope those Syn controllers are as good as everyone says."

The display was divided into thirds. The left side was a live view of one of the ten Syn-control centers containing thousands of controllers wearing bright white synaptic helmets. Each controller was physically located in the control room, but synaptically synced to his or her new Synman that had been embedded into society somewhere on the planet. I recognized many of the controllers and was friends with some of them. Around each was a holographic display that allowed the controller to track the attacking Synships while simultaneously seeing through the eyes of their new Synmen. Looking at the large screen, I saw each controller concentrating, calm and focused, completely immersed in a Syn interface.

The middle of the display showed a large group of young men and women lounging around in what seemed to be a warehouse converted into barracks. Like Elle's, their heads were partially shaved and scarred from being stuck with wires. Armed guards stood at the entrance and watched their every move.

The right view showed the advancing Syn fleet. There were a dozen ships, each massive and packed with hundreds of thousands of Synmen. As large as they were, I knew they held far less than the millions of Synmen and thousands of Synships that were unaccounted for. Where were the others? The twelve massive Synships orbited the planet, descending closer each rotation.

"Where's Elle?" I demanded.

A soldier, closer to the screen than I, turned and looked back. The squad leader nodded. A moment later, the display switched from thirds to fourths, adding the new view on the right side. I saw Elle. She lay in a bed in what appeared to be a larger, more sophisticated version of the room where I had just seen her. Wires protruded, not just from her head but from her entire body, and ran into large computers that lined the walls. Scientists crowded the room. Ten tended to computers, and four surrounded Elle. One held her hand.

"Take me to her," I said, standing up.

Alvin stood with me. "We will, but we can't now," he said.

The right side of the display panned from Elle toward the door and into the hallway. Dozens of heavily armed soldiers stood guard. The leader continued.

"Elite guards, totally loyal to the scientists. They won't hurt her. The men you encountered were escaped criminals and deserters."

Alvin must have sensed my disbelief. Soldiers didn't desert, ever, except for me. He explained, "A few years ago, tourists discovered scientists had been kidnapping and using other tourists as guinea pigs in experiments to understand how to defeat Synmen. Thousands had been sacrificed, including children, and the tourists rebelled. The army splintered. Most soldiers remained with the scientists. Some refused and tried to make it to the surface, but the scientists closed the doors."

"Your squad?" I asked.

"We fight only for tourists now, not scientists. There are others, but not many."

"The soldiers who were going to hurt Elle?" I asked.

"Criminals disguised as soldiers. They escaped during the revolt. They roam the cavern, terrorizing scientists and tourists alike. We were hunting them. That's how we found you. We thought you were one of them, so we stunned you. Sorry about that. When we realized our mistake, we barely got you out of there."

"You left Elle behind," I said accusingly, looking at the display. The scientist who had been holding her hand was leaning over her, whispering something to her.

"We didn't know how to remove the wires. We were afraid we'd hurt her, or worse."

I stiffened. A scientist approached Elle, lifted her head, and stuck a wire into the back of her neck. She yelped.

"Monsters!" I shouted, fuming. "What are they doing to her?" I'd felt Elle's pain in my dreams but never knew the cause.

"Your friend defeated the Synmen, disabled all of them with some kind of energy from her mind. The scientists are trying to replicate the energy as a backup plan in case the new Synmen fail."

A tear fell from Elle's cheek. The scientist who held her hand wiped the tear away.

"Who's he?" I demanded.

Alvin touched my shoulder. "We'll save her, Ramien," he said. "They can't keep those guards on her forever."

"The hundred clones in the warehouse are a backup plan too," said a soldier behind me.

I looked at the display. The view on the left still showed one of the Syn-control centers. The controllers in the center buzzed with excitement. The fighting would begin soon, and the controllers were confident. I was too. I had personally trained many of them. The original Synmen, no matter who was controlling them, would be wiped out by the new versions. That's when I remembered one hundred was the exact number of children who had been sent to the surface, including me, and also the number who'd been returned to Fitz for his experiments.

"Who are the *one hundred*?" I asked.

"Clones," replied Alvin. "Of your friend, Elle."

"Show me their faces," I said. The middle display zoomed in on several of the group of young men and women in the warehouse. I recognized many of them.

"Those aren't clones. They don't even look like Elle," I said.

"Synaptic clones," said Alvin. "They're tourist children."

"They *were* tourist children," said a soldier. "Now, they're Elle, every last synaptic impulse, thought, and connection."

Alvin nodded and continued. "Scientists cloned one hundred copies of Elle's mind and replaced the minds of the children with minds cloned from Elle."

"Why?" I asked, feeling sick.

He shrugged. "Maybe to have more copies of Elle's mind for experiments. Maybe to re-create a hundred times Elle's energy that disabled the Synmen. Maybe because Fitz is an evil, sick kid."

"Sir, look!" interrupted a soldier, pointing at the display.

The Synships had descended so low it seemed that they would crash into trees and buildings. Then the ships ascended into the sky once more and hovered over large fields.

"They've chosen their landing sites," said one of the soldiers. "Close to population centers, and one right above the cavern."

"New Synmen, designed to assume shapes of regular people, are embedded in every city," I said. "A new Synman can kill hundreds of originals. The originals won't know what hit them."

"Who do you think is controlling them?" asked a soldier.

"Good question," said another, eyeing me. I confessed I didn't know.

"No one knows," said Alvin. "The real enemy is whoever is controlling the Synmen. After we defeated the Synmen last time, I joined a team that searched every planet, moon, and sector in the solar system. We didn't find a single portal that had been used to control the invading Synmen."

60

ELLE TAKES CHARGE

THE SCIENTISTS SHOULD HAVE KNOWN that although the original Synmen had either collapsed or fled, the real enemy remained with us, in the cavern and on the surface, the whole time.

Confident of victory, from the makeshift command center with a rogue group of tourist soldiers, I watched the attack commence. All the while, I kept an eye on Elle, waiting for the moment her guards redeployed so we could rescue her.

Inside the Syn-control center, each controller concentrated, unafraid, focused, completely immersed in his or her Syn interface. I felt proud. They were ready and would perform exactly as trained.

But then, without warning, a controller stood and disconnected from his portal. Then another, and another. Some ran. In a moment, I saw why. Ten small Synships had appeared and were racing straight at each of the ten control centers on an unmistakable collision course. The enemy knew about the scientists' plan!

There was a bright flash, then the section of the display showing the Syn-control center went black.

On the left view of the display, thousands of original Synmen poured from the Synships and into the cities.

In the middle of the display, the guards drew their weapons, secured the doors, and ordered the clones to the center of the room.

On the right, scientists rushed to Elle and to the equipment on the walls, frantically checking connections and turning dials, urging her to disable the Synmen. Elle's scientist friend stayed at her side. Suddenly, panicked guards burst into the room.

"Run! Synmen are coming!" they shouted.

I jumped up, as did Alvin and his squad.

"How can that be?" said a soldier watching with Alvin and me. "It should take the Synmen years to break in."

"Not new Synmen," I said. "They'd break into the original cavern instantly. The enemy must have taken control of our new Synmen!"

The scientists fled, leaving my Elle behind, hooked with hundreds of wires to her bed. Elle's scientist friend also ran, although he stopped in the doorway and looked back at her. I remember her warm blue eyes as she looked at the scientist. Then he turned and ran too, leaving her alone.

"Everyone, move out, now!" Alvin ordered. "We're going to get her." Soldiers scrambled for their weapons.

I ran to the door, wondering how the new Synmen could have known where Elle was. It was as if they'd gone straight to her.

"Look!" shouted a soldier, pointing back at the display. We stayed and watched.

Five new Synmen had crashed into Elle's room. Elle lay terrified, trapped in her bed. She watched as the Synmen surrounded her. I saw her eyes again and shivered. Her eyes were pitch-black. Only a moment before, I swear, my Elle's eyes had been blue. A Synman disconnected her from the equipment, meticulously removing each wire. Another Synman helped her out of the bed, appearing to be careful not to hurt her. The Synman picked up Elle and set her down gently. It held her steady, not letting go until she had her balance.

Then my beautiful Elle walked out of the room, leading the way.

"Track her," ordered Alvin.

The Synmen followed Elle toward the surface. She walked slowly. Whenever she lost her balance, a Synman caught her. Along the way, Synmen gathered scientists who were hiding and made them follow. I recognized one, Fred, the chief scientist, the father of Fitz.

"That's odd. Elle appears to be in charge," said a soldier.

"Maybe that's good," said another.

Remembering Elle's pitch-black eyes, I suddenly felt sick.

"I don't think so," I said.

61

TWITCH OF A FINGER

ELLE and her entourage arrived at the surface and stepped onto the large field above the cavern. Two Synmen flanked her. A Synship that had delivered the returning original Synmen stood in the center of the field.

Elle looked up at the sky. Descending rapidly toward them was a massive Synship. It landed next to the smaller Synship. A thousand-foot-wide door on the larger Synship opened, and thousands of Synmen carried out an odd thing: an old gray concrete building.

The Synmen carried the building onto the field. It rested on a tall foundation, so high that its doors were forty feet above ground. The materials and architecture appeared ancient.

"That's not from our planet," said Alvin.

The building's doors swung open, revealing two Synmen, with several more visible behind them. Abruptly, Elle turned as if she knew from which angle our display was capturing the scene, and I could see her face straight on.

I expected her to be crying and frightened, but she was neither. Instead, she seemed pleased and even smiled. It would have been a beautiful smile, perhaps the most beautiful smile I had ever seen, except for her eyes. Her eyes were bottomless icy-black.

Synmen herded the captured cavern scientists and hundreds of others from the surrounding area toward the building. Once the people were bunched together in front of the building, everything came to a standstill. The intention seemed to be that the crowd should go inside, but the entrance was high above their heads. None of the Synmen knew what to do.

The Synmen looked at Elle. I remembered when she was a little girl, how blue her eyes were, and how her smile made me happy. Now I saw how cruel she looked. Her smile was still there, but it made me want to cry.

Elle's right hand pointed at the crowd of frightened people, many of them scientists. Chief Scientist Fred broke from the crowd and ran toward her, begging her to let him go. One of the Synmen at Elle's side grabbed Fred and held him out to her, as if on a platter.

Elle waved her arm in a wide, whirling circle and pointed at the building. The Synman whirled Fred, round and round, and let him fly. Fred smashed into the building so hard that his mushed body stuck to the side, dripping red goo onto the people below.

Elle smiled, whirled her arms again, and pointed at the door. Synmen grabbed people from the crowd and whirled them toward the door. Some flew straight through and were caught and dragged inside by Synmen. Some struck the side of the doorway, breaking body and limb, and were dragged inside by laughing Synmen. Others missed completely, hitting the wall of the building as Fred had, then falling to the ground. If still alive, a Synman whirled them again. Finally, the only living person on the field was my lover and best friend Elle.

We watched, transfixed by the horror she orchestrated.

Alvin's commanding voice snapped us out of it. "We need to see inside. Switch to the mass-wave sensors," he ordered.

All displays were connected to a bank of mass-wave sensors that didn't require light to create images. Long ago, scientists had discovered that all objects in the universe generate waves, but unlike light or sound waves, an object's mass-waves travel through space unhindered. Using mass-wave sensors, we would be able to see inside the building, but without color or sound.

The display flickered on. Inside were rows of steel chairs. We watched the people who had been whirled through the doorway being dragged to the chairs. Each person was strapped into one and fitted with a helmet. Then a Synman pulled a switch and the person died. Getting the dead out of the chairs slowed the process until the Synmen realized the bodies didn't have to come out in one piece.

Before long, every person inside and outside the concrete building was gone. The Synmen inside returned to the front door and stood facing Elle, waiting.

She walked calmly toward the building. Synmen in the doorway jumped to the ground, formed a tight group, then climbed atop each other and positioned their backs to form a ramp toward the door. Assisted by the two Synmen at her sides, Elle walked up the ramp. After she stepped from the backs of the Synmen into the building, the Synmen followed her inside.

My beautiful Elle walked through the building, past room after room packed with bloody limbless bodies, looking to each side as if walking through a garden. She stopped in front of the row of steel chairs, now wet and gory from bodies having been torn from them. She looked up and down the row, choosing. It seemed to me she chose the goriest chair.

A Synman helped her into the chair, carefully attaching her to the apparatus. At a nod of her head, the Synman reached to pull the switch.

Then it stopped. Elle had raised one of her fingers.

At a twitch of her finger, two Synmen approached, unstrapped her arms from the chair, and ripped them off. Then they unstrapped her legs and ripped them off. Blood shot from my Elle's torso as the switch came down.

I CAN'T DESCRIBE how I felt. Who can describe the unimaginable? I convinced myself it was a dream. I heard soldiers discussing what had happened.

"Who took over the new Synmen?"

"Why'd she rip her arms and legs off?"

"Sir, we can save all one hundred clones if we hurry."

"Where are the clones now?" asked Alvin.

"Still in the original cavern, sir, same as us. We can escort them to the new cavern, but we have to leave immediately."

Alvin grabbed my shoulders. He shook me.

"Ramien, we have to go. We can still save the clones."

I broke free of his grasp. Suddenly, I couldn't breathe. That felt good. I'd failed to save Elle. I didn't deserve to breathe.

"Ramien, the clones *are* Elle!" shouted Alvin.

62

LOVE US, RAMIEN

ALVIN LED THE WAY, with me and his squad close behind. Sprinting down aisleway after aisleway, he knew exactly where he was going. At each turn, he stopped to check for Synmen around the corner. If we encountered original Synmen, we'd have a fighting chance. Our weapons were designed to stop originals, at least temporarily. But we wouldn't have a chance if we encountered new Synmen. At last, Alvin stopped outside a large door. He turned and looked at me.

"You ready for this?" he asked.

"Hurry," I said. I should have known what he meant.

Alvin motioned to a soldier, who waved a small device across the door. It slid open and we ran inside.

"Follow us," Alvin yelled. "I know a place where you will be safe!"

All one hundred clones turned toward us, and all at once, they smiled. I felt their joy magnified one hundred times. All one hundred rushed me. The nearest, a man with a scarred face and wires from a recent experiment still protruding from his neck, kissed me. A young woman took my hand and held it to her cheek. Another man caressed my neck. Hands stroked my face and grabbed my legs.

"We missed you, Ramien."

"Love us, Ramien."

I shrank back instinctively, but the clones were everywhere, struggling to get at me. Alvin forced his way to my side.

"Ramien, they're Elle, all of them. Let them love you."

I tripped and would have fallen if not for Alvin, who caught me. The clones began chanting.

"Strawberries and cherries. Best-friend berries."

I shook my head. These clones weren't Elle. My Elle was gone. I closed my eyes. She came to me. I saw her, my beautiful Elle.

"Save them, Ramien, all of them," she said.

I opened my eyes and saw what had tripped me. The man who'd kissed me had fallen. I picked him up.

"I will save them, my love," I said.

"Sir, Synmen are coming!" said a soldier.

"Move out! Now!" commanded Alvin.

An instant later, we were running down a hallway. Alvin led the way, followed by me, the hundred Elles, and in the rear, Alvin's squad.

"Where are we going?" I asked.

"To a newly built part of the cavern, an area strong enough to resist new Synmen," he replied.

The clones were slow. Some had to be carried. We stopped, I thought to allow the clones to catch up, then Alvin waved a device, and part of the wall slid open.

"Hurry, we're here!" Alvin yelled to the clones.

Waiting for them to catch up, I felt his hand on my shoulder. "Ramien, the same beautiful girl you knew, the little girl with warm blue eyes, a beautiful smile, and soft brown hair, the most beautiful girl in the world, she's right there, in every one of them. She loves you. You're the luckiest man in the universe."

I looked up at Alvin, stunned. I didn't know what to say. The clones caught up just as a soldier from behind screamed. Objects sailed above the heads of the clones and smashed into the wall near Alvin and me—torsos and limbs of Alvin's soldiers.

"Run inside!" Alvin yelled, pointing at the newly opened entranceway, about ten feet long. On the other side, it opened into a large room where I heard a commotion and people yelling. "Synmen are coming! Shut the door!"

"These are clones, Elle's backups to fight the Synmen. Don't shut the door!" shouted Alvin.

Clones ran through the entranceway. Alvin and I stayed in the hallway, hurrying the remaining clones through. Synmen rounded the corner, overtaking the last of Alvin's soldiers. Only myself, Alvin, and two clones remained. The two clones could barely move, too damaged from the scientists' experiments. Alvin grabbed me and the two clones.

"Get inside!" he shouted.

I heard a loud, wrenching noise from above and looked up. The entranceway's ceiling was descending. It was going to crush us! I pushed the two clones down the entranceway to the other side and turned back to Alvin just as a whirled soldier smashed into him, knocking him into me, and both of us to the floor. I jumped up. Alvin was conscious but hurt and couldn't move. Shrieking Synmen raced toward us. The ceiling was almost on top of us. I grabbed Alvin by his arms and pulled him away from the Synmen farther down the entranceway. Two Synmen dived into the opening and scrambled to grab Alvin's feet.

I was highly trained, every muscle perfectly developed and easily strong enough to pull Alvin to safety. But not if a Synman had him, much less two. Alvin knew it too. He looked at me. I realized that besides Elle, he was my first friend. Our eyes locked. Whatever it is that connects one human to another connected me to Alvin. I pulled with all my might. Abruptly, he jerked, twisted his arms from my grasp, crawled backward, and kicked the Synman in the face. He was sacrificing himself for me.

"No, Alvin!" I lunged for him, hindered by the descending ceiling, now pressing against my back. I had his wrists in my hands, but without his help, I couldn't pull him to safety. Suddenly, large hands encased mine, hands of the two Synmen. They spun around, one's foot shoved Alvin, the other's legs shoved me. The two Synmen were saving me and Alvin!

The next instant, a flash blinded me and intense heat burned me. The Synman's hands that held my hands tight to Alvin loosened and fell away. I lost my grip too. Frantically, I reached for Alvin, but the Synman's kick knocked me down the entranceway and out the other side. I landed on my back, smacking my head against the floor, hearing a sickening crack. When my eyes opened, the entranceway's ceiling lay flush against the floor. Blood seeped from between. I blacked out.

63

ONE LAST KISS

I WOKE IN A HOSPITAL ROOM. My head hurt. My arms were reddened. I was alone in the room except for an armed guard standing at the door. I sat up and swung my legs to the floor. The guard pointed his weapon at me and told me to stay where I was. A moment later, the door opened and Fitz, the boy scientist now a young man, walked in. A patch that looked taped onto his lab coat read *Chief Scientist Fitz*.

"Sorry about your friend getting crushed," he said. "If the Synmen had gotten inside, we'd all be dead now." He glanced at my arms.

"Sorry about that too. That's from the Syn vaporizers, weapons that don't actually stop Synmen but temporarily weaken them. In this case, so the ceiling could crush them."

"Sorry about your father," I said, as cruelly as I could.

Fitz laughed. "Elle's gone and your friend and his soldiers are dead because of that idiot. If not for his arrogance, Elle and the clones would have been inside this new area all along."

"Where are the clones?" I demanded.

"That reminds me," he said. "I've been meaning to thank you. Remember that day we stuck needles in your brain? You provided the key to Elle's deepest love. You."

I thought back and remembered Fitz and his father sticking needles into my head. It was right after Elle had defeated the Synmen. But I didn't know what he meant by a key. Fitz continued.

"Your stupid sayings, you idiot. 'A billion teeny, tiny bits. Strawberries and cherries, and best-friend berries.' They were critical to the cloning experiments."

I wanted to kill him. I'd never wanted to kill anyone before. I think he sensed my hate, and it made him laugh again. He turned to go, then turned back.

"Why do you think the Synmen were helping you escape?" he asked.

I glared back at him. I had no idea.

TOURIST GUARDS CAME the next morning and escorted me down a dozen flights of stairs into a large, low-ceilinged room below the hospital. Many tourist soldiers, scientists, and all one hundred Elles were already there. The clones rushed to welcome me, but the guards warned them back. Behind me, the door swished shut, and I felt the floor dropping. The room was a large elevator! As we dropped, I looked at the scientists and the tourists, who clearly knew about this place. The clones, like me, wondered where we were going and why.

After about ten minutes, we stopped, and the doors slid open revealing a vast underground space, complete with newly built buildings and automated walkways.

The guards led us into a large theater inside one of the buildings, with a gigantic, curved screen that wrapped nearly all around us. The theater probably held a thousand people. The guards ordered the clones to sit down in the center of the room, and I was made to sit in the center of the clones. I noticed our chairs were different from all the other chairs in the theater.

Ours had shiny black headrests. A faint light pulsed from within the headrests. We sat while the scientists were ushered into the room. Unlike our chairs, the scientists sat at conventional computer workstations. When everyone was seated, the doors shut, the lights dimmed, and a man walked onto the stage.

"You're all safe now. We've thought of everything. This was the backup plan in case the plan to defeat the Synmen failed. We are deep beneath the surface of the planet. The walls are ten times thicker than the walls of the original cavern, built with material from the new Synman production line. It's impossible for the new Synmen to break in. We will live here together as a family until the completion of a special weapon. Even today, the weapon might be ready, thanks to all of you."

I suddenly realized the man on the stage was talking only to the clones and me. The scientists weren't even listening to the speech. They were busy manipulating instruments built into their workstations: typing, analyzing, taking notes. Our chairs were just shiny black chairs, with no advanced computer systems except the strange headrest contraption. The man walked off the stage and the lights dimmed. The scientists stopped using their keyboards.

"Ramien, what's happening?" the Elle clone on my right asked. The clone on my left took my hand. A guard rushed over and slapped our hands apart.

The large screen flashed, and an image appeared. The image was black, but there was something hidden in the blackness. A blacker black lay within the image. It had tentacles and strands. When I looked closer, it moved away. As I kept looking, the black thing with the tentacles moved beyond my peripheral vision. I tried to track it but couldn't.

What were we looking at? Why was I drawn to it? The theater seemed to be getting darker. The blackness in the screen sucked the light out of the room. I heard scientists punching their keyboards, then quiet. The blackness sucked the sound out too.

The man from the stage appeared right in front of us, startling the clones and me. We struggled to look at him instead of the screen. The black within the black seemed to draw us in, along with the light and the sound.

"We don't have much time," the man said urgently. He seemed terrified. "It's a superportal."

I finally understood. I'd heard rumors of a superportal while on the surface, some kind of portal made for Elle, but now I knew. The superportal wasn't for Elle but for her one hundred clones. It would multiply the strength of Elle a hundredfold to stop the Synmen.

Using a superportal, the clones were to take control of all the Synmen simultaneously. That's why all one hundred were in the theater. The headrests behind us were interfaces that connected each clone to the superportal.

"We need all of you to engage the portal," bellowed the man. "Get the enemy who has taken control of our Synmen to talk. Get them to tell you who they are, where they are. The scientists will hear everything." The man looked back at the superportal. The room was now perfectly quiet. The man kept talking, shouting actually, but we could hardly hear him.

"Find them!" he yelled. "Go, now! Engage the portal!"

The clones didn't move, too transfixed by the screaming, terrified man and the black blackness that loomed behind him. He leaned toward us and yelled again. I smelled terror on his breath.

"Engage the portal," he screamed. "It works just like the individual portals you already know how to use."

At last, the clones did as the man commanded. I felt a fist rap my shoulder and a knife at my throat.

"You too," growled a guard.

I twisted, flung my legs, flipped over him, grabbed his chin, and snapped his neck. As he sighed his last breath, I realized something evil had gotten inside me and was making me mean. From that point forward, I vowed to resist the evil. I laid the guard down gently and closed his eyes.

Then I returned to my chair, leaned my head back, and engaged the portal.

The next instant, I felt Elle, just as I had previously felt her in my mind, only now magnified one hundred times. The portal blended all one hundred of her together, overwhelming me with her love. As souls, no longer in the bodies of others, I saw them all as my one and only, my beautiful Elle.

Time didn't exist. We laughed and played in her front yard. We yearned for each other. We cried when I found her, and when we were torn apart. Forever and an instant were the same. I told her I loved her. One hundred Elles said I love you back.

This occurred entirely in our minds. We tried talking in sentences, but that was confusing. We began exchanging concepts and ideas. One Elle told me of a book she had read, every word, with a single thought. Another Elle told me of a painting she'd drawn.

Suddenly, an Elle screamed. Then another. Then I screamed. I'd never screamed before. My lover caused my first scream. A scream is worse if you can't actually scream. We had no mouths or throats, so our minds screamed, all parts of our minds, the parts that think, the parts that remember, the parts in the past and in the future. My lover made us scream until we were an icy-black nothing. I understand screaming now. My lover taught me.

"My true love," said my lover. "Wait here, I'll be right back."

All at once, my hundred Elles quieted, then became spots of deep, dark, writhing black. Worms twisted and slithered around each Elle, swarming the carcass of something newly dead. The worms transformed into black maggots, feeding on the remains of my hundred Elles. The maggots blended into one, became an icy-black blackness, and came to me.

"I'm back, my love," said my lover.

I tried to back away, but her icy-black was all around me.

"You will join me, and we'll love each other forever," she said.

I didn't reply. I was still in shock she'd killed all one hundred Elles.

"I didn't kill those freaks. I ate them. They're part of me now, where they belong. Besides, you killed the guard for no reason, you two-faced hypocrite."

"You made me. That was you," I said.

She moved closer. She squeezed me with her icy-black. "Ramien, my love, you promised we'd be together forever. Remember strawberries and cherries, best-friend berries?"

I tried to get away, but she held me tight.

"Join me, Ramien. We'll rule the blackness."

Never, I thought with all my might.

"One last kiss," she said.

I couldn't stop her. I felt icy-black pain. Her kiss had torn a tiny bit of me.

"I hate you, Ramien. I will tear you apart into a billion teeny, tiny bits. A billion times I will make you scream. See this first bit of you, this white light? I take only this bit and replace it with my icy-black. Go back to your pitiful underground city with your frightened scientist friends. Tell them your Black Lover is there too. My Synmen will break in soon. I'll be back for you, Ramien. A billion times I will be back for you, and when I take every last bit of your billion bits of white, you'll be my Black Lover too."

I don't know how I got out. Hands pulled me from the portal. I opened my eyes. One hundred clones lie dead all around me.

64

BIKE-ME

ALTHOUGH I WAS a prisoner with no way to escape, I was allowed to walk around. It didn't take long to explore the new area. Two scientists followed me, whispering and taking notes, but they let me go wherever I pleased.

On other planets, scientists stored Syn machines in vast warehouses. This new refuge must have been a warehouse as well. Brand-new buildings took up half the massive space. Surrounding the buildings sat thousands of Syn machines that had been moved to create space.

I saw personal Synships, built for three or four passengers. I saw Synmen too, both original and new versions. All were disabled, but they made me nervous. I knew that all around us, all the time, my Elle hovered, hoping to enter an enabled Synman. Oddly, many other common items were also stored in the area, devices like bikes, cars, household appliances, and piles of cloth.

A bike that stood at an angle, held up by a folding steel rod, caught my attention and I stopped to look. I had never ridden a bike, but I understood the physics of bicycling and knew the importance of keeping one's balance until the wheels were spinning. I looked back at the two scientists following me, and they didn't seem to mind, so I got on the bike. As I swung my leg over, I noticed a knit cap attached to the handlebars, hanging by a hook that was built into the bike specially for the cap. I let it be, but the cap nagged at me. It provided no protection. What could its purpose be?

It was funny, in an ironic way. I was deep underground, distrusted by the last of my people, and my lover had been ripped apart and had sworn to rip me into a billion teeny bits. Yet, I was wondering about a cap dangling from a bike.

I grabbed the handlebars and sat on the bike. My feet easily reached the ground. I put a foot on a pedal, but my knee seemed too high. I guessed it was a kid's bike. If a child could ride it, so could the most highly trained tourist fighter on the planet.

The two scientists following me hadn't moved, but they shook their heads and smiled at each other. They were laughing at me. I thought I recognized one of them but couldn't be sure. Their laughing made me feel like not riding the bike. If I fell, they would laugh. If I started out wobbly, they would laugh. They were thinking I was too afraid, or maybe that I didn't even know it was a bike. I felt self-conscious for the first time in my life. Then I was embarrassed that I worried about what they might think. The whole thing made me angry, all over my riding a stupid bike in front of two stupid men. I looked at them, and they looked back.

"Glare at them. Make the idiots look away," I told myself.

I hated them for making me feel embarrassed. I'd get on the stupid bike, and then maybe I'd ride the stupid bike right into them. I'd knock them over, maybe hurt them. Maybe I'd help them up, or maybe I wouldn't. Maybe I'd laugh at them first. I realized the two clowns were walking toward me. They were upon me before I could think of what to do or say. Again, I had that certainty that I recognized one of them but couldn't place from where.

"Can we try after you?" one man asked.

"Maybe you could teach us?" asked the other.

After the second man's question, I understood. My lover Elle hovered nearby. When I was strong, she waited. When I was vulnerable or weak, she attacked. That's why I'd killed the guard. I realized Elle couldn't have been the first. There were other evil souls too. My once good and beautiful people never had a chance. I remembered Elle's promise that she would be inside us. Slowly, relentlessly, Elle's evil would transform all of us. She was in my mind, egging me on about the two scientists. With all my might, I acted as if she wasn't.

"I was actually hoping you could teach me!" I said, imagining my evil Elle laughing at my weakness. I had been visualizing running them over with the bike. She had taken a bit of good from me and replaced it with a bit of evil. I was changed, and I knew it.

The two men helped me, holding the bike steady while I put my feet on the pedals. Then they held me up and ran alongside the bike until I was going fast enough. I felt a rush of joy when they let go. The moment was pure and wonderful. In that instant, whatever darkness had wormed inside me was pushed away, and I felt happy. I rode the bike around, wobbling recklessly, my legs pumping high. I felt a breeze on my face. You can cover a lot of ground on a bike. The two men cheered me on. They saw my happiness and wanted to feel that way too. I made a final circle around the vast warehouse and returned to the men.

"Your turn," I proclaimed, smiling from ear to ear.

The man I somewhat recognized took the bike, thanked me, and swung his leg over the seat. He'd probably be a natural and ride away with no wobbles at all. He waited while the second man readied himself on one side of the bike and I readied myself on the other. The man decided the cloth cap dangling from the handlebars was in his way, so he handed it to me, and off he went. I stuffed the cap in my pocket.

The bike wobbled, but the man rode better than me, and

he loved it too. Smiling as I'd never seen anyone smile in my life, he rode the bike all around the warehouse.

The second man wanted a turn, but he was nervous. We encouraged him, gave him a push, and off he went. His riding was wobblier, but he did it. We cheered him loudly. As he rounded a corner out of sight for a moment, I took the cap out of my pocket and held it in my hand. The first man and I laughed, saying we three were the best bike riders in the history of our planet. Then I did what one does with a cap. I put it on my head.

The man on the bike came hurtling around a corner, wobblier than ever, but laughing and having great fun. To our amazement, his hands were up in the air! I realized he was out of control and was going to run into me, head-on.

Suddenly, something strange happened. The second man wasn't coming at me. *I was coming at me.* I was the bike, yet the bike was coming at me. I jumped left as I jerked my bike-me handlebars left and slammed my brakes, throwing the man, still laughing, over the top of the handlebars. I ducked, but the man crashed into me, knocking me back. He must have hit the first man too, because all three of us went tumbling.

The two of them were laughing and having a wonderful time. I laughed too, but there were two of me. Bike-me nearly fell over without a rider to keep me up. I pulled my handlebars straight, and bike-me pedaled away without a rider, while me-me tumbled, rolled, and laughed with my two new friends.

During the tumbling and tussling with the two men, the cap came off, and at that exact instant, bike-me was gone. Only me-me remained. The two men sitting beside me slapped my back, tousled my hair, and handed me the cap. We three looked, laughing still, for the bike. It had crashed twenty feet away. We wondered how the bike had gone so far. I looked at the cap and had an idea about that.

Sitting next to the two men, I put the cap back on.

Instantly, I was bike-me again, lying on the ground with my tire spinning. The cap made me one with the bike.

My new friends picked themselves up, and I got up too, disoriented at first by being both me-me and bike-me. When me-me stood up, bike-me rose too. This caught the attention of my friends. I focused, separated my two selves, and the bike fell back down. My friends and I looked at each other and shook our heads, but I was asking different questions than they were.

On the surface, I'd heard old survivors tell stories about these devices, Syn products made for play and other household uses that were controlled by dedicated wearable portals. Long ago, all nonessential Syn products had been put in storage when the Syn technology began malfunctioning. There was a rumor that the cloth caps for controlling Syn toys were making children afraid. The cap must be a portal, specially made for the bike. I remembered the piles of cloth I'd seen in the storage area. I wondered if the cloths were made of the same material as the cap, a general-purpose portal, not yet tailored for a particular device. I wondered if Elle's evil could reach me more easily through the cap.

One of my friends walked over and picked up the bike and wheeled it to where I had first found it. Laughing and talking about how much fun we'd had, we began walking back to the center of the cavern. We walked right by the pile of cloths stacked atop a pitch-black cube. I made a show of coughing and sneezing. My new friends asked if I was okay. I grabbed two cloths and wiped my nose with one.

"Thanks. I feel better now," I said, pocketing a cloth while placing the other back on the stack. My heart raced. I'd never stolen anything before.

"Nice try, but that didn't work," said one of my new friends, walking toward me.

I'd been caught. I readied for a fight, but he walked right by me and knelt in front of the cube.

"A Syn Blaster," he said.

"What's its purpose?" I asked.

"It was designed to stop the returning Synmen by blasting them with the exact same synaptic waves Elle created when she first disabled the Synmen. When that didn't work, scientists embedded threats into the wave, hoping to frighten them away."

He pointed at the stack of cloths on top of the Syn Blaster. "Those are generic synaptic cloths, used to clean synaptic dust from the Syn Blaster surface that might distort the signal. Scientists planned to put Syn Blasters inside Synships and fly them around our solar system, continuously broadcasting. Obviously, it's down here because it's junk."

"Syn junk," I said, feigning a smile. Inside, I was furious. The pitch-black cube represented another cruel experiment that had been performed on my lover.

My two new friends escorted me back to my room. Both encouraged me to take a walk the next day so they could ride the bike again. They said goodbye and left me alone.

Upon inspecting the cloth and the cap, I learned they were made of the same material. I put on the cap, and as before, I became the bike. I controlled it, moving its pedals and squeezing its brakes. I could see the area all around the bike. I took the cap off and inspected the cloth. Wondering what might happen, I laid it on top of my head. Nothing. The cap was paired with the bike. However, the cloth hadn't been made into anything, so maybe the cloth was still just a cloth.

I concentrated on the cloth but nothing happened. I tried harder, but for some reason, I couldn't focus. My mind kept seeing the big warehouse, the hallways, the buildings, doors, windows, walkways, the Syn machines, and the bike, still lying where we'd left it. I pulled the cloth off my head and sat back.

Suddenly, I understood. I wasn't remembering the warehouse and the hallways, *I was actually seeing them!*

The cloth was a map. No, not just a map. The cloth, I

realized, connected me to the area as it was at that moment. Apparently, these cloths weren't just for cleaning Syn Blasters.

I grabbed the cloth and stared at it intensely. Nothing happened. I closed my eyes, calming myself, and then opened them again. The cloth was gone, and in its place was the area around me. I realized the cloth was a portal, not paired to anything specific yet, so it projected me everywhere.

I wondered what else the cloth could do.

Footsteps sounded outside my room. I hid the cap and cloth under my bed and opened my door. I looked up and down the hallway. No one was there, though I was sure I'd heard someone. Returning to the cloth, I tried concentrating once more. I could see everything and began to explore around the building. I heard voices. With the cloth, I could not only see, I could hear! I followed the voices to a room where scientists were meeting. Inside, I recognized Chief Scientist Fitz.

"We will torture and kill Ramien tomorrow," he said. "Then maybe that demon freak Elle will leave us alone."

65

SHIP-ME

I KNEW FITZ WAS WRONG. My death would cheat Elle of her promise to tear me into a billion teeny, tiny bits. Either way, I was done for.

I decided that whatever I did next would likely be the last thing I ever did before fighting for my life, so I decided to ride the bike again. I grabbed the portal-cap, wondering what it would be like for me-me to ride bike-me. I would be happy on my last day. Not many people get to plan their last moments.

I used the cloth to guide me out of the building. It wasn't far, but I worried the scientists would be watching. They weren't. Why would they? Where could I go?

The bike was exactly where I'd left it. I thought of my two friends, wondering if they would be the ones who came for me. And I still didn't know, where had I seen one of them before? I didn't even know their names.

I picked up the bike, but something felt wrong. Pedaling wasn't as much fun. I was too afraid. Elle was hovering around me, and her black hate ruined my fun. My lover was trying to make me angry, but I'd show her.

I put on the cap, knowing I was letting her in. I became the bike and simply held on. I had the time of my life as I raced around the whole cavern. Round and round I rode, letting my mind go, daring my lover to come and get me. I laughed, purposefully thinking about the scientists' plan to kill me and ruin my lover's revenge.

That last thought probably caused my lover to do what she did next. The fourth time around, the bike slowed when I passed one of the Synships, and not because of me. The next time around, the bike stopped at the same Synship. I didn't stop it. Bike-me didn't either. Wondering what was wrong with my bike, I got off to examine it. Everything seemed fine, though I had no idea what to look for. I closed my eyes, slipping deeper into the bike: tires, chain, brakes, all seemed okay. Out of nowhere, I felt attracted to the Synship.

Something beckoned me inside. I walked my bike inside the ship's hatch and laid it down. Bike-me saw things lying along the floor: specks of dirt, the legs of chairs, and a stack of cloths atop a pitch-black cube in a corner of the ship.

Another Syn Blaster, I thought, suddenly angry. The floor view was disorienting, so me-me took my cap off. My anger instantly faded.

I was standing in an amazing vessel made in a past era of great scientific advancement. The ship had been designed by scientists for scientists. It had three beds, three workstations, and a captain's chair. Draped over the captain's chair was a cap. I laughed, imagining I would fly around and have some fun before Fitz and his scientists came for me.

How hard could flying a spaceship underground be, especially if I wore the ship's controlling cap? I sat down in the captain's chair, put the cap on, and immediately became the ship. Me-me looked at the cloth map and charted a path around the cavern. Ship-me closed my door and started my engines.

Both ship-me and me-me heard voices in the distance. I detected scientists approaching through the ship's sensors. Inexplicably, I felt drawn to my cloth map again. I had planned to simply fly around, but the cloth map showed me a path out into space! I realized all these ships had been flown into the cavern, so there must be a way out! On the map in front of me was my escape route. Ship-me and me-me could escape!

I heard shouting outside the ship and sensed a large group of people. They banged on the ship's door. My two bike-riding friends were there. They told the others to back off, and then once I felt safe, maybe they could persuade me to come out.

"Come on out, Ramien. We need to talk to you," one friend said.

"Open the damn door, Ramien!" my other friend yelled.

Ship-me was connected to the ship's synaptic portal, so I heard his thoughts: *Ramien is my friend. I'm going to help him.*

"Okay, I'm coming out!" I yelled. Ship-me extended toward my bike friends, and thought aloud, forcefully enough so that their minds could hear me, *My two friends, please move away. I'm going to fly this Synship out of here, and don't want the ship to hurt you.*

The banging stopped. My friends had moved the men back. I closed my eyes and focused on the ship. There was a soft hum, and the spaceship lifted off. I immediately realized my folly. Elle had used the cloth to trick me. I had no chance of escape. The map showed an opening directly above, but straight up was a thick titanium ceiling. Seconds remained until I crashed.

Goodbye, I thought to my new friends.

Amazingly, the ceiling parted and I flew straight through! I was excited until I saw another titanium wall ahead. Then it too parted. Massive door after massive door opened before me until I emerged from the cavern.

Smoke covered the planet. My ship's sensors detected burning acid in the air. Synmen, blackened with soot, walked around, shrieking. With no people remaining on the surface, they were fighting and whirling one another.

I flew away, leaving my planet behind. Ship-me scanned my provisions. I sensed I would be able to survive forever aboard the ship. The beds were actually sleep chambers that would let me sleep for minutes or millennia without aging. Food synthesizers would feed me. I flew out into space. I could go anywhere, and that's where I would go.

The next moment, a black wall appeared in my path, an evil horde of squirming, shrieking, furious hate. I knew the evil was spiritual and assumed it was Elle. I could have turned back, but behind me lay certain death.

Here I come, my Black Lover, I thought and flew straight into the writhing black.

A tiny hole formed in the midst of the icy-black wall. The hole grew, then contracted, as if trying repeatedly to grab me. It seemed like something held it back. The hole became a tunnel, as large as my ship. I flew straight in, a frenzy of evil shrieking on all sides of me.

My brain began to freeze. Elle's icy-black had entered me. Black needles stabbed my head, coming from my cap, so I ripped it off. I was no longer flying the ship. I don't know how long I was in the tunnel. Then the tunnel was gone, and I was in open space. I put my cap back on.

Stars shone all around me. Luckily, the stars were far enough away that I didn't fly into one. I looked behind me as I flew away. The shrieking evil struggled, trying to follow, but was held back by an unseen force, my lover. I was free.

I sat back in my chair. A moment later, my heart raced, and my stomach knotted. I realized my Elle had taken another bit of me. She'd planned for me to escape. She'd shown me the map and drawn me to the spaceship. She'd made the tunnel in the wall and stopped it from grabbing me. I wondered how she'd opened the ceiling. Maybe my two bike friends did that.

I shivered at the implication. My lover hated me. She wanted to tear me apart bit by bit. She'd not let people kill me or evil demons harm me. I was *her* prey, all billion bits of me. Then I heard laughter.

"Hello, my Ramien. Remember me? I'm your Black Lover. I will soon come for you. Another kiss I have for you."

I gasped. My evil Elle was still inside me.

"Let me see now, little Ramien. Before I leave, I will take a larger bit so you don't forget me. Ready, Ramien? This might hurt a little."

A terrible hate swept through me. I imagined killing her. I imagined killing my dead friend Alvin too, and my lover's coward scientist friend who had run—the final act that enabled icy-black hate to completely overcome her.

"There now, Ramien, that wasn't so bad. That's all for now, but I'll be back." My Black Lover laughed wickedly.

I realized that each piece she took from me changed me and made me a little bit more evil. Me-me trembled, and ship-me shook so violently I felt my hull beginning to break. The cap gave my Black Lover direct access to me and the ship. I ripped the cap off, and the ship stopped shaking.

Having escaped, I had to determine where to go. I looked for a control panel to help me navigate my ship and found nothing, not a single control. This was a pure Synship, designed for the days when Syn technology did everything.

To pilot the ship, I used the cap again. Thankfully, my Black Lover was gone. I learned to make food and to use the bed. I instructed my ship to find a nice planet and to wake me when we got there. I took off the cap and went to sleep. A few hundred thousand years later, my ship crash-landed right here.

I awoke in what seems like a brand-new universe, with light and warmth all around me, making me happy.

I feel joy in the air, happiness in the sun. I know I'm all alone on this planet, yet somehow I feel connected to others.

I discovered that my Synship has a long-range synaptic

portal, the one I'm using now. It's thousands of times more powerful than my cap, and I can see far into space.

I looked into it to see if my Black Lover was coming for me. Every day when I wake, I look. That's when I first saw demons raging through the universe, chasing you.

Behind the raging demons, I saw the terrible blackness that you call the black spot. The black spot is my Elle, my Black Lover.

Billy, I'm sorry. My lover killed your mother.

66
SAVE THE UNIVERSE

JIMEE, Brill, and Stevens hovered close to Billy, wary of him charging the hate wave to attack the Black Lover.

After a few minutes, Billy asked a question. "Why did Elle order the Synmen to tear her arms and legs off?"

"To experience fear and pain during her transfer, so her soul would transfer as pure hate," replied Jimee.

"The scientists asked that question too," said Ramien. "Also, who took control of our Synships and Synmen."

Jimee sensed sadness within Stevens.

Billy rushed to Stevens. "It's not your fault. We were all part of it."

"Part of what?" asked Ramien.

Jimee waited for Stevens to calm, then addressed Ramien directly. "I can elaborate on part of your story. You described an old gray concrete building containing chairs. That building was from our planet. Our people created the chairs, called transfer chairs, so our souls could separate from our bodies and explore the universe. But many souls became lonely and missed their bodies. I think some came upon your planet, discovered the Synmen, and hoping to become physical again, caused the twitches and jerks in your Synmen while trying to manipulate the synaptic interfaces. Meanwhile, a new generation of people evolved on our planet who were unusually cruel because of the hate wave. They found the chairs and used them to execute millions of criminals, unknowingly transferring them. Those criminal souls became evil demons. The demons took over the Synmen, eventually leaning how to control the interfaces, and attacked your people. When the Synmen fled your planet, they must have returned to our planet and retrieved the building containing the transfer chairs."

"The chairs still worked, but no longer vaporized the bodies, just like on our last day," said Billy.

"What about Elle?" asked Ramien.

"I think she had unusual psychic abilities," said Jimee. "When you were being tortured by the Synman, her love for you somehow created an energy wave that disabled the synaptic interfaces in Synmen and drove away the demons, at least temporarily. After Elle defeated the Synmen, scientists experimented on her, attempting to weaponize her psychic abilities. They knew their experiments might kill her, so they developed synaptic clones. The experiments worked, making Elle even more powerful, but also growing her hate for the scientists. When the demons and Synmen returned, she didn't disable them. Instead, she took command."

"Why did she eat the clones?" asked Billy.

"To become even stronger," said Jimee. "By consuming the clones, she became a hundred times more powerful."

"Enabling her to create a tunnel in the demon wall so I could escape," said Ramien.

Jimee nodded. "By now, I'd guess she's in control of every demon in the universe, and that means every Synman and Synship. Every planet with humans is at risk."

"We need to stop her," said Billy.

"First things first," interjected Brill. "Ramien needs to leave. The hate wave and Elle will overtake this planet soon."

Ramien shook his head. "The ship's thrusters work, but

only for a few seconds, just enough to break free of the dirt that accumulates around the ship. Additionally, the radiation shield and temperature controls are damaged. I can't leave."

"You need another ship," said Billy.

"There are millions of Synships," said Stevens.

"Maybe we could find one in a warehouse," said Billy.

"Not likely," said Jimee. "Demons will have co-opted every Synman and Synship. By now, they're likely torturing and transferring people on other planets, adding to their demon army. There could be billions by now. Everyone in the entire universe is at risk of being made a demon."

"We can steal a ship from the demons," said Stevens.

"It's not stealing if it's for Ramien," said Billy. "Right, Jimee?"

Jimee hesitated before speaking. "Legally, I think you're right, depending on which planet's—"

"Even if we acquire a Synship, we'd still need to outrun the demons," said Brill. "Synships fly much slower than demons. We'd be ripped apart trying to escape."

Jimee sensed Ramien tiring. While time meant nothing to disembodied minds, Ramien was human. She suggested he go to sleep. Whatever plan they executed required finding a spaceship, which would take many times longer than a human could live.

Ramien prepared his sleep chamber. "How long should I set the timer? The auto-awake system was damaged in the crash."

"Once we find a ship, we'll need to wake you the moment we arrive," said Brill. "I'll extend into the ship's cloth-cap portal to study the sleep chamber design. Join me from your own portal, and we'll blend. As I learn how to modify the chamber so we can wake you from outside, you'll learn along with me."

Ramien joined Brill studying the chamber design. An

instant later, he disconnected from his portal, looking quizzically at Brill.

"You understand?" asked Brill.

Jimee sensed something had gone wrong.

Ramien disengaged from the portal, retrieved some tools, and opened a panel on the sleep chamber. A few minutes later, he closed the panel. Brill tested the modifications affirming they were correct. Ramien stood in silence beside the chamber, one hand on the lid.

"Don't worry, Ramien. You won't sleep forever," said Billy. "I promise we'll be back to wake you."

"He can't hear you, Billy," said Stevens.

Ramien re-engaged his ship's portal.

Jimee waited a few seconds to be certain he heard her. "Ramien, we made a promise and intend to keep it."

Visibly upset, Ramien shook his head. "Brill, I'm so sorry."

"About what?" she asked.

"I have to make you face the death of your family. I'm so, so sorry."

Brill pulled back. "How do you know about my family?"

"Ramien, don't do this," said Stevens.

"For the sake of all of us, for the sake of everyone, everywhere in the universe, I have to," replied Ramien.

"No, you don't," said Billy.

Ramien persisted. "Brill, when you and I became one so you could blend your knowledge with mine, I couldn't help but see your wall. I tried to ignore it and focus only on the chamber modifications. Still, I couldn't help but wonder about your wall. It was such a mystery. I saw a crack in the wall with the tiniest light peeking through. While you were thinking, I looked through the crack. I don't think you even remember all that is behind your wall. I apologize, but you need to look, and let your friends look too."

Brill shrunk back.

"Stop, Ramien!" yelled Billy, wrapping himself around Brill, then reaching out for Jimee and Stevens. All three joined with Brill, interweaving their energy with hers to absorb her sadness. Brill opened her essence, fully welcoming the comfort of her friends. All four became one, their thoughts, their emotions, their memories. Jimee sensed a thick wall deep inside Brill and realized that she too had a wall. She didn't try to look through Brill's and avoided even a single glance at her own.

"Everyone has walls. That's where their pain goes, and that's where it should stay," she said. "Don't worry, Brill, we won't look behind your wall."

"I'm sure Ramien meant well," said Stevens.

"He shouldn't have looked. That was mean," said Billy.

"What did he mean by for the sake of the universe?" asked Jimee.

"Ramien's a good person. I trust him. I'm going to look behind my wall," said Brill.

Blended with her friends, Brill peeked through the crack in her wall. All four saw what she saw; her husband and children, laughing, and playing, they became separated, her husband called out, her daughter screamed, then nothing, only Brill, alone, weeping. She reached for a control panel to program a fleet of—

"Spaceships!" yelled Billy.

The four friends deblended. Ramien's essence, still projecting through the ship's portal, hovered a short distance away.

Brill looked into space toward her planet, at the coming hate wave, then at Ramien. "I configured the spaceships to be controlled by a synaptic interface just before I transferred. The hate wave is still thousands of years away. There's time if I hurry."

The friends discussed the most expedient plan to get Brill's ships. Brill argued she should go alone because the evil on the black side of the hate wave was too thick with demons. The light from two souls would certainly be detected, and all would be lost.

"Plus, I'm the only one who knows how to interface with the ships," said Brill.

Reluctantly, Jimee and the others agreed.

"Ramien, before you go to sleep, I'm curious about the Syn Blaster," said Brill.

"According to my bike friends, it didn't work," replied Ramien.

"I think it did, but not how the scientists intended," said Brill. "I analyzed the Syn Blaster while you were telling your story. The problem wasn't the threats sent by the scientists. The problem was that Synmen never actually heard the threats."

"What do you mean?" asked Stevens.

Brill continued. "Ramien's bike friends said the Syn Blaster was designed to disable Synmen by transmitting an exact replica of the energy Elle created when she first stopped them. My analysis verifies that it works by transmitting into the fabric, much like my people used the fabric to communicate."

"Ramien said the Syn Blaster didn't work," said Stevens.

"Correct, it didn't," said Brill.

"Why not?" asked Billy.

Brill moved her essence to hover atop the Syn Blaster. "Communication within the particle fabric is point to point," she explained. "That means both a sender and receiver are required, and they are paired to one another. The Syn Blaster is the sender, blasting energy into the fabric, but because its target was millions of Synmen, there wasn't a specifically paired receiver, so the message disappeared, and is forever going back in time."

"Who was Elle's receiver when she created the energy that disabled the Synmen?" asked Stevens.

"Ramien," replied Brill. "When he was being tortured, I think Elle sent Ramien a massive wave of love, so strong it created a white-hot surge in the fabric. Because Elle's love wave had a receiver, it remained in present time. The resulting white-hot surge disabled Syn circuitry and scared the demons away, at least temporarily."

"Ironically, the scientists tried saving themselves by blasting the exact opposite, icy-black hate," said Jimee. "Even if demons had heard the Syn Blaster, it only would have fueled their anger."

"What was the scientists' message?" asked Billy.

"Ramien, can you turn the Syn Blaster on?" asked Brill.

Ramien disconnected from his portal, walked to the Syn Blaster, and removed the stack of cloths from the top, exposing a black button on the pitch-black surface. He touched the button and returned to his portal.

All five friends heard the message blasting from the Syn Blaster.

STAY AWAY OR DIE!

"Oh my," said Jimee.

"I don't understand," said Stevens.

"Me either," said Billy.

"What's there to understand?" asked Ramien.

"Blend with me," Jimee said, opening her mind.

Brill, Stevens and Billy blended. Ramien held back.

"You too," said Brill.

"You're one of us now," said Billy.

"Also, your memories are part of the explanation," said Jimee.

All five friends became one. They heard Ramien's bike friends describe how the Syn Blaster sent threats into the fabric to frighten demons. They heard Brill's explanation about synaptic messages going back in time forever and ever, if there was no receiver. They saw Jimee on Stevens's deck billions of years ago, looking at a recording of a sunrise captured by a synaptic imager. From Stevens's deck, they saw the message.

STAY AWAY OR DIE!

Still blended, the five friends imagined how the universe would still be loving and good if the message had been received sooner, in time to stop the Great Advance.

Billy separated from the blending. "I guess that explains the mystery of the sunrise. Let's help Ramien," he said.

RAMIEN CLIMBED into the sleep chamber and went to sleep. Brill prepared to cross the crest of the hate wave, thinning herself to avoid detection, a skill, Jimee now realized from looking behind Brill's wall, that Brill had acquired while trying to end her sadness.

"Be safe, Brill. See you in a few thousand years," said Stevens.

Jimee felt strength when she heard Brill's reply.

"I'll get the ships, Jimee. You make a plan. Together, we'll rescue Ramien."

Jimee felt hope when she heard Billy.

"Then we'll save the universe from the Black Lover!"